ORDINARY PROBLEMS OF A COLLEGE VAMPIRE

VAMPIRE INNOCENT
BOOK SEVEN

MATTHEW S. COX

DIVISION ZERO PRESS

Ordinary Problems of a College Vampire

Vampire Innocent #7

© 2019 Matthew S. Cox
All Rights Reserved

Cover & interior art by: Alexandria Thompson

ISBN (ebook): 978-1-950738-06-9

ISBN (paperback): 978-1-950738-07-6

CONTENTS

THE ZEN OF ALTERNATE DIMENSIONS

P eace.

  If death had anything going for it, I might have once said 'they're at peace now' or something hokey like if someone I knew passed away. Once. At least before I got to experience death personally. As it turns out, being dead is anything but peaceful—at least in general. Moments like this, where I'm soaking in a nice hot 'orange creamsicle' bath bomb, are the exception.

  Okay, to be completely fair, I'm not dead. Not all the way. Let's just say I had a really strange day last summer. Within the span of a few hours, I went from being a reasonably typical girl who'd recently graduated high school to a murder victim who knows vampires are real. *How* did I discover vampires exist? Simple—I turned into one. Not by choice, mind you. But yeah, I'm a vampire.

  One could say it made for somewhat compelling evidence.

  However, I have to say becoming a vampire is the best worst thing to ever happen to me. I'd say it's the best thing to ever happen in my life, but technically speaking, my life ended before it happened. So, there's that. Anyway, ever since I found myself in a morgue cooler a couple days after my 'death,' my unlife has been a little on the crazy side. Okay, a *lot* on the crazy side. The only thing I want is to be as normal as possible and enjoy the time I have with my family.

  But for some reason, the Universe has other plans.

And, I really am bending over backward to be normal. Seriously, how many vampires go to college? The latest insanity du jour is my little sister, Sophia, has resumed having nightmares about a monster she made up when she'd been three. She calls it Fuzzydoom. It's basically a massive black pom-pom with itty bitty wings, like the size of the ones you get fried from a Chinese restaurant. I'm not entirely sure how something so silly looking could scare anyone, even a three-year-old, but this *is* Soph after all. Poor kid spent fifteen minutes once when she'd been like two trying to run away from her own shadow. She's nowhere near as bad now, but she's still super high strung.

Normally, if a ten-year-old started to have 'wake up screaming' nightmares about a huge, furry pom-pom monster they invented at three, it would probably be time to start considering a therapist. However, in our case, there's a perfectly reasonable explanation for her fear: we saw the damn thing in a parallel dimension after going through a mirror.

I did say, *reasonable*, right?

Okay, so theoretically speaking, if even one strand of the monster's fur touches something, it'll kill it. But that thing *crept* along. Like, we're talking makes the DMV look fast. Another mark in the plus column is I'm not entirely sure the thing is real. And yeah, weird as it sounds, I literally am debating the actual existence of a figment of my kid sister's bizarre imagination.

Did I mention she's got magical ability?

So, the whole alternate world behind the mirror thing may or may not have really happened. It *might* have merely been some sort of mass-hallucination illusion Sophia planted into our heads. Part of me is inclined to believe the entire escapade happened for real, but I am trying to be in denial here. Stuff like parallel mirror universe full of acid-trippy monsters simply doesn't happen... right?

Then again, neither does a small invasion of imps.

What's an imp you ask? A minor demon type critter that evidently adores playing pranks. They're also not particularly concerned with the victim surviving said prank. While the little bastards don't *try* to hurt people, if someone gets maimed or killed, they find it hilarious. My sisters wanted to do something spooky for Halloween and ended up summoning a ton of those things by accident. Every liquor store within driving distance of my neighborhood has to be wondering why business is booming lately.

I'm still in awe that the PIBs didn't show up to ask a whole ton of questions about where the imps came from.

What's a PIB you ask? Persons In Black. Government agents who are in on the whole 'vampires are real' thing. They got wind of my less-than-stealthy escape from the morgue and came to visit. Their visit mostly felt like they wanted me to know they knew about me, and bad stuff would happen if I didn't behave myself. I wonder if they visit all new vampires or if I got lucky? And for that matter, how long has the government known about all this weird stuff without telling anyone? There *has* to be magic involved. No one can keep secrets that long, that perfectly.

Right. Back to the peace issue, or lack thereof.

Two in the morning is like the vampire equivalent of eight at night, except for me. I could be out partying or doing stuff with other undead, but not even dying changed me that much. I've never been into hitting nightclubs or bars or simply going to random places and hanging out. For the last half of grade school and all of high school, 'fun' usually consisted of hanging out at home with my friends or maybe a mall trip. As soon as we got licenses to drive, we started hitting the occasional restaurant together for something of a girls' night out, but still never really went wherever the 'cool kids' go. Yeah, we were kinda nerdy. So, I'm staying in my room.

If Ashley and Michelle—or my boyfriend Hunter—happened to be around, it would be different. But, our schedules have mostly gone in two entirely different directions. They can't stay up this late anymore due to school and jobs.

I'm going to classes, too. At Seattle Central College. Night school if it's not obvious. The type of vampire I am—Innocent—gives me a little leeway with the damn ball of nope in the sky that most normal people call the sun, but attending classes on a normal teenage schedule is out of the question. My inner nature forces a hard sleep on me the instant the sun rises. Most vampires are stuck as still as corpses until sunset. I consider myself lucky to wake up by two in the afternoon most days... unless I've had my ass kicked.

Fortunately, I've managed to avoid ass kickings for a good while now.

Between chasing imps around, leaping across dimensions—twice, dammit—having a psychotic vampire bitch wanting to tear my head off, and narrowly avoiding a war between vampire elders, I've had a heck of a few months. It's hard to believe it's *only* been five. And ugh... Thanksgiving is coming up soon. That's going to be interesting. Actually, hang on. Maybe it won't be as bad as I'm thinking. Thanksgiving ten years from now is going to be strange when all the relatives we only see twice a year start noticing I still look like I'm eigh—sixteen. Grr. If there is anything I'm not totally thrilled with about becoming a vampire, it's how it made me look younger.

And yeah, I get that 'looking younger' happens to almost every vampire, but usually we're talking about a thirtysomething who could pass for their hot twenties or a forty-to-fifty-year-old who looks thirty. Me? I legit look like a freakin' sophomore again. I mean, I didn't get any shorter or anything but something about my face...

Everyone thinks I'm a kid again.

Has to be the 'Innocent' blood. My best defenses are: being underestimated by other vampires who think my kind are weak, and looking as harmless as possible. It does have a rather compelling upside though. While awake, I appear totally alive. Lifelike color, body heat, still appear to be breathing, blinking, sweating, and a normal heartbeat. When I sleep? Not so much. No one has yet shown me a picture, but the parents 'can't bear to look at me' when I'm out cold because I evidently resemble a corpse.

And in the most bizarre twist the universe could ever come up with, Sophia doesn't at all mind how I look while sleeping. Well, I mean she *minds*, or else she wouldn't use me for a cosmetics crash test dummy, but she doesn't freak out and scream. This is the same girl my brother Sam once reduced to shrieking tears of terror by wearing a werewolf mask and sneaking up beside her bed.

So, I'm less frightening than a five-dollar Halloween mask. Go me.

Sophia's present glitch is worrying Fuzzydoom will somehow escape the mirror dimension into reality and come after her. Sierra and I have both been trying to convince her the creature is a product of her mind so she has total control over it. No, I don't know this for a fact, but undeath requires a certain degree of guesswork. My fangs didn't exactly include an instruction manual. Most vampires spend a couple years 'living' with the one who gave them the Transference, learning the ropes so to speak.

Did I mention the guy who made me a vampire is a bit, umm, unreliable?

Okay, some of that is my fault after all. Most vampires spend their first few years in their sire's shadow and don't decide to run home as fast as possible to their mortal families like me. However, I have zero regrets about my decision.

What I do have is an orange creamsicle bath bomb and a bathroom all to myself for several hours.

Oh, and there's Aurélie. She's like a four-century-old vampiress who has—for some strange reason—taken a particular liking to me. Sure it kinda felt weird and creepy at first, but what 400-year-old woman with an entire room full of haunted old dolls wouldn't be a little weird and creepy, amirite? Naturally, nothing in life—or death—is free, but so far, the only thing she's wanted from me is going to fancy vampire parties with her while dressed up in a ridiculous gown. Oh, that and posing for paintings. Not creepy paintings, or even nudes. She dolls me up in these super elaborate gowns. But the woman is hard to look at without feeling emotions of some kind. I'm straight, but she could make me question myself. While she's physically beautiful, the attraction mainly comes from her constant mental radiance.

Good thing she's taken on a maternal vibe with me or I might've found myself getting *way* strange with her. She already seduced my friend Ashley without even trying. Ash is at least bi, so being attracted to women is normal for her. But I think Aurélie is so old she's merely stopped caring about trivial things like what kind of plumbing someone has. People talk about the French for being great in the bedroom, and after existing for centuries, if an act is possible, I'm sure Aurélie has done it until it's become boring.

Shudder.

I really hope she keeps thinking of me as a daughter. Or she waits until I'm old enough that cracks start appearing in my sanity. Pretty sure every vampire eventually gets a little odd in the head once they've gone well past a normal human lifespan.

But, like the teenager I still really am, I shouldn't be worried about what's going to happen a week from now, much less a century. Okay, so there are *two* things about becoming a vampire I find annoying: being mistaken for sixteen and this weird precocious maturity thing. How many eighteen-year-olds think about the future this deeply?

Anyway...

It's two-something in the morning, all my friends are asleep, my entire family is asleep, and I'm all caught up with homework. So, I'm treating myself to a soak. Most of the people—I don't say kids because I'm going to night classes and a good portion of my classmates are over thirty—at school constantly grumble among themselves at never having enough time to do their homework. Even Ashley and Michelle do, and they're going to normal morning classes like ordinary freshmen who the sun won't incinerate. Both of them are taking more classes than I am this semester and they have jobs.

I have no job and a buttload of time when everyone's asleep. College coursework is barely a burden when there's not much else to do. No parties, dorm craziness, sports, job, or other distractions in my life other than the paranormal insanity. Speaking of… it's been almost three weeks since my kid sister ripped open a hole into another world. Feels like I'm about due for something to blow up in my face.

Sigh.

Some girls get drunk when they want to cope. Me? I lie here underwater in the bathtub. Breathing is for lesser mortals. Only, I'm having trouble relaxing with my brain poking me about two tests coming up this week as well as a project due for biology, plus the supernatural stuff.

The bathroom door opens. Someone small walks by the tub toward the toilet.

What the heck? I *know* for a fact I locked it this time.

I sit up slow like a prop from a haunted house—dead girl in the bathtub—and peer around the shower curtain. A tiny figure stands on the toilet seat, about the size of a three-year-old with batlike wings and glowing red eyes.

Sam's closet imp.

Wow. Okay. Whatever. Screw it. Just a minor daemon taking a post-midnight whiz. Who am I to criticize? I lower myself flat again under the nearly opaque orange water, unsure what I find the most strange:

Imps exist.

There's one in our house who's apparently decided to make friends with my brother and not prank anyone.

Imps have to pee.

He's using the actual toilet.

And apparently, imp pee glows lime green.

Any one of those things would leave most people scratching their head. Since the little guy plays video games, I suppose it's not too bizarre he's figured out how toilets work. Pretty sure Mom wouldn't appreciate cleaning smoking messes up off the rug.

No, I'm more hung up on the whole 'imps really exist' thing, because it also means the mirrorverse we went into is probably real and my little sister has magical abilities. Yeah, I'm a *vampire* who's struggling to believe in supernatural things. How is it I've taken becoming an undead in stride but stuff like magic and demons still feels implausible?

A flush breaks the silence in the bathroom. Seconds later, the door closes and the lock secures with a faint, metallic *snap.*

That stuff really happened. Great. Does this mean *Alice in Wonderland* might have been real? Things we saw in there certainly qualified as trippy, but definitely had a darker overtone. Hmm. Mirrors are reflective. Perhaps what occurs on the other side is a reflection of the person who opened the door?

Or maybe I've been underwater too long.

And… I lied before. I'm not all caught up on my schoolwork. I'm done with the small assignments. I still have that project for biology to do, and a paper to write for computer science. Would it be wrong to make my biology project about blood? I'll probably wind up doing something lame like trying to demonstrate which type of cheese grows mold the fastest or maybe I'll do a study on oceanic coral. I probably *still* have pieces of it inside my left lung from that stupid rapier.

Grr. I reluctantly get out of the water and grab a towel.

By 2:48 a.m., I'm down in my basement bedroom staring at a blank word processor. There might be some people in the world who would find writing about the evolution of digital storage media fascinating. I'm not one of those people. Like, do I really need to care old computers used paper punch cards to store data, and how the technology gradually developed across various storage mediums to the multi-terabyte hard drives of today? Oh sure, a ten-megabyte hard disk used to weigh as much as a Prius. How is that important to know?

Ugh. It probably is, but it's boring as hell. Sierra would probably like this stuff. She's far more of a tech geek than I am. Going into programming happened as a kind of dart-throw 'why not' decision. My father writes code for a living and it's a theoretical job I could do at home without requiring I go anywhere during daylight hours. Theoretical, because almost no one hires a newbie programmer for a work-at-home gig.

Then again, I wouldn't be an ordinary newbie programmer. Any future boss of mine would give me whatever hours or work arrangements I want them to. That would be a seriously unfair advantage if we worked actual jobs. Whoever heard of a vampire with a day job? My unlife has already defied tradition in staying with my mortal family. Would going into the workforce break the gears of the universe further? And for that matter, dare I condemn myself to a job I don't really love?

My dad has to be brain damaged. The man can sit in front of a computer for fourteen hours straight—barring bathroom and meal breaks—and it doesn't bother him. I could never do that even playing games, and he's not even having fun, just staring at a screen full of letters. Sierra is the same way. She can play video games all damn day and still grumble when the parents pull her away from the PlayStation. Going into computer programming for me could be a mistake, even if I have no sincere need to make any sort of living at it.

Guess it's technically kinda hard for me to make a *living* at anything.

Great. I've reached an advanced stage of undeath: I'm thinking in dad jokes.

There are two main reasons my butt warms a seat in a college classroom, and neither one of them is the desire to obtain a career capable of supporting me. One, I'd spent the last year or so of my life stressing out over getting into college. While Seattle Central isn't exactly sunny California—big upside for my new vampire self—it gave me a scrap of normality I craved, as if I could pretend none of this weird crap happened. Nope. Nothing to see here. No such thing as vampires. I'm just an ordinary girl still going to college who happens to have a severe allergic reaction to daylight.

Somehow, I doubt claiming to be Irish would've explained away *that* sunburn. Besides, SCC doesn't allow smoking in the hallways.

The second reason I'm going to school despite these theoretical claims of my evident status as a powerful—relatively speaking—immortal being, is my parents. They wanted and expected me to go. Perhaps in the same way I tried to cling to normality, it lets them pretend our new normal isn't anywhere near as messed up as it is.

Though, any attempt at normal probably went out the window the moment my mother played Wak-a-Rat with her cast iron skillet during the great imp invasion. If Dad ever convinces her to try D&D, she should totally go with a two-handed-weapon using barbarian. Knowing Dad, he'd even give her character an enchanted skillet with a damage bonus on minor demons.

Alas, Mom will never play D&D. She's far too serious. Weird, though, since she loves books and movies. Maybe it's the roleplaying part. Yeah, she's a lawyer and has to speak in front of people all the time. But, that's all super serious. I don't think she can handle being a humorous focus of attention. I had to get my social anxiety from somewhere. Thanks, Mom.

I type out 'The Evolution of Digital Information Storage by Sarah Wright for Computer Science 101 – Professor Garcia' and proceed to stare at it for ten minutes.

It's not too late to change my major. Only problem is, I have no idea what I'd change it to. I could go with English, maybe. Not like I'm going to need to build a career off a degree. Maybe I'm wasting time with college. Whenever I'm sitting in class, it's time I could be spending with my siblings or parents. The littles won't stay tweens long. Though, our family clinginess in the wake of my almost death has eased off a bit. I no longer have this desperate need to spend every waking moment surrounded by my family. Not that being around them bothers me at all. Clinging to them still feels awesome, but it's not an overriding demand. Everyone's finally accepted that I didn't die for keeps.

Fortunately, the arguing and rivalry has stayed gone. On that note, I shouldn't smother the littles or they might start resenting me. So I can't use inflated guilt over family time as a reason to shirk off college. Can't even use time in general. Four years isn't anything at all to me now.

After a few more minutes staring at a blank screen, I come to the astute conclusion this report won't write itself. See, I have keen vampire senses. Unfortunately, none of my immortal powers comes with a pre-written boring-ass paper on digital storage. I'm going to have to write this paper the usual way.

Four years might not mean much to an immortal, but at the moment, it sure does feel like an eternity.

2

OUR WORST FEARS

Throughout my life, I've had several strange relationships.

In eighth grade, I briefly dated this kid Tommy Quinones. Before our first date, I had to sit before the council of judgement. And by that I mean his grandmother, mother, aunt, and older sister. They apparently didn't disapprove of me, but at least one of them stayed in eyesight of us the whole trip to the mall, the movie, and the restaurant after. Yeah, awkward.

I have a new strange relationship, and no, not with Hunter... with sleep.

They say people with higher intelligence or who are intensely creative always have trouble falling asleep at night, often spending long periods staring at the ceiling. That used to be me. I still think the most awesome part of becoming a vampire is being able to fly, but it is damn nice to be able to go to sleep in an instant.

Though, sometimes passing out so fast can be inconvenient depending on where I happen to be when the sun comes up. I've ended up sleeping draped over my computer desk a few times. Once, I even collapsed on the floor while trying to walk to bed. My new semi-underground room doesn't have any windows, so if I'm really absorbed in something like schoolwork or a video game and not looking at the clock, sunrise can sorta sneak up on me. In my new reality, once those feelings of drowsiness start up, there is no 'aww mom, just a few more minutes.' The instant the sun peeks over the horizon, I'm out cold no matter where I am.

Except if I'm outside or near a window. Being exposed to daylight prevents instant unconsciousness, though it has other complications... like spontaneous combustion, temporary feral insanity, involuntary murder of anyone between me and a dark place to hide—so yeah, best to avoid ending up outside near dawn.

I did manage to get a few pages into my research paper before the nag of approaching sunlight tugged at my bones. As far as my brain wants to tell me, my body isn't crashed on the floor or draped over my desk. Seems as though I made it to bed. Vampire sleep comes in two varieties: either it feels instantaneous or brings bizarre dreams. Given how close to the wire last night pushed it and how it barely feels as if I even blinked, my guess is option one today. It is, after all, the far more common mode of sleep.

Another minor nitpicky complaint about being a vampire: I no longer wake up feeling energized by a good night's sleep unless my ass got kicked the night before. It's more like I'm some kind of robot being turned off for a few hours then back on. And yeah, that's a tiny thing to grumble about. However, it is still possible for me to be lazy and lie here after regaining consciousness, enjoying my soft bed.

Know what's kinda creepy and weird? Consciously being aware of an utter lack of body heat gradually warming up. It's kinda cold for a moment or two until my insane metabolism furnace kicks back on.

Sophia's soft whispery voice breaks the silence on my right, low to the ground. She's probably sitting on the floor. From the sound of her muttering, she's playing with dolls. Okay, more than a little strange. Yeah, she's girly as heck but she's been more into reading or drawing lately than having a doll tea party. Maybe we're spending too much time around Aurélie? No, the woman doesn't play with her dolls, merely collects them. But she does speak to them. Can't blame her for doing it though—most of them answer her.

Again, shudder.

Yanno, I really should stop being freaked out by stuff like this. What are haunted dolls going to do, kill me?

My kid sister does voices for her various dolls having court with royalty. Not until she addresses 'Duchess Sierra' do my alarm bells go off. The older of my two kid sisters hates dolls. She's no tomboy, more like a small adult woman... totally not into the frilly, girly stuff. Also, not into outdoorsy activities or whatnot. The girl likes her video games and science fiction.

But, for some reason, she's playing dolls.

Danger Wilhelmina Robinson.

I sit up, open my eyes, and almost faint back asleep when my brain processes the scene.

Sophia, in a puffy, iridescent black-and-red gown, sits at the head of an imaginary table of creepy dolls, having a tea party with Sierra—who is balanced stiff as a board on a small plastic chair. Too many things are wrong with this image.

Sophia has fangs.

Sierra's skin is grey and sunken, as if dead for a long time.

Sophia does not own a dress that extra. She's halfway between a French noble and one of Aurélie's dolls.

Oh, and the dolls are moving, sipping blood from tiny teacups.

It's too much for me to even think of words. Next to seeing Sophia with fangs and Sierra dead, living dolls barely register... at least until they all turn their heads to look at me.

"Gah what the hell!" I rasp.

"Hi!" chirps Sophia. "I saved you a spot." She pats the rug beside her. "You can sit between me and Princess Isabella."

A blonde porcelain-faced doll waves at me and emits the creepiest giggle I've ever heard in my life.

"What the..." I gesture at her, then Sierra. "What happened? Who..." I leap out of bed and land next to her, grasping her puffy shoulders. "Please tell me you've used magic to give yourself fake fangs and make Sierra look..." The word 'dead' won't even come out of me.

"Duh." Sophia rolls her eyes. "It's still light out. Not even two-thirty yet. You know she and Sam can't wake up until the sun goes down."

I stare at her for a moment before looking at Sierra. She looks like a mannequin leaned against a chair, stiff as a plank. "Sam, too! What? I don't remember... how did..."

"Wow, you must've had a bad night." Sophia 'pours' tea into a plastic cup and hands it to me. "Sierra's a Sybarite. She can't wake up as early as we can."

"What!?" I shout.

"No, doofus. She makes video games. Not like that slutty blonde. What's wrong with you?" Sophia grins, showing off her fangs—the most unsettling thing I've ever seen.

"How? No… how are you three vampires?"

Sophia stares at me out from under flat eyebrows, a total look of *'really?'* "Are you messing with me?"

"I could ask you the same question. You did some kind of illusion magic to freak me out, didn't you? C'mon, Sierra, knock it off. Is that really her?" I grasp my 'dead' sister's arm, unable to tell if it's a real body or a high-quality fake carved out of wood and covered with silicone skin.

"Are you okay, Sare?" Sophia sets her teacup down and hugs me. "You've had it rough ever since Hunter threw himself into the sun."

"Wait. What?" I stare into space. "Hunter was a vampire?"

"Wow. You seriously don't remember?"

I glance back at the creepy person who kinda looks like Sophia, all dolled up like something out of a morbid *Alice in Wonderland*. "No…"

She huffs. "School shooting like twenty years ago. Got all three of us. You totally lost your mind and turned us. I'm an Innocent like you, Sierra went Sybarite, and Sam's…"

"A Lost One," I whisper. He would go his own way. "But… why don't I remember any of that?"

Sophia 'sips' her pretend tea, shrugging.

"Blocked it out most likely," says a brunette doll in an unfamiliar woman's voice.

The bedroom door creaks open. Grandma pokes her head in, smiling. "Oh, you're awake."

"Gram?" I ask.

"Ha ha." The seventy-something woman smirks at me. "I wish you'd stop teasing me."

It hits me the voice belongs to my mother, not Grandma.

Okay, there's no way in hell I went to bed last night and slept for like thirty years.

"Shit. I'm dreaming."

Sophia grins. "Yep. Took you long enough to realize that."

"Wiseass," I mutter.

She makes this 'excuse me' face. "You do realize I'm only a product of your unconscious mind right? You're the wiseass."

"Right. So how the heck do I wake up out of this incredibly depressing dream?"

Sophia pouts. "Aww, being with us forever is depressing?"

"Yes… no. I mean… you guys deserve to grow up and be normal."

"What if I *want* to stay small and cute forever, and be with my favoritest sister?" She leans against me.

"Umm. Not thinking about that right now. Wake up."

Sierra's eyes snap open. She emits a scraping hiss and flings herself at me, mouth wide. I catch her, but she hits me with the weight of a grown adult and knocks me flat on my back. The instant my head hits the carpet, I realize I'm in bed again.

I gingerly roll my head to the right to look at my room. No super creepy tea party. No vampire little girls. No moving dolls.

"Ugh." I rub both hands down my face. "Guess I was wrong about not having a dream. Wait." I splay my fingers, peering between them at the room. "What are the chances I'm *still* dreaming and woke up for the second time in a dream?" Argh. I never should have watched *Inception*.

Mercifully, nothing answers me.

The alarm clock reads 2:23 p.m.

Dreaming about waking up has got to be one of the most unnerving, unsettling, weird things to ever happen to me. I don't know if I'm really awake or still sleeping. Afraid to find out, I just lay there hoping I'd merely had a nightmare based on my worst fears and not some sort of undead prophetic vision of the future. The girls didn't look older than they should be. Great. I'm going to be a paranoid wreck about something happening to them any day now.

In the past, getting sick would almost always give me bad dreams. Not all of them woke me up in the night screaming, but every single time I had a cold or something, I'd have a nightmare. Suppose death isn't much different to my body. Every dream I've had thus far since becoming an undead has been freaky and scary. While 'sparkle goth vampire Sophia' did have a certain degree of cute, I could never get past the idea of her having to die first. Thinking of any of my siblings as vampires is way too damn depressing.

"Am I really awake?" I look around again. "Okay, it's been ten minutes and nothing has happened. Guess this is reality."

Though my new vampire body is incapable of waking up groggy—in the absence of a severe beating the prior night—I still yawn, stretch, and wipe my eyes out of habit. After a dream like that, it seems proper not to be well rested. Also, with the memory of tween vampires in my head, focusing on finishing my paper isn't happening. Worry eats at me until I can't take it anymore and head out my door, and left to the basement bathroom.

It's small, with a toilet and Plexiglas shower stall, no tub. However, it does have a mirror.

At least with the kids going to school now, Sophia doesn't have the time to paint my face before I'm awake. Like some eighth grader about to dare Bloody Mary, I lean on the sink and stare into the mirror.

"Coralie? Are you out there?"

No idea why I'm talking to a mirror. Pretty sure it would be absolutely solid if I tapped it. I'm a vampire, not a warper of reality. But, having been drawn into an otherworld, it feels like talking to a mirror might let ghosts hear me more easily.

"Coralie? If you're not too busy, can I ask you a question?"

The hairs on the back of my neck stand up as the sense I'm no longer alone becomes quite distinct.

"Sarah," says Coralie from behind me.

Hooray for amplified senses. Knowing she'd appeared—if only a split second before she spoke—stops me from shrieking and breaking my face on the sink while falling to the floor. Still, I twitch before releasing my grip on the porcelain and turning.

Coralie Hall stands between me and the door out, still in the same black dress she'd worn the day she died in 1849. It's hard to think of a woman her age being married—she'd been twenty—but that far back, people often married quite young. She tilts her head in curiosity. "What is it you wish to ask? Forgive me if I startled you."

"It's fine. Kinda surprised calling for you worked." I let out a deep breath. "So, I just had this weird dream..."

She listens as I explain the details of the dream, her expression giving away no hint of worry... or much of any emotion, really. I'm sure she's used to questions like what I'm about to ask. The order of mystics she'd belonged to in life, the Aurora Aurea, the same people who'd kept her mummified remains in their vault, referred to her as an oracle. Something about a magical ritual they'd conducted—and led to her death—gave her the ability to see the future.

It didn't work out like her former husband had hoped. While she did gain the ability to receive random, nonspecific glimpses of the future, she ended up dead with no way for him to benefit from her foresight. Eventually, he worked out how to communicate with spirits, but died soon after himself.

"Anyway, my question is... did I have a vision or just a nightmare?"

Coralie stands there like a three-dimensional oil painting. It shouldn't creep me out a ghost isn't breathing, but her total stillness unnerves me even more than her partial transparency. A few minutes of silence later, she reanimates and offers a weak smile.

"Umm?" I ask.

"You had a nightmare, not a prophetic vision."

"Whew." I nearly collapse into a puddle with relief. "Awesome. So, I'm not gonna make them vampires?"

She shakes her head. "I cannot see one way or the other. However, I feel strongly they will not perish at their school as you—and Sierra—fear." She glances off into space. "I do think her first relationship will end poorly."

"Ack. Not as poorly as mine I hope."

"Scott was not your first." She flashes a wan smile. "I know what you meant even though it is not what you said. For Sierra, I don't think there will be anything worse than tears."

"Okay. Cool. Tears I can handle. Just a dream." I pace around, scratching the back of my head. "Guess since I'm not mourning the life I might've had anymore, the brain needs to torture me with other things."

She shrugs. "Nightmares are a natural process. Even I have them sometimes."

"Uhh…" I stop pacing and raise an eyebrow at her. "But, you're a ghost."

"Yes. We rest. I am unable to explain the mechanism involved, but dreams are still an aspect of my existence. They are far more real than any dream I had in life. Perhaps because as a being of pure energy, I *become* the dream rather than experience it."

"Whoa. I haven't had enough coffee yet today to think about that. Anyway, cool. Thanks for coming to help." I glance at the mirror. "Did you hear me because I spoke at the mirror or because you have like a spiritual ear turned my way?"

"Being near a mirror does make it easier, yes."

I blink. "Next thing, you're going to tell me the Bloody Mary thing really happens."

She raises her eyebrows slightly, lips pursed. "Well, I will say certain apparitions may occasionally be drawn to those who are opening themselves to the paranormal. However, to the best of my knowledge, 'Bloody Mary' isn't one single entity. Sometimes, the visitor is friendly, other times, not so."

Okay, I'm kinda glad I never let Ash or 'Chelle talk me into doing that when we were little. I *really* need to make sure Sophia doesn't try playing the 'Bloody Mary' game now. "Umm… if Sophia does it, will bad things happen?"

"It depends on what her expectations and desires are at the moment she does so."

"She has magic…"

Coralie nods. "That is a way of expressing it, yes."

"Does she need to like learn stuff? They don't really have schools for it, do they?"

"There are small groups, such as the Aurora Aurea here and there. Different mystical traditions abound. Far more have been lost to time than remain known to anyone alive, though that statement was true before my death. In your sister's case, she is not an adherent of any particular 'school' so to speak."

"School?"

"Such as voodoo, Thelema, Wicca, Sumerian demonology, and so on. There are some people who obtain what many would call 'magic' via the intercession of external beings. The mechanisms of action governing the interplay between said beings and humans often requires specific rituals, writings, gestures, and so on. Sophia's power originates from within her. She does not *need* to follow any particular set of 'rules' for using her gift. Her desire is enough. But…" Coralie clasps her hands in front of her. "If she does utilize the trappings of an 'established' form of occultism, it could shape the effect she has on reality purely because it will alter what she believes will happen."

I nod, sorta getting the idea. "That's where the imps came from, because they found the 'spell' online and it had demonic-ish overtones?"

"Yes."

"Okay. Umm. So, this mirror universe stuff, gateways, the damn troll… all of it is real?"

Coralie nods.

"How? I mean… no, not how. That's way too long a question. If this stuff is real, why does everyone think magic is made up? Heck, *I* used to think it was all fake."

She ponders, then gives me a blank look. "The world is far more paranormal than the collective consciousness of humanity is willing to accept. Whenever most people witness an event they cannot explain, their subconscious mind disregards it or fabricates a more logical explanation."

"That simultaneously makes sense and makes no sense." I chuckle. "Do you think Sophia should get some kind of training? Like, would it be bad to let the mystics work with her? Or is it better to let her figure this stuff out on her own?"

"Is it dangerous? Possibly." She smiles. "But so, too would be leaving her to her own devices. It is not a good idea to give a child so young the ability to alter reality and leave them unsupervised. Especially for someone like her who is so easily startled. She has a gentle heart, and could be easily swayed by outside influences. Remember, our worst fears are what we make for ourselves."

Okay, that one leaves me scratching my head. "Umm... Oh, you mean like Fuzzydoom?"

"In a manner of speaking, yes."

I cringe. "Could she theoretically let the thing loose in the real world?"

"Highly unlikely, at least any time soon. Perhaps, she may eventually understand her abilities sufficient to gather the power necessary to do such a thing, though I suspect it would require the use of a ley line nexus, or some other great source of spiritual energy."

None of it makes any sense to me, which means there's no way Sophia would understand it. Gonna call it a no then. She won't be able to summon Fuzzydoom. Unless, of course, she gets a dog and names it that. But there's no way my parents will agree to a dog in the house. At least, not without me tampering with their heads... and I promised never to do it. The only way a pet would stay here is if it could turn invisible. Them allowing Sam to keep two frogs in a tank is a miracle already. If they ever find out my brother has an imp in his room, prank-ma-geddon from a couple weeks ago is going to look like amateur hour.

Maybe I could convince them he's more of a friend than a pet? Last time I checked, pets don't hang out and play video games. Of course, my 'rents probably won't be rational enough to accept any arguments if they discover him. Well, Dad might be okay with the idea. Mom will likely wallop the imp with her skillet.

Lucky for him, he can stay invisible.

3

A FEW MINUTES OF FOREVER

Remember that thing about me promising not to use my powers of mind control on my parents?

The next afternoon a little over an hour after I wake up, the temptation to cheat my promise rears up. A large pile of schoolwork sits in front of me, it's about three-thirty on a Friday afternoon, and my mother wants me to take Sophia to her dance class. Several things help me keep my promise. One: she's texting me. I haven't yet figured out how to make vampiric powers work over an iPhone yet. Two: Sophia needs me and I care more about her than schoolwork. I'd say 'Three: it's daylight and my powers are offline' but it's not totally true as long as I stay in my windowless bedroom.

I lean back in my chair, smiling at Mom's text. She's unable to get out of work early and Dad's already left to take Sam and Sierra to taekwondo. After her ending up eyeball deep in imps, she's become highly interested in learning how to fight. It hits me I experienced my pre-death instinctual reaction to such a request from Mom—trying to dodge it. Whoa.

Holy crap, maybe I'm coping.

While the urge to duck out of having to take Soph to dance class happened, it's easy to brush aside and help my kid sis.

Holy crap, maybe I'm growing up.

Ugh. I slump forward and bonk my head on the desk.

Sunset time around now—mid November—is roughly ten minutes to five depending on cloud cover. Her dance class runs from four to five. My first class starts at six. I should have plenty of time to get to school if I fly. There is, however, another slight problem. I don't have my own car and Dad will have the Sentra. I sit up again and text ‹Flying doesn't work at this hour.›

Mom replies with ‹Take the Sentra.›

‹Isn't Dad using it?›

‹Lol! No. He picked up the new one today. Silver Sentra is officially yours.›

Oh, yay. I should be thrilled, but... flying is way cooler than driving. My sense of independence isn't dangling off a keyring, it's dependent on the stupid sun going down. Still, they didn't *have* to give me the car. It might be like ten years old, but free is free. ‹Awesome! Okay. I'll take her.›

Mom sends back an explosion of seemingly random emoticons. I swear, people over thirty don't know how to text.

Well, hmm. Can't exactly work on the digital storage paper at the dance—crap! It's due tonight. I'm going to have to find a way to finish it at the dance studio. Mom's fault, so I'm going to help myself to her laptop for the night. After saving the in-progress paper to the cloud, I throw on jeans and a T-shirt, then run upstairs. Sophia, evidently also in text-communication with Mom, waits near the front door already in her dance costume. Nothing fancy, just a plain black one-piece and white leggings. No recital or performance tonight, purely studio practice.

She gives me a confused stare when I zoom past her and go upstairs. "Sare? You lost?"

"Nope," I yell. "One sec."

Mom's laptop is set up on a little desk in the parents' bedroom, thankfully at full charge. I grab the power cord in case of emergency and head back downstairs to throw on a coat. The chill doesn't bother me much, but I'd look out of place walking around outside in November without a coat on. Sophia bundles up in her coat with a scarf plus wool hat, and we head outside.

The sky is in one of those bipolar type moods where it keeps going back and forth from kinda gloomy to kinda-not-gloomy. I feel like the hotdog at the very edge of the grill that only gets cooked on one side, so half of it is still fridge cold while the other half is too hot to bite. Thankfully, it's not bright enough to cause serious pain or smoke. The light does, however, mess with my eyes, so after getting in the Sentra, I pull the sunglasses down from the window shade. I shouldn't be this nervous about driving. Honestly, I'm not nervous about driving—I'm nervous about *crashing* since I'm kinda vulnerable right now. As far as Aurélie thinks, if I get hurt or killed while exploiting my ability to withstand low levels of sunlight, the injuries might become permanent or at least take a really damn long time to heal. Death, on the other hand, would likely be final.

I never really worried about death before actually dying. Sounds weird to say, right? But, it's not something people, especially people my age, think about. School shooting drills aside… those freaked me out. Still not sure if being murdered made me more aware of death than I'd been before, or if it's simply knowing I've got quite a bit more time to lose now.

"Dad got a new car today," says Sophia after getting in.

"Mom told me. What did he get?"

She rolls her eyes. "Another Sentra I think. Something small."

I back out of the driveway and whirl around the cul-de-sac in reverse until facing out, then accelerate off down the road. "He barely drives, so he doesn't need anything large. Surprised he didn't get one of those smart car things."

"Those are too small. Dad could run over a squirrel and wind up in the hospital."

"Hah!"

She eyes the backseat. "You're stealing Mom's laptop?"

"I've got a paper due for a class tonight and I've kinda been putting it off to do other stuff because it's super boring."

"Wow." She blinks at me. "You've never slacked off on school stuff before. Is that a side-effect of the vampire thing?"

"I haven't been slacking on school stuff in general, just this project. The other things taking up my time *are* school related."

She shivers. "Okay, that's just wrong. You can stay up all night and *still* can't keep up with the work? Scary. Remind me not to study whatever you took."

"I'm backed up a bit over this stupid paper." I nearly miss our turn due to being lost in a conversation, but manage to get over to the left in time without breaking any traffic laws or even making my sister cling to the door handle. "Wasted hours staring at the screen I should've used doing other work. Thinking of changing my major."

"Why?"

I spend the rest of the ride to the dance studio rambling about how boring it is to write a paper about data storage. Sophia cheers me up a bit by suggesting it isn't computer science I'm bored with but history. Really though, it's not even that. Certain history is fascinating. Writing about old hard drives which used to weigh half a ton isn't. But, she's got a point. Bad idea to let one dreadful assignment change my major. Unlike everyone else in my school, if I get a degree in a field I end up not being able to stand, it's not going to be the end of the world. I have all the time I want.

Living with my parents aside, my existence doesn't rely on money for anything. My food can't be purchased, and if it came down to it, finding a place to live would be as easy as a little minimally-invasive mind control. My plan is to stay home for as long as possible. The place might begin to feel weird after my parents grow old and pass on and the siblings all move out. Perhaps I'd want to be rid of it then to escape painful memories. Or what if one of the littles wants the house for their family? Would it be fair of me to keep lingering in the basement? Wait, no. They'll all be grown up, moved out, and re-homed before Mom and Dad are gone. So, yeah, dibs on the house for as long as I can handle the memories associated with it.

And there I go again, not acting my age.

Dammit, I'm eighteen. I'm not supposed to have this much foresight at this age! I need to start making half-baked decisions that sound fun in the moment but bring heaping piles of regret down on me when least expected. Well, a snap decision didn't quite work out for me too well last time, did it? Oh, I'll just take my cheating boyfriend off alone into the woods at night to break up with him. What could possibly go wrong there?

Sigh.

We arrive at the shopping center at two minutes to four in the afternoon. As soon as the car comes to a stop, Sophia's out the door and running for the studio before the engine is even off. Naturally, the sun decides to intensify at that exact moment, almost like it knew I got out of the car. The burn hurts, but it's not quite bad enough to cause smoke. Grumbling, I grab the laptop and haul ass inside, mingling in among the various other parents seated in the 'audience' area.

I'm a little surprised to see Mrs. Snow here. She's the tiger mom who basically tortured her daughter Alexis. Figured the poor girl would've quit going once she had the opportunity to, but maybe it's become fun to her since her mother is no longer driving her along like a manic Olympic coach hopped up on cocaine and Vicodin, desperate for one last shot at glory. I take an empty seat near the corner and cast a casual glance over the class, all doing warm-up stretches. Alexis is wearing a costume still a bit too much on the skimpy side for a tween, but nowhere near as bad as what her mother had been encouraging her to wear before my brain corrections. Seriously… who *encourages* girls so young to show skin to get ahead in the dance world? Ugh. So damn creepy.

Everything seems normal with the class, so I take a spot in the corner, as far away from a window as possible, set up the laptop, and get to work on my paper that's due in two hours. Ten minutes in, it's pretty obvious this is not going to cut it. The only way this paper's getting done in time is an absence of daylight. Or, there's always mentally tweaking Professor Garcia to give me until Wednesday next week. Hmm. Possible, but I'd still have to endure the embarrassment of openly admitting to the whole class I didn't finish it when she collects the papers.

Nah.

I head to the bathroom, located in a short hallway near the back end of the dance floor. My hunch pans out and there aren't any windows here. As soon as the door shuts behind me, the tingle of my vampire nature coming online washes over me. It's not a huge bathroom, only three stalls, a counter with two sinks, plus a tiny sofa near the door. Something floral hangs in the air. The little couch is ideal. No need to take up a toilet.

Boredom is a state of mind. I can choose to surrender to it or overcome it. Life has many tedious situations that can't be avoided. Unlife is full of dangerous things with a strong desire to eat me, like a two-ton tarantula-scorpion whatever the hell that critter was. You know, boredom doesn't seem all bad. I'd much rather be sitting here writing a dryer-than-melba-toast report about ones and zeroes than *ever* seeing an abomination like that again.

The world plunges into slow motion in response to me pushing my body to the limit of vampiric reflexes. Most normal undead use their powers for cool things like racing up the sides of buildings, dodging or catching bullets out of midair, clawing the crap out of each other, and so on.

Me? I type at like 650 words a minute or some ridiculous number like that… probably even faster if the subject's entertaining. Alas. Any mortal walking into the bathroom at the moment would probably hear buzzing rather than keyboard clicking. It does take some concentration on my part to only use speed and dexterity, not strength. Mom would be kinda mad at me if I punched my finger straight through her new laptop.

Another weird thing happens… I'm having an easier time

remembering all the research I did without having to look stuff up. Could it be another little-known-of vampire perk or a side effect of staring at this crap for a whole week? Meh.

In a little over twenty minutes, I finish a reasonable first draft of a fourteen-page paper. Dad once joked about how he hated writing papers in school. A teacher would give him an assignment for a two- or three-thousand word project and he'd feel like he'd been sentenced to the guillotine. Now, for his job, he writes hundreds of thousands of words—granted, it's program code—without batting an eye at it.

Grunt work done, I get up and leave the bathroom, grimacing the instant sunlight shuts me down. Don't get me wrong—feeling normal is amazing. But, the normal I want to feel is having a family, being home with them, and going about my life. 'Losing my powers' normal still sucks.

Again seated in the waiting area, it's time to proofread, which is a whole lot faster than trying to come up with crap to say about drive platters and file allocation algorithms. The two older women are in the midst of a conversation about their lack of success dating the theoretical, hunky Latin pool guy named Raul.

Right. For once, going offline is a good thing. My sense of hearing isn't abnormally acute. Alas, they're *still* distracting enough to trick my brain into trying to figure out if they seriously want to seduce a guy half their age or if they're merely fantasizing. Before my frustration level builds to the point I get up to ask them, they switch topics to an upcoming Las Vegas trip the black-haired woman is planning next week.

The thought of playing blackjack or some other casino card game with the ability to read minds makes me smile. Not that I have the first clue how to play, though the basics ought to be easy enough to pick up with a bit of research. I could see myself 'vampire cheating' at cards for a laugh, but using my abilities to steal money would make me feel too damn guilty. Yeah, so what if I fail at vampire. Though, if ever my butt wound up stranded in Vegas and I seriously needed cash for an emergency, I'd probably do it.

Grr. Enough distractions. Back to proofreading.

Parents around me read their Kindles, chat on the phone with their significant others, or—as in the case of the two cougars—talk about gambling in Vegas. Mrs. Snow sits there in silence with an eerie not-all-there smile. Pretty sure some part of her is still watching her daughter, Alexis, in the class and wanting to scream at her for not being unattainably perfect. Fortunately, I hit her brain pretty hard. Her 'valium calm' face is coming from my compulsion, not because she took a sleeping pill then drank ten espressos. Her spaciness almost makes me feel bad, but the smile on her daughter's face—the kid is sincerely enjoying the class now—kills any guilt.

Aurélie told me vampiric compulsions generally last as long as it takes a mortal to complete whatever task. A command/compulsion of the kind I gave to Mrs. Snow may or may not be permanent since there's no specific end to the task, but even if it does wear off, her daughter will be an adult before it happens.

I largely tune out the blur of small bodies spinning back and forth doing jumps and pirouettes and focus on rereading my school assignment. This paper kinda makes me understand how a normal (not-Innocent) vampire must feel if they force themselves awake before sundown: it takes every bit of willpower I have not to fall asleep. This topic bored me to death and it shows. Reading is usually fun for me, but no one in their right mind reads technical manuals for enjoyment.

A pale pink blur catches my eye because it's going somewhere it shouldn't: straight up.

What the hell?

I peer over the top of the laptop at the class, my jaw dropping open at the sight of Megan—the slightly chubby girl Sophia befriended—floating well off the floor, still in a pose like a leaping ballerina. Only her enormous eyes give away she knows something isn't quite right.

Sophia's standing right beside Megan, her expression like she just stumbled and dropped a whole birthday cake on the floor. Uh oh. When she makes eye contact with me, I don't even need telepathy to ask 'what the heck did you do?' My sister flashes a brief 'help me' look before grabbing the other girl's waist and tugging her back down. By some complete miracle, no one else in the room notices her breaking the law of gravity. My sister lets go, but Megan begins gliding upward again—until she grabs on and struggles to keep herself oriented in a standing position. Her body seems to be trying to float up horizontally. Whatever's going on here, she's not negatively buoyant enough to lift Sophia into the air with her.

Her feet slide out from under her and she winds up half-sideways, clinging to Sophia... but it almost looks like they're doing a dance maneuver where scrawny Sophia is lifting Megan off the floor.

My sister stares at me mouthing 'Help!'

If I get up and walk out among the students, it'll draw attention, so I make this 'what am I supposed to do here' type face while sorta-shrugging at her. Good grief, Megan is ten. She's not supposed to be getting high yet.

After a few seconds of looking around in a mild state of panic, Megan recovers her balance and gets her feet back on the floor, but it's obvious —at least to me—they aren't supporting any of her weight. Sophia takes her by the hand and tows her across the room to where I'm sitting. Two of the dance instructors look over, but neither makes a move to intercept her. Guess they're doing freestyle practice. Nothing obvious appears to be out of the ordinary, except how the padded floor mats squish a little under my sister's feet, but remain perfectly flat under Megan's.

"Sare!" whispers Sophia.

"You did something."

She bites her lip.

"What?"

"Umm. Meg was having a little trouble with the jumps, so I wanted to help, only I helped a little too much."

Megan gives her side eye. Perhaps the only thing stopping her from screaming 'what the heck did you do to me?' is not wanting to become the center of the entire room's attention.

"Okay. No need to panic. Think about what you did, and want it to stop."

Sophia closes her eyes for a few seconds, concentrating.

Megan's weight sinks onto her feet again. The poor girl looks so relieved *I* feel better. "So weird."

"Sorry." Sophia flashes a cheesy smile at her friend before fake-wiping sweat from her forehead at me. "Thanks."

"I didn't do anything."

"You gave me the idea to cancel it instead of trying to do the opposite thing. That might have squished her."

Megan raises a hand. "Umm, I would like not to be squished."

"Girls?" asks Ms. Ramirez, the head instructor. "Is everything all right?"

"Yes!" chime the kids together.

They run back to their positions and resume practicing.

Holy crap. Sophia just used magic in public at dance class and nearly sent her friend up to the ceiling. I am so not equipped for this level of weird. Keeping one eye on her every few minutes makes my tedious proofreading even more frustrating. After a little while, I'm fairly sure she's not going to try doing anything else supernatural.

Whew.

About fifteen minutes before the end of class, the instructors gather the kids in lines and guide them through a controlled rehearsal of the technique they'd been practicing. From the look of it, only about half of them are doing it right. I smile a bit at seeing Sophia, Megan, and Alexis all getting nods of approval from the teachers. Another cool thing happens around then: the sun decides to call it a night early thanks to some clouds.

This girl is online. Aww yeah.

A few minutes later, boots scuff up to the front door, and the metal emits a painfully loud—to me—squeak. I don't pay it much attention until all the parents fall silent at the same time, even the two talking about Vegas. Naturally, I'm expecting something super freaky like a giant imp, maybe a vampire with their fangs out, or heck, it wouldn't surprise me to see a huge black pom-pom monster. Considering Sophia hasn't started screaming, safe bet Fuzzydoom isn't floating in the door.

I finish reading the paragraph in front of me, then glance over at the source of the parental silence. This giant dude in a black biker jacket, blue bandana on his head, beard, and jeans is standing near the entrance like the Hells Angel version of Paul Bunyan. Seriously, he looks like he'd walk into a burger place and flip a coin to decide whether or not he wanted the meat cooked first.

The parents are all staring at this guy like they're expecting him to pull out a gun and rob them or start punching people at random—except for the two cougars. They're looking at him in a slightly different way. Oh, ick. And no, I don't have a problem with women in their late fifties being interested in guys. I'd feel every bit the same level of ick watching an old guy check out a woman who could be his daughter.

None of the kids seem to care one bit about the guy.

He shifts to the right so he's no longer blocking the door, folds his arms, and focuses his attention on the kids, a hint of a disapproving bend to his lips. The instructors aren't freaking out so I'm guessing this isn't some random dude showing up at a dance class to stare at little girls. His body language isn't throwing off creepy vibes, so I content myself to observe for now. Though, pre-vampire me would've been petrified of annoying this guy and probably would have walked rapidly in the other direction.

The big biker continues watching the kids with an unsettling frown. Okay, he's past my limit of tolerance, so I peek into his head. He's focused on one of the two boys in the room, specifically the white kid who's so thin and flexible he could pass for an elf—and he's annoyed his son is still doing the same technique they worked on last class instead of learning new stuff.

Oh, okay. Wow. Looking at this guy, the *last* thing most people would expect is for him to be totally cool with his *son* taking dance class. Right, so this guy's a non-issue. No threat. I resume proofreading. With the sun down, I squeeze roughly forty minutes of work into the twelve or so left in the class' time.

Eventually, the kids give off a group cheer of encouragement to each other and come running over in a mob toward their respective guardians. I'm not terribly surprised to see a maybe fourteen-year-old who could pass for twenty approach the cougars. I'm also not surprised to hear her call the black-haired woman 'grandma.' Evidently, the blonde is the woman's friend and doesn't have a kid of her own in this class.

Sophia runs over to me and starts pulling on her puffy raspberry-colored winter coat, then hugs me before whispering, "Should Megan forget floating?"

Hmm. "Yeah, probably."

My sister's friend isn't too far away in a teal coat, waiting patiently while her mother puts her—matching—coat on. I stare at the girl until the weight of my mental influence makes her look toward me. It only takes me a few seconds to eliminate her memory of magical levitation. Of course, this leaves her staring into space like a zombie for three-ish minutes while her mother's trying to get her to follow her to the door.

"All set."

"Thanks." Sophia grins. "Sorry. I thought it would just help her a little without being obvious."

I pat her on the head. "Finesse like that takes practice."

"Yeah." She kicks at the padded floor. "Sorry. I won't do it again."

The slender, almost elven, boy—one of only two boys in the class—breaks off from a small group of kids who'd been talking, and runs up to the giant biker dude.

"He must be *so* proud of his son," whispers a thirtysomething man, father of a pair of twin girls, the two littlest ones in the class at about six. He looks like an extra from the movie *Office Space*. Total cube dweller. "Poor kid."

Ryan glances over, evidently having heard us. Initial shock gives way to shame and the sort of embarrassment that only comes from frequent teasing.

"Actually, I am." The big guy—who I'm now sure is Ryan's dad—takes a few steps closer and looms at the man. "My son's doing what he loves, and he's good at it. You're damn right I'm proud of him."

Ryan's mood does a one-eighty and he stands there grinning.

"I… uhh…" The polo-shirt-guy peers up at the biker like a mouse watching the eagle coming for it. If that man could open a mirror and crawl out of reality, he probably would do it right now. "Nothing against him dancing, just… you, umm, didn't look like the kinda guy who'd approve."

Okay, I admit I had the same initial thought about him. I bite my lip and bonk myself on the head with the laptop twice. Bad Sarah. Shouldn't assume things about giant bikers.

"Why are you being a dork?" asks Sophia.

"Hey, you usually hit Starbucks after this. Wanna?" I smile.

"Aren't you going to be late for school?"

I throw my coat on, grab her hand, and head out the door. The Starbucks shares the parking lot with the dance place, all the way on the left end of the huge U-shaped strip mall. "Cutting it close, but I have forever to repeat classes. You won't be a kid forever."

She squeezes my hand tight the whole way across the lot. As soon as we join the line at Starbucks, she hugs me.

"What?" I pat the back of her puffy coat.

"What you said. Guess I'm still clingy."

"Aww, it's okay."

"I could if you wanted me to." She peers up.

"Huh?"

"Stay a kid forever."

A shiver runs down my body, remembering the dream. "Please don't joke about that."

She strikes a pose. "What? I'd look totally adorable as an eternal tween, wouldn't I?"

Her tone and posture makes me laugh despite the somberness of the thought. "You would, yeah. But don't you want to grow up and stuff? Spending eternity having to go to bed at nine would suck."

"Bedtimes wouldn't really work. I dunno. Mom always complains about how much 'adulting' sucks. That's not exactly a ringing endorsement to growing up."

"Hah!" I grin. "True."

The kid might have a point. Our mother does often complain endlessly about how stressful her life is. For a person who wouldn't mind remaining dependent on others and having no freedom, I suppose an eternity without any responsibilities could be appealing. No job, no worries about taxes, insurance, and so on. Just sit around at home, play, read, do whatever. Though, it would have to get old eventually, right? At some point, the eternal child would surely start to resent being treated like a kid all the time. But I suppose it depends on how the mind reacts to vampirism. Would Sophia's personality remain permanently like ten-year-old, or would she turn into an adult woman trapped in the body of a child?

Ugh. I don't want to think about it.

"So why were you acting like a dork?"

"Oh. Umm. Just bonking myself for thinking poorly of that big guy. Thought he'd give Ryan attitude for being into dance."

"Nah, Mr. Bowman's pretty cool. Ryan said his dad even built him a little dance studio in the basement so he can practice at home. They also go rock climbing together."

"Cool." It's nice to feel like we're not the only family in the world with a good dad. Thinking of Hunter's father makes me cringe. And yeah, I know there are worse parents out there than even that, but still.

We stand in line for a few minutes discussing the floating Megan situation in obscure terms so the other people around us don't think we're crazy. Framing the discussion in terms like we're talking about fictional characters in a nonexistent book series allows us to discuss weird stuff without breaking secrecy. Sophia's not really sure how trying to help her friend jump resulted in the girl 'becoming floaty' as she puts it.

"Well, in the book world, people who can do magic have to keep it hidden because society isn't ready for it."

"Yeah." Sophia kicks at the floor. "That's true."

When we're third from the register, the mom-aged woman at the head of the line begins asking the clerk all sorts of questions about what's in the various coffees. Ugh. This woman is apparently vegan, anti-GMO, says she's avoiding gluten because 'it's what people do' and doesn't want anything with high-fructose corn syrup, processed in a place with peanuts, or made with 'bad vibes'. She's even got the classic 'I want to talk to the manager' haircut.

People behind us fidget in annoyance as two minutes become six. The poor girl behind the counter, who can't be much older than fifteen, looks like she's about to scream and quit her job to get away from this woman grilling her over every little ingredient. I'm already playing it close with the clock. There's no time for jackassery of this magnitude.

I lean around the man in front of me and tap the indecisive woman on the arm. As soon as she looks at me, her brain is mine. Once confident the woman has no legit health concerns and merely decided to be super picky because she's super picky, I narrow my eyes. "Order something."

She rotates to face the kid behind the register and gets a matcha latte.

The blonde teen gives me a grateful smile, then rings the woman up.

"Did you?" whispers Sophia.

"Yep." I rock heel to toe.

"Nice." She grins.

The guy ahead of us gets a cappuccino plus a hot sandwich. Finally, I step up to the girl.

"Hi. Welcome to Starbucks." She smiles at me, then blinks. "Oh, you're that kid everyone thought died, right?"

"Police messed up. I didn't die." I emit a fake sad sigh. "Some other poor young woman did and we kinda look alike. But yeah, that's me. Can I have a skinny mocha latte? And… umm, whatever she wants."

Sophia smiles. "Grande white chai? But only if it's got good vibes."

The clerk and a few people behind us chuckle.

"Cool," says the girl, Mindy according to her name tag. "Did you know my sister, Bree?"

I blink. "Mindy Swanson?"

"Yep." She grins. "Go ahead and swipe your card or phone whenever."

Sophia's expression hardens, but she's far too sweet to comment about my ex-boyfriend cheating on me with Bree.

"I know Bree, but we didn't exactly hang out in the same circles." I pull out cash, hoping the math won't confuse this kid. Oh, that's bitchy of me. She might be blonde, and related to Bree, but she can probably count. Or at least type in numbers. And really, I don't blame Bree for what happened. Scott lied to her about us breaking up.

"Oh, cool." Mindy takes the $20 bill and makes change.

"How is she doing anyway? Haven't seen her since graduation."

Mindy shrugs one shoulder. "I miss her. She's doing okay. Went to

Texas A&M. Kinda worried about her, too. She had a really bad break-up with her last boyfriend. It's left her all spacey and weird for a while. Like, her whole personality changed. Far as I know, she still isn't dating anyone and for Bree, that's bizarre."

"Yeah. Sorry, the situation was kind of a mess." I step to the right so the woman behind us can order. "Next time you talk to her, let her know I hope she's doing okay?"

Sophia blinks at me.

"Sure." Mindy smiles, then faces the woman. "Hi. Welcome to Starbucks."

I head to the end of the counter to wait for our drinks.

"Sare, the girl kidnapped Sierra. And cheated on you."

"Nah. Bree was under the influence."

"Still. I can't believe you forgave her so fast."

The woman behind the counter sets our drinks up. "Here you go."

"Thanks!" I collect the cups and walk with Sophia to a small table. "She's another victim. Nothing to be mad at."

"Okay." Sophia flops in the chair and sips her chai.

We spend a few minutes talking about random stuff: her schoolwork, an upcoming movie adaptation of a book she likes—she's afraid the movie will stink—and so on for a little while. Eventually, she confesses to having nightmares about Fuzzydoom again.

"They're not *that* bad. I still wake up scared, but not so much there's screaming or crying. Just freaked out." She slurps chai. "Kinda stupid, huh?"

"Not really. People who are bitten by snakes when they're really small can develop lifelong phobias. You should consider yourself lucky you're phobic of a mutant pom-pom demon. Not like you're going to run into it… at least not in the real world. And no one will ever know you're afraid of it unless you tell them."

She laughs. "Yeah. Umm. You don't think he's going to come out of the mirror? I mean, we *saw* him in there."

"Still not sure if it really happened. But, I spoke to Coralie, and she's confident Fuzzydoom can't leave the mirrorverse. And I'm also sure you wouldn't try summoning it on purpose."

"No way." Sophia shakes her head so hard, her blonde hair ends up covering her face. "I didn't even want to see it when we did. So, umm… do you think I should talk to those mystics? Maybe they could help me figure out how to do stuff—or not do stuff by accident?"

"Hmm." I swirl mocha around in my cup. "Got a feeling you learning magic isn't the sort of after-school activity Mom and Dad ever had in mind."

"Pff. Dad would adore it." She wags her eyebrows at me while drinking. "Totally adore it. I can hear the Hogwarts puns already."

"Owl bet you do," I mutter.

"Ugh." She shakes her head. "You're supposed to be undead not un-dad."

"Ouch." I cringe. "Wait. If I'm *un*-dad, wouldn't that mean my puns are actually funny?"

She laughs.

"Hmm. It might not be an awful idea to ask if they can help you figure things out. I'd hate to see you float Megan or some other kid up into the clouds and lose them."

"Eep!" Her eyes go wide. "Yeah, that would be bad."

"Let's see how Mom and Dad feel about it. If they're okay with it, I'll approach Darren and see if he'll talk to you."

Sophia grins. "Cool."

We continue talking about random stuff for a few minutes as we work on our drinks. Sophia gets a mischievous glint in her eye and fixates on a table across the room for a moment. A minor commotion erupts when a guy's man bun bursts free from its moorings and explodes into a fluffy poof. The two women and other guy sitting with him all come close to choking on their drinks at the sudden explosion.

"Soph... behave. It's cruel to abuse hipsters."

She snickers.

After we finish our drinks, we head outside. I should have enough time to print my paper and fly to school. My attention drifts sideways to a late-twenties guy in a cheap grey suit, standing on the curb outside, rambling at his cell phone about setting up a meeting with a business client to do a demo. He's thin, tanned, bit of beard scruff with a hint of Italian or Spanish in him. He looks over at us as we pass, giving me a 'hey baby' wag of the eyebrows.

You know, I went out in the sun today.

At my stopping short and walking toward him, the guy blinks in shock. "Let me call you back, Jake, okay?"

"Sure," says the voice from the phone.

"Hey. You have really pretty eyes." He smiles at me for a few seconds until I get close enough for him to get a better look at me. The instant he thinks I appear underage, he stammers, "Umm, is something wrong, kiddo?"

Heh. Nice backpedal. "Thanks. Come with me a sec?"

His expression slackens. Like an automaton, he follows me to a small alcove behind the Starbucks where they keep the dumpsters. Sophia stands at the corner of the building on lookout while I back the guy into the wall, stand up on tiptoe, and bite him on the neck. A burst of hot blood fills my mouth, surging in time with his heartbeat. The flavor of tacos... maybe burritos... overwhelms me, but not in a totally bad way.

Clicking footsteps approach the corner.

Sophia ducks back out of sight from the parking lot, hiding as a person goes by. Without looking back, she gives a thumbs-up as if to say I'm safe. In truth, it's a little unnerving to have my ten-year-old sister standing guard while I drink some dude's blood. Like, my biting this guy is as normal to her as stopping at a hotdog wagon randomly for a snack. If anyone ever needed proof there's nothing whatsoever sexually appealing about a vampire feeding—at least for me—that I can still do it with Sophia watching me is concrete evidence.

I can barely hold hands with Hunter when the littles are in sight. Kissing him while my sisters watched would be way mortifying. And, I say sisters because Sam wouldn't bother to watch.

"Hungry?" asks Sophia. "Duh, obviously. You're eating. What's he taste like?"

I'll take 'things a ten-year-old should never ask' for $200.

Once I've had my fill, I seal the bite and give the guy a mental prod to forget ever seeing us. Also, a compulsion to go into Starbucks and get a cookie. Gotta take care of blood donors, right?

"Tacos," I say, walking toward the parking lot.

Sophia falls in step at my side when I pass her. "Weird."

"More weird than vampires and magic?"

"Hmm. Yeah, a little. He looks like steak. Or burgers."

I raise an eyebrow at her. "How do you figure that?"

"He's a sales weasel. Probably takes people to like TGI Friday's for meetings all the time."

"Hah! Yeah, probably."

Crap. Ran a little long. I hop in and start the engine while Sophia buckles up. Meh, who cares? I might be a few minutes late to class, even flying there, but spending time with her is worth it.

Besides, the teacher won't remember I'm late.

4

HOW TO DEAL WITH ANNOYANCES

The worst part about night school is having friends who go to day classes and work jobs.

Usually, by the time I'm done with school for the day, my friends are eyeball deep in homework, still at work, or too damn tired to do anything. This, of course, has the not-unwelcome side effect of me spending more time hanging out with Glim. He likes to sit on the roof of a building at the apartment complex where his ex-wife lives with his two sons, at least until they go to sleep.

It's kinda sad watching him hover at the edges of his old life. Unlike me, he won't reveal himself to his mortal family due to his appearance. As a Shadow, he's pretty striking—and not in an aesthetically pleasing way. Pale grey skin, glowing yellow eyes, big fangs, bigger claws… generally ghoulish. They're also skilled with illusions, making people see things that aren't there. Most often, though, they use it to force people *not* to see them.

He thinks it's kinder to let his wife and sons go on with their lives. They believe he died over in Iraq. To be completely technical, he *did* die in Iraq, and spent several years there under the wing of his sire, Saeed El-Amin. Glim hasn't told me much about the guy other than making him sound wicked and creepy, and not the sort of creature anyone mortal would enjoy meeting.

So, whenever I find myself having a night alone with no homework in need of doing, I've been hanging out with Glim. Once his wife and sons go to sleep, we sometimes go flying around sightseeing or sneaking into museums or whatever and messing with the security guards. Breaking into places with him is beyond easy. He leaps into the shadow dimension for a few seconds and goes right past walls or doors. Once we're inside, he can keep us both from being seen as long as I hold his hand. Guards in at least a dozen places around Seattle Downtown are now firm believers in ghosts.

I've been asking him to let me try playing around with some of the shadow stuff with a blood loan, but he's super hesitant. No idea how true it is or if he's a big softie, but he's afraid if he temporarily lets me borrow some Shadow abilities, it might start having an effect on how I look. Even if it doesn't cause my eyes to go yellow or my teeth to resemble those of a gargoyle, it could steal my lifelike appearance and leave me with an obviously dead complexion.

Or at least, it's what Glim's afraid of.

Apparently, Shadows are one of the more potent bloodlines, perhaps the Universe making a tradeoff for how badly they get screwed in terms of appearance. My one strength among vampire kind is how I look perfectly alive while I'm conscious. It's pretty obvious he's jealous, at least a little, of it, and doesn't want to be responsible should anything happen. Okay, it's understandable despite being annoying. But, if there is any truth to his fears, it would freak my family out to see me walking around with grey skin—not to mention end any chance of me pretending to be normal. No college, going out in public with my friends, or anything really.

It would be one thing to take the risk for an emergency, but just farting around to have fun? Yeah, not worth the chance. Even if it does turn out to be complete paranoia with no basis in fact, oh well. No big deal. I mean, he's borrowed my ability to tolerate food and his appearance hasn't improved, but nothing about my new reality even remotely follows logic.

Enormous troll in a pocket dimension. 'Nuff said.

Of course, the more time I spend with Glim, the more confusion I have regarding my feelings toward him. No, I love Hunter and it isn't going to change... at least not unless he randomly turns into an asshole. (Gonna call it unlikely.) However, there's the distinct possibility due to his being a mortal, he isn't going to live forever. Maybe it's creepy and odd of me to think of, but once I'm done mourning his eventual death,

I'm not so sure being romantic with another mortal would be a good idea.

Then again, I'm not exactly having romantic feelings for Glim. He's become this quirky combination of best friend, older sibling, foster dad, and the guy at work who's been there forever, knows everything and kinda-sorta likes me. With him, I don't need to hold back any secrets or talk in circles to allude at stuff that can't be said in mixed (mortal) company.

Unfortunately, Ashley, Michelle, and Hunter are all hammered with schoolwork and actual work. Plus, Hunter's doing stuff around his house in his spare time. They have a huge place, but it's in 'horror movie house' shape, basically a never-ending repair project. Worst part is, they can barely afford the supplies to do the limited repairs he's doing, much less hire professionals. So anything Hunter can't teach himself to fix stays broken. Except for important stuff like if the furnace craps out and their heat stops. If something big or complicated blows up, his mother would call a pro.

Another 'unfortunately' is how I've been absorbing quite a bit of homework as well lately. It's not more than I can keep up with being up all night, but I've been too damn busy to have fun with Glim for a while now—which is frustrating. I need some cooldown time. Guess that's what weekends are for.

The remainder of the week passes without anything too unusual happening, though the parents did have to go to the littles' school once. Some boy who'd decided to start picking on Sam wound up stuck in his locker, claiming to have been pushed from behind. No one saw it happen, but the kid blamed Sam for it. Fortunately, a teacher vouched for my brother, having seen him walking out of a classroom on the other side of the building at the time.

Naturally, I blamed the imp.

My mouth, however, stayed shut. If the kid decided to bully Sam, his new supernatural friend did him a solid. The other boy didn't get hurt, only a little rattled. Hopefully, he'll leave my brother alone from now on.

So, yeah. The long-awaited weekend finally showed up. One good thing: my classwork has become more interesting. Though, to be fair, only the one comp-sci assignment bored me to tears. The other classes are fine. Maybe introduction to computer science is hyper boring on purpose as sort of a gatekeeper thing to make sure the unworthy fall before the altar of technology.

I awake Saturday afternoon at 2:37 p.m. The smell of cosmetics in the air informs me Sophia has been in my room. Hopefully, my face looks like I'm about to have a professional photoshoot, not perform in a circus or try to sell hamburgers. She's been getting better. Last few times I've been 'decorated,' the effect has been more 'drunk prostitute' than rodeo clown. Okay, I'm being harsh. More like a heavily made up *sober* prostitute.

She's been watching videos online, makeup tutorials. Sophia's passionate about cosmetics and novels. I really think she's going to end up doing makeup for theater or movies someday. If it's what she wants to do, I am not above using my powers of mental influence to ensure she gets a job somewhere in the field. Cheating with mind powers doesn't bother me when someone else benefits. It only feels like stealing or being naughty if I'm enriching myself.

A slight stiffness in my bones warns me it's a little nuclear outside, but not *too* bad. No point cooking myself without good cause. Since I haven't eaten regular food in a while, nothing wants out, so I have no reason to get out of bed or move. I do, however, sit up, grab my phone, and proceed to text the usual three suspects: Ashley, Michelle, and Hunter.

Ashley's at the vet place, Michelle's *still* at the law firm putting paperwork back in drawers. Ugh. I wonder if I could convince Sam's pet imp—I mean friend—to undo that? Hunter's presently replacing a toilet in his house, and needs to go to work at Mi Tierra in like an hour.

Argh! This is truly starting to suck. I'd have been willing to suffer a light broiling to hang out with my friends today. Schedule conflicts have also kept my Hunter time pretty limited as well, which is beyond frustrating. Though, to be fair, it wouldn't have been much different for mortal me since then, we'd both have day classes. He'd still be doing stuff around his house plus homework, then going to his job. I'd also have a job if the sun didn't mess with me so bad. At least if I remained alive, I could've gone over and helped him around his house during the day. That's still spending time with him even if it's work.

So, I can't blame the fangs for my inability to see him much lately. We do sit on the phone together sometimes while he's working. I loaned him my Bluetooth earbud. Whenever he's not talking to customers, he can 'mutter to himself,' talking to me. His boss might fire him if he gets caught being on the phone, but it's nothing I can't smooth over. Most likely, he'd only be yelled at the first time, in which case, we'll stop.

Thinking about him gets me in the mood. Alas, as soon as I start taking matters into my own hands so to speak, Sophia's rapid thumping footsteps go by overhead. Crap. It's Saturday. Consequently, I can't guarantee a roughly twenty-minute child-free time where I don't have to worry about someone barging in on me at an embarrassing moment. Sure, Dad's usually home, but he'd knock… and I'd hear him coming a mile away.

How weird is it that I can recognize my family purely from the sounds they make while walking around above me?

Sophia's footfalls are kind of rabbit-like. Soft, quick. I think she pretty much keeps all her weight on the front of her feet. Sierra's a heel-thudder, but she doesn't weigh as much as Sam despite being two years older than him. Or maybe it's just something about boys. He's almost as loud as Dad, especially when he charges down the stairs. Mom and Dad are both fairly obvious due to them being adults.

Ugh. I have too much schoolwork waiting to sit here bored and analyzing ceiling thumps.

Screw it. I jump out of bed, lock my door, and deal with my frustrations. Wonder if Hunter's ears are burning from how hard I'm thinking about him?

<hr />

YOU KNOW WHAT'S WEIRD ABOUT BEING A VAMPIRE?

Okay, a lot of things. But… getting myself off, in fact sex in general, leaves me breathless, sweating, and kinda tired like it would have normally. Yet, I can run full speed for like a half hour and barely notice the fatigue. Talk about highly awkward things to ask one's sire. Hell, I'm not even going to bring it up to Aurélie. Doing so would set off a long, bizarre conversation I'd rather avoid.

Meh. It's probably psychosomatic.

I grab a cute top, skirt, and underthings, then dash across the basement to the downstairs shower. While it doesn't feel painfully sunny today, no sense burning through my blood reserves purely to take a bath upstairs instead. Sure enough, Sophia painted my face, though impressively, she didn't do too bad of a job. It wouldn't be embarrassing to go out like this, other than it being way more makeup than usual for my taste. Anyway, the instant I'm back in my room, cleaned and dressed, Mom walks in. Can't call it 'barging' because I left my door open.

"Hon? Would you be able to take Sam and his friends to the movies?

Your father's already out with the girls at soccer and I have a ridiculous amount of prep to do for litigation next week."

Mom leading with justification makes me cringe a little, since it reminds me of before my death. Most reasonable people wouldn't have considered me abnormally bitchy for a teenager, but I'd almost always argue and protest whenever she asked me to do something like this because of plans to hang with Ashley and Michelle. It's like she's bracing for the argument her subconscious mind expects to happen.

"Sure, no problem. Umm. What kind of mood is the sun in?"

"Hiding. It's kinda rainy." Slight tension in my mother's face relaxes.

"Ahh. Guess the girls are playing soccer indoors then?"

"Yeah."

I stand out of my computer desk chair and give her a quick hug. "Sorry."

"What did you do this time?"

"Heh. Nothing."

Fists on her hips, she quirks an eyebrow. "So why are you apologizing?"

"For all the arguments we used to have whenever you asked me to do stuff. I could tell you'd mentally prepared yourself for a fight, even if you didn't consciously intend to do it."

Mom's expression turns guilty. "Just a habit. You have to admit you were a bit selfish before."

"Yeah, I know. Hence the 'sorry.'" I wink. "So, when do they want to go?"

"The movie's starting in about forty minutes." Mom shakes her head at the ceiling. "So, naturally the boy asks for a ride two minutes ago. He actually thought I'd leave him at the theater on his own at nine."

"Oof." I grimace. "Sophia would have better odds of talking you into letting her get a cat."

Mom laughs. "Hmm. Hard call there. Thank you, sweetie."

"Sure. Drat."

"Hmm?"

I wiggle my toes. "This is going to require socks. It's November. I'll get weird looks for walking around in flip-flops."

"Don't you dare." Mom shivers. "That makes me cold even thinking about it."

Chuckling, I trade the skirt I'd intended to wear around the house all day for jeans and socks, then head upstairs. Sam, plus his two friends

Daryl and Jordan are waiting by the door. To most people, Jordan's skinny, but not compared to my family's genetics. I consider him average. Daryl's a little heavy, and I can still smell birthday cake on him since he turned ten a week ago on November fourth. Or, wait, maybe I'm smelling *him.*

Nah. Can't be. It's too 'daylighty' in the room. My senses aren't any sharper than normal at the moment.

"Thanks for driving us!" Sam hugs me.

"Yeah, thanks, Sarah." Daryl gives me a double thumbs-up.

"Sweet." Jordan grins. "Your sister's cool."

"Not so cool I'm going to scam you guys into an R-rated movie. Which one are you going to see?"

"The new *Avengers* one," says Sam.

I blink. "Didn't they kill them all off?"

All three boys laugh. "Naw."

"At least not yet," says Sam, deadpan.

After I step into my sneakers, we hurry out to the old Sentra, none of the boys bothering with umbrellas. I've got a compact pink Hello Kitty one Ashley gave me for my seventeenth birthday. Naturally, Sophia saw it and had to have one like it. I swear, that girl… if Brussels sprouts were pink, she'd adore them.

Not quite four minutes into the ride, the stench of forty-thousand dead souls assaults my nostrils.

"Aww, man!" yells Jordan. "Dude!"

"Lies!" Daryl punches him on the shoulder. "He's lying. He thinks you'll blame the fat kid."

I cough, eyes nearly watering. Good grief, that's worse than anything Dad ever summoned and none of these boys are even half his size.

"You're not fat, Daryl. Tim Dearborn is fat." Sam eyes the door, but appears unfazed by the horror in the air. "We can't open the windows because it's raining too hard. Seriously unsportsmanlike."

"C'mon, Sam." Jordan leans into the front seat. "Good one. You should be laughing."

Sam sighs and glances at him. "My sister is in the car. Not cool to shred the atmosphere around her. She has to breathe too." He sneaks a little wink at me the boys can't see.

The kid has a point. I stop breathing for a while.

Daryl continues to gag while pantomime-clawing at the window like he's trapped in a chamber of toxic gas. This, of course, only makes Jordan laugh louder. Fortunately, even with rainy roads, it doesn't take us too long to get to the theater. The boys leap out and run for the entrance as soon as I park. Not wanting to become drenched, I walk like a normal vampire with an umbrella.

Upon noticing them in line at a ticket kiosk, it occurs to me Mom didn't give me any money for tickets. Evidently, Daryl's covering the boys' tickets with his birthday money. I briefly debate mental trickery to get in. Stealing still feels wrong, even a movie ticket. Of course, I don't have a job or any money of my own left. That means, I either cheat my way in or the parents are paying for me. Pretty sure Mom expected to cover my ticket since she asked me to take the boys, so I don't feel any guilt whipping out the authorized-user credit card they gave me.

Okay, that's a lie. As soon as I see it, my brain leaps to thinking about how Hunter doesn't have one. Heck, I'm not sure his mother even has a credit card at all. My parents can afford to trust me with access to their credit card account. The moment of awkwardness passes when I blame society for such inequalities. My life hasn't been comfortable because my parents exploited anyone, so there's nothing for me to feel ashamed of. It's the human dragons sitting on their piles of gold with fourteen yachts, six mansions, and more money than anyone could spend in a hundred lifetimes who should be ashamed of themselves. And yeah, I extend the same contempt toward a handful of vampires, too. Aurélie has a crapton of money, but she's also been around for several centuries, and she *still* has a lot less than some mortals. Doesn't stop me from wishing Hunter's family wasn't in such a position. Or any family for that matter.

Anyway, I get my ticket and follow the kids straight to the snack counter. We go deep enough in the building that combined with the gloominess outside, my powers come online unexpectedly. I fake a sneeze to distract anyone who might be looking right at me from noticing the brief red glow in my eyes.

Right. Movie snack counter. Here, I have no qualms using my powers. In the hierarchy of scoundrel scumminess, you have simple thieves, people who embezzle millions, those who scam elderly couples out of their life savings, people who steal money from children's charities, and finally movie theater snack merchants. No problems exploiting my powers here.

Daryl approaches the guy behind the register, who's probably like sixteen or seventeen. He stares right over the boy's head at me and smiles. Ugh. Here comes the lame pick-up line. Since he obligingly made eye contact already, I give him a compulsion to charge the boys only for one soda and popcorn. Still, for what they cost, it's more than fair for three orders. I could make like six times the amount of popcorn at home for the same price.

Once he's bucketed the kids' orders and handed over the sodas, the guy leans on the counter and wags his eyebrows at me. "Hey. I'm Nathan. What's your name?"

"Sarah."

"Cool. Got plans for after the movie?"

"She's got a boyfriend," adds Sam in a slightly raised voice.

Nathan leans back, giving me an almost insulted look. "Really? What's his name?"

"I don't have to justify myself to you."

"Thought so." He tries to revert to the suave smile, but is still giving off irritation. "You don't need to use the fake boyfriend excuse. Girls shouldn't lie. It's not sexy. C'mon. You know you're not busy after the movie."

I narrow my eyes at him, trying to come up with something to say or do to him that won't get the Persons In Black knocking on my door. Compelling him to run around the theater shouting 'I am an asshole' probably wouldn't go over too well.

Before anything comes to mind, the soda fountain to Nathan's left explodes in a spray of multicolored syrup, dousing him—and the area around him—liberally. He screams, flails, and promptly falls on his ass in the slippery puddle. Within seconds of him crashing to the floor, the eruption from the soda fountain stops.

Sam, Daryl, and Jordan burst into laughter.

Oh, this has imp all over it. Even though the little bugger can't make himself invisible from me when my abilities are online, I don't see him around. Still, not going to complain.

"Nice," I whisper.

My brother's backpack twitches.

Aha. Wow. Guess he really has become more of a friend than a pet.

While Nathan struggles to get to his feet, I shoo the boys down a huge hall decorated in dark red curtains and movie posters among the theater entrances. Naturally, ours has the longest line, all along the right side wall behind those irritating fuzzy rope barriers. It's not a big deal though since we have guaranteed seats. Another teen employee goes by, apologizing for the delay and informing us the theater is still in use, should be open in about ten minutes.

The absolutely weird fact that occurs to me a minute or two later is the boys and I are probably the youngest people in line for a comic book movie. Almost everyone around us is thirty or older. Sure, there's a handful of kids, but three out of five people waiting for this movie are neither parents nor very young. Conversations about characters, powers, and plot lines abound. It mostly goes over my head as I've never been much of a superhero fan. My dad, Sierra, and Sam are nuts for it, so a certain degree of information-by-osmosis has occurred.

Sam, in a moment of highly uncharacteristic extroversion, inserts himself into a conversation among three grown men about some story arc involving a secondary hammer or something like that. Other than a brief glimpse at each guy's head to make sure they're not a threat to my li'l bro, I largely tune their conversation out.

My ears pick up an older guy screaming at Nathan for making a mess. Heh.

Eventually, the theater doors open and a river of people shambles out. Most are ashen-faced, like they'd just witnessed some horrible tragedy unfold. A few seem excited, one or two look highly pissed off. One such angry guy glances over at the conversation going on between my brother, his friends, and the three guys still discussing the hammer.

"Thor dies!" shouts the angry guy.

A collective gasp comes from the line around me. The next thing I know, like fifteen people jump the rope barrier and pounce on this guy, beating the snot out of him. He crashes to the floor, screaming for help and trying to defend his face. A little girl who can't be older than like eight scurries out there and furiously kicks him repeatedly in the leg.

Sam, Daryl, and Jordan stare at the melee with expressions of heartbreak.

Three movie theater employees run over, yelling at people to calm down. Some of the attackers slip back into line.

The little girl gets in one more cheap shot to the guy's balls, yells, "Spoilers suck!" and darts back to her father.

I grasp Sam's shoulder. "Don't worry about the spoiler. He could be lying. But either way, it won't ruin the movie for you."

"What?" He peers up at me. Disappointment evaporates a few seconds later. "Oh! Yeah! Please."

Once the people back away from the guy, I delete the last five minutes of the man's memory. Hey, not condoning assault or anything, but spoiling a movie? Yeah, he deserved a bit of a beating. He also gets a temporary compulsion limiting his ability to speak for about an hour. No matter what he tries to say, he's going to blurt 'I'm a jackass.' Next, I give the theater people an urge to walk away and forget they saw a fight.

Everyone more or less goes back to normal and we stand there in peace—despite much complaining and grumbling from the people in line about the spoiler—while the employees clean up the theater. Minutes later, we shuffle in and take our assigned seats. As soon as we're comfortable, I erase the spoiler from the boys' memory.

A short delay later, the lights dim and the preview reel starts.

"What kind of dickhead yells a spoiler like that?" asks a guy in the row behind us.

"Spoiler?" Sam looks at me, confused. Realization sets in, and he hugs me. "You're an awesome big sister."

"You're a pretty awesome li'l bro, too."

So, yeah. A bunch of fan-favorite characters went through the meat grinder.

My brother, his friends, and the people shuffling out of the theater at the end of the movie have the same shell-shocked expressions as the group ahead of us. The boys quietly mutter to each other about the odds the deaths are some kind of trick. Either everyone will get brought back to life by a powerful demigod or new people will assume the identities of the fallen heroes.

Since I haven't been following the story arc over the past three movies, my emotional reaction isn't as deep. It's a bit after six at night now, so the sun's gone down. Hooray for winter, right? At least the boys don't regret going to see it. This might be the first time Sam has seen a movie so soon after it released. I text Mom on the walk to the front of the theater, letting her know the movie's over and we're on the way home.

Besides spoilers, you know what else sucks? Prey instinct.

Not in and of itself, mind you. The sucky part is that I have it. More to the point, girls tend to develop it as soon as they realize the world is *not* a safe place for them. Ashley and I knew never to go to a public bathroom alone ever since we turned like nine. We never questioned it, just did it. The craptitude of the whole paradigm never really occurred to me until I rose to the top of the food chain. Like, I grew up trained to consider myself vulnerable to attack at any moment along with the nervous guilt from being conditioned to accept if someone did something to me, it would've been considered my fault because I screwed up and let my guard down.

Despite being immortal, my hopes of living long enough to see a world that stops blaming girls for everything done to them is pretty dim.

Anyway, as soon as we reach the front room with all the ticket kiosks, my prey instinct returns—and I don't like it. I shouldn't have prey instinct anymore. The feeling has returned because I *feel* someone staring at me the way no young woman ever wants to be stared at. It doesn't take me long to locate the source: a twentyish Hispanic dude leaning against the wall on the right, acting far too casual. His hair is super short and dark smudges mark the sides of his face and neck, probably tattoos. Hard to gauge his build under a winter coat, but he definitely doesn't look like he's used to the weather here—and he's also staring straight at me.

That's pretty telling given the number of people in the room between us. Plenty of young women, quite a few I'd say are way hotter than I am. No, this dude is interested in *me* for some reason. This is no random creep looking for a girl to hit on, or even a darker creep with worse intentions. It's fairly obvious he's a human, but for reasons beyond my understanding, his thoughts are walled off from my sight.

Okay, now I know for sure something supernatural is about to bite me square on the ass.

Hmm. Do I storm over there and confront him in a public place where there's less chance he'll do something violent? Having my brother and his friends with me adds another layer of complexity. If anything happened to them, I'd never forgive myself. So, the best course of action is to get the hell out of here.

As casual as possible, I usher the boys out the doors to the parking lot while keeping one eye on the dude. Could he be another hunter, one who's far more competent than the last group? That's probably not likely since he looks like some kind of gangbanger. Admittedly, the winter coat makes him a little funny. Like this dude is trying to look so 'hard,' but he's shivering, and it's sorta amusing.

Predictably, he follows us out to the lot, tailing us two rows over. Rain's still falling, but more of a drizzle than the aquatic pounding from earlier. It's tempting to run for the car before he can make a move, but he's not some random creep. This guy is clearly interested in me on a deep, personal level and I don't at all feel like getting touchy-feely with him. At least, not without claws being involved. Since he's already at the theater waiting for me, I figure he knows what my car looks like. He had to have trailed us here, and simply eluded my awareness during the daylight. When we reach the Sentra, the guy can't help himself but sneer a little.

Okay, he *didn't* know what I drove. Weird. And hey, this creep is stalking me and he's got the nerve to critique my ten-year-old ride? Screw you, pal. Drat. Now he knows what my car looks like. How the heck did he find me at the theater if he hadn't followed me in? Not recognizing the Sentra means he also doesn't know where we live.

Maybe I can lose him on the road?

"That dude's following us," says Sam.

"Yeah, I know." I shoot the guy a 'back off' look before dropping in behind the wheel and closing my door. "Hurry up and get in."

Sam jumps into the passenger seat while his friends cram into the back. "Is he…"

"Probably has a gun." says Jordan.

"Dude." Daryl hunkers down, peering over the seatback out the rear window. "You can't just assume a Latin looking guy with tats is carrying a gun."

"Then why are you ducking?" Jordan folds his arms. "The guy looks like he's straight out of GTA."

I back out of the space and drive a little fast down the row.

"Because, sometimes people who look like gang members *are* gang members." Daryl pivots to keep watching the guy as the car turns.

"You contradicted yourself." Sam looks back at his friend.

"Not really. Jordan's thinking he's carrying a gun because he looks kinda rough and has tats on his face. I'm thinking he's dangerous because he's following us and staring at your sister like he's gonna do something bad."

The boys proceed to debate the concept of stereotyping people while I focus on not crashing. Between the damnable sky water and traffic, I'm not going to be doing any *Fast and the Furious* type stuff tonight. More like the *Sluggish and Mildly Perturbed.* That's probably what they're going to call the fortieth movie in the franchise when everyone's elderly. Maybe they'll be driving their electric scooters recklessly around the aisles of Walmart while a security guard on a Segway chases them.

"Hey, can we go to the VR place?" asks Jordan.

"Sam's gotta be home by seven for dinner."

"Aww," chorus all three boys.

Conversation shifts back to the movie for a little while once we're on the highway and up to a reasonable speed. With three kids in the car, I'm driving like a responsible person despite wanting to fly (metaphorically) to get away from the guy. Unfortunately, there's a small Toyota a few car lengths back that's been there for most of the ride.

Dammit.

The instant I have enough of a straightaway to take my eyes off the road for a few seconds, I look at the side mirror and zoom my vision in the same way Glim taught me. Sure enough, it's the guy. Ugh, dude's got nerve grimacing at my car when he's driving an oversized wind-up toy. I didn't think Toyota made cars so little. It's not exactly Smart Car little, but cub scouts might steal it for a pine derby racer.

"Dammit," I mutter.

Sam, twisted around in the passenger seat to converse with his friends, leans back enough to look at me. "What?"

"The guy is following us. I don't want him to find out where we live. But I can't drive like a maniac with you guys in the car. Especially on wet roads."

"What's he want?"

"I don't know."

"You said he's not a... umm." Sam bites his lip.

"Pretty sure he's not. But I can't see for some reason. This is definitely more weird stuff."

Sam nods. "Okay. No problem. Hey, Blix. Can you get that guy off our tail?"

Blix? He named it? Okay, sure. Lots of guys name their pet imps, but most don't have wings and fly around on their own.

The soft *zzzzt* of a backpack zipper precedes a small grey hand reaching up. Sure enough, my brother's closet imp climbs out of the backpack. The boys in the backseat don't react to him at all, a good sign he's invisible to them. I can't tell if Sam can't see him or simply acts like he can't to help his new friend stay hidden.

Blix turns his slightly oversized head and floppy ears toward me.

"Little blue Toyota, behind the Chevy pickup," I whisper.

The imp nods once, then disappears.

Okay, not what I expected.

Seconds later, the Nissan loses speed rapidly. It swerves hard to the right, losing both left wheels—which keep on rolling down the highway as the car slides, sparks flying, onto the shoulder. The cars behind the guy slam on their brakes to avoid rear-ending him. A mini-SUV spins into a side-slide for a few seconds but the driver manages to save it and resumes going straight again—at least until she pulls over.

Probably to change her underwear.

Wow.

The boys, all three of them watching out the rear window, laugh. Okay, no one got hurt, so it's not *too* wrong to consider it funny. Two runaway wheels going down the road, anyone's guess where the lug nuts went, yeah… the guy's going to be delayed a bit.

Scary, but effective. I suppose since an *imp* caused it, we should be grateful no one ended up mauled or dead.

Blix reappears on the floor in front of Sam's seat and climbs into the backpack again. Before he sinks out of view, I nod at him. He grins, flashing bright yellow teeth. It's so weird to think of an imp as friendly and 'creepy cute.' Weeks ago, I killed dozens of the little bastards with my bare hands. Not sure this one seems to care. They didn't have much of a sense of solidarity with each other. Though, it probably is stupid to expect anything orderly or sensible from creatures of chaos.

"Wow," I mutter. "Nice. Guy's off our tail."

"Yeah." Sam grins at me. "Blix is a cool friend."

5

SWORDS, SORCERY, AND DAEMONS

W e got home okay, unfollowed and unhurt.

Mom really landed up to her eyeballs in work, but Dad saved the day—or at least disappointed the pizza guy—by cooking dinner. Before I died, the whole family sitting down for meals happened sometimes, but hardly as a matter of routine. Now, we try to do it whenever possible even if I don't get any physical benefit from ordinary food. Still, I can appreciate the taste, and the time spent with the family is priceless. That, and watching me eat helps the parents feel normal.

The girls had a league game tonight, which ended up moved to an indoor soccer field due to rain. Their team didn't win (2-3) but Sophia had fun playing. Sierra, being more competitive, is frustrated and complains about some girl named Melanie on their team who just happened to be standing in the wrong place at the wrong time. Someone kicked the ball away from their goal and it hit Melanie in the head, rebounding into the net. Even though she essentially scored against her own team merely by existing in a particular space, the refs let the point stand.

After dinner, I head downstairs to my room. A quick round of texts confirms my dreaded expectation: Hunter and Michelle are still at their jobs, and Ashley's overloaded with homework. It sucks how I'm unable to really help Michelle put those files back where they go using my accelerated reflexes. Superhuman speed doesn't make up for not having the first clue where to put what. So, yeah, another night alone.

Maybe I should get a job like my friends. Nah. What the heck could I even do? Night shift security? Bleh. Who would hire a girl who looks like she's sixteen for *that* job? I couldn't intimidate a Brownie scout with a bad attitude. Besides, for the time being, anything with the potential to take even more time from me I could spend with my family is bad. Maybe it's spoiled of me to think, but the money isn't necessary. Skipping extra clothes, video games, fun money, or whatever else I'd waste it on is not a big deal. And yeah, that's like total feel my forehead and ask what's wrong with me for a girl my age; however, being murdered kinda rearranged my priorities.

Sigh. Mom always says 'adulting sucks,' and I'm starting to see why. At least she has Dad. The last time she hung out with her friends happened years ago. Like, 'my butt was still in grade school' years ago. Granted, all of her friends except one moved out of state. Time is a cruel master. The idea of freezing my family as they are by giving them all the Transference does have a certain kind of romantic/nostalgic appeal—if I glaze over the moderately inconvenient truth I'd essentially be murdering them. No serious chance of that happening exists. The *only* way I'd ever make them immortal is if something else killed them and I managed to get to them fast enough.

According to Professor Heath—who also happens to be a vampire— we've got about a minute or two after a person dies to initiate the Transference. Wait too long, and the corpse gets back up as an abomination called a *sefil*, basically a demon filling in the body after the soul went bye-bye. Looks like the person, but it's not.

There's also the slight problem of the vampire community at large frowning on bestowing the Transference on children. In the USA, it's not as big a deal since no one has established any kind of organized vampire 'law' or anything beyond the whims of small groups of elders in each city, basically a whole bunch of little separate kingdoms. Over in Europe, there's supposedly a council of elders or some such thing that oversees all of vampire kind. They can hand down decrees of annihilation if a vampire does something really bad... like make a *sefil* on purpose, run around hunting other vampires, turn kids into undead, or mix Skittles and M&Ms in the same bowl.

From what Heath told me, it's not even any high-minded morality at work there. They don't feel particularly bad about kids. It's purely because children who don't grow up risk exposure of our existence to normal people. A vampire with the physical appearance of a child would need to live forever in hiding, stay somewhere super remote, or constantly move from place to place so no one realizes they aren't growing up.

I do get some odd looks for being 'too young.' Though, my legal age of eighteen at the time of Transference makes me acceptable, even overseas. However, I have zero plans to go anywhere… at least while my family is still around.

Might as well attack my homework since it's either that or video games. Not quite fifteen minutes into reading what I need to cover for English lit on Monday, Dad pokes his head in.

"Hey, hon. You up for movie night?"

"What particular form of cheese are you treating us to?" I smile, mark the place in the book, and set it on the desk. The littles won't be up too late. Spending two-ish hours with the family for an old movie is just the kind of thing to help my mood. Once the kids go to bed, I can stretch the remaining time before sunrise out to almost five times its effective duration by speeding myself up.

Comes in as handy for doing homework as it does for dodging bullets or trading claw swipes with a pissed-off vampire. Wonder if a super-old vampire from like the 1400s would consider me using my powers to compel people to buy Girl Scout cookies or compress my homework into less real time as insulting?

"*Conan the Barbarian.*" Dad grins, striking a pose like he's holding a big sword.

"Sounds fun. Homework can wait a bit. Gonna be awake all night anyway." I get up and follow him to the stairs. "Pretty sure you made me watch that years ago but it's been so long the memory's fuzzy."

"Never a good reason not to re-watch a classic." Dad hurries to the living room.

Mom's already got two giant bowls of popcorn ready, one faintly orange—probably cheese flavored. We squeeze together on the sofa. Mom and Dad in the middle, Sam leaning on Dad from the left. Sierra squishes herself into a burrow between Sam and the armrest. I flop on Mom's right, with Sophia snuggled up to my side.

Another two years or so and we won't all fit on this couch. Dad will need to get a sectional then. Something tells me even when the littles are all grown up, 'family Eighties movie night' will continue, even if it's once a month. The movie tradition is far easier to maintain than the summer road trip thing. At least, assuming none of the littles move out of state when they get jobs. Given Sophia's interest in movie makeup, she's probably going to end up in California.

Roughly a third of the way into the movie, we run out of popcorn. Mom gets up to make more while the littles race for bathrooms. I sit there on the couch licking fake cheese off my fingers—until Mom screams.

My literal flight into the kitchen is so fast, I nearly leave my clothes on the sofa. I land behind her, claws out, ready for some crap to go down, but nothing appears out of the ordinary. No open door, no blood, no vampires or gangbangers anywhere in sight… not even a spider.

"What's wrong?"

Mom turns toward me and yelps again. "Oh, God, Sarah…"

"What?"

"You're in dire need of a manicure." She stares at my hands. "Good grief."

"Oh… Umm." I flash a weak smile and retract the claws. "Sorry. Why are you screaming?"

She points at the cabinet where the snacks dwell. "I could've sworn I saw a pair of glowing red eyes staring at me from in there."

"Huh?"

"It looked like one of those imp things. Are you sure you got them all?"

"Nothing's out of place right?"

"No. Everything seems normal… but I could've sworn we had three bags of corn chips in here. But there's only two."

"Maybe Sam and his friends motored through it earlier?"

"No. He'd have asked first. And it still doesn't explain two glowing eyes in the cabinet when I opened it. They disappeared so fast I'm starting to wonder if I imagined it."

Crap. I don't think Blix would be reckless enough to tease Mom. Doing so would jeopardize his ability to remain Sam's friend. Though, it's possible she opened the door and caught him unexpectedly. Guess their ability to go invisible is something they need to concentrate on. He let his guard down thinking the cabinet kept him hidden.

"Umm. Pretty sure all the dangerous imps were pulled back into the portal when Soph broke the enchantment." Hah. Qualified that with 'dangerous' imps. Not technically a lie.

Mom eyes the cabinet again. "Your sister better not have summoned more paranormal creatures."

"After what happened last time, I'm sure she wouldn't dare."

"Okay, well. Stay alert." Mom grabs two more pouches of popcorn.

"Will do." I grimace to myself when she's not looking and scurry back to the sofa.

When the 'rents go to sleep, I'm going to need to have a chat with Blix. Wow. So weird how Sam named him. Makes it difficult to think about killing him if he gets out of control. Guess it's something like having chickens. They're food until you give them names.

Though, I am not eating an imp. Nope. Not happening.

Eventually, we resume the movie, popcorn stock replenished.

Sierra is clearly unimpressed by some of the special effects, but she doesn't seem to dislike the movie, more snickering here and there. Out of the corner of my eye, I notice Sam tossing the occasional piece of popcorn up over his shoulder.

Blix is perched on the sofa back behind him, watching the movie with us. The instant my expression radiates 'oh crap,' Sophia covers her mouth to hold in a laugh. I glance at her. She looks straight at the imp and grins.

You can see it? I ask, telepathically.

She nods, and thinks it's way cool I have telepathic abilities. Also, my girly-girl sister who's afraid of just about everything in the world doesn't mind Blix being around. Even after imps trapped her for hours in a dumpster at school and tried to shred us in the mirrorverse. She senses something about Blix being different, nonthreatening. Okay. Works for me.

But, I'm not going to try convincing Mom to accept having an imp around. That's all Sam's job if she discovers the little guy.

"Dad," says Sierra. "I want to learn how to fight with a sword."

Mom coughs on her popcorn.

"Uhh." Dad glances at her. "That's a bit more, erm, drastic than taekwondo, isn't it? Do places even still teach sword combat?"

"Obviously." She gestures at the screen. "Someone had to train the actors and stunt doubles."

"They made that movie in ancient times, when Mom and Dad were our age," says Sam.

Dad playfully swats him across the head, making him laugh.

"Could be fake fighting." Sophia shrugs. "Just teaching them how to look good on camera. Would they know how to use a sword in a real fight?"

"Are we seriously discussing Sierra learning how to use a sword?" asks Mom in a slightly raised voice.

"You can't be Conan. You're a girl," says Sam, no emotion in his voice or expression.

Sierra glares at him, likely seconds from answering with a fist.

He looks up at her, smiling. "You'd be *Red Sonja.*"

Her anger melts.

Dad ruffles his hair, beaming with pride. "This is my son."

"There is no way Mom is going to let you wear a chain mail bikini," says Sophia.

"They're stupid anyway." Sam stuffs a whole handful of popcorn in his mouth. "Why does she only wear armor on her boobs? Her heart and stomach are totally open to be stabbed."

"It's not… umm." Dad fumbles over his words for a moment. "She's wearing that… umm."

"Because a man directed the movie," snaps Sierra.

Sophia points at the screen. "Conan doesn't have much on either."

"Yeah, but those massive pecs would probably stop a sword," I mutter.

Mom coughs.

"Still. Can I try sword lessons?" Sierra smiles.

"What possible reason would you have for wanting to learn how to fight with a sword?" Mom leans forward to peer past Dad and Sam at her.

"Because our life is weird now. Soph's like magical and Sarah has a sword."

Mom redirects her shock at me. "You what?"

"No, I don't have a sword. The blade broke off in the giant wasp-tarantula-thing's face."

After a long moment of Mom staring at me, she whispers, "I'm not sure I even want to know."

"You don't," deadpans Sophia.

Sierra laughs. "At least that thing was actually scary. Not like a giant pom-pom."

"Fuzzydoom is terrifying!" shouts Sophia.

The 'rents snicker.

"Great, so what's Sam gonna do?" Dad stretches his left arm around Sierra and Sam, snugging them close. "Soph's a wizard, Sarah's straight up supernatural, Sierra's going to become *Red Sonja*. What about the boy?"

"I'm gonna make friends with demons," replies Sam, completely serious.

Mom and Dad laugh.

Oh boy. They're used to taking my brother's flat tone as joking. He says off-the-wall stuff so often in that voice it's nearly impossible to tell when he's kidding. Considering Blix, I'm pretty sure he's being serious. My brother plans to cavort with demons.

Uh oh.

Wait, not strong enough.

Crap.

Nope, still not quite there.

Shit.

AFTER THE MOVIE ENDS, THE LITTLES HEAD UPSTAIRS TO GET READY FOR BED.

When I'm sure they've gone far enough to get out of earshot, I clear my throat. "So, umm…"

Dad, halfway to his feet, pauses and sits back down. "Something on your mind?"

"You're not embroiled in another vampire elder war are you, dear?" asks Mom.

"No." I chuckle. "At least I sure hope not."

"What's that supposed to mean?" asks Dad.

I fill them in on being followed earlier. "No idea why. I haven't done anything even remotely involving other vampires. Sure, Glim and I fly around sometimes, but he would have warned me if anything we did offended someone. Besides, he's far too careful for that. Anyway, what I wanted to ask you guys about… I think it might be a good idea for Sophia to meet those mystics, maybe ask them if they could possibly teach her how to better control whatever ability she's got."

"Hmm. Not a totally bad idea." Dad rubs his chin. "What will that involve? They're not going to demand she live with them as an apprentice or anything? If so, my answer is a hard no."

"Jonathan…" Mom fidgets. "I'm not sure that's wise. Aren't those mystics the same people who attacked her in the first place and pulled her spirit out of her body?"

"Yeah, but what they did was more spying on me than attacking Soph. It wouldn't have hurt her… I think. Just borrowing her body for a little while."

"Still!" Mom slightly shakes her head.

I raise both eyebrows at her. "Do you know any other mages in the area who might be willing to guide her? Also, do you really want to let her abilities develop completely wild? She almost launched one of her dance classmates into low-Earth orbit."

Dad cracks up so bad he's crying. Mom merely gawks at me.

"Okay." I laugh. "Little exaggeration there."

By the time I'm done explaining 'weightless Megan,' both of my parents are laughing. "Okay, so Sophia with magic is like arming a child with a nerf gun... capable of punching holes across dimensions. She might be cute and harmless, with innocent intentions, but you see how much weird crap is gravitating to us with me around. I think she needs to learn how to protect herself from unwanted outside interference."

"That's what steel chairs are for," says Dad.

"Jon. This isn't wrestling." Mom wipes laugh tears away, her lip quivering as if she's fighting a smile.

He wiggles his eyebrows. "Admit you just pictured Sophia walloping something over the head with a steel chair."

"You are impossible." Mom resumes laughing for a few seconds, then goes serious. "You'll keep an eye on her?"

"As much as possible. I'm still not entirely sure I believe it's real."

"If I had a dollar for every time I thought that about what happened to you..." Mom hugs me. "Just be careful. All right. I don't want her accidentally hurting herself. Talk to them and ask what they think, but let your father and I know before you do anything?"

"Sure."

"When are you going to contact them?" asks Dad.

"Maybe tomorrow. Right now, I have a crapload of homework to finish." I hug them one after the next, then stand. "Night, guys."

"Night, hon." Dad yawns. "You know, I think I'm going to call it an early night."

"Not me. I've still got so much to do for a case coming up." Mom inherits Dad's yawn.

"Sleep. Come to bed now. Wake up earlier. You'll only drown in paperwork if you try to do it while tired."

"Oh, Dad? Isn't there a sequel? *Conan the Destroyer*? Next Saturday?"

He points at me. "Confirmed. Now, go get your homework done."

"Okay." I hug him again, and run off to the stairs.

6

THE NARAJ CUBE

L ate afternoon Sunday, I'm in the car with Sophia, driving to Seattle for a meeting with Darren Anderson at the Brass Tap. I'm not entirely sure if the mystics' eagerness to meet her is a bad sign or not. When I called him last night, he suggested a brief face-to-face as soon as I could be there.

Mom's not terribly thrilled with the idea and almost walked away from her mountain of work to come with us. Sophia's a little nervous, too, but she's also eager to get a better understanding of whatever it is she can do. Whenever she's nervous, she can't stop talking. So, the ride is anything but quiet. Another habit of hers while nervous is to leap from topic to topic without any apparent connection between them. She also has the bizarre ability to ramble between subjects so easily her conversation sounds like it flows even if it's nearly impossible to follow.

By the time I park in downtown Seattle, I'm fully informed about the trials and tribulations of her classroom's five hamsters, the soap-opera saga going on among the characters in the fictional world she intends to write books in some day, what she thought of her lunch yesterday, random ideas of what Fuzzydoom might do if it managed to emerge from the mirror, and her friend Megan's insecurities of being on stage for a dance recital. The girl's a little thick, and being in a class where everyone else is slim makes her feel conspicuous.

Oh, and Sophia's worried she'll look stupid in front of the mystics.

The ride is reasonably brief and I even find a parking spot on the same block as the bar.

"I changed my mind. Can we go home?" asks Sophia as soon as the engine's off.

"Seriously? What happened?"

She shrugs. "I look like a dork."

My kid sister is wearing a pink dress, white leggings, and ballet flats. If she had her hair up in pigtails, she'd resemble a tall six-year-old, but it's loose.

I'd call her adorable, but that would only make her insecurities worse. "No you don't. You look normal. They're not going to be expecting you to wear a robe or anything. Wizards only wear robes in stories."

She fidgets. We sit there in silence for a minute or so.

"Up to you." I put the key back in the ignition. "You don't *have* to do this. If you wanna go home, we can go home."

Sophia stares at her peeling nail polish. "Are they going to laugh at me or think I'm a nerd?"

"These guys are nerds, too."

"Are they gonna hurt me?"

"If I had the slightest fear of that, we wouldn't be here right now. And if they do something unexpected, I'll rip their heads off."

She grins. "Like Scott. Or are you being figurative?"

"Depends on what happens." I wink.

"Okay." She exhales hard. "We can at least talk to them."

We get out of the car and head inside. At a little after four on a Sunday afternoon, there aren't too many people here. In addition to being a bar, the place is also a restaurant, so a ten-year-old walking in the door doesn't raise too many eyebrows. Then again, people would give me weird looks if I tried to go into a bar. Admittedly, eighteen *is* too young for a bar, but I don't even appear to be that old. Grr.

"Wow. Someone really likes steampunk," whispers Sophia while gazing around at all the brass.

"Yeah. I think the owner of this place is into brass like you're into pink stuff."

She sticks her tongue out at me.

I spot Darren, Landon, and Callum sitting at a round table in a corner booth, one big enough for like eight people. Sophia's grip on my hand might break fingers if not for my vampiric toughness. Poor kid's terrified.

It's almost enough to make me change my mind, but the idea of what she might end up doing by accident worries me more.

All three guys look over at us when we approach the table. As soon as they spot Soph, they make faces like an adorable cat picture just scrolled by on Facebook. When she sees that, her grip relaxes. Perhaps one day, she'll outgrow liking it when people think she's adorable. Sierra hated it from like age nine up. Not sure exactly when I bristled at people 'awwing' at me, but it happened years before I had the nerve to tell people it bothered me. Curse of being the oldest I guess.

"Sarah…" Darren nods in greeting. "This must be Sophia."

My sister steps closer. "You should recognize me. Didn't one of you kick my ghost out?"

The men emit nervous chuckles.

"Actually, Pippa did that." Landon scoots in to make room on the C-shaped bench. "Seemed most appropriate to have a woman cast the distant seeing spell on a girl."

I pat Sophia on the back. "You wanna sit closer to them or be on the edge?"

She glances at the room, then unzips her coat. "I'd rather have you between me and bad guys."

I'm not entirely sure who she's referring to, and the mystics all seem equally confused as to whether or not she'd insulted them. However, before any of us can ask her to explain, she hangs her coat on the peg above the seat and crawls in to sit right next to Landon. Guess 'bad guys' are theoretical problems who haven't shown up yet. The men smile upon realizing she hadn't called them evil.

Landon shakes her hand. "A pleasure to meet you, Miss Sophia."

"The pleasure is mine, but I'm afraid I do not yet know your name, kind sir."

Darren and Callum chuckle. Landon raises both eyebrows.

I hop into the bench seat, leaning on the table. "She plays with dolls a lot."

Sophia's face goes scarlet.

"… and she's read more regency romance novels than any ten-year-old ought to have."

"Landon York, at your service." He shifts from shaking hands to kissing her knuckle.

"Callum Bailey." He nods in greeting.

"And I am Darren Anderson." Darren offers a slight bow.

Sophia glances at his long black hair, small round glasses, and somewhat dated suit. "Is he trying to look like 'human Dracula' on purpose?"

Darren coughs, while the other two stifle chuckles.

"Oops." Sophia goes wide-eyed. "Sorry. I mean, you look pretty cool. Just wondering if you do it on purpose."

"I'm fond of the aesthetic." Darren smiles at me. "I appreciate you bringing her to speak with us."

I salute him with two fingers. "Sure. No problem. So, can you guys help her?"

"It is too early to say." Callum stares at Sophia with an intensity that would've totally creeped me out if I didn't know he was a mystic studying something about her aura or whatever.

A waitress stops at the table, giving me a nod. "Hi. Welcome to the Brass Tap. Can I get you girls anything?"

"Sprite?" asks Sophia.

Meh. Might as well order a drink to keep up appearances. "Just an iced tea, thanks."

"Long Island?" Callum winks.

The waitress raises an eyebrow at him in an 'are you kidding' way. "Need to see some ID, hon."

I chuckle. "No, definitely not Long Island. Normal iced tea."

She smiles. "Okay. Anything to munch on?"

A momentary flashback to the buffalo nuggets from the ninth layer of hell makes me squirm. They tasted great, but oh-em-gee they hurt on the way out. Yeah, being able to still eat normal food is cool and all, but I *can't* do spicy anymore. As the old saying goes, what goes in, comes out. I give Sophia the 'wanna snack?' look. She shrugs.

"Why don't we get a sampler plate?" Darren nods at the waitress. "That way we can all pick at whatever."

I give a thumbs-up. "Sounds good."

"Be right back with the drinks." The waitress whisks off.

"What has happened thus far?" asks Landon.

"You saw the imps…" I put an arm around my sister and explain the whole mirrorverse trip, pausing while the waitress drops off our drinks so she doesn't overhear anything too strange.

The men nod along, unfazed by everything—including the mega-nope-a-saurus. That kinda freaks me out. Like, if a truck-sized wasp-tarantula-scorpion thing doesn't make them flinch, what the hell else might be out there? Of course, they could simply think I'm nuts...

"Have you done anything since?" Callum sets a plain, wooden box on the table, resting his hands on it. It's about the size of Mom's jewelry box, pretty old looking, and covered in a dark varnish that lets the wood grain show.

"Yeah. A friend in dance class was having trouble jumping, so I tried to help her. But it didn't really work. She floated like a balloon. I had to hold her down."

The men all nod.

"How long did the effect last?" Darren jots something down in a small notebook.

"I dunno. Maybe ten minutes." She scratches her head. "I was kinda freaking out not wanting anyone to notice Megan had no gravity. Sarah suggested I try to undo the spell, so I did, and it stopped."

Darren jots feverishly, his old-timey quill wobbling into a white blur.

We all sit there trying to appear innocent while the waitress approaches carrying an enormous platter of various appetizer nibbles. Chicken fingers, jalapeno poppers, wings, buffalo nuggets, loaded potato skins, mozzarella sticks, cheesy fries drenched in bacon bits, and stuffed mushrooms.

"Thank you," says Darren. "Might I request a refill?"

"Sure." She takes his wine glass. "Be right back."

"Alright." Callum slides the top off the box sideways, exposing numerous small items bundled inside. "If you don't mind, we'd like you to take a little test just to confirm you have some ability."

"Okay." Sophia squeezes my hand and exhales.

Callum removes a small cloth bag from the box, opens it, and dumps out an assortment of metal bars. Most are L-shaped, a few have ninety-degree bends on both sides, and one piece is a weird little starburst-shaped nugget full of sockets. "This is a Naraj cube. All of these pieces fit together to form a single, solid block. The complexity is such that it would take a person days to do by hand. It is an excellent way to calm the mind and pave the way for a deeper connection to the universe."

"However, for the purposes of this evaluation, we'd ask only for you attempt to put it together using whatever ability you have with magic." Landon gestures at the pile of metal bits.

The pieces leap up, scrambling around like a bunch of kids at a birthday party playing musical chairs. Delicate clinking and pinging continues for a little over twenty seconds before the last segment slides into place with a *click*, resulting in a complete four-inch metal cube with sun pattern engravings on all six sides.

"Wow," whispers Sophia. "That's *so* cool."

Darren picks it up and turns it over in his hands, letting the light gleam off each face in turn. The instant he mutters a strange foreign-sounding word, a rain of loose pieces falls between his fingers back to the table. "Please, Sophia. You try."

The waitress returns with a glass of red wine for Darren, then hurries off.

My sister leans forward, holding her hands over the parts, a fascinated expression on her face. A second or two later, a distinct note of 'ooh!' glints in her eyes. I'd almost swear she's having a telepathic conversation with a bunch of metal scraps. The glower of deep concentration takes over. One of the tiny rods twitches. Despite the minimal reaction of the puzzle box, the minuscule motion seems to leave the mystics awestruck.

Sophia's determination curls her lip. A faint waft of light races away from her chest, bounces off the table, and flies across the room to the bar where it hits an occupied stool—that promptly bursts apart into loose pieces as though all the screws, glue, or nails holding it together ceased existing. The man sitting on it drops straight down, landing on his ass so hard watching it gives *me* a headache. He didn't even have time to scream in surprise before crashing to the floor. Sprawled on his side, he emits an anguished gargle.

Ouch. I squirm, sympathetic pain riding up my spine into the bottom of my skull. People at the bar rush to help the older guy up. Pieces of barstool roll back together and reassemble at the precise moment no one's paying any attention to it—other than me. By the time they get the dude on his feet, it doesn't look like anything happened to the stool. The man appears to be unhurt—at least as far as serious injuries go—but highly confused.

The mystics didn't react to the energy projectile, or to the man falling.

I'm not sure how in the heck no one noticed the thing collapse to pieces and put itself back together, but maybe there is something to the whole 'human brains just reject magic' thing Coralie mentioned. A rapid metallic tapping noise comes from the table in front of me. By the time I look away from the scene at the bar, there's an intact cube sitting in front of Sophia.

And she's grinning big time. As if rewarding herself, she grabs a potato skin from the tray.

"Most impressive," says Landon. "It usually takes quite a few years to be able to invoke even minor magic like this without chanting aloud."

"You did it without saying anything," says Sophia.

"I chanted in my mind. Which invocation did you use?"

"Umm." She grimaces. "No idea. I just stared at it until it put itself together."

Darren blinks. "The Naraj cube is primed with arcane energy, making it quite easy to affect with magic, hence why we use it as a test to confirm ability. However, most prospective mystics use some manner of evocation spell, intended to move objects."

"I don't know any 'spells.' I just picture what I want to happen and concentrate on making it happen." Sophia bites her lip. "Did I do it wrong?"

"You guys missed the barstool." I point at the guy standing beside said stool, tapping and pulling at it.

"What?" Darren looks at me.

I explain what happened.

"Oops," whispers Sophia. "I didn't wanna hurt anyone."

"You saw something fly out from her?" Callum stares at me in a way that makes me feel like a lab specimen.

"Ever watch one of those ghost shows where they capture a 'light anomaly' on video? It kinda looked like those. Really faint."

Sophia tries to pick up the cube, grunts, then grabs it in both hands, gawking at its weight. "I got frustrated it didn't want to work. Pretty sure I felt it when the energy happened."

"Sounds like a focus issue." Landon strokes his short beard. "She invoked an assembling force but had trouble directing it to the intended target."

I tilt my head. "But it took the stool apart... Wouldn't an 'assembling' force put something back together?"

"Didn't it?" Landon smiles. "Magic is not always sequentially iterative. Casting a reassembly spell on an object composed of multiple parts when it is not currently *in* multiple pieces will often disassemble it so the subject of the magic is in a state receptive to the intent of the spell."

Yeah, okay. I'll pretend what he said is perfectly logical. "Oh. I suppose that makes sense. So, did she pass?"

The men nod.

"Quite so." Darren reaches across the table and gently takes her hand, turning it palm up like a fortune teller. "Fascinating."

"Are you gonna read my palm?" asks Sophia around a mouthful of potato, cheese, sour cream, and bacon bits.

He chuckles. "No, child. I'm studying the residual energy leaking from your fingertips." He lets go, satisfied. "I'd like to ask you to take a few more evaluations, but not here. It will take us a little time to make the necessary preparations. Would you be willing to meet with us at the lodge tomorrow afternoon? As early as your sister is able to go outside?"

Sophia looks up at me. "Okay, but it's up to Sarah."

"We'll run it by the parents first," I say. "Can I call you in a few hours?"

"Of course." Darren smiles. "I shall be waiting with extreme anticipation."

7

OOPSIE

One of the things I never imagined I'd ever have to ask my parents is 'Hey, can I take Sophia to a mystic's lodge so they can teach her magic?' It's weird seeing her *this* interested in something other than dance class or makeup artistry. The whole ride home, she rambled about having magic abilities and worried Mom would refuse to let her see the mystics.

Whatever fear she had of those guys before is gone.

Guess she's forgiven them for kicking her out of her body and stealing it for a while. I can understand how she got over it though. For one thing, it didn't hurt her, and more importantly, being targeted with magic is what unlocked her abilities. At least, that's what the mystics said. I'm still a little suspicious though. No one in our family—at least anyone I've ever heard about—has any connection whatsoever to things paranormal or strange. You'd think if Sophia had latent magical ability all along she could never have unlocked herself, there would have been something in our past to hint at it. Some eccentric relative surrounded by strange stories or some such thing. Granted, my father's side of the family came from England... so maybe we *do* have a weird relative but they're way, way back.

I spend the rest of Saturday worrying my presence here is having unintended consequences. Sort of like how putting a heavy object in the middle of my bed creates a well that causes other, smaller objects to roll toward it. What if being a vampire is a paranormal magnet and it's attracting energy to my house? It may not be a bad thing, actually. At least in Soph's case. I'd much rather she have some ability to protect herself against whatever clawed, fanged bullcrap messes with me.

Anyway, we managed to get Mom's approval. Mostly, because I played up the worry of accidents if her abilities ran wild. Darren asked me to meet him with Sophia tomorrow at Woodland Park's rose garden. So, she's on cloud nine, like tomorrow's Christmas. Again, it's surreal to see her into something this much that isn't dance. But making objects move with magic is infinitely cooler than zooming around in tights leaping and spinning.

Doubtful she's going to lose interest in dance, but she's pumped about magic.

Ugh. This could go wrong in an infinite number of ways.

I'm supposed to be studying, but I wind up doodling Fuzzydoom chasing faceless little people. Okay, enough. Work time.

MONDAY IS HIGH ON THE SUN-BITCHINESS INDEX.

Figures now that I *want* it to be gloomy in Seattle, the sun decides to become an exhibitionist. And yeah, it is far more likely nothing is different and my perceptions are skewed. Prior to my death, I adored sunny days because they felt few and far between. It's doubtful my immortal powers are strong enough to affect the solar system. Logic says the fiery ball isn't showing itself more often to spite me. I'm merely paying attention to it now.

Because it's a pain in my ass.

At least it's November, so bundling myself up to ridiculousness won't seem too weird. I'm going to be hungry tonight from this, but it's worth it to protect Sophia—and keep everyone else safe from what she might do without meaning to. And speaking of keeping safe from things, it's astounding Blix hasn't played any pranks in the house. This gets me wondering about the true nature of imps.

Anyway, a little after three, I race out the front door as covered as possible: winter coat, jeans, boots, gloves, scarf around my face, sunglasses, and a wool hat. Only a little bit of skin right below my eyes is exposed to daylight… and holy hell this hurts.

I jump into the Sentra and slam the door.

Sophia climbs in, coughing and waving her hands at the smoke hanging in the air. "Wow, Sare. You're smoking. Maybe this isn't a great idea."

"I'm already in the car."

She looks me up and down. "Want me to see if I can protect you from the sun somehow?"

"If all my clothes fly off, I'm going to give you a mental command to wear that bunny costume Grandma Sheridan made for you last year to school tomorrow." Mom's mom is super sweet. She tries *so* hard but... yeah. She still thinks we're all four years old.

"Eep!" She blushes. "You wouldn't! You promised you wouldn't mind control us!"

I start the engine and back out of the driveway. "Runaway magic creates an exigent circumstance."

Sophia jabs a finger at me. "Don't go into lawyer mode! You promised. Sare!"

I grin. "Okay, fine. I'm just kidding. I can handle this... probably. Look, if I legit catch fire, then go ahead and try, but until you know what you're doing, the accidents might be worse. Remember the stool."

"Okay. I'm just worried. I don't want you to burn to ashes."

"Great. That's two of us."

She's quiet for a few minutes watching me try to navigate the street away from the house, driving as slow as if it's my first time behind the wheel. Even with sunglasses on, the world is a nuclear glowing blur to me. Maybe I shouldn't be driving at all given I can barely see anything but ouch.

"Sare!" shouts Sophia. "Look out!"

I jam on the brakes, only noticing the black Labrador in the road after we screech to a stop. The dog looks at me for a second, then darts off. Ugh. "This is a bad idea. We should go back and let Dad drive us."

"He's with Sam and Sierra at karate."

"Taekwondo?"

She raspberries me. "Whatever. Kicky-punchy stuff."

I laugh, remembering Sam referring to it as 'yoga with screaming.'

"It's not funny." Sophia pulls at my arm.

"You're right. This isn't safe. I don't want you getting hurt. We need to do this when it's gloomy out or when Mom or Dad can drive us."

Sophia tilts her head to the right. "Ashley?"

"In class."

She tilts her head to the left. "Michelle?"

"Work."

"Ooh. Hunter?" Sophia grins.

"Probably homework in the few hours he has between class and his job." I grumble. "Notice how little he's been around lately?"

She sighs. "Wow. You need it bad."

I gasp. "What?"

Sophia looks up at me, all innocence. "Time with Hunter, maybe a hug. You relax when you're with him, and you're all wound up right now. Why are you gasping?"

"Umm." Great. At least she can't see me blushing with the scarf over my face at what I thought she meant. "Painful sunlight."

Sophia emits a grunt of annoyance while thrusting her hand toward the windshield—which darkens like a giant sunglass lens.

"Whoa."

"Holy crap it worked!" She squeals in delight. "Awesome! Umm, does that help?"

"Yeah, actually." Straight ahead is still a little painful to look at, but it's not washed-out white. "Great. I'm going to get pulled over for having too much tint."

She shakes her head. "If we get pulled over, I'll change it back."

"Okay... but please don't turn the cop into a frog."

Sophia laughs. "That would be *toad*-ally rude."

"Ouch." I groan.

The drive into Seattle is nerve wracking, to say the least. Makes me think of our grandfather on Dad's side. His eyesight isn't the greatest, so he hates driving at night. I'm the reverse. Day driving blows. I'm so worried about getting into an accident my brain starts hallucinating vampire-Sophia in the passenger seat. But even that won't happen. If we crash bad, I'll end up mauled, too and won't be able to do anything to help her before it's too late.

So, yeah. There's a lot of beeping and middle fingers coming my way for merely driving the speed limit.

We make it to the park without causing or suffering serious injury. Conveniently, the place has a parking lot right across from the rose garden. After stashing the Sentra in the rearmost row due to ample tree shade, I hop out and move a few steps deeper into cover, taking a moment to enjoy not feeling like I'm standing in a giant microwave being high-beamed to extra crispy.

"Umm, Sare, the garden's that way." She points.

"Yeah, I know. But there's shade here. Need a moment."

"Okay."

Not long after we get out of the car, a red minivan pulls in to park two spaces away from my Sentra. A man and woman in their later thirties emerge from it. He pauses, sniffing the air while the woman pulls open the side door for a pair of seven-year-old-ish boys.

"You smell that, hon?" asks the guy. "Something's on fire. Almost"—he sniffs—"smells like steak but, the meat's gone south."

Screw you too, pal.

"Brakes?" The woman sniffs at the front wheel. "Yeah, I smell it. It's stronger up front."

"I just had the pads replaced." He reopens the door and pulls the hood release. "Maybe I hit something and there's roadkill roasting on the engine."

Sophia tugs on my arm.

I sigh. "Yeah, good idea."

Before the guy's nose can lead him to me and he starts asking why the smell of burned meat is coming from a person, we head to the east, crossing the street into the rose garden. I'd say it's pretty, but that would largely be a guess. My vision is full of painful white light—and I walk straight into a tree where the paved path abruptly becomes a circle. Sophia laughs, but takes my hand, leading me like a blind person. Good enough. Might as well close my eyes to stop the pain. She's considerate enough to move in quick scurries from shade patch to shade patch. This really is a bad idea. If the feeble cloud cover in the sky decides to clear up at some point, I'm going to be in big trouble.

Eventually, she stops short and swerves to the left. "I see Darren."

"Great. Lead on."

We walk for another minute or so, off paving and onto grass. There's no shade on this route, so I cringe in on myself while hurrying along wishing for the burning to stop. It's tempting to jump headfirst into a giant deep fryer so I can cool off.

"Oh, my," says Darren. "You should have postponed. Quick, inside."

He grasps my left hand and hurriedly drags me forward. As soon as the burning lessens from being in shade, I risk a peek. We've entered a tiny, beige gazebo in front of a wall of trees. Darren mutters a word or three in a foreign language, then grasps a ring on his left hand, twisting it around his finger.

The world outside the gazebo changes from an outdoor rose garden to a smaller, indoor garden under a greenhouse roof. A similar gazebo stands against the wall of an old manor house. It takes a second or two for the disorientation to wear off.

"Whoa. Did we just teleport?" I ask.

"Not exactly." Darren smiles. "We're essentially in the same place, but we've moved in the fourth dimension. It would be more correct to say we passed through a doorway than 'teleported.' Let's go inside before you roast."

"Sure…" I'm in too much discomfort to protest.

Darren leads us down a short stone path past a fountain to an ancient black wood door covered in bas-relief cherubs. Inside, a hallway lined with oil lamps hung from wall mounts leads into a mansion stolen straight from the early 1800s. It makes sense why Darren wears such odd suits. He fits right in here. Oh, please don't be insane. This guy better not be loopy.

We make our way along a corridor lined in blue-patterned wallpaper and dark wood wainscoting to a set of double doors on the left. Though a set of floor-to-ceiling windows at the end of the hall lets in a flood of light, they're far enough away I'm no longer burning—merely standing outside on a 110-degree August day. Or at least what I imagine it would feel like, since it's never been that hot up here in my lifetime.

Darren pulls the doors open, then gestures for us to go in.

Sophia clings to my arm as we enter a large room somewhere between library and 1800s-mad-scientist lab. Several long tables on the right hold disorganized stacks of books and candelabras. More books are stacked here and there on the floor, several piles taller than I am. Shelves on the left hold yet more books, everything coated with a layer of dust so thick my mother would probably have a seizure if she saw this place. Cabinets line the back wall in the spaces between three massive windows that appear to also be glass doors out to a courtyard.

Darren again mutters an incomprehensible word. Dense burgundy curtains at each window come unbound as if in response to his command, draping closed. Darkness washes over me like a moving wall of air conditioning. The transition in temperature is so stark and sudden it makes me shiver from the chill for a few seconds. In fact, the curtains are so thick, they block the light enough for me to come online.

"Gah!" blurts Sophia. "It's dark."

"Yes. Your sister is not enjoying the daylight." He snaps his fingers and a hundred or so candles spontaneously ignite all around the room.

To me, absolute darkness looks like normal lighting. However, I can still tell the room is dimmer than normal electric light. Darren waves for us to follow him, then proceeds to weave around the various stacks of books, boxes, and junk into the maze of shelves. More books. Good grief, there's an entire rainforest of dead trees in here. On one shelf above my head level, an imp floats dead in a big jar of amber-colored liquid. Hard to say since they mostly look identical, but I think it's the same one I killed at the veterinary clinic and dropped on the table at the Brass Tap a couple weeks ago.

Other jars hold the remains of various small animals like bats, serpents, and a few I don't recognize. Pretty sure they're normal, albeit exotic, animals, not like demons or magical beasts. Darren takes a right turn to a small chamber surrounded by shelves deep inside the maze. A square table stands at the center, littered with objects both recognizable (bowls, candles, yet more books, boxes) and some unrecognizable stuff like metal crescents, weird crystal polygons and so on.

Callum and Landon are waiting for us by the table.

Sophia leans close to me and whispers, "This is so weird. It's like we went back in time."

"Seriously."

"Welcome, Sophia." Darren takes a place by the edge of the table and rests his hands on the dark wood. "You have demonstrated that you possess magical abilities. Today, our goal is to measure your knowledge and get a feel for where any instruction would need to begin."

"What school are you familiar with?" asks Callum.

Sophia blinks. "Cottage Lake Elementary."

The guys chuckle.

"We mean magical schools." Landon brings his hands together. "What sort of mystical tradition are you following?"

"What like evocation, abjuration, illusion?" asks Sophia.

They exchange glances.

"That stuff's from a roleplaying game," I whisper. "It's not what they're talking about... but I think it's kinda close in concept."

"The Aurora Aurea, our order, is derived from a school once referred to as Thelema. It has changed somewhat from the 1900s." Darren's body language gets all sorts of awkward. He kind of looks like Dad when he gave me the talk about sex.

I peek into his head. Oh, he's thinking of someone named Crowley and a lot of messed-up sex magic. Ugh. Really? Sex magic is like a thing? Eww. Aha. No, he's thinking the guy was just a creep who wanted to sleep with a lot of different women.

"Regardless. That is just one tradition." Darren smiles. "There are others. Druidy, Wicca, Santeria, voodoo, various branch-offs of witchcraft or other nonspecific occultism, several strains of Sumerian diabolism... though I doubt a small girl in the Pacific Northwest would've stumbled across something so dark by chance."

"Umm." Sophia shakes her head. "None of that. I'm not reading any books... except for the one stupid thing we found on the internet. But you guys didn't think it was real magic."

"Interesting." Callum rubs his chin.

"Coralie said she's like a natural or something." I pick up a weird little metal star and look it over. Oddly, the flickering candles all over the room don't reflect from its surface.

"That's curious." Darren walks around the table to us, gently grasps Sophia's cheeks, and stares into her eyes. "Yes. I do believe she is correct. There are some things you should know about her particular type of magic."

"Such as?" I ask.

He folds his arms, tapping a finger to his chin. "True mystics as she appears to be 'work in the here and now' as we call it. Before you ask what I mean, she does magic when she wants to with little preparation or ritual involved. The advantage, of course, is not spending hours or days gathering reagents, etching circles, and so on."

"Saves quite a bit of money on components." Landon grins.

Sophia chuckles, as does Callum.

"There's a downside, isn't there?" I lean on the table. "There's always a downside."

Darren laughs. "But of course. However, it isn't a crippling one. A natural mystic trades control for freedom and spontaneity. With ritual magic, some of the burden of powering it is drawn from reagents, the natural world, even the rigidity of performing the ritualistic actions." He faces my sister. "In your case, *all* the energy is coming from inside. You run the risk of exhausting yourself, or in extreme situations, harming yourself."

Sophia leans back with a gasp.

"Oh, don't worry just yet. It will take years of practice before you are able to channel so much energy into a spell you can accidentally feed it your life."

"Umm." She shivers. "I can kill myself doing magic?"

"Whoa." I put a hand on her shoulder. "Maybe we shouldn't go down this road after all. No one said anything about her being able to drop dead."

Darren waves dismissively. "It is nothing that could ever happen without her knowing full well what she was about to do. A spell so severe it would consume her life essence would be the sort of thing she knowingly releases to perform some great feat of magic she considers worth sacrificing her life over."

"So, I couldn't like try to snap my fingers and turn the lights on and accidentally give myself a heart attack?" Sophia swallows hard.

"No, my dear. Say a high-rise building was about to collapse on top of you and a big crowd. You might channel sufficient power to hold it up and prevent it from falling, but collapse afterward from the strain."

Sophia looks up at me with an 'it's okay, let's keep going' face.

I relax—a little.

"The advantage in ritual preparation is that the magical energies are collected, focused, and sent forth in a highly predictable manner. While it may take hours, days, or even months in some cases to complete a ritual, most of the time, the magic will do exactly what it's intended to. And those sorts of spells tend to have more power because they draw not only on your inner resources of energy but the objects associated with the ritual. Now, the good part is, should you choose to study a traditional form of magic, there is nothing preventing you from using rituals as well."

"Oh, neat." She smiles.

"All right then. Let us begin." Darren faces the table and gestures at a giant candle near the middle. "Please use your magic to light that. However, know this is a special candle. It will resist you. If you are able to overcome it, do so. Don't worry if you cannot make the fire spring to life. It is not failure, merely an indication your abilities are undertrained."

"Okay." Sophia widens her stance and stares at the silvery wick like an Old West gunslinger about to throw down.

I look around at the various shelves full of dry books, bottles, bundles of burlap-wrapped junk, and tons of dust. "Last time, her magic didn't exactly go where she wanted it to. You're asking her to summon fire in *here*? You guys do have a fire extinguisher somewhere, right?"

Sophia huffs. "Not funny. You're breaking my concentration."

The mystics take up positions on the three sides of the table where my sister isn't. At least they look as if they're bracing to contain runaway magical energy. Or maybe I'm imagining that from their 'goalie like' posture. Soon, Sophia's expression shifts among intensity, annoyance, determination, and the same sort of face Sierra makes whenever someone kills her character in an online game. Uh oh. I think the candle just pissed her off.

About five minutes into the staring contest, Sophia's face reddens. The men start to relax their postures, as if accepting she won't be able to ignite it. She clutches her hands into fists at her sides and screams, "Light!"

A fizzling *pop* comes from the wick and it erupts in a tall, pure-white flame.

All three men lean back, wide-eyed.

"There." Sophia folds her arms. "Stupid thing wasn't listening."

I glance at Darren. "What's with the 'oh shit' face?"

They continue staring at the candle for a while.

"That's… wow." Landon whistles.

"Did I do something wrong?" Sophia leans closer, eyeing the flame. "Why is it white? Fire isn't supposed to be white."

Darren walks around the table to us and pats her on the shoulder. "I wasn't completely truthful with you earlier. We expected you would not be able to light the candle at all. Almost no one, even natural mystics, can ignite a dragonwick on their first try with no training."

"Whoa. Dragons? Seriously?" I gawk.

The men chuckle. Darren shakes his head. "No, it's merely called that."

"The white." Callum fidgets, a bit of guilt in his expression. "Well, I suppose it might not be so unusual given her young age."

"Hello," says Sophia. "I'm still completely lost here."

Darren smiles. "When someone manages to magically ignite this candle without understanding its true nature, the color of the resulting flame is a fairly accurate measure of the person. A white flame means she is pure and innocent, highly altruistic."

"A gentle soul," adds Landon.

Sophia blushes a little.

"Once a person understands the nature of a dragonwick candle, it becomes possible to manipulate the resulting color so any reading of essence is suspect. However, holding the necessary focus on an appropriate mindset to fool the candle makes it more difficult to ignite." Darren leans over the table and pulls two mason jars closer. One empty, one containing blue liquid. "See if you can move the liquid from the full jar to the empty jar."

Sophia picks up the empty jar and starts opening the lid.

Darren chuckles. "With magic."

"Oh. Duh." She puts the lid back on and sets the jar on the table again.

After a moment of staring at them, she picks up the full jar and sets it on top of the empty jar, lid to lid upside down. Again, she focuses on the stacked jars. Seconds later, the fluid falls into the bottom jar as if both lids became intangibly ghostly. The sight of it is enough to shock a gasp out of me. Smiling, Sophia picks up the top jar, demonstrating an intact lid, and sets it flat on the table beside its twin.

"Interesting. What made you decide to put them on top of each other like that?" asks Landon.

She points at them. "I thought it would take less effort to make a hole in two thin lids than literally move a quart of whatever the stuff is across space."

Darren appears proud of her. "All right. Two more tests to go." He pushes the jars away, opens another jewelry-box sized container, and deposits a handful of reddish dirt in a pile in front of her. "For this test, concentrate on this powder and attempt to magically change it into something else."

I lean closer to examine it. "Looks like red clay."

"It's dried and ground faerie's perch, a mushroom not native to this dimension." Darren brushes the pile a bit tighter. "Highly charged with magical energy, so it will not take much out of you to do anything to it."

Sophia nods, then leans her hands on the table, staring at the pile while Callum and Landon pepper her with tips on how to mentally frame the desire to transform one substance into another object. Callum suggests she try making it into a wooden or stone sphere.

Over the course of the next minute or three, smoke begins wisping up from the powdered mushroom. The substance appears to moisten, going from a pile of dust to a gooey blob of mud. My sister squats down so she's eye-level with the table surface, gazing at the shifting goop with the mesmerized expression of a tween at an Ariana Grande concert. Four tendrils stretch out from the blob approximating legs, then a fifth, much thinner one extends from one side. The opposite end to the small tentacle swells up into a secondary pod. The whole thing goes from brick red to charcoal colored... and in a puff of smoke and light, turns into a fuzzy kitten with piercing teal eyes.

Sophia squeals in delight.

"Mew," says the kitten.

"My word." Callum points. "She managed a live transmutation in minutes, with no prior training."

"The girl is definitely a natural mystic." Darren plucks the kitten from the table and examines it. "Tell me, child. How is it you made a kitten?"

Sophia stands there for a second with an expression as though he'd asked her why she breathes. "I wanted one."

I whistle. "Yeah. She really does want one. Bad. Is it a real kitten or is it going to like fall apart into dust in a few minutes?"

"No," whines Sophia in a quiet voice. "Please don't fall apart."

Darren holds the critter up, turning it to examine from multiple angles. The other two crowd in, also curious. The whole time, the little furball mews constantly, almost seeming like it wants to get away from them and go to Sophia. Eventually, Darren offers it to her and the little cat eagerly leaps into her arms.

"As far as I can tell, it is quite close to an actual cat. However, it may have some unusual properties." Darren pauses to think for a moment. "There are certain rituals that cancel magic. Such an effect would likely convert it back into a pile of faerie's perch. It may or may not mature into an adult cat. Depends on if it is actually alive or merely a construct in the shape of a kitten."

"More study would be needed, though it is not harmful." Landon pats the little cat on the head.

"Mew," says the kitten.

"Mom's gonna kill us." I gaze at the ceiling and let out a defeated sigh mostly because I know Sophia's going to insist we bring the kitten home... and I also know I'm going to cave in and let her. Might as well skip past the pleading argument and proceed straight to the inevitable conclusion.

Sophia hugs the kitten. "Mom will melt as soon as she sees her."

"Here's hoping," I mutter.

"One last test for today." Darren makes a 'come here' gesture with one finger. A huge glass vessel the size of a water cooler bottle near the middle of the table slides on its own toward him. It's mounted in a wooden frame kinda like an hourglass, only there's no crimp in the center of the bottle. "This is a ghost jar. Focus your magic on it until a light orb appears inside."

"There already is an orb inside that jar." Sophia looks up at him like he's nuts.

I squint at it. Sure enough, a faint sphere about the size of an orange drifts around inside. For no particular reason, it makes me feel frustrated and lonely to look at it.

"You see a spirit already?" Darren glances from her to me. "I'd imagine Sarah might be able to see a trace of something in there, but most living people can't."

Sophia flaps her arms. "Guess I'm a small medium."

Callum sighs. Landon covers his mouth to hide his smile.

The way Darren glances at me makes me peek at his thoughts. He suspects Coralie may have done something to Sophia to either amplify or give her this ability. Possible, but he doesn't know about Rebecca the haunted doll spending a whole night in Sophia's room. Plus whatever being exposed to the mirrorverse did. Then again, Sophia has been able to see ghosts ever since the mystics kicked her spirit out of her still-living body.

"Right, well. Can you try to make it appear so we all can see it?" asks Darren.

Sophia, still cradling the kitten, focuses her stare on the giant jar. The orb inside ceases drifting around at random and hovers close to the near side, almost like a strange fish come to the edge of its tank to watch the people watching it. Minutes pass. My sister doesn't appear to be straining herself, though her attention is locked on the orb.

Darren gently rests a hand on her shoulder. "It's all right if you can't. Not everyone is able—"

The ghost jar explodes in a flash of glimmering glass bits. Emitting a keening wail, the orb stretches upward into a smear, taking on the shape of a pallid bare-chested gaunt man with black eyes, black teeth, a freakishly long neck, and long claw-like fingernails. Darren screams and jumps back as the apparition slashes his chest, tearing slits in his old-timey shirt.

"No!" shouts Sophia.

Palpable anger wafts from the apparition, but he hesitates, turning his head to look at my kid sister. Dark blood seeps from his lips, disappearing about midway down his chest before striking the floor. Landon and Callum edge back from the table, bumping into shelves, both men seemingly terrified to make the slightest sound or move too fast.

"I agreed to let you out, but you promised not to hurt anyone." Sophia looks about ready to faint from fear, but keeps a stern expression.

The apparition casts a final withering glare at the mystics, then fades away.

"What the hell?" rasps Darren, examining his sliced shirt.

Sophia leans against me. She's trembling, but not enough to see, only feel. "He was trapped in that bottle for a long time. It's cruel. He was really sad and lonely. So, I let him out 'cause he asked me to set him free."

"Umm… he was *not* a nice man." Darren shoots me a look like my little sister just broke a priceless artifact and I'm going to need to pay for it. "He killed several dozen people during his lifetime in most unpleasant ways."

"I made him promise he wouldn't hurt anyone." Sophia looks down, guilty. "Sorry. I didn't know he was bad."

Callum and Landon whisper to each other about setting up some protections in case the spirit comes back for revenge after Sophia leaves. They both think he lied about not hurting anyone.

Ugh. I gaze at the ceiling. "This is going to bite me square in the ass, isn't it?"

Darren shrugs. "No real telling what he'll do. We didn't put him in the jar, so he shouldn't have too much motivation to cause trouble here. The two most likely outcomes are he returns to the place where he died or goes wherever spirits go when they're done in this world."

"Where'd he die?"

"The gallows at Tyburn in or around 1760," says Callum. "London."

I exhale out my nose. Great. "That someone trapped a 300-year-old serial killer in a jar shouldn't surprise me. Why anyone would want to keep such a thing around, however, is beyond my grip. And now it's loose."

"He's got little cause to remain in this area." Callum chuckles. "Though our mates in London might have a bit of a surprise."

"Perhaps we should warn them?" Landon fidgets.

"Aye. Good idea." Darren nods at him before facing Sophia. "It's quite clear to us you are both gifted and in need of training. If your parents are amenable to an arrangement, we can work out a schedule of some kind. Perhaps one or two Saturdays a month?"

"Twice a month?" asks Sophia.

Darren smiles. "Yes, did you expect us to take you from your parents as a live-in apprentice? This isn't the 1300s anymore."

She emits a nervous laugh.

"Oh, relax, child." He grasps her right hand and gently shakes it. "The days of apprentices being little more than household servants are past. I think a few hours twice a month of instruction will be sufficient."

"Mew," says the kitten.

"See? She agrees." Darren pats the kitten on the head.

I can't help but stare at the smashed remains of the ghost jar, already feeling the proverbial teeth closing around my butt. Letting this ghost out is going to blow up in my face, eventually. Then again, there isn't much I can do about spirits except yell at them.

Yeah. This guy's someone else's problem.

Just hope it's not Sophia's.

8

MINOR ACCIDENTS

A little after five that afternoon, I'm in my room doing school work.

No matter how often I glance up at the clock, it remains Monday. How cool would it be to look at the clock and have it suddenly be Tuesday? Meh, not too cool. It'd probably be a sign of dementia to lose half a day. At least I have a little extra time tonight. My bio class doesn't start until seven. And, being November, it's quite well dark before it's time for me to leave home.

Guess what? This girl doesn't have to deal with traffic tonight. Whee!

I didn't bother changing after showering, still wearing two towels: one in my hair, the other wrapped around me like a shift dress. The clothes I wore to the park earlier had become saturated with the reek of burning me. So as to avoid contaminating the rest of the laundry in the house, I threw them in the machine by themselves. Not much I can do about my winter coat. Not supposed to wash it in a machine. Though, it didn't pick up the smell too bad—at least compared to the rest of my outfit.

Bath towels are surprisingly comfortable as clothing, kinda like the sweat pants version of a dress. Their tendency to slip loose and fall off, however, makes them impractical for anything other than lazing around in the privacy of my bedroom. I'll probably head out the door at quarter to seven, which will let me have dinner with the family, even if I don't eat anything. The brutal sun exposure from earlier has me famished, which is partly the reason for my self-imposed isolation.

Maybe I should sneak around the cul-de-sac and feed on Mr. Neidermayer. Nah. His blood would probably taste like those awful dry cookies that come in the blue tin, plus be loaded with a bajillion prescription drugs. Bleh.

Mom runs around the house complaining about her missing car keys. She had them when she got home from work a little while ago and in the time it took her to change out of her office clothes, they've vanished. Sierra's lost her 'lucky wristband' she wears when she wants to dominate at *Call of Duty*. Naturally, she blames the imp, so an argument starts up in Sam's room. I can't understand what the little guy's saying, but Sam relays he's denying involvement. Dad ends up driving, and the parents head out to buy groceries.

IT'S GOTTEN PRETTY DARK BY A LITTLE AFTER FIVE. BUT, I'M TOO LAZY TO fly all the way to Seattle to feed then come back to keep doing schoolwork and join the fam for dinner. Fortunately, I'm not *starving*. Controlling myself and not biting anyone I love should be possible.

A shrill scream comes from the backyard.

At first, I'm sure Sophia somehow wound up with a reptile of some form down the back of her dress, but the scream changes pitch and turns into a boy crying. The 'rents don't intercede, so they must still be out shopping. Great. I'm the adult in the house.

We're in deep trouble.

In a blur of supernatural speed, I fling the towels off and pull on my sweat pants, T-shirt, and hoodie, then fly upstairs to the kitchen, heading for the patio door to the backyard and out onto the deck.

Sam, Sierra, Nicole, Megan, and Jordan stand around Daryl, who's curled up on the ground holding his face and howling in pain. Sierra has a look to her like she just did something really wrong and expects to get in a ton of trouble, but is trying to act casual and tough about it. She's also holding a big ass stick. A similar stick lays on the ground by Daryl.

Shaking my head, I hurry down the deck steps to the grass, wet with rain that ought to be icy to my bare feet but registers only as cool. "What happened?"

"We were practicing with swords." Sierra gestures at her stick. "I guess maybe I got a little too into it."

"Daryl failed to block," says Sam in a matter-of-fact tone.

Ugh. I crouch by Daryl—who's giving off a strong smell like Hostess chocolate cupcakes. Crap. He's bleeding. "Hey. Let me have a look, 'kay?"

Sierra leans down and whispers, "Please make him forget? I don't wanna get in trouble."

"Did you try doing it the normal way first?" I ask.

She stares at me. "The normal way of making people forget stuff? I don't have any sodium thiopental handy."

I stop trying to pull Daryl's hands away from his face and stare at my sister. "How the heck do you even know what that is?"

"You *do* remember who our father is, right? Movies."

"I meant the usual way by apologizing. Perhaps bribing him with large amounts of chocolate." Again, I tug at his arms. "C'mon, Daryl, let me see."

He moans in pain.

"Sare, he's a boy, not a moody girlfriend. Chocolate isn't going to help."

Sam holds a finger up. "I beg to differ. I am highly susceptible to bribes involving copious amounts of chocolate. Preferably dark."

"Eww," says Nicole. "Dark chocolate is nasty."

"Says the uncultured heathen," mutters Sam.

"Sierra, your brother is a dork." Nicole rolls her eyes.

Daryl pulls his hands away from his face, revealing a split lip gushing blood. I don't think any of his teeth are damaged, but it's difficult to focus on anything but the sight of the red stuff. As hungry as I am, the bright color triggers an involuntary growl and a minor flash of light in my eyes.

A soft, squeaky fart escapes the boy and most of the color drains out of his cheeks.

Oops.

Okay, *that* I will delete from his memory. With every ounce of my self-control, I resist the urge to act like an overly affectionate golden retriever and lick the blood off his face. Considering my first thought isn't how weird and inappropriate licking him would look is a big ass warning I've let myself go too far without feeding.

Daryl's eyes glaze over as I erase his memory of seeing my eyes glow.

"Awesome," whispers Sierra.

Once I'm sure the boy has lost any memory I'm anything more than his friend's *extremely normal and boring* older sister, I look up at her. *That's not what I made him forget. You should still apologize. He agreed to play swordfight with you, so if you get in trouble, so will he.*

"Okay, it's just a split lip," I say, before pulling the boy upright. "C'mon, I'll clean it up."

Sierra follows as I guide Daryl into the house and the downstairs bathroom.

My hands shake a little from the war going on inside me. It's so damn tempting to take a little taste, but I'm afraid of losing control. One bit of chocolate-flavored blood hits my tongue and I might end up having to give this kid the Transference because hunger wouldn't let me stop in time. Sierra probably followed me because she noticed my reaction to the blood, knows I'm hungry, and hopes to blackmail me by offering not to tell the parents I fed off Daryl if I make him forget she walloped him with a stick.

Sierra loves me, but she's shrewd.

I wet a wad of TP and dab at Daryl's face. It doesn't look like she got him too hard. Teeth aren't damaged. A few scratches on his cheek and a split lip. He could've hurt himself worse taking a spill off a bike.

"How bab if it?" mutters Daryl.

"Small cut and a fat lip. Don't worry about the amount of blood. Cuts to the face and scalp bleed a lot."

He nods.

"Sorry," says Sierra. "You dropped your guard and I took the opening. Didn't mean to hit you so hard. Only trying to get in before you defended."

Daryl mumbles, "It's okay. Accidents happen"–or at least the fat lip version thereof.

Relief melts off Sierra. "Maybe we should do something else instead of sword practice."

He nods.

Pretty sure I know what happened. In the heat of the moment, Sierra mentally jumped back to fighting off the imp swarm to protect Sophia. 'Playing with stick swords' turned into a real life-or-death fight in her head. Once I get Daryl cleaned up and sent on his way, I hug her.

"What now?" deadpans Sierra. "You don't usually get clingy for no reason."

No need burdening an eleven-year-old with my guilt over how she's facing a completely abnormal rest-of-childhood because of something that happened to me. "I'm proud of you for wanting to help protect Sophia and Sam from all the crap following me around these days."

She hugs me back. "Don't go away. It's okay. I don't mind the weird stuff."

"I won't."

"Sweet." She looks me in the eye. "Now can you stop being mushy before someone sees us?"

I laugh. "Sure."

She heads out to the yard. A momentary trancelike state comes over me when my gaze falls on the bloody lump of TP in the waste bin. Both so I don't try eating it, and the parents don't ask about it—damn sure they're going to become inquisitive upon noticing a bloody wad of paper—I decide to flush it.

And, yeah. Homework can wait. I need a snack, stat.

THE BEST LAID PLANS OF MICE AND VAMPIRES OFTEN FALL APART DUE entirely to circumstances beyond control. I had planned to fly in tonight, but despite being super sunny most of the day, Mom Nature decided to be annoying at night, dumping the kind of rain on us that soaks through clothes in seconds. Dashing from the front door to the driveway without an umbrella would've drenched me as bad as jumping into a lake.

If I had a waterproof bag, saving time and avoiding traffic might have tempted me to fly in a bathing suit and change at school, but no such bag. Flying is awesome. Flying in the rain, considerably less awesome. Sitting in class wearing saturated clothes is the exact opposite of awesome. So, I drive. Doing so shaves time away from my studying since I have to leave the house earlier. At least I'm mostly caught up on work. This only means I won't have as much free time tomorrow.

Professor Kendall is like the generic template from which the world generates university teachers. Like, if reality was a roleplaying game, he's the dead average 'professor' character class with mediocre stats and all the usual proficiencies and feats. Add a bunch of humor and personality to this template, you get Professor Connolly. Add a pedantic drive for perfection, and you get Doctor Mercer. And so on.

The man's not boring, but he's not interesting either. Fortunately, I can't fall asleep unless the sun's out. Also, I kind of overdid it earlier when

I flew into town before the rain started, feeding from two big dudes. I'm a little dazed from the vampire version of a food coma.

He hits us with a pop quiz, and I once again find myself in the Chinese Hell of Torturous Sounds only vampire ears can hear. Today's symphonic performance is brought to you by the letter B—for bodily functions. Gurgles, rumbles, squeaks, scratching, burps, and of course, a thermonuclear fart from the back row. I don't know what the woman in front of me had for dinner, but it damn sure isn't going down without a fight. Her stomach's either trying to sing the background melody from *The Lion Sleeps Tonight* or the *Day-O* song from *Beetlejuice.*

That's it...

I fish my earbuds out of my purse and drown the annoyances in music.

Naturally, Professor Kendall starts walking over to give me grief about it, as if I'm going to cheat on a pop quiz in English lit by calling a friend with a lifeline. Seriously? I lock stares and give him a compulsion to go back to his desk and ignore my music. He stops short, turns on his heel, and returns to his chair.

One advantage of mega-sensitive ears? I can have my music on at a barely-audible volume—to normal people—so it sounds fine to me, but no one else can hear a thing. This room is so damn quiet, listening to music with headphones at normal volume would be basically playing for the whole class.

Shielded from distractions, I attack the test like old times. And okay, maybe I was a bit of a geek in high school, usually among the first three or four kids done with tests.

I ABUSE MY POWERS TWICE IN CLASS TONIGHT.

Professor Kendall was about to assign us to do an analysis of the underlying themes of *Fahrenheit 451*. While I have nothing against the book, the English teachers at my high school must have shrines set up to it. Every year for four years in a row, we had to do reports on it. So, nope. Not doing it five years in a row, even if the college-level version would've gone deeper. We're going to analyze the underlying themes of *Do Androids Dream of Electric Sheep* instead.

Yeah, I know, changing our assignment was a bit of a Dick move.

And argh! It's still pouring when I leave the building after class.

Umbrella for the win. At least it's not too windy.

I feel watched on the way from the school building to the parking garage, but don't see anyone obviously staring at me. My guess is the same dude from the movie theater has picked up my trail again, but he's not showing himself this time. Either that or the spirit Sophia let out of the jar is sniffing me out. Not sure why he'd mess with me, unless my 'aura' or whatever is unusual to him. Maybe he's never seen a vampire before? I really don't like the feeling of having to keep my head on a swivel while walking around alone at night. Feeling scared should have ended when I became a vampire. Let some creep grab me now and see what happens to him. But, the idea of another vampire—or something darker—becoming a possible threat to me hadn't occurred. Maybe my safety isn't as iron-clad as it might seem.

But honestly, I've been laying really low in terms of vampire stuff. My involvement with the local undead is limited entirely to Aurélie dragging me to those fancy parties. It still bugs me they have brain-zonked mortals hanging around like living snacks, but it's not like they murder them. One or two might end up hospitalized due to losing a little too much blood, but they survive.

My non-involvement with the 'scene' here should mostly protect me from some other vamp getting their fangs in a twist over something I did. So, there really is no good reason for this guy to be shadowing me.

Shadowing.

Good idea. I should ask Glim to sniff this guy out the next time I see him. Maybe he can discover what's put a target on my back this time.

Nothing jumps out at me on the walk to the Sentra. The parking garage is packed since everyone tried to avoid having to leave their car on the uppermost floor, out in the rain. My Sentra is on the small side, so I squeezed it into an end spot on the third level that's probably not supposed to be a parking space. The lack of a ticket or notice on the window is a good indication no one cared about me parking there—or maybe the security staff is lazy.

Anyway, time to go home.

Getting into the car requires a little flying and an open window. Fully leaving the parking space requires me backing straight up, hopping out, grabbing the front bumper, and dragging the nose around toward the aisle. The corner of the garage doesn't have enough room for a K turn. Maybe the security guy had been too mystified at how someone got a car into the space to begin with he figured I deserved to be able to use it without a penalty.

Shrug.

Still no sign of anyone following me, though a sense of someone staring at me remains. I stand beside the car looking around for a bit, but he's staying out of sight. No point standing here, so I give up and decide to go home.

I'm on edge for the first few minutes of the drive. Darkness doesn't hinder my ability to see, but the rain is ridiculous and it sounds like a million tiny hammers beating the crap out of the roof. You know how some people—*moi* included—turn down the music in the car while looking for a parking spot? Yeah, I want to turn down the rain so the roar isn't so distracting, but I can't. The constant din is as unnerving as it is distracting. Ahead of me, the world's a blur of red lights and the blinding glare of oncoming traffic. Since driving gives me no choice but to stare toward the headlights of approaching cars, I need to throttle back my eyes. This, of course, makes the road ahead dimmer and scarier.

It's almost a good thing my friends are all too busy to hang out during the week. The ride is slow and nerve wracking enough without the pressure to hurry up because I'm late for something. In fact, it's damn tempting to stash the car somewhere and fly home even if I end up soaked. Wouldn't be so bad going home. No need to *stay* in wet clothes there like I'd have to do in class.

Wobbly lights in the oncoming lane don't look like they're pointing quite in the proper direction.

It hurts, but I focus in that direction, trying to see past them. The front end of a semi clarifies out of the rain-blurred night, swerving out of its lane. For a brief instant in near-frozen time, I can clearly make out a panicky youngish driver just sitting there, paralyzed by indecision… his truck veering into my lane.

With total disregard for what might be on my right, I yank the wheel and swerve one lane over. Accelerated reflexes are the only reason I don't plow headfirst into a Peterbilt going way too fast for wet roads. Miraculously, there's no car in my way. The Sentra slips past the tractor-trailer's bumper with so little room to spare I'd have wet my pants if I still had normal biology. The rapid lane change causes my tires to lose their grip on the paving, sending me sliding toward the edge of the road. I crank the wheel to the left, succeeding only in throwing the car into a sideways slide, still heading for the ditch.

Screaming, I mash myself against the door, trying to use my vampiric flight to push the car while steering into the skid. The tires catch a grip, straightening the Sentra out with only a little bit of fishtailing. Too frazzled to think about doing anything else, I pull onto the shoulder and stop.

The door mirror lets me see the taillights of the semi receding into the distance. He, too, appears to have regained control of his rig, put it back in the proper lane, and didn't even slow down. For a moment, I'm pissed at him for not stopping… but then I second-guess myself. We had a near miss. No one got hurt, not even paint scratched. Are drivers required to stop for that? Admittedly, it *should* have been a nasty accident. During the day or if I'd been mortal, I'd have gone flying out the windshield and probably landed in the sleeper box of the truck.

Did the ghost Sophia set loose just try to kill me or was it merely a newbie driver letting his rig get away from him in the rain? I could sit here for hours pondering unanswerable questions like what happened here, or where wads of pocket lint come from. Or why drive-through ATMs have braille on the keys, or why the Kardashians are famous.

Sigh. Some things humanity will simply never understand.

Anyway, I might as well get going before a cop decides to check out why I'm sitting on the side of the road.

DRIVING FROM SEATTLE TO COTTAGE LAKE SHOULD NORMALLY HAVE BEEN about a thirty-minute trip, but it takes me over an hour to get home.

Seriously considering going with the waterproof bag.

Vampires are not made for night driving in the rain. At least, not on highways where oncoming traffic is a magma flow of headlights. Despite it only being like a twenty-foot walk from car to door, I still pop the umbrella, finally noticing how badly my hand is shaking. Not sure if it's adrenaline given my altered biology, but it feels the same. Narrowly avoiding a head-on collision with a giant truck at night shouldn't rattle me as bad as it did. It couldn't have killed me or even inflicted any injuries I wouldn't have recovered from in a few hours.

Still shaking, I quietly make my way down to my room, scooting past the 'rents watching the evening news. After changing into my sweats, I flop on the bed and send Hunter a 'call?' text. There's no way focus on homework is going to be possible at least for an hour. Maybe longer.

My phone rings.

"Hey," I say.

"Is something wrong?" asks Hunter.

"I miss hearing the sound of your voice."

"You sound a little freaked out. What happened?"

Eyes closed, I imagine myself leaning against him. "Bad ride home. Almost got into an accident but it wasn't my fault."

"Crap. Are you okay?"

That makes me chuckle. "Yeah. Even if I *did* crash, it wouldn't have hurt me… much. Not sure why I'm freaking out about it." I explain what happened and even tell him about the spirit.

"Doesn't make sense to me the spirit would go after you. I mean, not unless you're a distant descendant of someone responsible for arresting and executing him."

"Uhh." I twirl a strand of hair around my finger. "Not that I'm aware of. But he died in the 1700s. I suppose it's possible. My dad's side of the family has roots in England, but I'm pretty sure my grandfather's great grandfather was already in the US. Even if I am related to someone who caused the guy to be hanged, would the spirit even know or care? Besides, I'm already dead."

"I dunno how long a ghost carries a grudge for, but wouldn't he be angrier at the people who put him in the jar?"

"Maybe. No point stressing out over it. If something else strange happens, then I'll worry. So what have you been doing?" I hold a foot up, debating toenail polish. Been awhile. Meh. Screw it. November. No one's gonna see it anyway.

Hunter rambles about school, work, and his mom. She's started a second job at night, part time. So, he's gotta stay home to watch Ronan or bring him to Mi Tierra while he works. Usually, the kid does his homework there, so he's not too bored when he's sitting around the back room.

Eventually, it gets late enough Hunter should go to sleep. He wants to stay on the line talking, but I shoo him off to bed. Hearing his voice has let me calm down enough to consider schoolwork despite—I think—a vampire stalking me and a semi nearly flattening me all the same night. Next to having an imp living in the house and a sister capable of doing magic, neither of those should seem strange.

But then again, I'm a vampire with a mountain of homework to do.

Nothing about my life is normal.

9

ALL THINGS WEIRD AND SARAH

Sierra's scream drags me out of sleep Tuesday afternoon.

I know that scream, so I don't panic. It's the sort of scream she lets out borne of shock, frustration, and outrage. Usually, the PlayStation causes it when someone's killed her ten times in a row. Other triggers include unexpected frogs in places they don't belong, accidental snot-rockets from a sneezing Sam, and one time, she fell in the yard behind the school and slid over a mountain of dog poop, ending up covered her from chest to knees. Oh, she also lets out the same particular yell if she encounters a toilet seat in the wrong position in the middle of the night.

Considering it's presently a little after three, this scream means someone did something to her. Rapid footsteps coming down the basement stairs make me jump to the conclusion it had to be either the imp or Sophia. If Sam or his friends did anything mundane, she'd have gone to Dad.

My bedroom door opens and Sierra barges in, smelling of bath soap and shampoo. Sophia's right behind her whispering rapid apologies, but I barely notice her due to the spectacle before my eyes.

Sierra has long, straight light brown hair a few inches shy of being a sitting hazard. At the moment, her hair is fluffed up into an enormous sphere. Every strand is sticking out of her head, pin-straight like a koosh ball.

Massive sphere of hair plus small enraged face equals Sarah laughing her ass off.

Predictably, this does not go over well with the little one.

"It's not funny!" shouts Sierra. "Make it stop!"

The doorbell rings.

Sierra screams again. "No! Don't let anyone see me like this!" She shakes her head, causing the hair orb to wobble.

I laugh until tears roll down my face.

"I'll get it," whispers Sophia.

"No." Sierra grabs her. "You did this. You gotta fix it."

"So why did you come to Sare's room?"

Sierra fumes. "I… I dunno. Just thought she could fix anything."

"Oh. My. God. You are adorable like that. Next year, Halloween, do it on purpose."

"No!" roars Sierra. "Not happening."

Sophia shrugs. "I could do it to my hair if I remember how."

"No, don't." Sierra pats at her orb of hair. "No hairspray invented will keep hair this long so straight. It's obviously unnatural."

"Dare I ask what you tried to do?" I swing my legs off the bed and sit on the edge. Hey, if I'm going to be forcibly jolted out of bed, waking up to laughter is an acceptable tradeoff.

"Some dipshit nailed us with a muddy puddle," says Sierra, scowling. "Again."

Sophia gasps at her for swearing. "We were walking home from the bus stop and a guy in a Beemer hit a puddle in the gutter and splashed us. Sierra took a bath once we got home, so I tried to dry her hair off fast… and that happened." She pokes a finger at Sierra's hair, marveling at the way the ends waver and go back into position after each disturbance. "So cool."

"Stop it." Sierra grabs her hand. "It's not cool. I look ridiculous."

"Be right back," I say, then hurry upstairs, leaving them to discuss the dekooshification of Sierra's hair.

The doorbell rings again. Yeah, yeah, I'm on the way. Fortunately, it's still kinda gloomy from the rain yesterday though it's not actively raining now. That makes it only irritatingly warm upstairs and not painful.

I'm surprised to see Hunter at the door when I open it. "Hey."

"Somehow managed to catch up on stuff and ended up with a free afternoon. I really wanted to see you." He smiles.

Ronan peers around him from behind, waving. "Hi."

He turned ten last August, but his short stature, big eyes, and longish blond hair make him look younger. The poor kid still has a generally fearful, quiet affect about him, a consequence of living with his abusive father. Sometimes, it's tempting to make the boy forget him entirely, but that's probably an overreach on my part. Or not. Trauma like he lived through can mess people up well into adulthood. Their mother doesn't know about the vampire stuff, so I'll talk it over with Hunter at some point. Ronan might be way happier forgetting all the nights he watched his dad scream at and hit his mother, slap Hunter around, and even hit him, too.

No, he definitely would be way happier without those memories.

"Hey, kiddo. C'mon in." Once they're inside, I shut the door.

"Don't mind Ro. Mom's at work." Hunter pats him on the head. "He's housebroken."

Ronan smirks. "I'm not a dog."

Of course, the first thing I want to do is be alone with Hunter. Dad's here, in his office working, so I don't need to be responsible for chaperoning children. And, yeah, it's big time awkward thinking about doing what I want to be doing while my father's in the same house and awake. However, the ability to erase memories makes up for a lot of risk taking. Pretty sure Dad would absolutely want to forget walking in on Hunter and me *in flagrante delicto.*

Sam emerges from the kitchen with a handful of cookies and a cup, heading for the stairs. He pauses upon noticing Ronan. I half expect them to circle and smell each other like strange dogs meeting by a familiar tree. Whatever assessment process happens between boys goes by in an instant.

"Hey," says Sam.

"'Sup." Ronan nods.

"Cookie? Mom just made them last night. Chocolate chip."

"Sure."

My brother gives Ronan his handful, then heads back to the kitchen to get more. When he returns, he stops near us again. "I'm Sam."

"Ronan."

"Wanna hang out and play video games?"

"Okay."

The boys go upstairs to Sam's room, discussing game systems, mostly my brother's shock that Ronan doesn't have one. Our house has two

PlayStations, one in the living room and one in Sam's bedroom, so I end up feeling awkward.

"Well, that was easy." Hunter chuckles.

"Want some tea or something? Cookies?" I start toward the kitchen.

"Sounds good. Your mom must make cookies in giant batches to keep up with four kids."

I laugh. "Yeah, when she bakes, she's cooking for an army."

Sophia and Sierra emerge from the basement door. They appear normal and calm, no more giant ball of hair. I assume they worked out the koosh problem without full contact martial arts. Given the way they fight sometimes—or should I say used to fight before my death—watching Sierra hurl herself at the imps to protect Sophia both shocked me and kinda made me want to cry from 'aww.' I'm sure nearly losing me gave both girls an unwanted lesson in mortality that dragged a protective streak out of Sierra. It's probably what kept things from getting physical. Also, Soph didn't prank her, she flubbed a spell.

A spell. I sigh at the floor. Seriously, when did my life get this weird?

Cookies and iced tea in hand, Hunter and I relocate to my bedroom for a date. Copious snuggling and a little making out follows while we sorta-watch a movie on my computer monitor. I'm not sure exactly what, but something keeps us from going all the way. Perhaps due to it being the middle of the afternoon with kids and at least one parent in the house. Maybe Hunter feels too awkward at the idea of bringing his little brother over on a booty call—so by keeping our date 'cute,' it's not a booty call.

It's obvious to me we both want it bad, but we end up just holding each other and talking. This is one of the few times in my life I've been tempted to skip school. In fact, I think it's gonna happen tonight. It's Tuesday, which means intro bio tonight. Probably nothing that couldn't be caught up on. Wouldn't take much effort to make Professor Connolly ignore my absence.

Ugh. Not even six months as a vampire and I'm already tempted to abuse my powers.

Okay, perhaps compelling people to buy Girl Scout cookies counts as an abuse, too, but that doesn't seem as bad as cheating the rules at school.

"What are you thinking?" asks Hunter, his breath right at my ear.

"How much I missed spending time with you."

He kisses me on the cheek. "Same. If I wasn't so damn busy, it would've been absolute torture. I don't have enough time to think about much so it's just plain torture."

I chuckle. "So you're off today?"

"Off in the sense of no homework waiting to be done and nothing to fix at the house. I still need to be at the restaurant later."

"Aww, darn. I was gonna skip class tonight."

He grins. "Don't give yourself more work. We can make time around our schedules."

I curl up against his side. "Wanna stop behaving ourselves?"

The look he gives me is one of total conflict. "There are at least four kids running around plus your father."

"Hmm. I could come over after you're done at the restaurant."

"That sounds wonderful." Hunter kisses me full on the lips.

Wednesday afternoon, I wake up, still smiling over the night before.

Yeah, Hunter stayed up way too late for him. When we realized the time—after one in the morning—I insisted he go to sleep. After helping myself to their shower, I flew to the Seattle outskirts and swung by the roof hoping to ask Glim about the tattooed guy who'd been watching me at the movie theater and who may or may not have followed me the other night. Though, given the time, he'd already gone elsewhere. He only haunts the roof so he can watch his boys and ex-wife. No idea how he's able to see her with another man and not let it rip him up inside. It has to be painful for him. Still loving her, wanting to be with her, but considering himself 'dead and gone' already. No telling how she'd react to seeing his true face. The woman might not even believe he's her husband. But… as far as Glim is concerned, Anthony Chavez died in Iraq.

I fished a Post-It out of my handbag, jotted down a quick note asking if he could look into the guy following me, and stashed it in the rain gutter by where he usually sits. Hopefully, we won't get another monsoon before tomorrow night.

For a little while, I lay awake in bed replaying my time last night with Hunter over and over in my head. Eventually, the nagging specter of responsibility pulls me out of bed, so I attack the homework I dodged yesterday. The only 'window' in my room is a life-sized printout of a photo my mom took of the window in my former bedroom looking out over a sunny summer backyard. Since it doesn't allow any actual sunlight into my room, my powers are at full strength. I still get kinda maudlin whenever I look at the fake window, but it's not over becoming a vampire or even losing the space that's become Sierra's room. Mostly, I miss my childhood. That view of the backyard had been mine for many hours sitting at my desk doing homework or playing around on the computer.

And yes, I'm fully aware I'm only eighteen. It doesn't make sense. Maybe it *does* have something to do with becoming a vampire. Dad sometimes talks about how he wishes he could be nine again so he didn't have to worry about responsibilities like a day job, taxes, bills, and so on—just spend all day playing video games or D&D with his friends.

Totally understandable for a guy his age. But me? I gotta be missing the lack of paranormal weird. It really hasn't been that long since Ashley and I could sit around goofing off for hours without worries. For the most part, we still kind of can. Neither one of us needs to work to survive. Though, pretty sure Mrs. Carter wouldn't be too happy with Ash for slacking off. Growing up I could've dealt with. Without dying, like most people, I probably would've rushed headlong into becoming an adult, not realizing what a mistake I made until hitting the late-thirties-red-wine-every-night phase of womanhood.

Growing up is highly overrated. I don't recommend it.

Of course, being a kid kinda stinks in some regards. Being a teen has its issues as well. Pretty sure everyone always feels like their present age is the worst time of their lives and either can't wait to get older or wants to be younger. What if true happiness only comes when a person becomes so old they enter the stage where they stop caring about what everyone else thinks and just follow their heart? Like that old guy two streets over with a corvette, or the elderly couple who live next door to my maternal grandparents. They tried to convince my grands to go skinny dipping with them. Talk about living wild and free. Okay, four elders skinny dipping is definitely a mental image I don't need. Sadly, staring at a mirror doesn't let me erase my own memories.

After a while of doing homework, an unexpected voice catches my ear from upstairs. My senses are sharp to the point where I can hear squirrels darting across the roof outside, two stories above me. This is typically why music is almost always on low in my room, to drown out a thousand random sounds that would drive me nuts. But, music with lyrics gets in the way of reading assignments for school.

However, Ronan appears to be in our house.

Curious, I head upstairs to Sam's room.

He and Ronan are on the floor, mesmerized by the PlayStation. They don't live *that* far away it's beyond belief for the boy to have taken his bike over here to hang with Sam, or even walked. Heck, Hunter might've dropped him off. Pretty sure Ronan prefers to be here playing games with Sam to sitting in the employee break room of Mi Tierra for hours, even if it includes a free burrito.

I'm about to head back to my room, but it occurs to me there's something not quite ordinary about the scene in front of me. Sam isn't playing the game, he's watching. Blix, the imp, sits between the boys with a controller in his minuscule hands... and Ronan is evidently aware of said imp and not freaking out.

My brother's blasé reaction to a small demon didn't bother me too much since, well, Sam. Pretty sure a tornado could rip off the front wall of our house and he'd calmly inform Dad the wind's a little strong.

The imp is playing video games with Sam and Ronan. Whatever.

I start to turn away, but Sam says, "Hey."

"Hey yourself." I lean in the door, eyeing Blix. "What's up?"

The imp salutes me with his tail since his hands are occupied.

"Hope it's cool Ronan's here." Sam grabs a corn chip from a bag in front of them. The bag Mom reported missing has been in here all along.

"Hi." Ronan tosses his head to get his hair off his face.

"Daryl and Jordan would be here, too, but they're both busy today and can't hang out." My brother gives me a pointed look, then a second later, taps the side of his head.

Aha.

I peek at his thoughts. Apparently, Ronan admitted to not having any friends because he's kinda small for his age and his long hair gets him picked on for looking girly. He's already confided in Sam he likes it long even if causes teasing because he's spiting his father who used to force him to keep it buzz cut short. He wants to learn guitar as soon as his mom can afford to get him one, and figures the long hair will work for when he's a musician. They've become quick friends and Sam really wants me not to be annoyed at Ronan for being here unannounced.

My ability to erase memories allows certain conversational shortcuts. "Not to put too obvious a point on it, but I'm guessing you realize your imp is hanging out."

Sam checks his fly, but laughs, clearly teasing me before I can say 'not that imp.'

"Wiseass."

He grins. "Yeah. Blix brought him here through the mirror world. If you're gonna marry Hunter someday, Ro's gonna be my cousin in law or something, so he's going to find out about stuff. He's good at keeping secret stuff secret."

"Swear." Ronan lets go of the controller for a second to raise a hand like in court.

Blix mashes buttons, using his tail to help.

"Hey, no fair," yells Ronan. "Tail foul."

Despite the extra button-pushing appendage, Ronan wins the match in whatever fighting game they're playing.

"Umm." I tap my foot. "Is that safe? We saw some *wild* stuff on the other side."

Blix looks up at me and tilts his hand side to side in a 'so-so' gesture, then babbles in a voice like Alvin the chipmunk played backwards.

"He said it's kinda dangerous but he's a good guide, so it's safe." Sam grabs and eats another corn chip.

Blix stares at the bag and a line of six chips launch out, gliding in an arc straight into his mouth.

"Umm." I gawk. "How is it you can understand him?"

"I dunno." Sam shrugs. "Just do."

The imp drapes an arm around both boys' shoulders, his little body dangling between them, grinning up at me. I can't read his thoughts, but he seems to be trying to project a sense of camaraderie. Best buds.

Okay. Whatever. Considering how weird my life has gotten, my brother making friends with a daemon isn't too terrible. Things could be far worse. Sophia could get her hands on a Ouija board. I don't even want to think about what would happen. Then again, it couldn't be any more of a disaster than an invasion of malicious imps, could it?

Wait. Hold that thought. Some questions should *not* be asked.

Sam's got a point. Hunter's little brother is going to wind up finding out about me eventually. Unless something funky happens, I'm fairly sure we'll be together for a long time. The boy's going to see me on holidays and probably figure out pretty quick my appearance isn't changing. Still not sure how I'm going to handle being in public with Hunter when he looks way older than me. Do I pretend to be his kid sister when he's in his late twenties? When he's forty, do I become the daughter? Eventually, granddaughter?

Ugh. Maybe the kind thing to do would be to make him forget ever knowing me, let him find a mortal girl and have a normal life. If I offer to do it for him again, he's going to be upset. Last—only—time I brought it up, he insisted he loved me and didn't care about not being normal. Should either of us ever desire to become parents, there's always adoption. Pretty sure the inner workings of my plumbing are shot. And really, would it be fair to the kid having a vampire for a mom? Especially one who's eternally more like big sis than a mother? Then again, a permanent home even with a vampire is probably a step up for them.

Right. I'm a teenager and I am breaking the fundamental laws of the universe by ruminating about the future. Chanting 'stop caring about stuff more than a day from now' over and over in my head, I return to my room to once again exploit my vampiric abilities for personal gain.

In this case, cramming six hours of studying into two.

Rawr. I am a fearsome creature of the night.

UGH. NOT AGAIN

More rain. Awesome.

By the time I need to start figuring out if I'm flying or driving to school Wednesday night, it's pouring outside. The storm isn't as bad as the other day at least. However, considering the harrowing ride, I don't want to drive in the rain again. People are idiots on the road already. Add water to the mix plus my constantly squinting at oncoming headlights? Yeah. No thanks. To be perfectly honest, my reaction to driving tonight isn't 'no thanks.' It's something my mother would gasp at me saying out loud, starting with an f and ending with 'that.'

Upstairs, Dad's asking Mom if she's seen his Fallout Boy figurine. It should be on his computer desk, but it's gone missing. The 'rents aren't going to grill Sam about the imp taking it because neither of them know we have an imp living in the house. Some kids have nightmares about a monster living in their closet. My brother, Sam, *has* a monster living in his closet and thinks it's the coolest thing.

My life. Seriously.

I pack a set of underwear, T-shirt, jeans, socks, and sneakers in a trash bag, add my backpack since it's not waterproof, and change into my swimsuit. Actually… no. I remove the bikini and grab the wetsuit I bought a few weeks ago. Black is harder to see in the sky than neon green plus my pale hide. Oh, yeah. A towel goes into the bag as well. And my umbrella. It will be much less awkward changing in the parking garage than walking into school barefoot in a wetsuit. Maybe if I lived in Portland or a surfing town, no one would bat an eyelash at that.

Comp sci starts at six, so I'm out the door and in the air by 5:30 p.m., trash bag slung over my back like some kind of morbid reimagining of a gender-swapped Santa Claus. Other than ending up soaked, flying in the rain doesn't suck as bad as expected. Honestly, the worst part of it would have been drenched clothes. There are no headlights—and no tractor trailers—up here. Though, the next time I do this, swimming goggles might not be a bad idea. Rain pelting me in the eyes is kind of annoying.

Before long, I swoop down out of the air, heading for the Harvard Garage across the street from school, slipping in via one of the giant openings right under the roof deck at the northwest corner, which provides the lowest chance of being seen. The worst part about this idea is going to be toweling off in a public parking garage after removing my wetsuit, but I can make people forget seeing me if need be. Compared to my first night as a vampire when I'd been stuck naked for twenty-four hours, this is nothing. I'd rather be caught streaking than cause a traffic accident.

Anyway, I find a nice secluded corner that's probably dark to mortals, set my trash bag down and pull the towel out.

"Sarah," says Glim. "I received your note."

He scares the crap out of me so bad I can't even scream… just go rigid. At least he decided to appear before I peeled off the wetsuit.

"Go ahead and change. I'm not looking and neither is anyone else."

I peek back over my shoulder—at a curtain of blackness. Oh, nice. He's giving me total privacy. Can't rely on him doing it every time I fly in the rain but I'll take it. "Thanks. One sec."

As fast as I can make myself move, I remove the wetsuit, towel off, and scramble into my dry clothes. The wetsuit goes into the inside-out trash bag, water to water, dry side facing out. "Okay, I'm decent."

The shadow wall drops, revealing Glim standing with his back to me. He does this melodramatic turn, then smiles. "Regarding your note… it seems you have somehow gained the interest of a group of vampires from Los Angeles. There isn't much information rattling around in the shadows about the whys."

"LA? Seriously?" I blink. "Why the heck would vampires from California be after me?"

"That, I have not been able to determine."

"Darn. Thanks for trying. Can you maybe warn me if I need to be on guard?"

"Of course." He bows like a butler.

"Stop that." I hug him. "Hey, question?"

"Hmm?" He leans back, one eyebrow up.

I explain the man from the movie theater. "Why would a guy who seems to be human be unreadable?"

"The three most likely explanations would be he is either a thrall, in possession of some mystical item capable of shielding his mind, or perhaps he may have trained himself to a point where his mind has become difficult to penetrate."

"Wow, people can do that?"

"It's unlikely to see in a man who appears to be a gangbanger. Typically, only ascetics and monks possess that degree of mastery over their thoughts." He gazes off into space, his yellow eyes glinting with a flicker of brighter light. "My guess is the man serves one of the LA vampires as a thrall."

I fold my arms, scowling. "A thrall is basically a human who drank vampire blood and got mind controlled, right?"

"Not necessarily controlled, though such things are possible. In much the same way vampires can share temporary gifts back and forth, it passes on some aspects of vampirism to a living mortal. If they regularly have blood, they cease aging, become tougher, a little stronger. Some develop night vision even."

"If the blood stops, do they rapidly age into a pile of dust if it's been long enough?" I snicker.

"No, they'd resume where they left off. However, the longer a human is enthralled, the more addicted they become to it. A person kept in thralldom beyond their natural lifespan would so crave the rush of vampiric blood that to deny it of them would drive them irredeemably insane. They'd devolve mentally into a nearly feral monster. Take the worst things you've ever heard about heroin addicts fiending for a fix and magnify it to supernatural degrees."

"Ouch. And whatever power the thrall has, the vampire loses?"

"Maintaining thralls does draw on the master's overall power, yes. That is why they are relatively rare or used only for short periods of time. The master can, however, see and hear everything the thrall is aware of."

I face-palm. "Another body thief spy then. Ugh."

"Another?"

"Sophia and the mystics?"

"Right. Not exactly the same but perhaps functionally similar. Unless the thrall belongs to an elder, they wouldn't pose a threat to you. Even if they did belong to an ancient one, the risk is relatively minimal. Thralls do not regenerate any faster than a normal person."

"Great. Okay, so this guy is merely spying on me for unknown reasons."

"That would seem to be the case." He nods.

"I've never been to LA."

"Innocents are rare. It could be someone has become curious." He grasps my arm. "You will be late for class."

Before I can even say anything, the parking garage around us blurs into a swimming mass of indigo and black, shadows upon shadows crawling like serpents across a void. Three seconds later, the bizarre scenery evaporates to the ladies' bathroom inside the building where my class is.

"Here you are. I hope you have a pleasant night." He flashes a toothy smile. "I really ought not to be in here."

With that, he poofs into a burst of black smoke.

So a vampire in LA might want to study me. Grr. I'm supposed to be staying under the radar! How the hell did someone so far away find out about me? Probably the same way Glim finds out about things. I smirk at myself in the mirror and spend a minute fussing at my damp hair before hurrying out of the bathroom to class, making it in the door with only two minutes to spare before the official start time. Professor Garcia is both on point and a decent speaker, so her class is a pleasure. If the rest of the teachers in the programming curriculum are this engaging, maybe I'll be able to handle this major.

A few students around me are discussing their nervousness about going into a career field so easily offshored. If programmers can work from home, they can work from Europe or Asia. Their conversation would probably worry me if I planned to rely on a legit job to survive. While I may have qualms about using my powers of mental influence in ways that feel like 'stealing,' no such guilt bothers me in any way in regard to keeping the house. I will mind control the crap out of anyone needed to retain ownership of the place I grew up once my parents are gone.

One of the guys says he thinks companies will always be interested in local programmers because there isn't a language barrier and it's a lot easier to make people showing up at an office work twelve hour days on weekends when a release date is looming.

Their worry session ends when Professor Garcia starts talking.

A bit of old me comes out from under all the supernatural stuff, and I listen intently to a class I'm really into.

WEDNESDAYS ARE ONE OF MY TWO-CLASS DAYS.

After comp sci, I have calculus. I've never really been best buddies with math, though it would be inaccurate to say I disliked it. To me, it's sorta like green beans: on the plate and I gotta eat it. Sierra always gave the 'rents a hard time with some green vegetables, chiefly broccoli and Brussels sprouts. Mom doesn't serve the latter so often anymore. Sierra deliberately got herself grounded to make a point. At nine, when Mom told her to eat the sprouts, she said 'F that.' And no, she didn't say 'eff.' She dropped a big ol' legit F-bomb straight on the table. As upset as Mom got with her for it, it's debatable if Sierra would've opted for another two-week grounding, but it did make a point. Sprouts have become rare.

Sophia always ate whatever the parents put in front of her. Some things, she took a lot longer to finish than others, but she choked it down, too non-confrontational to put up any resistance. And Sam? I think his taste buds are dead. As long as I've known him, he's never even flinched at anything on his plate. Of course he has favorites like cake, chicken nuggets, French fries… and oddly, fried fish sticks. But even if the parents served liver and onions, he'd probably inhale it. Fortunately, they haven't tried. Sierra would absolutely drop another F-bomb and go to bed hungry. Dad might, too. Besides, the liver is like the body's filter. Whoever got the bright idea to eat the part that absorbs all the toxic crap?

So anyway, back to math. Calculus is kind of like Brussels sprouts. I wouldn't call it terribly fun, but it's there and I gotta do it. Programming is going to be a bunch of math. At least I'm ambivalent about it instead of loathing. Sierra *likes* math. Sophia not so much. Sam is pretty blasé about everything in school. He doesn't seem particularly fond of anything nor does he complain about any subject.

I do kind of dread calculus if I'm honest, but it has nothing to do with math. It's the teacher. Dr. Mercer is highly knowledgeable, but holy crap, the woman speaks in slow motion. Guaranteed this class goes fifteen to thirty minutes late every single time. I have a one-hour break between classes. Only like three people from my comp sci class also have calc today, and I haven't bothered to make friends with them since they're all adults.

So, I hang out alone in the cafeteria, basically killing time. Tonight, I decide to feed two quarters to one of the old arcade machines in the alcove at the back. *Ikari Warriors*. The graphics are laughably crappy, but this game is like as old as Dad. It takes me a moment to get the hang of using the rotating joysticks, but with reflexes like mine, video games, in general, are kinda easy.

"Hey," says a guy on my left.

I give him a quick glance, then focus back on the game. He's probably around twenty with short black hair. Fairly handsome in a slightly nerdy Zac Efron sort of way, though not quite that cute. And he's giving off douchebag vibes.

"Hi."

"You're pretty good. Play a lot of games?"

I shrug and try out my best 'ancient Chinese martial art master' voice. "A lot to some, barely any to others."

"Waiting on a class?"

"No, I just drove a half hour to stand here playing a thirty-year-old video game in an almost empty cafeteria."

He laughs. "Nice. Yeah, I walked into that one didn't I? I'm Brandon. How'd you feel about grabbing coffee sometime?"

"Thanks, but I'm already in a relationship."

"It's okay if you're not interested. No need to make up a boyfriend. I hate how we live in a society where women are afraid to say no."

Sigh. "I appreciate that, but my guess is you're just trying to get me to say I don't really have a boyfriend so you can resume trying to talk me into going out with you. Hate to break the news, but sometimes when a girl says they have a boyfriend, they actually do."

"Okay. Chill out. No need to get all emotional." He takes a step back.

Oh, yeah. Douche. I'm about to compel him to go dunk his head in a toilet bowl and jiggle the handle a few times, but a better idea hits me. This jackass is now a self-delivering meal. A quick mental poke stalls him in place while I keep playing. Alas—or fortunately as the case may be— these old school games are kinda hard. Even with accelerated reflexes, not being familiar with what's going to scroll down on the map gets me trapped and killed. Oh well. I would've had to stop at some point for class anyway.

I lure Brandon to the rear of the arcade section and tuck in between two machines in the corner to feed. No idea what about him made my brain translate the flavor of his blood to cheese steak, but it's far from the worst thing that could've happened. He does save me the trouble of going hunting after class. Feeding is always annoying in the rain anyway. Besides, now I can go straight home to my room and get tonight's assignments done early.

When I finish feeding, I delete myself from his memory and... crap. He's in my calculus class. All right, rewind. I replace his attempt to ask me out with the idea I am already in a relationship and not interested. If I were Sierra, I'd compel the guy to still flush his head in the toilet a few times, but I'm not as vicious.

I leave him standing there amid a mental fog and head to the ladies' room for a quick mirror check to make sure there's no blood on my face before going to the classroom. Brandon shows up about six minutes after I take my seat and doesn't even look at me. Good. And wow. Two guys in under a week hit on me and think I'm lying about having a boyfriend already. Wait. No, that's not unusual.

That's being a woman going anywhere alone.

Grr.

Dr. Mercer gets up from her desk at 8:00 p.m. on the dot and begins the lecture. Is it wrong for me to be irritated at her for being so precise at the start of class but ignoring its official end time? Given how slow she talks, it would basically be shortchanging myself if I ducked out at nine. My weird mood and desire to go home get the better of me. As soon as Dr. Mercer looks in my general direction, I stab her in the brain with a minor compulsion to speak at the pace of a normal person.

The whole class emits a collective murmur of surprise when she accelerates. It's kind of like playing a song at 130 percent speed, only her voice doesn't go up in pitch. Unfortunately, by the time this class rolls around again, the minor compulsion will have worn off. But, at least tonight I can enjoy not being stuck here late.

⁂

CLASS DOES, IN FACT, GET OUT ON TIME.

Eerily precise as a matter of fact. At 8:59, she reaches the end of her lesson plan for the day. Everyone exchanges glances of awe and wonder at the miracle we just witnessed, but no one says a word about it. I pretend to be astonished as well, and waste no time ducking out the door. Alas, Glim isn't here to shadow-slip me back to the parking garage—or home. Second alas: it's still raining.

Huddled under my umbrella, I scurry south down the street to the parking garage, planning to change back into the wetsuit for the flight home. My ears tell me someone's walking behind me, which isn't necessarily an unusual thing after class. Those who drove in need their cars. I reach the parking deck and the same set of footsteps continues to tail me. When the guy follows me to the stairs and out onto the second story, it becomes pretty obvious he's not merely going in the same direction.

My initial thought is Brandon's come back to slap me around for saying no to him, but I rearranged his memory. No, it's gotta be the strange guy from the movie theater. Okay. Enough of this.

I stop and spin.

The guy tailing me isn't the same one from the movie theater, though he does share a few similarities. Hispanic, young twenties, short hair, and tattoos. Almost the same black leather jacket and jeans. Wow, do they 3D print these guys?

"What the heck do you want?" I ask, not quite yelling but still a bit louder than normal.

He keeps walking straight at me with this look like he's already made up his mind we're getting into a fight. And... shit. This one's a vampire. Grr. At least the expensive wetsuit is still in the trash bag and won't get shredded. I toss the bag and my backpack off to the side a second before he's in my face. He doesn't do anything worse than loom at me—yet.

"Where is he?"

"Gee, guy. Can you vague that up a little more?"

His right hand flies up toward my throat blurry fast, too quick for me to fully dodge. My attempt to jump away redirects his grab from my neck to a handful of my shirt collar. He shoves me against the nearest concrete column. I snarl and push at him, but he's significantly stronger than me. We're not quite as mismatched as normal me trying to fend off a guy this size, but I still can't budge him.

"Where is he?"

"Seriously, dude. Where is who?"

He pushes harder into my chest, close to breaking my collarbone. "The one who made you."

"How should I know?" I rasp due to his nearly crushing my trachea. "I haven't seen him in weeks. What did he steal this time?"

The asshole eases back a little on the pressure, giving me an up-and-down look before emitting a dismissive *pff.* "Just a pretend vampire."

I roll my eyes. "So? You're a genuine douche and I'm not jealous."

He gives off an angry snarl, then flings me at the back end of a big white SUV. My attempt to slam on the brakes with flying doesn't stop me before impact, though it causes me to crash into the window rather than punching through it like a human javelin.

The part of my personality most like Sierra comes out to play. Growling, I launch myself at him, irrational anger making me go for a punch to the jaw. He blurs to the side, catching my fist and slamming me into the column with my right arm chicken-winged up behind me. Great. I feel like a nameless bad guy setting herself up to be owned in a Stephen Segal movie. Just charge in like a freakin' moron.

Did I mention my father likes Eighties movies?

"You're a cute little girl," mutters the guy. "So I'm gonna let that slide. Your sire did some real stupid shit in LA. The boss wants his head on a spike. We find out you're covering for him, your unlife is gonna be real short."

Being up against a concrete surface does give me the advantage of leverage. He might be stronger than me, but he still only weighs about 190 and even a weak vampire like me can drag a car around. I push off the column hard enough to send us both tumbling. This dude apparently can't fly since he goes straight over on his back and slides halfway under a Jeep. I catch myself in midair and land on my feet, claws out, shaking from adrenaline as much from fear. He's stronger than me but I could be at least close in speed. Claws might put me on even footing... but is taking things up a notch a mistake?

Damn. Not thinking straight. Too pissed about being manhandled.

He slides out from under the Jeep and stands, chuckling at me. "You best put those things away before you get hurt *niñita.*" My attempt to glare likely fails to hide my lack of confidence, since he laughs at me again. "Lucky thing I believe you haven't seen him." He shakes his head. "Not surprised he left you to fend for yourself. Like fishing. Too weak, throw it back."

It doesn't feel like he's going to attack me again. No longer afraid for my unlife, I let go of some anger at being grabbed and threatened. Dalton did something stupid and somehow this guy traced him back to me.

Honestly, I'm more pissed off over feeling weak than I am at his threats. The best part about being a vampire is supposed to be not having to be afraid of guys anymore. Well, there's flying. Okay, the second best part is not having to live in constant fear. I'm simultaneously furious at losing that as I am scared. My pride isn't worth escalating this confrontation to a bloody mess of claws, especially when there's a real good chance it's going to be me getting the worst of it.

He keeps staring at me until I shrink my claws back to normal fingernails. His 'yeah, I thought so' smirk almost makes me leap at him to tear his throat out, but I'm more mellow than that. Really. This isn't my fight.

The guy gives me a pitying head shake, then walks off. It takes me a few minutes of standing there to calm down enough to realize I still need to fly home... and grab the trash bag holding my wetsuit. Damn. I can't win. Still going to get home like twenty minutes late even after putting Dr. Mercer on fast forward.

———————————————

As soon as I'm in my bedroom, I pull my cell phone out and call Dalton.

It goes straight to voicemail.

"Hey. It's me. Some dick from LA just showed up here and threatened me. What happened? Are you still alive? Wait... dumb question. You know what I mean. Look, I have no idea what's going on or where you are—or if this number still even goes to you. Whatever. Just be careful."

Ugh.

I hang up, toss the phone on the bed, and peel myself out of the wetsuit. After drying off, I slip into sweat pants and a loose shirt, then flop on my bed. So much for doing schoolwork tonight. I'm too damn worried. Calling Aurélie might help, but could also obligate me to go back out in the rain since she will probably invite me over. Laziness and the urge to stay dry wins. The LA douche just threatened me. Since I don't actually know what the heck Dalton did or where he is, I'm not *too* worried. Maybe it's a good thing the idiot thinks I'm a 'fake vampire.' Not sure if he meant it as a dig on being an Innocent or me being only five months old. Pretty sure anyone my age as an undead is on the weak side.

Grr. I hate being made to feel helpless, but perhaps, in this case, it works to my advantage. They'll either ignore me entirely or underestimate me. Honestly, I'd just as soon stay the hell out of whatever crapstorm Dalton set off.

Right. Okay. I'm good. Homework might even help me relax, especially the reading assignment. Nice warm bed, safe bedroom... wait. Something's missing.

I think I'm going to make myself some tea.

DEALS WITH DARKNESS

Hunter and I have epic sex in the middle of a sprawling forest.

In my dream.

I wake up Thursday afternoon in a haze of delirious passion that gradually mutates to the disappointment of realizing I'm not surrounded by massive snowy pine trees, but the rather ordinary confines of my bedroom. My craving to be in his presence almost pulls me straight out the door despite broad daylight. Grr. This is so frustrating. Bright days feel like I'm trapped in a dungeon cell.

In fact, a literal dungeon might be preferable. At least it would offer the physical stress relief of attacking a locked door and fighting to escape. I groan in irritation, roll over, and grab my phone from the nightstand. It's 2:18 p.m., and the weather app shows 'light clouds.' Hmm. Is my internal sun detection wonky or is the internet wrong? *Feels* like it's a bright one out there due to the overall lethargy plaguing my body.

Though, I suppose it could be actual lethargy.

My plan worked: all caught up with school stuff, so I am free and clear of any responsibility to do anything until after class tonight if/when there's more homework assigned. My cheese samples are gradually gathering mold in the outer basement inside a glass tank. The freedom of having several hours to myself is nice, but the idiot from last night is still on my mind.

It occurs to me my left foot feels a little cold. One of my pink fuzzy socks is missing. Sure, they're big on me and it's possible it might've slipped off in the middle of the night—but I don't toss and turn anymore. When I'm out, I'm *out*. E.g. I sleep quite literally like a corpse. Stealing one sock off a sleeping Sarah doesn't sound like something Blix would do. It also doesn't really sound like something any of my siblings would do. Is there a new ghost around?

My wardrobe doesn't contain much pink. These socks happened three years ago as a birthday gift from Grandma Sheridan. Super fuzzy pink socks with rubberized treads on the bottom. They're basically meant to be worn to bed or around the house, not inside shoes. I try to keep pink at arms' length, but these I like. Sentimental value and all. Grr. Annoying, but there are more pressing things on my mind at the moment than tearing my room apart to find a stray sock.

Dalton's number is still going to voicemail. As much as I'm hoping to stay the heck out of whatever he got himself involved with, it's in my nature to worry. The guy did save my life—relatively speaking. Without him, I'd be dead, my family all kinds of messed up. Ashley… ugh. The girl would have been a complete wreck for years if I'd died. I hate to say it, but Michelle probably would've handled it the best. She's tough. And I haven't known her as long as Ash. Yeah, she'd have been sad for a while but, like I said, she's tough.

No point calling Aurélie now. She's definitely not an Innocent vampire. And at her age, she's way *out* when the sun is up. The gift of consciousness during the day is one of the bigger advantages I have. Apparently, Innocents are rare enough that many vampires don't believe they exist or even that it's possible for a vampire to wake up easily before the sun goes down. This gets me wondering if the one who threatened me understood what I am. About the only real thing I have over them is possibly invading their sanctuary before sundown. Which is great if all I do is sneak around or steal stuff. Trying to kill them in their sleep would not end well for me.

They'd spring awake and be kinda mad. Though, if it's just a single guy sleeping alone, I'd be able to lop his head off pretty easily—at least physically. Not sure about the mentally part. It takes a certain kind of personality to be able to chop the head off someone who's helpless, and I am definitely not that kind of personality. Nope. Not me. And why am I debating murdering other vampires?

After a huge yawn, I stretch and get out of bed, creeping to the door to check the light levels of the basement. Dad covered all the windows down here with five layers of automotive tint film, so even when it's brutally sunny outside, I have the run of the entire basement. I suspect this is part of the parents' nefarious plan to keep me as a laundry slave. Just throw the dirty clothes down the stairs and the creature in the basement goes to work.

Chuckling to myself, I head up the stairs to the kitchen door. Really, it doesn't bother me at all to take over the laundry. Mom's definitely got her hands full with other things. Heck, on nights when there isn't a load of homework in front of me, I often go on cleaning benders around the house. Mostly to kill boredom and help out. It's the least I can do since I'm basically an adult freeloader at this point. It helps they no longer have to feed me, so all they're really 'spending' on me is a room that would've been empty anyway.

But, I know they want me here. The clinginess to my family that came over me after realizing I'd been murdered also hit the parents. Both of them had been looking forward to a lessening of the chaos by having one baby bird leave the nest and move to California for school. Now, they'd guilt trip me if I tried to go anywhere else. Mom's almost even gotten used to me doing housework unprompted. Okay, admittedly, prior to my Transference, I hadn't exactly been the most helpful almost-adult daughter around the house. We never really fought, but I'd go out of my way to disappear before she could ask me to do stuff, and when she did catch me, I'd grumble as I worked.

Weird how death can change someone's attitude, right?

The kitchen is bright, but not nuclear. Feels like my face is hovering in front of an oven set to 350. It's also a complete disaster. What the hell?

I lean out the door a little more, looking around at an array of spilled sugar, glasses all over the counter, big spoons, a few puddles, and half a grocery store's worth of Swiss Miss boxes. What in the heck? Back to my room I go, to trade my nightie for a purple long-sleeved sweatshirt and jeans. With my powers online in my lightless room, the voices of several tween girls reach my ears. Both sisters, and probably Megan and Nicole as well. They sound oddly far away and they're talking about hot cocoa for sale.

Well, that explains the explosion in the kitchen.

Once dressed, I brave the over-amped warmth of the upstairs world and peek out the living room window. The girls plus Sam have set up shop with a small table at the corner where our cul-de-sac joins the street. A chain of Dad's extension cords runs straight from the front of our house, out over the road, all the way to the table. At each point where cords join together, they're propped up out of the slush on cinder blocks. Reasonable children sell lemonade in the summer, not hot cocoa in mid-November. I don't even want to know whose idea this was or how it got started.

Sierra, Sophia, and Nicole pretty much look the same from behind while bundled up in winter coats. All three are skinny, though Nicole's not quite as stringbeany as my siblings. I can, however, tell them apart from hair color. Sophia's blonde. Sierra's got light brown hair, and Nicole's is black. Megan is both taller and thicker than the other three.

They have three electric kettles on the table to boil water. Since we don't own three electric kettles, Megan and Nicole likely brought one each. Seems they expect to do quite a bit of business for some reason. No idea why. We're not exactly in a high-traffic area here. Also, there's probably a good reason why everyone knows what a lemonade stand is and no one has ever heard of a hot-cocoa stand.

What could they possibly feel the need to generate money for?

Naturally, suspicion falls on the dance studio, but those places usually make the kids sell overpriced chocolate bars as fundraisers. And as far as I can recall, they aren't planning an organized trip anywhere to compete or perform in some national thing. And, Sam's out there. Then again, he'd be happy to help his sisters with something like this.

Whatever.

I'm about to ignore this particular new weirdness, but a police car rolls to a stop by the table. Crap. They didn't drive by, spot the stand, and circle around—they came straight to it. That tells me someone probably called them to complain. What is wrong with people? I dash out the door and run across the slushy cul-de-sac, squinting at the intense light. Without a house above me, the sun prickles at my exposed skin—fortunately, only my face, hands, and bare feet. It's definitely ouchy enough to compel me to go inside if at all possible, but I'm not emitting smoke and my sisters need me. What's a little flaming discomfort for family?

Sierra's in the midst of explaining to a big, bald officer how they saw a story on the news about spouses and kids of soldiers killed or injured overseas struggling financially, so they wanted to raise money to donate to a charity that helps them. They're selling hot cocoa for three bucks a cup with all the profits going to the charity.

"That's very thoughtful of you girls," says the cop.

"Are we doing something wrong?" asks Sophia in a small voice.

He leans back, thumbs hooked on his utility belt. "Technically, any sort of vendor stand requires a permit, but... a bunch of ten-year-olds doesn't strike me as a 'commercial venture.' What do you think, Ed?"

The other cop grins. "Nah. Carry on. And"—he pulls out a wallet—"I'll take a cup."

All four girls cheer and get to work preparing two cups of cocoa. The bald cop makes a radio call 'for backup,' explaining the situation here. Within fifteen minutes, I think the entire Cottage Lake PD and even some Woodinville officers show up to buy cocoa. Sierra finally notices I'm standing barefoot in a slushy puddle and gives me this 'eep' look before shivering in sympathetic chill. I don't really notice the cold. Looks worse than it feels to me.

Controlled chaos continues for a little over a half hour. A few firefighters and even an ambulance crew or three show up to buy cocoa. Sam and Megan operate the e-kettles, the boy making frequent runs back and forth to the house to refill with water. I'm not entirely sure where so much cocoa mix came from, but this has the stink of Dad's handiwork to it.

When the dust settles and all the emergency personnel have left, I nudge Sierra. "So, umm. What happened?"

"Some ass—I mean jerk called the police on us." She peers up at me with this 'beyond done' expression. "Take a wild guess who around here would be mortally offended that people under the age of eighteen exist."

I chuckle. "Neidermayer."

"He was staring at us while the cops were here," says Sam. "Seemed kinda angry."

"Oh, that's awesome." Sierra grins. "The prick complained, then he had to stand there watching the police buy cocoa. Sometimes, I love karma."

"Police karma," mutters Sam.

Megan and Sophia groan.

I glance over my shoulder at Neidermayer's. He's on the left side of the cul-de-sac in the house closest to the street. Sure enough, the old bastard's in the window glaring at my siblings and their friends. The look on his face, you'd think he observed a pack of hooligans spray painting graffiti on people's houses and cars, not selling people hot cocoa to raise money for charity. Any chance of me letting it go dies a withering death when he shoots *me* a nasty stare. Like, what the heck did I do but stand here being sort of adulty?

Grr. That man.

The kids seem to have things reasonably under control, so I head back inside to get away from the irritating sun daggers stabbing me in the face. The pain stops the second I'm out of direct sunlight, though it's still uncomfortably warm. For a few minutes, I stand there in the living room fuming about Mr. Neidermayer being such a prig. I'm eighteen and mature. So, letting something like this go is a perfectly normal adult thing to do. Right?

Only, I'm not as mature as I pretend to be.

Eyes narrowed, I head upstairs to Sam's bedroom. It *looks* empty, but I know better. "Blix?"

The closet door creaks open and a small grey head pokes out, one floppy ear dangling.

"How would you feel about a little deal?"

A tiny hand grips the edge of the door. He regards me for a moment with a measuring stare, then walks out into the room. He's not quite even up to my knee, but folds his arms in an 'okay, I'm listening' sort of posture.

I sit on the rug so as not to tower over him so much. "Neidermayer."

Blix emits a sound I assume to be impish for 'ugh.'

"Right?" I roll my eyes. "So, he just tried to mess with Sam and the girls in a big way. Think that deserves some payback. I want you to mess with him—and yes, I'm giving you permission to prank someone—but no injuries, okay? Get him back for Sam. I'll let you pick a new Ps4 game in return. Sound okay?"

Blix grasps his chin in three fingers, head tilted in contemplation. A moment later, he gives a thumbs-up and holds out a hand to shake.

This may or may not be wise, but I accept the handshake.

"Remember, no injuries. He's kinda old. No injuries includes not giving him a heart attack. No permanent damage."

Blix holds up his right hand as if swearing an oath.

"Great."

The little guy looks at me and emits a gurgling 'ooo' noise that gives off a sense of questioning.

"You want to know what happened?"

He nods.

I explain about the cocoa stand and Neidermayer calling the cops. Blix narrows his eyes, gives me a firm nod, and zips back into the closet. Okay. Guess that's that then? I head downstairs, wondering where on the scale of grandiose mistakes making deals with an imp ranks… probably somewhere between saying 'whatever you want' to a child picking a movie to watch and starting a land war in Asia.

Clicking from Dad's office tells me he's in there working, so I change course to bring him up to date.

I lean in the door. "Hey."

"Morning?" He looks up from his screen, one eyebrow raised in question.

"I've been up for a little while. You know about the hot cocoa stand?"

"Yeah. The kids saw this ad on TV for a veteran's charity or some such. Not the worst thing they could be doing with their afternoon."

I jab a thumb toward the front of the house. "Our jackass neighbor called the cops on them."

"Aww crap." Dad rolls back in his chair, about to stand. "They busted my dealers? It's only a matter of time before they trace the supply back to me. I'm the Heisenberg of hot cocoa."

"Nah, it's handled. The cops were really cool about it. Most of the force showed up to buy a cup. Good thing you bought an industrial quantity."

He sinks back into the seat, chuckling. "Well, you know my motto. Anything worth doing is worth overdoing."

"They still have an entire unopened case. We have enough hot chocolate for *me* to drink one cup a day for the rest of my existence and probably still not run out."

Dad snickers. "So, the kids are good?"

"Yeah. Just thought you should know what happened."

Sam walks in, squeezing past me into the office. "Dad? The girls are cold and wanna come inside. Can you help with the table?"

"Sure." He gets up.

"Right. I'm gonna retreat from the inferno. Be downstairs if anyone needs me."

And yeah, I just bribed a minor demon with a video game to play pranks on an old guy. Is that bad? Do imps legit count as demons? Wow. It blows my mind I'm even asking myself these questions. Another good thing about being a vampire? I can have a double-portion mug of hot cocoa without guilt.

THE SUN SETS AT A FEW MINUTES TO FIVE THAT NIGHT.

My foray into the light has left me hungry, so I duck out of the house and go for a fly into Seattle. Tonight's class is philosophy and sociology, which starts at eight. Out of laziness, I bring my books with me to avoid having to make another back-and-forth trip home before going to school.

A delivery driver emerging from the kitchen entrance of a restaurant in downtown Seattle with an empty hand truck makes for a convenient meal. I follow him into the back of his truck and pull the door down for some privacy. He whirls, but succumbs to my mental influence before he can yell at me. Among boxes of various breads and buns, I clamp on and feed. His blood tastes like a grilled chicken, bacon, and cheese sandwich—probably because the area outside smells the same.

After finishing, I head out via the front passenger side door, slip into the shadowy alley between the restaurant and the next building, and go back into the air, heading for Glim's usual haunt. An afternoon of trading texts with Ashley, Michelle, and Hunter has put me in a lonely mood since they're all busy again. It makes me feel like a total slacker to be sitting around at home all afternoon while everyone I consider a friend—or more—is out there busting their butt. Maybe it's too harsh of me to call myself a lazy slug. It's not as if much choice is involved. As a vampire, it really isn't feasible for me to be out and about when the sun's up, or working a real job. So, I am kinda stuck in my room at least until the sun goes down. No one thinks a guy in a wheelchair is being lazy for not taking the stairs. Would they expect a dead girl to get a day job?

I swoop in to land beside Glim on his favorite roof. The breeze has a distinct chill tonight, enough for my breaths to make foggy puffs. Not really sure how it works since I don't *have* to breathe anymore. But, my body does have warmth while I'm conscious, so it has to be part of the living illusion. Or something. I've been to alternate dimensions. Little weird things my body does shouldn't surprise me at all.

"Hello, Sarah," says Glim, not looking at me.

"Something wrong?" I plop down to sit beside him.

"Not really. Ana Maria and her new man got into a fight earlier. It's fine, nothing abnormal. Just reminded me of arguments we had sometimes." He lets out a long, heavy sigh. "The heaviest weights on the heart are those moments in time I can't go back to undo."

Ugh. I put an arm around him. "What did you guys fight about?"

"The worst one happened a day before I left to go overseas. She knew I couldn't just say no and resign from the Army, but she still wanted me to try. It's almost like she sensed she'd never see me again. Ana Maria spent the whole next morning moody. Didn't speak to me again until like ten minutes before I had to go out the door."

"I'm sorry."

"Thanks. You seem troubled as well."

"Ehh." I shrug. "I might have made a deal with a demon. Not sure if I messed up."

He blinks at me.

I explain what happened with Neidermayer.

Glim laughs. "I think your eternal soul is safe."

"Blix is a weird imp. He doesn't seem so driven to constantly prank everyone. It's like he just wants to play video games with my little brother. And weirder still, Sam can understand him when he talks."

"The imp most likely bestowed the knowledge of its language on Sam."

I glance over at him. "Are there French or Spanish imps? I gotta take two years of a language and I'm really not looking forward to that."

"Not sure about imps, but I've heard rumors some Academics can transfer knowledge via paranormal means."

"What, like they make a potion or something and people drink and know things?"

"Essentially. Though I'm not sure it takes the form of potions. Could be blood transfer or telepathy. You should ask Dalton, too. Those who pass along the Transference can also impart knowledge along the sire-progeny mind link."

Tempting... but asking favors from an elder sounds even more dangerous than bribing an imp. And Dalton? Yeah, maybe if I needed to learn a Cockney accent for school. No idea if he knows any other languages. Speaking of which, I'm going to need to find a way to make some cash. Can't really ask the parents to cover my deal with Blix, and the money I earned from my last part time job is pretty much gone.

"Is there a moralistic difference between compelling someone to hand me a hundred bucks or compelling someone to hire me for a night?"

"Probably, though it's splitting hairs. I think you'll find the longer you remain around as a vampire, the looser your opinions become regarding mortals."

I frown at the night sky... and the first traces of snow starting to fall. Tiny white flecks drift around in front of the vast blackness of the Universe. "Hope not. At least, I don't see myself getting jaded."

"Would you stick a piece of bread around your little brother's head and put a photograph of it on the internet for amusement?"

"Hah. Maybe."

He chuckles. "You were supposed to say no so I could reply with 'but you'd do it to your cat without thinking about it.'"

"I don't have a cat. Well... maybe we do." Somehow, Sophia has managed to keep it hidden from the parents. At least, if they are aware of it and an argument happened, it went down while I slept.

"Oh?"

I tell him about Sophia and the mystics and the kitten, which gets him laughing. "So anyway, I promised to get the imp a video game if he played tricks on the jackass neighbor. Trying to decide if I should basically shoplift the game or encourage someone to give me a temporary job. Both feel like stealing. But the job option seems less bad. Can't figure out what I could do that pays under the table right away and won't require a long-term commitment. And no, I'm not dancing in a strip club."

"Glad to hear it." He flashes a fanged grin. "Hmm. You could wait tables or wash dishes at a small restaurant for cash. Babysitting even."

"That's a thought. Oh, maybe I'll make the manager at Mi Tierra let me work there for a night or two. I'd get to be around Hunter a little more."

"Just remember to pay attention to the job if you do." He winks.

"Yeah." Snow flurries against the dark sky strike me as oddly mesmerizing, occupying my brain for a minute or two before another thought crashes in from the side. "Oh, did you find out anything more about the LA thing?"

He leans back, nodding. "Yes. The situation there is somewhat different. While the traditionalists maintain a society along the lines of what you're used to seeing here, Southern California also has a surprising number of individual groups constantly warring over territory. They tend to be on the younger side, both as vampires and in appearance. Some are anarchists, others merely adore the fighting."

"So, basically gangs... but vampires?"

"Yeah, that's a reasonably accurate analogy. In fact, many of them trade in drugs purely for the financial gain."

I lean forward and bury my face in my hands. "Crap. Dalton, what the hell did you do?"

"Considering the number of different groups at each other's throats down there, men like Dalton have no shortage of opportunity to make money or kill boredom."

"You think he stole drugs?" I groan and flop over backward, staring up into the sky. "He's kind of a sketchy sorta guy, but his heart's in the right place. I can't see him doing that."

Something in his family's apartment distracts Glim for a few minutes. Eventually, he pulls his attention off the window and back to me. "I was thinking more along the lines of mercenary type work. Participating in the territorial wars for profit or the excitement of it. Perhaps he owed someone a favor? Regardless of what one does in that case, it's guaranteed to make enemies. And it sounds like he made some enemies."

"Darn." I groan again. "He must've done something bad if they threatened me all the way back here."

"Probably."

I pick at my jeans. "The guy threw me around pretty easily. When I got mad and charged at him, he like totally owned me. Should I get used to feeling so weak? Is it like an Innocent thing or just an age-as-vampire thing?"

"Perhaps a bit of both. I'm hardly an authority on your bloodline, but I think the 'weakness' commonly attributed to the Innocents largely involves *other* powers."

"Other powers?"

He falls quiet a moment watching his wife's apartment, then looks at me. "All vampires have the common traits of being stronger, faster, and tougher than mortals. In terms of sheer physicality, I don't think the Innocents are at a great disadvantage. Each bloodline has a proclivity toward various additional powers beyond the basic aspects of vampiredom. Academics become inhumanly intelligent or delve into mysticism. The Old Guard often have charming powers. Beasts and Furies are endowed with additional strength above and beyond normal vampires, and so on."

"So, basically, you're telling me I'm a multi-class character who never gets access to high-circle spells?"

He blinks. "I'm afraid you have utterly stumped me with your analogy."

"Heh. My Dad and Sierra like roleplaying games. Some characters have really powerful abilities but if you mix two different character types together into a hybrid, you can't access the big guns so to speak. You're trying to tell me that as an Innocent, I should be fairly even with any other vampire for speed and strength, I just don't get the super fancy stuff like turning into a wolf or mist or mind-controlling an entire room at once."

"More or less, yes. But, again, you are the first Innocent I've ever met in person."

"Yay me. I'm a celebrity."

He chuckles.

"Do we keep getting stronger and faster the older we get or is there like a, umm, plateau where we hit full maturity?"

"Typically, a vampire reaches nominal physical prowess about twenty years after the Transference. Though, extremely old ones have been known to possess even greater strength. I'm unsure if it's due to intrinsic nature or some other form of temporary boost."

"Right. Okay. So, wow. Yeah. I really am still a baby. I haven't even existed for twenty years as a mortal."

"Your plan to stay out of the spotlight is a good one. Vampires who call attention to themselves seldom last long in the grand scheme of things."

"Yeah, but my plan isn't exactly working out too well. How the hell did they find me anyway? Or even know I exist?" I peer up at him. "That's kinda unnerving."

Glim reaches out, catching a snowflake on the tip of his finger. It perches there, not melting, gleaming in the moonlight. "There is most likely an Academic involved."

"So they 'scienced' me out of thin air?"

He chuckles. "Not all Academics pursue scientific fields considered legitimate. Some are much like the mystics you have tentatively befriended."

"Oh great." I sit up and catch a snowflake, too. Watching it melt as soon as it touches my finger makes me awkwardly aware of being simultaneously alive and dead. I'm Schrodinger's teenager.

"If true, it would also mean they had access to Dalton's blood. A vampire with the appropriate power could 'read' the blood to discover any other vampires with whom the subject has a direct connection. Sires, progeny, even thralls."

My fascination with the snow dies as fast as the molten flake on my finger. I wipe my hand on my jeans, sit up, and fold my arms across the tops of my knees. "So that's how they found me. Should I be worried? I really don't have any idea where he is or what he did."

"If they do have an Academic with those talents, they could likely use your blood as a means to attack Dalton."

"Umm. That sounds bad." I cringe. "Probably painful."

Glim rubs my back. "It wouldn't kill him, or you... though it would be highly unpleasant for you both. I can ask if any Shadows in Los Angeles are aware of what's going on."

"Thank you." I lean over and wrap my arms around him. An unexpected surge of gratitude and relief makes me cling tight. He's neither my father, my boyfriend, my best friend—that's Ashley—nor my older brother, but some inexplicable combination of all four. With him, I can talk about anything, even the vampire bits Dad or Hunter couldn't possibly understand. For no reason I can understand, talking to him is even easier than Aurélie. Wait, no... I *can* understand it. She feels so far above me in age and social status, I'm constantly afraid of offending her or coming off as a helpless mooch. "Now I feel guilty."

"About?"

I sit back from the hug and pull my hair off my face to smile at him. "I'm always asking you for help and never doing anything really for you... other than bringing beer sometimes."

Glim turns his head toward me, the moonlight playing off his brutal features—but the ghoulishness of his presence doesn't register. Despite the grey skin, elongated teeth, glowing yellow eyes, and lack of hair... I can easily picture the man he used to be. Anthony Chavez is still very much present.

"You are my friend." He grasps my hand. "That is already a gift beyond measure."

"Aww." I hug him again. "Still though, it's like I'm taking advantage."

"This might sound belittling..."

I laugh. "No problem. I get it. I'm new."

"Iraq has the kind of daytime sunlight that teaches mortals what it feels like to be a vampire." He grins. "Many times when my unit was out doing things, it felt like I was about to evaporate from heat. So there we are, and this little boy shows up. And you'd be wondering, what on Earth could this six-year-old child do to help a group of highly trained, heavily armed soldiers. Well, this kid had a wagon with water bottles. Walked right out in the middle of a dangerous street where he could've been shot to bring us water."

"This is a comparison to me bringing you beer?" I smile.

"A bit. Both you and that boy ended up stuck in the middle of a bad situation through no fault of your own."

I shrug. "I'm not an emo-pire. What I am isn't a bad situation. It's kinda cool."

"I meant the LA thing." He wags his eyebrows. "And now that you mention it, I am kind of thirsty."

"Hah." I pull out my phone. "Okay. I have time before class. Be right back. Ooh!"

"What?" He raises both eyebrows.

"Just got an idea for how I could earn a little cash. Delivering pizza by air."

Glim throws his head back and laughs, startling a few people down in the parking lot. They look around but don't appear able to see us.

Heh. Neat trick. Making people not see him—or anyone near him. One of those neato abilities I'll never have. But hey, at least it's comforting to know I won't need to spend the rest of eternity feeling weak. That guy had to be older than me by a good margin. Cool. My confidence is back, but I'm still annoyed at Dalton even though I doubt he intended to drag me into this situation.

The least my vampiric sire could do is return my voicemail.

LIVING PRECARIOUSLY

On the way out of school Thursday night, my phone rings.
With everything going on, the sudden noise and vibration causes me to jump and emit a yelp. A few other students look over at me with varying degrees of concern or amusement. Blushing, I pause under a tree on the sidewalk to answer. Seeing Hunter's face on the incoming call screen sets off a mixture of elation and worry. Dalton still hasn't called me back or even texted, but I'm happy to talk to my boyfriend.

"Hey," I say by way of answering. "What's up?"

"I don't have to be at the restaurant tonight. Wondered if you wanted to go out."

It's hard not to bounce with glee. "Sweet! Yeah. What did you wanna do?"

We toss several ideas around, but I can't ask him to spend a ton of cash he doesn't have. And I don't mean him paying for me. We cover ourselves. I meant paying for himself at some places is a strain on his budget. A fun night is a worthwhile escape, but he's already stretching it thin money wise. I end up nudging him to a simple date: dinner at a sit-down Chinese place in Woodinville. It's not much more expensive than ordering take out, and the food's way better. After we eat, we'll probably do the movie thing at home.

I agree to meet him at his house, then fly home to drop off my backpack and change into something a little less casual than a T-shirt and jeans. While gliding in over the cul-de-sac, I notice Mr. Neidermayer's house is glowing. Every single light inside the place is on and a steady stream of shouted curses leak out the windows. The old man's dropping some choice profanity tonight. Enough to wilt the flowers in earshot.

Oh, my innocent ears.

Curiosity pulls me in for a closer look. Going by the shouting, I head for the window where it's loudest and peer in. Neidermayer, in a tank top, boxer briefs, and a bathrobe, storms down the hall waving a golf club over his head. I'm not sure what he's chasing, but he runs full on into a doorway covered in clear plastic film, bounces off, and lands flat on his back. For a few seconds, he makes no attempt to move or get up, then lets out this horrendous scream of rage.

It's almost enough to make me feel guilty, but not quite. Hopefully, my 'no harm' rule means the imp won't give him a heart attack.

He gets up and chops at the plastic wrap with the golf club.

Looks like Mr. Neidermayer's in for a fun night.

Snickering to myself, I glide home to change.

WITH ECHOES OF SIERRA YELLING AT SOPHIA TO HELP HER FIND A MISSING sneaker rattling around in my head, I fly the relatively short distance to Hunter's house. I can't help it but hum the song *Defying Gravity* on the way. It's easy to spot the house from the air. The place is huge, but in bad shape. It's hardly about to collapse in on itself, but it definitely looks like it needs a significant amount of work or at least a pressure wash.

Hunter's waiting outside by his Buick. I land in the trees on the left side of the house to minimize the chances any neighbors see me, and walk out to meet him. We kiss for a little while, then get into his car and drive to the restaurant while talking about this and that. Our conversation is pretty mundane. No need to bother him with anything about Dalton, imps, or a whole gang of vampires from LA with their knickers in a twist. I do tell him about the neighbor though.

"Pretty sure Blix did something to the wiring so all the lights are stuck on."

He laughs himself almost to tears. "Poor guy."

"Not so much. He's a real piece of work. Mean as heck to the kids."

"Think tormenting him is going to teach him a lesson or only make him meaner?" asks Hunter.

"Unless he starts causing physical harm to kids, I don't think it's possible he could become meaner."

"Wow. That bad?"

For the last few minutes of the ride, and in between looking over menus, I share several stories about various times the old guy made me cry when I was little, or shouted at Sierra, Sophia, and Sam. There used to be a boy, Kevin, in the cul-de-sac who moved away when I was like twelve. He went to war one whole summer with Mr. Neidermayer after the man stole a soccer ball that strayed into the yard by accident. Fireworks, baseballs through windows, paper baggies full of dog poop lit on fire at the front door, all sorts of stuff.

"Wow," says Hunter. "The guy ought to move into one of those fifty-five plus places where they don't allow kids."

"Or put up an isolation fence." I shake my head. "Just can't understand what makes people so miserable they need to suck the joy out of other people's lives, especially kids."

"Well, some kids can be terrors. Couple houses up from mine, family there used to have a pack of four who'd run around shredding flowerbeds or ripping up lawns with their bikes on purpose."

"That's different. Yelling at delinquents is understandable. This guy just screams at kids for having the audacity to exist."

The waiter brings our food over. Orange chicken for him. I got beef lo mein. It really is amazing how subtly different eat-in Chinese food is.

"So, about Ronan…"

He looks up, worried.

"Oh, nothing's wrong. I was just thinking how he's so quiet and kinda flinchy. Do you think I should try getting rid of his memories of your father entirely? Would he be happier?"

Hunter teases his fork at a breaded lump of chicken, thinking. "I don't know. Who would he even be if all his memories are happy? He'd totally change. Maybe that would be better for him. Mom would probably be thrilled to see him come out of his shell. But, is it fair to do?"

"My dilemma exactly. Is it cruel to leave those memories in there when I have the ability to remove them, or is it more wrong to tamper?"

"There probably wouldn't be much left if you removed the bad stuff. It would be like he went from toddler to ten in an instant." Hunter lets out a sad chuckle. "He's just quiet. I don't think he's in any trouble. Actually, he's starting to come around a bit. Sam's the first real friend he's ever had. That's helping a ton."

I grin. "Cool. My brother doesn't usually make friends so fast. It's like he expects us to stay together. To him, you and Ronan are already part of the family, so hanging out with him is no big deal. Sam's even shown your brother his imp."

Hunter coughs, then cracks up.

"Oh, for... why does everyone take that the wrong way?" I roll my eyes. "The actual imp."

"I know." He dabs a napkin at his mouth. "It just sounds funny. Seriously though, Ro didn't flip out?"

"No. Blix even brings him across the mirrorverse."

He nearly drops his fork. "Say what?"

"Shortcut to come over and hang out. They go into a mirror at your house and come out of one at mine."

Hunter does this rapid blink thing and ends up staring at me like he's been lobotomized.

Hmm. Maybe I should make him forget I mentioned it?

"Whoa. That's real?"

"I know, right?" I exhale. "I'm still trying to sort out if I believe it even though I've been there, too."

"He's been hanging out at your house a lot, which is cool since my mom is never home now and I'm busy as hell."

Ugh. I twirl lo mein noodles onto my fork. I'd try to use chopsticks, but I'm merely a vampire with superhuman dexterity. "Okay, another question."

"Yes."

"Huh?"

"You're going to ask me if I want to go back to your place after dinner."

"That's already asked and answered." I wink.

"Your mother is a lawyer."

"Yeah, so?"

He chuckles. "Asked and answered sounds like something from a legal movie."

"Oh. Yeah. Mom says that sometimes." I biff myself in the head. "Guess I absorbed it. No, what I was going to ask... do you want me to maybe help your mom get a better job so she doesn't have to work two of them?"

"Umm." Hunter shrugs. "If you want. Isn't it kinda like stealing, or bad?"

"I dunno. It's not benefiting me personally, so it doesn't make me feel guilty."

"How would it even work?"

"Hmm." I eat a few forkfuls while pondering the best way to do this. "Okay. Got it. For now, let's leave your mother out of the supernatural loop. So, we'll need to be a little sneaky. Encourage her to apply for a job she wants that'll be enough income. When she does, you tell me where it is and I'll go talk to whoever is going to make the hiring decision."

Hunter wags his empty fork at me until he finishes chewing. "She's been turned down so much I don't think she has the nerve to try anymore. What if I can't convince her to interview?"

"Up to you, but I could give her a nudge, too."

A hint of a grimace appears before he can override his face reacting to his brain. "Let me try to talk to her first."

"It's okay. I understand exactly how you feel. The idea of tinkering with my family's brains is ick to me, too. You have my word I'll never do anything you don't know about and want."

He smiles. "Cool. So, wow. You can, uhh, just talk them into hiring her?"

"Yep."

"Really kinda weird to think about." Hunter stares as though he's trying to figure out what to make of me. "It says a lot about who you are that you don't run wild with the ability to get people to do whatever you want."

I point my fork at him. "When you first approached me in the admissions office, I told you my life was complicated."

"Complicated." He chuckles. "I don't think that word means what you think it does."

I can't help but giggle. "Someone's been watching old movies."

"Yeah. I figured it would help me the next time I ended up in a conversation with your dad."

Laughter almost makes me choke on lo mein. Fortunately, I don't need air—but, my body still objects to noodles going down the trachea.

"You certainly did say that. At the time, I didn't entirely understand what you meant. Now that I do... nothing's changed." He grins. "I'm still the happiest I've ever been."

Warmth blooms inside my chest, tinged with guilt. Who am I to take this boy away from a normal girl who could give him a normal life? My smile must be giving away more than I want it to, because his expression goes from adoring to concerned.

"Something's bothering you?"

"Dalton..." I suppress a sigh. "He did something in LA to stir up trouble, and it's come after me. No idea what happened down there, but I had a knuckle-dragger show up to give me attitude over it, as if I would somehow know everything about where he is."

"Uh oh. That doesn't sound good. How can I help?"

My turn to grimace. "I'm not sure it's possible for anyone to help with this." Of course, by 'anyone,' I mean mortals. "He hasn't even called me. I'm honestly not involved at all, so I don't think it's going to be an issue. Though, something weird *is* going on at the house."

"Like?"

"Stuff missing. Lost a sock the other day. Mom's car keys vanished. Dad had a figurine on his computer desk that walked away. Might be a bored ghost or maybe Sophia's new hobby is causing unintentional side effects."

Hunter nods, already aware of my sister's developing magical abilities. Maybe I shouldn't say stuff like this over the phone so freely. Can't help it. Wanting to hear the sound of his voice gets me saying anything I can think of to keep talking. Over the rest of dinner, I fill him in on what's happening with the LA vampire situation, the threat, being followed, and so on.

"I'm worried about you, Sarah. Maybe I can't do anything to help, but you should talk to the woman who's taken a liking to you."

I stare at my empty plate. The food tasted awesome, but noodle mush is going to feel *funky* later coming out. "Yeah, maybe. I've got a small confession to get off my chest."

"Uh oh." He chuckles, but it sounds more nervous than amused.

"It feels like our relationship is unfair to you. And before you freak out —no. I don't want to break up with you at all. I love you, Hunter. I just feel guilty about it. Things are never going to be normal for us. It's gonna get super awkward in a few decades. And, being around me could put you in danger."

He slides a hand across the table and grasps mine. "I'm okay with whatever risks are involved. You're totally worth any danger. Even if we have to play weird games in public when I look old enough to be your grandfather, there's nothing anyone could offer me to walk away from having you in my life."

My eyes tear up a bit from happiness and I damn near crawl over the table to cuddle with him. "So, umm, wanna head back to my place. Netflix and chill?"

Hunter flashes a big grin.

"Actually... I'm kinda being literal. I wanna snuggle with you and watch something."

His grin doesn't shrink. "Cool. Can't think of a better way to spend our night."

13

EWW

So, yeah. Things escalated, and I hadn't planned on it. Honest.

Literal Netflix and chill turned into metaphorical Netflix and chill. I'm presently lying in bed naked with Hunter beside me, also naked. There's almost a sheet on top of us. Soon after he fell asleep, I had to sneak away to the bathroom for reasons. Chinese reasons. Fortunately, it did not burn. Also took a shower to deal with certain other issues related to what we did.

While I literally *can't* sleep at night, it is comfortable and relaxing to simply rest. Also, having Hunter here with me is reassuring in the way a teddy bear is. And, much like a teddy bear, if some Los Angeles vampire shows up to cause trouble, there isn't a whole lot he'd be able to do about it.

Still, I adore being with him.

A few soft creaks pique my ears, but it could be the house shifting in the wind. Of course, it could also be one of Dalton's new 'friends' coming to attack me. Ever since Glim said they could do weird things with my blood, the worry they might want to kidnap me has been lingering at the back of my mind. With any luck, the phenomenon that lets women lift cars off their children works for vampires, too.

I'm about to hop out of bed and sprout my claws when my bedroom door flies open and Sierra runs in sobbing. Time drags to a near standstill as my vampiric reflexes kick up into combat mode. Instead of clawing someone's face off, I grab the sheet and yank it up to cover Hunter, while mentally scolding myself for not pestering Dad to replace this doorknob with one that has a lock.

Apparently, the warning sock I hung outside the door has also gone missing. Though, given Sierra's present emotional state, I'm not sure she would have cared. She leaps onto the bed and lands hugging me. It's only slightly embarrassing. Sierra has, after all, seen me with no clothes on occasion. It's happened a few times when we've gone camping and ended up changing into swimsuits in the same tent. Also, four kids in a house with two bathrooms is bound to have the occasional lack of privacy during emergencies.

However, having her clinging to me in tears while I'm naked feels *way* wrong.

I stare into her eyes and put her brain on pause. She goes from freaking out to a mannequin in an instant. After extricating myself from her grip, I throw on a long T-shirt, adjust the blankets to completely cover Hunter, then sit on the edge of the bed and alter Sierra's memory to see us as wearing clothes the whole time. She didn't consciously realize the nudity in front of her due to her terrified emotional state, but I'm not taking any chances. Nope. My kid sister lives in a G-rated world until she's in her thirties. At least if I have anything to say about it.

Now that the bare essentials are covered, I sit on the edge of the bed, grasping Sierra by the shoulders. "Okay, you may continue your meltdown." A small mental prod takes her off 'pause.'

She resumes bawling. I hold her for a little while, patting her back until she calms enough to blubber about having a nightmare about being caught in a school shooting. My eleven-year-old sister trembles while telling me about how she scrambled to crawl into a storage cubby already full of other kids while gunfire went off outside in the hall. She woke up right as a shadow fell over the window in the door.

"Just a dream." I hug her, rocking side to side.

Sobbing fades to soft crying for a little while, then silence. "I'm being a baby."

"It's okay. That sounds scary as hell."

She leans back, wiping her face, her expression total frustration. "I'm acting like a little kid having a bad dream."

I grasp her head in both hands and look into her eyes. "Sierra, it's fine. Those drills are traumatizing. They scared the heck out of me, too. I know it's hard, but try not to let it get to you. Nothing's gonna happen."

"Sure. Nothing's gonna happen. That's the same thing they said at every place where it's happened." She shivers.

The most frustrating thing about this is I can't think of a single person to blame. I want to be furious at whoever created this world in which little kids are acutely aware of their own mortality and think any single day they go to school might be the last time they ever see their parents or friends alive. My kid sister should not be waking up in the middle of the night freaking out about this. I'm way more heartbroken at the terror in her eyes than I am over my death.

I hug her tight. In the privacy of my basement bedroom, with no parents, other siblings, or friends to see her, Sierra lets her guard down and clings like the frightened child she really is inside. Eventually, she relaxes her grip and stares into space.

"Hey. Don't worry too much. We have Coralie, remember? She told me you're not going to be hurt at school. And, if something else is going to happen, she'll warn us."

Sierra looks up at me, relief in her eyes. "Oh. Yeah. I forgot." She exhales hard. "Duh. Stupid little kid with bad dreams."

"At least you're not afraid of a big pom-pom."

She laughs. "Seriously. Where did she ever come up with that? Umm, sorry for just running in when Hunter's here."

"It's okay. I was up anyway."

"Hah." Sierra sticks out her tongue, then blinks, looks around, and narrows her eyes at me. "Hey. I can't remember running in." Her cheeks go bright red. "*Gawd.* You guys were doing *stuff*, weren't you?" She shivers. "Ugh! Thank you for making me forget seeing that."

Snickering, I poke her in the side. "Relax. You didn't see anything. We were just lying there."

"Eww."

"This will be you someday. And Sophia. Another couple years, you'll feel differently about boys."

"Eww." She shudders.

"Or girls. Whatever."

"You think I'm gay?" Sierra blinks.

"I don't think anything. Just saying it's fine whatever." I pat her on the head. "Someday, it'll be me, Dad, or Mom barging in on you when you've got someone."

"Eww." Sierra shakes her head. "There is no way that's happening in Mom and Dad's house. I don't know how you can even do it."

"When you're older—"

"Eww." She jumps up. "I'm going back to bed. Thanks for helping me calm down. And if you tell anyone, there will be consequences."

I draw an X over my heart.

"Oh, and hang a sock on your door." She trudges out.

"I did."

Sierra pauses a step outside in the basement. "There's no sock on your door."

"The ghost probably took it."

"Which ghost?"

I get up and pad over there to look around. Sure enough, no sign of any sock. "The same one that's been stealing everything else."

"My Halo guy disappeared, too. It better not be Blix." She folds her arms, scowling. "Or I'm gonna use him for a sword dummy."

"You don't have a sword."

"There are brooms in this house. Close enough."

I chuckle. "Really doesn't seem like something an imp would do."

She yawns. "Gonna go back to bed."

"Night."

Sierra trudges off to the stairs.

I check the dryer and the basement laundry basket for the missing sock, but both are empty. On the surface, the random thefts of small objects seems like nothing I should be concerned about, but the way things are going lately, anything could be a sign of imminent badness. Today, a missing sock, tomorrow an apocalyptic collision of multiple divergent planes of existence.

And for all I know, Sophia's new kitten is going to explode with the force of an atomic bomb.

It's utterly astounding how she's managed to keep it hidden from the parents thus far. Kitten secrecy can't last much longer. Eventually, someone will notice she's using her allowance money on cat food and litter… and there's a cat box somewhere in her bedroom.

At least, *hopefully*, there's a cat box in her bedroom.

Then again, does this kitten poop? She made it out of fungus dust.

It *is* eating, so it stands to reason there will be poop. I stare down at my hands, gripped by the sudden dissociative worry I'm not real. Vampires don't exist. Magic doesn't exist. Right now, I'm either asleep in my old bedroom on the night before SATs having a stress-induced nightmare. Or maybe I'm still bleeding to death in the woods after Scott stabbed me and the past five months have really all happened over the course of like fifteen seconds.

Nah. I haven't taken anywhere near enough drugs to imagine one third of the crap that's happened to me since the night Dalton found me near death.

The eerie feeling of un-reality fades. I head back into my room, grab the phone, and call Dalton. Again, right to voicemail. Drat. Really don't wanna get involved, but it's becoming harder not to worry about him.

I hang another sock on the doorknob, close the door, and slip back into bed with Hunter after depositing my long T-shirt on the floor in easy reach. I've barely had three seconds to adore the sensation of our bodies pressed together before noises outside put me on edge. Sounds like someone rummaging around and trying—unsuccessfully—to be quiet about it.

Dammit. I'm really not in the mood for an abduction tonight.

Grumbling, I get out of bed and pull on a pair of jeans and a T-shirt I won't care about losing. Vampire fights aren't exactly kind to my wardrobe. So damn frustrating. Kinda redefines the term 'naked aggression.' The rustling from outside sounds farther away, but I'm on my feet and dressed already, so no point ignoring it. I head upstairs to the kitchen and go out the patio to the deck. The faint rattling of a stepladder comes from the left side of the house. Oh, that can't be good. Expecting something ridiculous rather than dangerous, I peer around the corner but there's no one trying to go in a second-floor window. The sound shifts, becoming obvious as an echo from a greater distance than right beside my house.

Okay, odd. I creep down the length of the house to the front yard, peering out at the cul-de-sac.

Mr. Neidermayer, wearing a bathrobe over pajamas and a cast on his right foot, struggles to position a ladder beside the roof of his porch. Oh, crap. He's hurt. Dammit. That wasn't supposed to happen. He drags himself up the ladder and starts mounting a small camera. Looks like he's gone full paranoid. Of course, given the circumstances, I can't really fault him. He probably blames my siblings for everything happening to him as retaliation for calling the cops but can't prove it. Given the kind of things imps can do, he's also likely questioning his sanity.

Confident there isn't a hostile vampire lurking about, I go back inside, but sneak up to Sam's room. Blix the imp is sitting cross-legged on the floor playing a video game with the sound off. Apparently, the light from the TV doesn't bother Sam at all, as he's sound asleep.

The imp pauses the game and peers up at me with a hopeful expression.

"Not yet. I need to make some money before I can get you a game. Probably do that tomorrow night or over the weekend."

He nods and gives me a thumbs-up.

"I just saw Neidermayer. His foot's in a cast. Didn't you agree not to hurt him?"

Blix drops the controller and waves both hands at me like he's trying to warn me away from driving off a cliff.

"You didn't do that?"

He shakes his head.

"What happened?"

Blix stands. He shakes his fists in the air, putting on a furious grimace, then kicks an imaginary object before grabbing his foot and hopping on the other leg.

"Oh. He got pissed and broke his own foot kicking something."

Blix nods again.

Is it cruel of me to find that funny? "Okay. Cool. No problem."

Mr. Neidermayer's scream precedes the crash of a collapsing ladder.

Blix puts a hand over his chest and rapidly shakes his head.

"Yeah, not you. I know. You're right here." I sigh. "Guess I should probably go make sure he doesn't need an ambulance."

The old man is quiet for a moment, but when he starts spouting curses insinuating what the guy who made the ladder does with goats, I decide he's okay enough to leave alone. Maybe someone will call in a noise complaint on him for installing video cameras at almost four in the morning.

Wouldn't that be karma?

14

TAINTED

I haz job.

Well, not entirely. I sort of *had* a job. Friday night after class, and Saturday after dark, I made good on my idea to earn some money delivering pizza. It didn't take much effort to convince the owner of the shop to both hire me for two nights and keep everything off the books. I wound up strapping my iPhone to my left forearm so I could see the screen while flying and holding a pizza warmer bag.

Somewhere, there's an ancient vampire walking around with a face like someone filled his knickers with lukewarm oatmeal. He doesn't know why he feels awkward, but some deep, inner part of his being objects to the mundanity of a vampire using their immortal powers to deliver freakin' pizza. The boss had this system where whatever driver happened to be available and waiting by the counter got the next order. So, by exploiting my ability to fly at over a hundred miles an hour—avoiding traffic and lights—I had pretty much every order to its destination in a few minutes. In the time a normal driver dropped off one order, I delivered three or four.

Naturally, the boss thought I merely went out back and tossed them in the dumpster, but when no one called to ask where their order ended up, he assumed I had a motorcycle or something and drove like an insane person.

Anyway, I made almost $350 in two nights' work, most of it tips. For a job, it actually wound up being kinda fun. It would absolutely suck in the rain, though. Also, can't do it too often since a few landings ended up being tricky on account of trying to remain unseen.

Saturday, Mr. Neidermayer let out this Tarzan scream at a few minutes past one in the morning, as if he'd channeled the pure quintessence of agonized frustration into audible form. I have no idea what the heck the imp did to make the old man produce *that* noise but it got me laughing like an idiot.

Sunday late afternoon, I took the littles plus Blix to the mall. The kids had some allowance money, Mom gave me the nod to use the credit card to grab a few things they needed, mostly clothes or school supplies, and deal with feeding them dinner. Mom and Dad are having a date tonight, going out to eat and maybe a movie in an actual theater. While at the mall, we hit a game store where Blix picked out his reward: a fantasy adventure where one of the playable characters looks like a succubus.

And, I got to spend some time with Hunter and my family. Sunday night, Dad put on *Conan the Destroyer*. Sam dubbed himself Conan the Destroyer—of popcorn.

All in all, I had a good weekend with much needed fun, time to wind down, and a bit of cuddling at Hunter's house.

Monday afternoon, I awake to find a grey kitten perched on my chest.

"Oh, hi there."

"Mew," says the kitten.

She stands, stretches, then disappears into thin air.

No, that's not weird at all.

But it does explain how Mom hasn't seen her yet.

My bones feel like they're made of lead, a good sign the sun is glaring today. I drag myself to my computer desk and start on the calculus homework dumped on me Friday. Computer science had a test, so Professor Garcia only gave us a short reading assignment, which I'll do after the more demanding math exercises.

A *ping* comes from my phone at 3:14 p.m.

Ashley: ‹Plz come over b4 I do smthg I'll regret.›

Aww shit. A panic bomb goes off inside my head. I scramble out of my nightgown into my clothes, then add gloves, a scarf, and a hoodie before running upstairs. The kitchen feels like I've thrown myself into a pizza oven. It's so nerve wracking and hot, I run straight out the door without stopping to grab shoes. Better to get to Ashley's faster than spend the twenty seconds standing still in sunlight.

I leave a smoke trail—literally—to Ash's house, four houses down the street from my cul-de-sac. The gravel walkway around the side to the back yard is like running on forks, but the pain barely registers to me past the sensation of being microwaved on high. I knock over their outdoor trashcan in my haste to get around into the backyard and onto the rear porch, which gives me some protection from the sun. It's enough to let me think again, rather than follow the primal cavegirl urge to get the hell out of the light as fast as possible. I grab the key from the fake plastic rock and let myself in.

"Ash?" I shout.

A faint moan comes from upstairs.

Crap! I'm too late. She's already done something to herself.

I sprint across the house to the living room and go upstairs to Ash's bedroom. Crying and sniffling inside gives me hope there might still be time to save her. I shove the door aside and barge in. Her thick, pink curtains are drawn closed over the windows tinting the room a shade of rose like a cheesy Sixties porno and reducing the sunlight from body surfing a hibachi table to broken tanning machine.

Ashley's curled up atop her bed in a long-sleeved pink sweater and jeans. She's barefoot, bawling her eyes out... and her right wrist is locked to the headboard by a set of fuzzy pink cuffs. Umm. Okay.

"Ash?" I ask barely over a whisper.

She sniffles. "Sare."

I close the door to block the sunlight from the hall and hurry to the side of the bed. A cloud of smoke continues seeping out of my clothes, hanging around me.

Her blue eyes widen. "Wow. You look like the L.L. Bean ninja. Oh, crap. You're on fire."

"Just a little superficial combustion. No open flame. What's up?" It's dim enough in here for me to take the sunglasses off without blinding myself. "What happened?"

"Thanks for coming over so fast. I didn't realize it was so bright." She sits up and wipes her eyes with her left hand. "You could've said too sunny."

I sit on the bed next to her. "Do I want to know why you're handcuffed to the headboard?"

"To stop myself from doing something I'm going to regret."

"Aww." I hug her. "It's not that bad. It's never that bad."

Ashley exhales. "No. No. Not that. I'm not gonna kill myself. I was close to eating an entire box of ice cream."

I stare at her. "Wait, you chained yourself to the bed over ice cream?"

Ashley tugs at her arm. "Not just ice cream. Rocky Road. It was an emergency. I had to stop myself or I'd have killed the whole box."

"Oy." I slouch, sighing. "Seriously?"

"Yes!" She puts on this sad fake-pouty face. "I have no willpower. Please don't be mad."

She's far too upset for me to be angry at her for scaring the hell out of me. "I'm not mad at you. Who did whatever that's got you crying like this?"

"Tabitha."

"Okay…" That name means nothing to me. "Umm. Who?"

Ashley cries on my shoulder for a little while, her right arm dangling from the fuzzy cuffs.

"Hey, where's the key?"

"Over there on the floor." She gestures at the corner by the door. "I threw it across the room."

"What if I couldn't get here?"

She shrugs. "Mom would've let me out eventually."

"Your mom knows you have fuzzy cuffs?"

"Not yet." She blushes.

"Since when do you have fuzzy cuffs?" I ask, eyebrow up.

"Umm. Since Aurélie. She, umm. Introduced me to some stuff. I, umm. Yeah. But this isn't anything like that. I just didn't want to run downstairs and whale a whole box of ice cream."

I fetch the key, which did its damndest to hide. Little tricky finding a pink-plastic covered key on a pink rug in a room awash with pink light. Honestly, I should've traded places in the birth order with Sophia so she'd have been the oldest and best friends with Ash. The two of them are *all about* pink. They would've been… wait. No. That much pink in one place would've caused Armageddon. No wonder the Universe sent me here first. It couldn't allow Sophia and Ashley to align.

Once I unlock her, she grabs me with both arms and cries for a little longer. "You gotta make sure I don't eat a billion calories."

"Okay."

She sniffles. "No, I mean it. Put it in my brain I don't want to do that."

"You want me to give you a mental compulsion?"

"Yes. But only a compulsion so I don't want to grief-eat."

I shrug. "Okay. But I can't yet. Too damn bright."

"Closet?"

"Wait, you want to go back into the closet?"

"Stop!" She laugh-cries, poking me. "Not funny. Okay. A little funny. Just for the darkness."

"Dark sounds good." I get up and walk with her to the bigger of her two bedroom closets, stuffing myself in among her dresses and coats.

Ash squeezes in after me, pulling the door shut. It's like going from a Middle Eastern desert in August to an industrial cooler, even if I am mushed into her wardrobe.

"Oh…. That's soooo nice." I moan in relief.

"Hey, stop making noises like that. If my mother comes home, she's going to get the wrong idea about what we're doing in here."

I laugh. "No, it's just so… awesome in here. Not sure if I ever told you, but the sunnier it is, the hotter it feels. It's like standing in a literal oven to me out there today."

"Oh, sorry." She hugs me. "You really should've told me you can't go outside in this light."

"Ash. You dropped a bomb on me so heavy I thought you were going to do something drastic."

She tries to look me in the eye, but she can't see in here. "Eating an entire box of rocky road ice cream in one sitting *is* drastic. If I didn't have those cuffs, you would've found me passed out on the floor in the kitchen in a diabetic coma."

"Dork. You know what I mean. And since when are you diabetic?"

"I'm not. But I would've been if I ate all that ice cream at once." She sniffles. "Okay, just go on and do the thing already."

"You seriously want me to give you a compulsion?"

"Yes. I want you to give me the strength to resist binge-eating ridiculous amounts of junk."

"Okay. I'll try." I grasp her head in both hands, stare into her eyes, and do my best to install the requested mental command. It's impossible not to see what's occupying the bulk of her thoughts because it's so foremost on her mind: she'd been dating this cute blonde girl with a pixie cut named Tabitha, a lesbian, who she *really* liked. But the girl freaked out over Ashley being bisexual. Called her 'tainted' for having been touched by boys. Eek. That bitch treated her like she had dog poop smeared all over her—which, considering where she works, is an actual possibility.

Grr. If I ever run into Tabitha, it'll be difficult for me to resist doing something to her for crushing my best friend's heart. Now for the hard part. No, not removing her urge to devour a whole box of ice cream in response to sadness. That's easy. The hard part is going to be acting like I don't already know why Ashley's despondent. She might be upset at me later, but the easiest thing I can think of to keep her off empty calories is to replace the urge to eat with the urge to cling to her stuffed animal army. I rewire her brain slightly to get the same sense of comfort from squeezing plushies as she might've gotten from overdosing on sugary dairy products. It's a lot easier and more permanent than simply leaving a blank space.

Fortunately, squeezing stuffed animals is totally guiltless.

A few minutes later, Ashley emerges from the mental fog and blinks rapidly. "Whoa. It worked. That's so cool. And weird."

"Yeah, well. I didn't erase your memory of wanting to eat the whole box of ice cream, or of asking me to help you resist it. So, now you don't want to do it but you remember wanting to."

"My head hurts."

"Heh. Okay, so spill. What happened?"

"Do we have to stay in the closet?"

"It's much more comfortable in the dark." I elbow one of her coats. "But it is a little cramped. It's okay. With the curtains closed, your room is only a little over-warm."

We re-emerge into a hot July day rendered in electric pink. I remove my scarf, hoodie, and gloves since they're not helping. Covering my skin is only a shield against *direct* sunlight, and her curtains are already blocking that.

"Oh, ouch." Ashley sits on her bed, pulling her giant stuffed unicorn into her lap as a reflex. When I get close enough, she grabs my hand, turning it to examine a strip of red burn where the North Face logo is clearly visible in white not-burned skin. "Sorry."

The gloves have a breathable mesh on the side with a plastic logo.

Guess a little light made it through the gloves after all. "It's okay. It should heal up in an hour or so."

"Umm. So, I met this girl Tabitha at the vet clinic last week. She came in with her mother and this adorable calico cat. We kinda got talking and ended up going on a couple dates."

"Okay..."

"Last night, we went out, had a nice date, came back here and cuddled on the couch." Ashley wipes a tear.

"Right..."

"We started kissing and stuff. She said something nasty about guys, I don't even remember what, and I said they're not *that* bad. When I told her I'm bi, she like totally freaked out. One minute we're falling down a rollercoaster and about to go all the way, the next, she's calling me disgusting and storming out the door."

"What?" I gasp. "The heck for?"

"She thinks it's disgusting that I've been with guys, and didn't want to touch me because she said it would be like doing it with a boy by proxy." She buries her face in her hands and starts sobbing again. "I really thought I'd fallen in love with her."

"Ash." I rest my hands on her shoulders. "You went on *two* dates with this girl. Why are you so upset over this?"

"I dunno. Maybe the Universe is telling me I'm gonna be alone."

"Don't overreact. The right person's out there somewhere, but it's okay to be single, too."

She lets out a long, hard breath and squeezes the unicorn plushie. "Okay, Hallmark."

I chuckle. "Kinda weird."

"What is?"

"Surprises me that a lesbian would be like so harsh to someone who's bi."

"Ugh." She flops over sideways. "Don't get me started. I get it from everyone."

I'm laughing before I realize it.

She rolls over onto her back and tries to glare at me, but ends up laughing. "Dammit, you know what I meant."

"I know. It's cool. I'm here for you. I literally lit myself on fire for you today."

"Hmm." Ashley twirls a strand of red hair around her finger, staring up at me. "You wanna go out, get drunk, and do a whole bunch of stuff we'll both regret tomorrow and will probably ruin our friendship?"

"Take me now, you beast," I deadpan.

She snickers.

"Seriously though, not a good idea. Besides. I can't get drunk." I swipe a finger over a strip of bare skin where her shirt pulled up.

She curls into a ball, laughing. "Eep!"

"Well, I *could* get drunk or at least tipsy, but it's a real pain in the ass. I'd have to drink blood from someone who's trashed."

"Yeah. I'm kidding. I don't really want to get romantic with you. Just saying stuff to fail at making jokes. Argh!" She pounds her fists into the bed in a mockery of a little kid having a temper tantrum.

Ash clearly needs 'friend time.' "Hey, wanna hang out like we used to before life got weird? And by weird, I mean the whole almost-an-adult crap hit us?"

She uncurls, hair sprawled everywhere, and grins impishly. "Movie, anime, games, doing our nails… or did you mean like the way we *used* to used to? Back yard swing set is out since you'd catch fire. Should I break out the dolls? Mom put them in the attic a few years ago. She wants to give them to my theoretical daughter someday."

"Dolls?" I laugh so hard I fall over onto the bed. "Hah. Sure. Whatever will make you feel better."

She gazes up at the ceiling, still intermittently chuckling. "If my mother catches us playing with dolls like a pair of eight-year-olds, I'm probably going to end up in therapy."

"If you end up in therapy, don't tell them your best friend is a vampire."

Ashley rolls over to muffle her laughter with the comforter. "No, that won't end well." She hugs herself. "I'll be in a straight jacket again."

I stop laughing and stare at her. "Again?"

"Aurélie." She glances sideways at me, then bursts into laughter. "Teasing. The look on your face!"

Whew. Holy crap. Thinking about my best friend in a romantic context is awkward enough, especially with the weird fetish stuff thrown in. Adding Aurélie is just beyond. She's kinda like a second mother to me and, well, she looks so innocent on the outside. It's difficult to imagine anyone who looks like her even being aware of what sex is… much less knowing more about it than anyone alive. The woman has probably seen

—and done—things that would make the average strip club owner feel faint. But I do not want to know about it.

Nor do I want to even think about sex while I'm in Ashley's room.

"Let's find an awful movie and make fun of it." Ashley jumps off the bed and runs over to turn her TV on.

"Sounds good." I fan at my face, but it doesn't help. The oppressive heat in the room isn't actual heat. Stupid sun.

Homework can wait for the wee hours. Ashley needs me now.

15

BAIT GOBLIN

I hang out at Ashley's until she shoos me off to school.

Her chasing me off is a good sign she's feeling better. She'd only met Tabitha a week ago and had two dates. Mostly, I think her emotions ran out of control for two reasons: the stress of school plus work, and the monthly friend is lurking around the corner. Hormones are going nuts. Ash's usual reaction to that time of the month is everything makes her cry. Happy stuff, sad stuff, a bowl of oatmeal that's a little too warm… the littlest thing sets off a storm of tears. But, she knows she's emotional because of stuff out of her control and she finds humor in it.

Ever hear someone laughing while sobbing? It's weird.

My monthly visitor usually made me antisocial. Just wanted to sit somewhere quiet and be alone. I could get kinda crabby too sometimes, which is Mom's reaction. She turns into this little mean old woman every so often, kinda like a female version of Mr. Neidermayer, but at least Mom always apologizes soon after.

But… that's a thing of the past for me.

I think if word got out vampires existed and becoming one ended period cramps, there'd be mobs of women chasing elder vampires up trees like packs of feral hounds after alley cats. Heck knows I sure don't mind being off that particular out-of-control train. Worrying about accidentally pissing off a powerful elder or being eaten by a three-ton wasp-scorpion-tarantula thing in an alternate dimension is a worthy exchange.

Monday is English lit from 7:00 p.m. to 8:45 p.m.

The class zips by in a relative blur since the discussion of *Do Androids Dream of Electric Sheep* is both interesting and fun. Professor Kendall made it a point to use the word 'ersatz' as often as possible.

As is my habit, I head out of the building and walk down the street to the parking garage even though the Sentra is back home. Did I mention how much flying rules? Right as I pass the former church on Harvard Ave —it's some kind of music school now—two men sprint out from behind the cinder block wall separating the building from the parking lot and rush at me.

I don't have enough time to respond to their burst of supernatural speed before they've grabbed me by the arms. Without a word, they drag me into the small parking lot toward a big, silver sedan with an open trunk.

Oh, hell no.

Despite my struggling, they drag me up to the rear bumper. I'm not strong enough to get away from their grip—until the guy on my right side lets go with one hand to pull a gun out of his pocket.

He raises it toward my head, smiles, and says, "Night night time."

Fear and anger give me the strength to wrench my arm free from his one handed grip and fling myself into a backward lean an instant before he would've shot me. A flash of heat and light washes over my face, the bullet corkscrewing in front of my eyes before burrowing into the clavicle of the guy holding my left arm.

I rake my right hand at his face, claws extending in mid-swing. Startled as if he'd never seen claws before, he jumps back, dragging me by his hold of my left arm, evidently forgetting he's only keeping me in range to slash him. I score three slices down his cheek. The guy screams, involuntarily releasing his hold to clutch his wound.

Vampire claws cause an amazing amount of pain. Way more than even being shot. They almost cause as much agony as listening to that collaboration album Metallica did with Lou Reed.

Speaking of… jackass number two tries to shoot me in the head again, but misses by an inch as I fling myself forward. Really not liking bending over in front of this guy, but it does put me in the perfect position to ram a kick backward into his groin.

He goes flying off his feet, landing a good distance away, sliding on his back.

"Bitch," mutters the guy I slashed.

I have less interest in getting into a fight with these two than walking in on my parents trying to give me a fourth sibling. Wait, no... given those choices, I'll take the claws. Scratch that. I have less interest in fighting these two idiots than streaking downtown Seattle—which is probably going to happen anyway if I get into a claw fight. Point being, I don't want to do either one—so I launch myself straight up.

Dalton must really have pissed someone off. He also must be doing okay. The LA vampires wouldn't be trying to kidnap me if they'd found him. Either Glim's right about them having some kind of magic they can attack him with using my blood, or it's a simpler case of kidnapping and threatening his progeny in hopes he cares about me enough to give in to their demands.

I don't doubt Dalton would try to play the gallant hero and rescue me. I doubt he'd pull it off successfully. Technically speaking, the first time he tried to save my life, he didn't quite do it. The man means well, but...

The vampire with the handgun fires into the air trying to hit me while the other one jumps skyward to chase. While I'm nowhere near as much of a gamer fiend as Sierra, I've played enough *Call of Duty* to know it's way harder to hit a target moving sideways than directly toward or away. So, I swerve to the left rather than flying straight up. It must work since no sharp nips of pain hit me anywhere.

However, the other guy—the one I slashed—gains on me, and doesn't look at all happy. Growling, I pour on as much speed as possible, wind threatening to rip my backpack off. The guy gets a hand on my sneaker; I pivot and dive straight down before he can reel me in. The maneuver causes him to overfly me and lose his grip. Miraculously, it doesn't cost me a shoe. Of course, the guy doesn't simply give up and keep going. He's gotta turn and come after me.

I level off, hoping for as much lateral speed as possible, but the LA douche is still gaining on me about as fast as a normal person walks. Down below, a stream of police cars goes by with their lights on, no doubt heading toward the gunfire. Hopefully, the other vampire is long gone and those cops won't have a bad night.

Still, outrunning this guy is not happening in a straight, open race. Going home wouldn't help me much, and puts my family in danger.

Something tells me vampires from LA don't give a rat's ass about Aurélie's decree.

Again, he grabs for my leg. I swerve to the right, rolling like a fighter jet and flying upside down for a few seconds. It's tempting to give the guy the finger, but he's already furious.

Wait… Aurélie.

Her charm aura is so damn strong she can affect other vampires with it. If I can evade this thug long enough to get to her apartment… she could totally flip this around. We'd be kidnapping one of them. Maybe she can figure out exactly what the heck happened.

The guy chasing me also pulls out a handgun.

Oh damn.

I hurl myself to the left as he starts firing.

Crap. Crap. Crap. This really is turning into *Top Gun*. Getting into a vampire dogfight is the last damn thing I ever wanted to do. And hey! No fair! I don't have a weapon. A bullet nips my backpack, so I pull upward, swerve to the right, then corkscrew down and left as two more *bangs* go off behind me. This idiot is going to hurt someone on the ground if he keeps shooting at me.

Against my better judgement, I swing around and fly straight into him, taking a bullet to the stomach for my trouble. My right knee finds his groin—hey, force of habit—the same instant I sink my claws into his right shoulder and grab his wrist with my left hand. We spin around and around a few times before I manage to bite him on the wrist. He yowls in agony, losing his grip on the handgun. It's gone in a blink, lost to the chaotic whirl of electric lights spinning below.

I think he hammers his fist into the side of my head, because I lose a few seconds, find myself a fair distance away from him, and my skull is throbbing. The burn tunnel the bullet tore into my gut has become a hell of itching.

A glassy smash stands out from the background din. I can't see it, but something tells me the dropped gun punched a hole in the window of a car. Oh, please let it just have scared someone or hit an empty car. The guy lurches at me again, so I take off, flying hard for center city where all the high-rises are.

Seconds later, I see a pigeon coming. More like, I'm hurtling toward the pigeon at 120 miles an hour and the poor feathery thing is just hanging still in midair waiting to detonate on my face. Most ordinary people limbo broom handles or sticks. Hello. I'm Sarah Wright. I limbo terrified pigeons. A quick leftward roll to the side lets me slip past the bird without hitting it, though the wind force of my going by sends feathers flying.

The man chasing me blurts something and starts gagging. Hah. I must have literally scared the crap out of that bird. I don't wanna look. If he took it in the mouth, it's gonna make me vomit even though I can't.

"Damn bitch," shouts the guy, before going off in a Spanish rant I can't follow.

Oh yeah. Call me a bitch. How original. I race for the skyscrapers, but the dude catches up to me and grabs my ankle again. Stomping at his face with my free leg doesn't make him let go. We're getting kinda close to a high-rise that's mostly glass with like orange stripes between the window rows. I fly straight at it while continually booting the guy in the head. It's an absolute shock he hasn't plunged claws into my leg yet to hold on. Not wasting time trying to figure out why though.

Rather than try to reel me in, he grabs my right ankle, too… probably to stop my sneaker from having a continued discussion with his face. Seconds before he pulls me in by both legs, I swerve to the left and kick, swinging us around into a flat spin and shaving him off with the corner of the building. He crashes through a window like three floors down from the roof as I cruise past the high-rise on the left, scraping the glass but not breaking it.

I slow to a stop about a block away, watching the building. My goal has changed from getting away from him to leading him to Aurélie's place. One of the things my Dad always does with goblins when he's running a D&D game for us is to have one run out and attack, then flee in an effort to lead us into an ambush situation. We only fell for it once, but he keeps trying it. Maybe he's doing it as a running joke. Right now, I feel like a bait goblin. The dude's probably a bloody mess inside the office or apartment or whatever it is. This would be a great time for me to get the hell out of here, but… I'm waiting for him to emerge from the building so I can lead him to Aurélie's. Though, if a piece of debris penetrated his brain, he's going to be out cold for a while. Maybe I should consider myself lucky and go home.

It is kinda hilarious to picture the guy cruising into a window at over a hundred miles an hour. Since the dude shot me in the gut, I don't feel the least bit bad about doing it. Unfortunately, he launches himself out another window like Superman, way faster than expected. Guess we heal faster as we age. That crash would've messed me up for a while.

Eep. Time to go. I zoom toward Aurélie's apartment building, something like the Cirrus Tower. The LA vampire is pissed. His anger level has to be affecting his flight speed. Okay, this isn't fun anymore.

I buy a little time with some rapid swerves around the various high-rise towers in the area. Despite flying to Aurélie's place reasonably often, I'm having trouble recognizing her building in the heat of panic. Like four towers look kinda the same, mostly bluish glass. I know it's not the oval-shaped one. He surges in close, grabbing for my backpack, so I roll to the side, causing him to cop a cheap feel of my boob by accident, but it beats his getting a hold of my pack and dragging me around like a seeing-eye dog in a harness.

He goes for my neck. I bring both legs up, plant my feet on his chest and kick. It more pushes me away than launches the guy, but any distance is good distance. We're both so strong the weight of our bodies is a mere triviality. He careens far enough away it's faster for him to cut around the opposite side of a high-rise. Guessing he wanted to avoid a repeat performance of window diving.

Steering away adds a few more seconds before he can get his hands on me again. As soon as he comes around the other corner of the building, he turns toward me and zooms, snarling so loud I can hear him from a few hundred feet away.

… and I spot Aurélie's place.

No idea if this is going to work, but I focus as much mental energy into wanting her to know I'm about to crash her pad and help is needed. I swoop down to her patio and break the door latch open barely a second before jackass lands behind me. He shoves me off my feet, but I catch myself flying before kissing the floor in her living room.

Unfortunately, she doesn't appear to be home. Dammit!

LA Man jumps on me, swings me around, and rams me into the wall, pinning my wrists together in one hand against my chest.

"Get off me!" I shout, ramming my knee up into his side.

The hit launches him, but he doesn't release my arms, dragging me along for the ride across the living room. We smash into the wall, knocking over a table with an abstract crystal sculpture. It's so heavy and brick-like it doesn't even chip when it hits the floor. Dude lands on top of me, still keeping my claws out of the fight with a vice grip on my wrists.

"Heh." He snags the big statue in his free hand, raising it up to mash me in the skull. "Nap time, sweetie."

I cringe, bracing for impact.

Shit.

Sometimes, the bait goblin dies before it can run away.

16

HARMLESS

T he crystal chunk falls toward my head in slow motion, thanks to
panicky vampire reflexes.

LA Man vanishes in a blur of white.

A little bewildered and a lot relieved, I sit up.

The thug lays in the corner of the living room, twisted into a human
pretzel knot. Aurélie stands a few feet from him in one of her elaborate
gowns, glaring down at him with an expression of profound disdain.

He unfolds himself and lunges upright into a punch. She seems to
shimmer, teleporting her body's width to the right, though I'm sure she
only moved too fast to see. Before the man's punch finishes traveling
forward, she spears her right hand into his chest, reaching up under the
ribs and ripping his heart out in her clawed hand as casually as if she
plucked an apple off a tree branch. The guy emits a bloody wheeze,
staring at her in pure shock.

Aurélie crushes the heart, spraying streamers of blood all over the guy.
While he stares at the crimson oozing between her fingers, she flicks her
left hand out past his throat. His head slides backward off his neck and
falls to the floor with a hollow *bonk*.

I've seen the look on Aurélie's face once before, but not on her.
Michelle's mother had the exact same expression the time their dog
pooped on their new sofa. Fortunately, Mrs. Gerard didn't behead
the dog.

"Whoa," I whisper.

Aurélie's disgust-riddled scowl softens to her normal reserved semi-smile. "Good evening, *cheri*. I would ask what brings you here unannounced, but I believe I understand." She flicks her fingers, tossing the lump of heart meat onto the body.

I scramble upright and walk over. Except for her right hand, she somehow managed not to get any blood on her dress. "Holy crap."

Only holes in the fingertips of her elbow-length glove give away she'd used claws. I'm not sure I want to know how she managed to behead the guy with *claws*. Pretty sure she doesn't have Glim's sword-sized nails. LA Vamp's neck's as clean cut as if he'd been guillotined. Eek.

She fans herself with her bloodless left hand. "Why do you seem so impressed? I am but a simple 'armless noblewoman."

Her dainty voice, her delicate French accent, watching her eviscerate a man so casually. Yeah, my brain is shorting out at the contradictions.

Aurélie laughs. "I jest."

"Yeah." I offer a numb nod. "That jackass chased me across Seattle."

"Why? Did he want to give you some literature about his church?" She sniffs her bloody fingers. "Hmm. A Scion."

"No, he had a big sedan, not one of those little things."

She gives me a curious look.

"Umm. Never mind. Stupid joke. Scion is a kind of car."

"Oh." She covers her mouth with her unbloodied hand and emits a courtly laugh. Probably merely to be polite. "No, he is a Scion."

"Is that the same thing as a thrall? And did you destroy him?"

"No, *cheri*. Scions are a relatively new bloodline. They started here in this country a little over a century ago. They are everything the Traditionalists are not. Spontaneous, thoughtless, careless, live in the here and now with little planning. They are so enamored with technology and modern conveniences they forget their true natures."

"Right. So, umm. What's their thing?"

"Their thing?" She raises her eyebrows at me.

"Yeah, like Beasts are really strong and dangerous."

"Oh. I'm not entirely sure." She peels her bloody glove off. "I am tempted to say they are merely vampires. A bloodline without direction."

I check my stomach. Hole in the shirt, but the wound is gone. "So, they're basically the OTC generic?"

She glances at me for a few seconds, then laughs. Pretty sure she had no idea what the hell I just said but read the meaning out of my mind.

That works. Saves me from explaining. "It is possible they have an inner strength but they are not introspective enough to find it. There are not too many of them in this area. They tend to favor cities with a much different energy than Seattle."

"Like Los Angeles."

"Yes. You know something of this man."

"Only that he's from LA."

She eases off on the aristocratic affect, shifting toward motherly. "Now it makes sense. Scions would not be given to respect my decree of protection even if they happened to reside here. One from so far away would surely ignore it."

"That's what I thought." I scratch at the bullet hole in my shirt. "Thanks for helping and sorry about your door."

"Oh, it is quite all right." She leans in and lightly kisses me on the cheek. "I am glad you are unharmed. A snapped latch is easy enough to replace. Why did this creature want to attack you?"

Two big guys enter via the front door that basically goes straight to an elevator. This entire floor is her apartment. They appear to be humans, though their thoughts are still open to me, so not thralls. The men are aware of her being a vampire and willingly in her employ. Pretty sure her charming personality helps ensure their loyalty even more than their generous salaries.

They gather the not-quite-corpse up and lug him out. Beheading a vampire doesn't cause final death, at least not in and of itself. Doesn't even really slow one down, e.g. Scott running around headless. Not sure about ripping the heart out causing final death. It only appears to have caused unconsciousness as well, since LA Vamp has stopped moving. However, it's a near certainty those two men aren't going to put this guy in a nice comfy bed so he can recover.

As soon as the elevator doors close behind them, Aurélie faces me with an expectant look.

I explain the guy following, then threatening me over something Dalton did. "Guess they can't find him so they tried to grab me. Glim thinks one of them can do some blood magic type thing. I have no idea where Dalton is, what he did, or what I should do."

She pats me on the cheek. "Do not fret, *cheri*. While these upstarts have no respect for my protection, they will regret crossing me."

"Thank you." Normally, I'd feel a bit too embarrassed to bow my head in thanks to someone, but this woman has literal power, not merely some title. And she just saved my ass. And I do regard her as a dear—if intimidating—friend.

She covers her mouth to mute a faint laugh.

"What should I do?"

"Stay alert." Aurélie nods once. "I will look into what's going on."

"Okay. What about the other guy? He didn't fly after me. And the other one could've clawed the crap out of me, but didn't."

"Yes. You should know by now not all abilities are universal. Only about a third of us can fly. Not having claws is much rarer. Some even lack any ability to mentally influence mortals."

"Beasts."

She smiles. "Yes. Lack of flight is sadly common among them, though they have some influence over animals." Her expression lights up. "Since you are here…" She gestures at the sofa. "Allow me to freshen up."

I do have homework, but there's no way it would be right to refuse her invitation. "Of course."

SOCIALIZING WITH AURÉLIE IS KINDA LIKE THE GROWN-UP VERSION OF playing with dolls.

Only, we become the dolls, sitting there talking and sipping blood from wine glasses. Except for the enormous television and electric lights, it's basically like going back in time and acting like young women did centuries ago. Yeah, I had to put on a gown. The jeans-and-T-shirt ensemble fell far below her standard for mundanity. What can I say, the woman has a thing for fancy. After a surprisingly pleasant few hours of conversation, she graciously suggests she has other matters requiring her attention. Basically, she's saying she's taken up enough of my time to start feeling guilty about it and I can leave without telling me I have to. It's all based on some strange system of elaborate social rules I can't even fathom. Had my response been something to the effect of expressing dismay over such a lovely evening having to end, she would've let me stay longer.

Right before I change back to my normal clothes, she drops the costume drama stuff and gives me a sincere, protective hug while assuring me she'll do whatever she can to stop the 'LA problem' from seeping into Seattle.

There are likely elder vampires in every major city. Question being, do they talk to each other at all? Though, from what Glim said regarding the particular group that has a problem with me, it sounds unlikely they'd care much about an old vampire up in a big building telling them what to do. Maybe their gang has an old-ish vampire, perhaps not an elder, running it. I really hope whoever is in charge of the LA group isn't as old as Aurélie.

Another thing that scares me? She's a charming, social creature who's content to spend her extremely long life painting and collecting haunted dolls. I highly doubt she participates in physical fights very often. After watching her rip the guy apart in seconds, I do *not* want to get on the bad side of a Fury her age. Aurélie's nearly 400 years old. Best I can recall, the oldest Fury around here is Arthur Wolent. He's a mere 180 or so. Not sure how much difference 220 years makes, but my desire to find out is quite small.

I fly home dwelling on feeling pretty damn weak as an Innocent.

Honestly, it doesn't really bother me to be underpowered compared to other vamps. All I want is to be left alone, out of the political BS. But hey, the powers Aurélie has out of my reach—all the charm stuff—doesn't affect her speed and strength. Maybe I will eventually become a total badass when I'm 'grown up' as a vampire.

Ugh. I just got done being a child, and I'm right back to being one... in vampire terms.

The LA vamp didn't throw me around because I'm an Innocent.

It's because I'm only five months old.

That's gotta be a violation of some fair play law somewhere, right?

As if. I have the distinct impression 'fair' is a four-letter word to most vampires.

17

A LITTLE BIT HEATED

Biology class Tuesday night is a tedious slog of lecture. Professor Connolly is perhaps one of the top four teachers I've ever had in terms of being funny and making topics interesting. But even he can't save this material. At least he joked about this being the worst night of the whole class right up front. If Professor Kendall, my English lit teacher, read this lesson plan, I think he'd be able to make a vampire sleep at night.

Though, maybe I'm having focus issues because I'm so on edge. My stress levels are insane right now over worrying more LA vampires are going to come after me at any minute, Sophia potentially having a magical accident, Sam's demon thing, Sierra's increasing fascination with swords... and random crap going missing from the house. I'm also worrying about what the heck Dalton got involved in as well as Ashley. She's not handling her rotten luck at dating well, and it scares me she might rush into a relationship with a total jackass just to convince herself she's in love.

If I get much guiltier about stealing Hunter's normal life, it might be tempting to play vampire matchmaker and put them together... but no. For one thing, I do love Hunter. For another, I've seen that movie. Forcing two people together *always* ends in tears.

At least no vampires try to kidnap me straight out of my classroom.

Once the driest lecture in the history of college ends, I hurry out with the crowd, but duck around the building into the little park-like area where Howell Street isn't an actual street for one block rather than going to the parking garage for takeoff like usual. It takes a few minutes of standing around before I'm sure there's no one looking at me. The science and math building is like five stories tall, so it gives me a decent amount of cover from view. Especially in the dark. People generally don't look up, and it's a bitch to see dark clothing against the night sky.

Someone might see my sneakers floating off, but hopefully, they'll mistake them for pigeons.

No one jumps into the air and chases me, but they could still be waiting for me to walk to the parking garage. Do the ones back in LA know one of their guys here got destroyed last night? Crap! What if they think I did that? As if I needed more to worry about. Aurélie could probably take on a whole swarm of those guys and still not have to use more than one hand. But me? Winning a fight with one of them would be a real task. If they think I destroyed the guy, it might make them want to retaliate in kind and come after me even worse. Before, they only wanted to kidnap me to get at Dalton. Of course, it's also possible they might reconsider coming after me out of fear.

My undead instruction hasn't exactly been textbook. But, from what I've picked up, the majority of fights between vampires end without final destruction. It's almost like a weird form of dueling. If two vampires have a problem and get into a fight, they'll rip the hell out of each other until one's clearly the loser. In most cases, the matter is considered resolved in favor of whoever won.

Actual, full-on destruction is usually more work than its worth. Usually when vampires want to *kill* each other permanently, the winner leaves the loser chained to a something heavy outside so they get a face full of sunlight. Or, as in the case of what I'm sure Aurélie had done to the guy last night, burn the remains before the unfortunate undead wakes back up. We don't regenerate from being cremated.

Anyway, talking about how to kill vampires over drinks with her last night while wearing a super elaborate gown has to be one of the most surreal things I'll ever do. She explained tearing the heart completely out takes longer to recover from than even brain damage, often putting a vampire to sleep for months or years depending on how old they are.

Going straight home feels like both a bad idea and a good idea. Bad if it leads danger to my family, but good because it makes me feel safe. It really shouldn't though. I'm going to need more than pulling my blanket up over my head to protect myself from a gang of out-of-state vampires. However, I'm still reasonably sure they don't know where I live. The more time I spend roaming around outside, the greater the chances someone looking for me will find me.

But, hang on… if they have some kind of blood magic to locate me in the first place, it's stupid of me to assume they don't know where I live. Being the world's lamest homebody of a vampire means I spend a ton of time there. Grr.

Great. Now I've worked myself up into a ball of worry about my family.

I can just see Dad charging at a vampire with a red tie around his head and a weed-eater in hand. Just don't see that working though.

Indecision becomes the desperate need to get home as fast as possible.

EVERYTHING LOOKS NORMAL WHEN I FLY IN OVER THE HOUSE.

Nothing's on fire, no one's screaming, and there's no broken glass. Okay, good sign. Something glimmers off to the right. I turn, hanging in midair and gawking at Mr. Neidermayer's backyard. Thin, pale lines of light crisscross the grass like something out of *Mission Impossible.* Holy crap. The guy's installed laser beams to detect people entering his yard.

Blix is gonna set those things off constantly until the guy goes legit nuts.

Hmm. Maybe I should ask him to stop? Yeah, retaliation is going a bit too far at this point. Enough for now. After landing on the deck, I pull my sneakers off as per Mom's law and head in via the patio door. Things appear under control. Both parents are in the living room watching television. The littles all sound like they're upstairs. Ronan's here as well. Wow, it's about twenty-to-ten. He's either sleeping over or planning to take a mirror home.

I just said 'take a mirror home' like it's something people do as part of everyday life.

Ugh.

"Oi, she's back," says Dalton from the living room. "Fanks for the chat. Excuse me a minnit."

My jaw drops open.

Dalton leap/flies over the sofa back and lands on his feet in view from the kitchen archway. He, too, obeys Mom's law, showing off a ridiculous pair of black dress socks polka-dotted with tiny, yellow smiley faces. As soon as he sees me staring at him, he flashes a grin and walks over. "Oi, luv. How's things?"

Were I a normal sort of person, I probably would bite his head off and start screaming. But, I have the distinct character flaw of being too nice. Not quite as bad as Ashley or Sophia, but still. There's also the minor issue of Dalton saving my life. It's really damn difficult to scream at the reason I'm not a ghost and my family isn't a complete mess.

"How's things? That's an interesting question, actually. Let's see. I've been stalked, threatened, chased, almost abducted, shot, and involved in a high-speed aerial duel." I blink at him. "That's how things are."

"Shot?" shouts Mom. She jumps up and runs into the kitchen. "When did you get shot? Why didn't you tell me!?"

"Umm. Last night. And I didn't tell you because it wasn't a big deal. Do you want me to tell you every time I stub my toe?"

Mom fusses over me like she's checking a six-year-old for ticks. "Where? Oh my God, Sarah. You were shot?"

Dad appears in the doorjamb, amused at my mother's freak out.

I pull my shirt up to expose my stomach. "Right here. Already healed back to normal. It's not a big deal, Mom. Only a bullet. Went straight through me."

She emits this noise part frustration, part worry. "I don't want you getting shot!"

"Yeah, Mom. I know you don't like body piercings."

Dalton snickers, as does Dad.

"This isn't funny, Sarah!" Mom stares at me caught between wanting to cry and screaming in anger—so she does neither.

"I'm fine, Mom." I hug her. "Please relax. Guns can't kill me."

"Not to split hairs but..." Dalton puts a finger to his lips, pausing. "Well, I suppose the ones large enough to kill us would be considered 'cannons,' not guns."

"You're not helping." I give him side eye, then look at Mom again. "The pain stopped in an hour. Stubbed toes hurt longer than that."

She squeezes me. "Sorry. You know this stuff is a bit much for me to handle sometimes."

"Yeah, Mom. I understand. And believe me, getting shot isn't on my list of fun diversionary activities. A total attack out of the blue. These guys tried to shoot me in the head and dump me into a trunk to kidnap me."

Mom goes pale. "That's murder, Sarah."

"No… shooting a vampire in the head is like using chloroform. Just a knockout."

"Should you report it to the police? Someone tried to mug you?" asks Dad.

"No. It's vampire stuff." I spin to face Dalton. "Which, I'm about to get an explanation for. What happened?"

"Nothing much. I owed a favor to someone and it got called in, so I headed down to LA to help them with a problem." He whistles innocently. "So, I was thinking I'd ask if you'd mind me spending a few days here. Aurélie's still looking out for you, yes?"

"Yeah." I smirk. "What did you steal this time?"

He holds his hands up. "Nothing, I promise. There is no legerdemain involved whatsoever."

"Really? So who are you hiding from then? And why are vampires coming after me?"

Dalton scratches his head. "You're sure this is this my doing?"

I set my hands on my hips and lean at him. This, of course, gets Dad grinning because it's the same pose Mom uses on the littles when they mess up. "Whatever you did in Los Angeles has really pissed some vampires off. Enough for them to come up here thinking I knew where you were. When that didn't work, they tried to kidnap me. Still don't know if they planned to use me as bait for you or if what Glim said about blood magic is true."

"Blood magic? Oh, that's just wonderful. I need wine." Mom walks over to the fridge and opens it. "The green bottle is still wine, right, not blood?"

"Yeah. I don't keep blood around at all, especially in the fridge with the littles here. Sierra would get halfway through the bottle before complaining the grape juice tastes weird."

Mom gags. Even Dad grimaces. Dalton chuckles.

While Mom pours herself some red wine, Dad walks over to grab a glass as well.

"Oh dear," mutters Dalton. "It seems it didn't work."

"What didn't work?" I ask.

"It's somewhat complicated." He leans on the island counter, offering a roguish smile.

"Everything is complicated. C'mon. Spill." I shrug my backpack off and set it on the floor by the wall.

"Perhaps we should discuss this downstairs?" asks Dalton. "Your mother doesn't seem to be ready for conversations like this."

Mom holds her glass up in toast. "I have wine now, I'm good."

"Okay then." Dalton stuffs his hands in his pockets. "Los Angeles is in the midst of a power struggle among vampires. There are a handful of elders who have each amassed groups of loyalists, a small cabal of elders who work together in a sort of shadow government, and a whole bunch of anarchists. Those in the cabal are trying to persuade the other elder factions to ally with them to keep order among our kind. However, they don't regard the smaller packs as worthy of the same courtesy."

"Let me guess. Lack of courtesy equals open warfare." I fidget. "Show fealty or die?"

"Something of that nature. An old acquaintance of mine realized I was in the area and asked me to do her a small favor."

I raise an eyebrow. "Someone you ticked off a few decades ago gave you a choice between seeing the sun again or doing her a favor?"

Dalton emits a humorless laugh. "Well, it wasn't *quite* so bad. But, amazing how long some people can hold grudges. She had a good point though. This lot did deserve to be thinned. Hazard to the innocent. Stray bullets going where they don't belong. However, to make a long story short, Simone and her friends had been quibbling over territory with this other group. She saw an opportunity to shift the power balance and it required my unique talents."

"So you *did* steal something?"

He chuckles. "No. I technically gave them something."

Dad sips from his wine glass. "You snuck into their lair and planted a bomb, didn't you?"

I sigh. "Dad, don't be ridiculous. This isn't a D&D campaign."

"Well, actually." Dalton gestures at him. "The man's almost correct."

"Hah!" Dad wags his glass at me. "Never underestimate the mind of a master tactician… or what her husband thinks."

Mom chuckles, nearly spraying wine everywhere.

"Almost? Wait, so you *did* bomb them? No wonder they're upset." I rake both hands through my hair. "Argh. And why didn't this Simone chick do that?"

"She's Old Guard. Not exactly the stealthy sort. Plus, she required plausible deniability." Dalton clasps the lapels of his tweed blazer. "I was able to get in with a giant incendiary device, then leave undetected."

"You dragged Rush Limbaugh into a vampire den?" asks Dad. "That had to be hard on your back."

Dalton cracks up. "See, two of the smaller vampire groups out there have been hostile to each other since the 1800s. Of course, things have evolved—and somewhat degenerated. It's not so much landowners and miners going at it these days. Basically, they're like any other LA gangs now, only blood and fangs instead of drugs and guns."

"They have guns. And you know they sell drugs to pay for their war."

He gives me this 'well I suppose' sort of eye roll. "Yes, but they're not *using* drugs."

"You still haven't told me exactly what you did."

He whistles innocently. "I'm sneaky."

"Yes, I'm aware," I deadpan.

"There may have been an incendiary device planted in a rather inconvenient place. Alas, it didn't quite go off as big as expected, so several of them may have survived."

"Can confirm," I mutter.

"Alas, it appears the vampires who survived have a slight grudge against said device's origin." He offers a weak shrug. "Hadn't intended any of them to walk away. Rather shocked those sods have shown up here."

"Ugh." I sigh at the ceiling. "You didn't get out as undetected as you thought. They know you did it and they are coming after me to get to you."

"Yes, well. That's why I was hoping to take advantage of Aurélie's protection. This house is off limits." The smile he flashes at the parents is so 'bad boy charming' it would probably make most people forgive him for burning their house down.

I'm less inclined to fall for it, but he *did* save my ass. "There's one small problem. The LA vampires don't care about her decree."

"That may be true, but she wouldn't stand by and permit anyone to threaten you or your family." Dalton smiles.

"No, she wouldn't. She already ended one of them." I slice my hand across the air in an 'away with you' gesture, mimicking her beheading slash. "In like two seconds. What if she objects to you being here and tells you to go?"

He flashes the same sly grin again. "I'll just need to explain things to her sufficiently. I can be quite charming."

I burst into laughter so hard I end up hanging on my father not to fall over.

Dalton raises an eyebrow.

"No... no..." I wave him off for a few seconds until the laughter stops. "Sure, you're charming. But this is Aurélie we're talking about. Charm?"

"Ahh." He cringes. "Yes, you're right. The woman could turn the head of Michelangelo's David. However, even if they don't abide her protection order, she could wipe them out if she cared to. Especially here, out of their territory and in her domain."

The parents exchange a look, shrug, and drain their wine glasses together.

"They know you gave me the Transference. According to Glim, that means they got your blood somehow. This is bad."

He stares down like a scolded schoolboy. "Sarah. If my presence here is a threat to you or your family, I'll bugger off."

There doesn't seem to be any sign of Coralie around screaming at me to watch out, so maybe having him here won't bring pain and suffering on the people I love the most. The instant his being here *does* turn into a problem, I'll ask him to go.

"I'm going to regret this, but I can't kick you out. After all, you did save my life... sorta."

Dalton looks up in shock, but he covers his surprise fast. "Sorry, lass. If I could've moved any faster..."

"Yeah. I know. You've said that already." I throw an arm around him. "Just promise me if something happens here, you'll do everything you can to keep my family safe."

"Aye." He nods, but a trace of guilt in his expression worries me.

I narrow my eyes at him, wondering what he isn't telling me.

Relax, luv. Not what you think, says Dalton inside my head.

"What is it then?"

"Well, Sarah looks tired. Has a bunch of schoolwork to do." Dalton nabs my backpack in one hand, my elbow in the other, and pulls me toward the basement stairs. "We'll get out of your hair."

Ugh. I roll my eyes. Clearly, he doesn't want to share something in front of the parents. It's kind of amazing, actually. A guy who looks like he's twenty-five or so is escorting me down to my bedroom and the 'rents *aren't* freaking out. Pretty sure they can tell there's absolutely no chance anything inappropriate will happen between us. You'd think a vampire's relationship with the one who made them would be somewhat like a parent and child. Nope. At least not for me. He's more like my slacker older brother who never quite has anything work out for him and keeps coming home to beg money off the parents. Hard to process he's really 161 years old. Ugh. Am I going to feel like I'm eighteen for the rest of time, or is Dalton special?

However, I can't complain. My sire is *way* better than Glim's. Eek.

Once we're in my bedroom with the door shut, Dalton lets his guard down. He hands me my backpack, then slouches a bit, no longer wearing the confidence of a Disney pirate like a tailored suit. "I mentioned a vampire named Simone earlier."

"Yeah?" I set the backpack on my desk.

"Quite a while ago, we ran in the same circles. Some other vampires in the North End didn't have much use for us Whitechapel folks."

I point at him. "If you tell me you're Jack the Ripper…"

"No." He chuckles. "And no, he wasn't a vampire. That mess happened during my sixth year as an undead. Wanted to find the bastard, but never quite managed it. But, in those days, we had a punch up at least twice a week. Sometimes things got… spirited. The reason Simone's carryin' a grudge is on account of me buggerin' off when I shouldn't have buggered off."

I sit in my computer chair. "You got her hurt?"

"Emotionally. Think about those blokes from LA comin' after ya. An' you're sittin' there watchin' an upstairs window in the back. Twenty of the bastards come charging at ya."

"Oh. You ran."

He chuckles. "Aye. Like bloody hell I ran. Not too long a vampire myself at that point, and them blokes would've been the end of it. They got inta the ol' warehouse we'd taken over. Torched the place. This other chap, Jameson, didn't make it out. They said a Molotov smashed straight over his bean. Burned him to a cinder."

"Sorry. Close friend?"

"Not entirely. I can't say I lost any personal sleep over the man's death… but he and Simone were lovers."

"Oh." I exhale. "She blames you for his death."

"Aye. 'Course, she's right to do so. I might've been able to hold the window for a little while, but for sure it would've been me on fire instead of him." He sits on the edge of my bed. "And, well, he might've been the revenge boyfriend."

"Revenge b—wait. You and Simone?"

"Quite past tense. Even at that point."

"You cheated on her."

He opens his mouth to say something, closes it. Raises a finger, lowers his arm. Sighs. "I suppose there isn't a point to making a justification."

"Really isn't any justification for cheating, but go ahead. I'm curious to see how you tried to weasel out of it."

"Didn't have any feelings for the woman she caught me with. Just a job. Information was often worth a lot of coin back then. I didn't think of it any different than an actor playing a character pretending to be in love with an actress playing his wife. All I wanted of that one was secrets. Simone only saw a moment and wouldn't let me explain."

Hmm. That's a little different. Spies sleep with the enemy sometimes even if they're married. Still bothers me, but maybe a little less than a fling for the heck of it. So she gets a revenge boyfriend who dies because Dalton chickened out. Now his guilty look makes sense. My asking him to help protect my family reminded him of the last time someone asked him to defend a place.

"Aye," says Dalton, a bit over a whisper, reacting to my thoughts. "I'll not make the same choice again. I'm a touch more comfortable with who I am now, and there's sprogs about."

"Huh? What do my brother's pets have to do with anything?"

He laughs. "No, luv. Sprogs, not frogs. Means children. A puffed up arse of a revenge shag is one thing, but I'll not leave your littles to face my problems."

It's beyond weird seeing Dalton so serious. History says otherwise, but I'm inclined to trust him.

18

SOFT SPOT

Our basement has two rooms that can be completely closed off from the sun: my bedroom and the space with the water heater and furnace. I couldn't even make Scott sleep in the machine closet since it's filthy, noisy, and cramped. Okay, bad example. I wouldn't even let him in the house. Still. Dalton's my roommate for the near future.

Dad even brought a cot down from the attic for him, which we set up on the opposite wall from my bed. It's not too awkward sharing my room with him. For one thing, being my sire, he already basically has full access to my thoughts. If he wanted to, he could eavesdrop on me in the shower or whatever. For another thing, he doesn't wake up until the sun is down. Granted, in November, it's only giving me a head start of about two hours or so. But, it's plenty to get out of bed and dressed before he's remotely aware of anything. No privacy concerns at all since I'm sharing a room with a corpse.

Kinda puts new meaning to the phrase dead tired.

When I wake up Wednesday afternoon, I hit the basement shower and spend a few minutes talking to Coralie—meaning talking at the mirror hoping she heard me—and asking her to please give me a warning if my family is in danger. She doesn't appear or say anything back, which hopefully means there's nothing to worry about and not simply that the mirror is having connectivity issues. Maybe I should upgrade it to a talk anywhere plan?

After taking some pictures and notes for my cheese mold project, I pass a few hours getting my work done for comp sci and calculus today. A few minutes before five in the evening, Dalton's corpselike appearance warms back to normal and he sits up.

"Evening, luv."

"Hey."

He looks around, shaking his head.

"What?"

"I've awoken in some truly strange places during my life, but a teen girl's bedroom hasn't been one of those places for a very long time."

I chuckle. "So what are your plans?"

"Oh, I figure I'll mostly lurk about here, keep your parents company. Perhaps play uncle to the sprogs if need be. Might tip out for a bite later." He pats himself down. "Oi, you've seen my lighter?"

"You smoke?"

"Only when lit on fire."

"Not funny."

"Hilarious." He winks. "I carry it around for utility purposes, but it's buggered off."

I gaze around, but don't notice anything obviously missing. "Things have been vanishing randomly around here for a while now. No idea what's causing it."

"You've an imp in the place." Dalton eyes the ceiling.

"It isn't Blix. He's behaving himself. Besides, imps don't play *subtle* pranks."

"I'll take your word for that. Think one of your siblings nicked it?"

"Don't see why they'd search your pockets in your sleep."

He leans off the side of the cot and examines the floor. "Might've fallen out."

I shrug.

"Bollocks."

"Lighters are hardly rare."

He pushes himself upright. "That one's a gift from Churchill himself."

"Wow. Impressive."

"Not too impressive. The man didn't exactly know he gave it to me." Dalton winks.

I laugh, shaking my head. "Good to see sometimes you get away with things."

He harrumphs. "More often than not, actually. Just always seems to be particularly troublesome during the 'not' parts."

"Yeah. 'Particularly troublesome' is one way to put it." I wag my eyebrows at him and resume doing calc.

DURING SCHOOL WEDNESDAY NIGHT, MY MIND KEEPS WANDERING AWAY from the class to worrying about home. Dalton being there is both scary and reassuring. I haven't been a vampire long enough to properly gauge how old another vampire is by getting into a scrap with them. The two guys who attacked me had definitely gotten past the 'newbie' stage at least, but whether they are twenty years a vampire or a hundred, I can't tell.

Still, I'm pretty confident Dalton could beat them, even two on one. Aurélie owned that guy pretty bad. She's almost 400. The most logical explanation would be to assume vampires gradually gain strength as they age, perhaps until they reach some 'full power' limit. She's gotta be there already—I hope. However easily he could kick their asses, his being at the house is potentially a magnet drawing the LA vampires right to my door.

So is it good to have him there since they've been attacking me anyway or bad because it will make them attack us more, even if he's quite capable of fighting them off?

Grr.

Fortunately, I am enough of a nerd that my brain multitasks well with academia. Even though my thoughts roam to supernatural topics so often, the class material still makes sense to me. Sorry, Dr. Mercer, gotta turn your speed setting up to normal again tonight. I need to be home.

She still runs long, but only by a few minutes.

Downside: she dropped a megaton bomb of homework on us.

Whatever. I have time. It's not due until Friday.

Famous last words. I shouldn't have thought about due dates. Gonna regret it, for sure.

A twinge of hunger nips at me while walking with the other students. It's highly tempting to lure one into the bathroom and feed, but it's risky to take meals anywhere I spend a large amount of time or see the same people often.

So, I make a stop on the flight home near this huge white building with a weird round part on the roof that looks kinda like an upside down old-timey paper coffee filter. No idea what the place is, but it takes up a whole city block. Right off Union Street, I ambush a guy out jogging at night. He's like forty or so, jogging suit, athletic and damn tall.

Looking like I'm sixteen does come in handy sometimes. Almost no one has their guard up when I approach them to ask for directions or something innocent sounding. After zapping his brain, I pull him up against a tree on 16th Ave and bite. Already have an excuse ready if some bystander decides to mistake us for a grown man making out with a kid: pretend he's my father and I'm crying on his shoulder. And blargh. He tastes like this Chinese tofu atrocity my high school used to serve. Must be the jogging/healthiness. Seriously. The cafeteria cooks shouldn't even try to do ethnic cuisine. They struggled to reheat frozen pizza into an edible state.

Fortunately, no one in the nearby houses is as nosy as Mr. Neidermayer, and my feeding goes uninterrupted—mostly. Someone comes around the corner, walking toward us, within seconds of me finishing and sealing the bite wound. I'm about to practice my horrible acting skills to cover for clinging to a guy who looks way older than me, but there's no need.

The guy walking toward me has got to be an LA vampire. Same sorta clothes, same tattoos on his neck and cheek. He's staring at me with purpose in his eye but not rushing in like he means to go straight to the fighting part.

"Crap," I mutter, shove away from the jogger, and leap into the air.

The other vampire jumps after me, following but not gaining on me. I get the feeling he's going to tail me to wherever I go. So... I swerve around and land on the flat part of the giant coffee filter building's roof— and holy crap the round part is huge. Gotta be six stories tall.

LA Man—not the same guy as the other night—lands in front of me.

"What?" I ask, managing not to sound too worried.

"We've decided to go about this a different way. It is interesting you have not severed ties with your mortal family." He rests his hands on his hips, sighing off to the side. "Never even thought about doing that, yanno? Might've been different for me, but it probably wouldn't have worked out. Parents were a bit too into church stuff to cope with vampires."

No idea why this guy is being social. Have they finally realized I had nothing to do with Dalton firebombing them? "Look. You're obviously a vampire. You know how stuff works. I have no control over what my sire does, nor could I stop him from doing something he wants to do. He's really damn old. It's barely been five months since my Transference, and he didn't even stick around to teach me much."

"Why does that not surprise me?" The guy laughs. "Ahh well. But you do obviously have a way to reach him. He is your maker. As I said, a different tactic. We have invited your brother and his three friends to be our guests. Your boy Dalton's got twenty-four hours to get his ass back to LA and answer for his bullshit, or we'll be having some sweets. Kid smells like chocolate. There's quite a few of us, so I wouldn't count on him surviving snack time."

He just threatened to kill Sam.

Anger hits me so fast I'm in midair with my claws out before consciously processing how pissed off I am. There's quite possibly some ragey-type-screaming going on. My lunge is evidently sudden and unexpected enough I score a cat scratch on his cheek before he can react. He catches my forearms and swings me around, hurling me into the coffee-filter dome. I bounce off it and flop to the roof.

Guess what? Concrete is harder than me.

Ouch.

Snarling, I jump to my feet and run at him, swiping my claws back and forth at his face and chest. He backpedals, dodging my first few attacks by leaning side to side. When he gets close to the edge of the roof, he catches my left arm, ducks my right hand, then grabs the wrist.

"Leave Sam out of it!" I shout, gradually forcing my claws closer to his throat.

His dismissive cockiness cracks to a look of surprised alarm. The tips of my claws come within a quarter inch of his throat before we stalemate. He grunts, lifting me an inch or two off my feet by his grip on my forearms. The instant my chances of overpowering him die, I plow my foot into his groin as hard as I can.

Something inside him cracks.

His jaw stiffens. He glares for a second, then releases my right arm to slug me in the face.

The punch launches me headfirst like a missile, but I stop myself before crashing into the giant dome. My jaw's busted, but so are his balls —and probably pelvis. He's doing a remarkable job of not looking as though he's in utter agony, but every blood vessel in his forehead is swollen up. Surprisingly, he hasn't gone red in the face. Still pale. A little too pale. Even the Old Guard look closer to being alive than this guy.

We both stand there staring at each other. I cradle my jaw in both hands waiting the few minutes for it to shift back into place and heal.

"Where the hell is my brother!" I yell. "Leave them out of it. They're kids."

"Yeah," grunts the guy. He exhales long and slow, the same way Dad does whenever he hurts himself. A bony crunch comes from his groin. "We know. Your boy Dalton's got a soft spot for them, right? We can dick around on this roof all damn night, but it ain't gonna help. Your bro is already in LA. All you're doing here is wasting the last day of his life."

A growl comes out of my throat, too deep to be a human voice, as I charge in again. Vampire or not, a shot to the balls slows him down. My second left-handed swipe slices bloody lines across his pectorals. Shallow, but painful. This time, I'm ready for the punch and duck it. Okay, these guys—or at least *this* guy—aren't too much more badass than me. They definitely have an advantage, but it's not impossible. Plus, I've got that 'mom-lifting-a-burning-car' thing going right now. Gotta protect Sam.

Still, I haven't taken any sort of fighting training so my pissed-off-housecat method of trying to shred this guy is only slightly more deadly than two girls getting into a scratching contest in a schoolyard. This guy has been in fights before, but he's not as good as the dude who Steven Segal'ed me into the floor.

I really need to stop charging in like a dumbass.

He stuns me with a rabbit punch to the forehead. Before I can reorient myself, he grabs two fistfuls of my jacket and pins me against the angled wall of the coffee-filter-shaped dome. "You're wasting time, girl. Go find your master and tell him. He knows where to go… if he's got the balls. Rumor has it, the man's got a soft spot for little kids."

The way he sneers at me makes it quite clear I'm included in the 'little kids' part.

I'm furious, but as much as it pisses me off to admit, he's got a point—assuming he isn't lying. Even if I rip this guy into six pieces and drop each one into a separate volcano, it's not going to matter to Sam, who's hundreds of miles away and likely surrounded by other vampires. Destroying this guy won't matter. He holds me pinned against the wall, more to keep me from attacking him than trying to hurt me.

I grab his wrists, gradually pushing him back. "If anything happens to my little brother, you and your entire bunch of friends are gonna be in a world of hurt." Ugh. I cringe. Dammit, Dad. It's your fault I sound like a cheesy Eighties movie when I try to threaten someone.

He rolls his eyes. "I'm trembling."

"It's not me you need to be afraid of," I snarl, then shove him back, taking a step after him. "It's my patron, Aurélie Merlier."

"Yeah right. The woman won't get involved. Maybe in Seattle, but elders are too confined with political bullshit to stir the pot in someone else's city." He snugs his jacket, ignoring my attempt to be intimidating.

"Keep telling yourself that. She adores Sam. Doubt she'll care about what town you hide in." I glare at him. So help me, if they hurt him, I don't care how dark it makes me... I will do anything necessary to kill every vampire associated with your gang.

He taps his wrist like he's got a watch on, then flies off.

"Shit." I grab for my phone, but stop myself. Calling home and finding out Sam really is missing would crush me too much. I need to be there in person.

Coralie didn't show up to warn me about this at all. I hope her lack of warning is a sign Sam's gonna be okay. Of course, she's hardly infallible. It's quite possible she might not have been able to see it, but I really don't need to be thinking worse case scenarios right now. My powers don't include anything like being an oracle or seeing the future, but I'm sensing a beating in my near future. Don't care. Whatever it takes to bring Sam home.

Channeling Sierra, I shout an F-bomb at the top of my lungs, then leap into the air, racing home.

Flying hurts my face.

I must be going faster than 140.

My home is a scene of absolute chaos.

Wait. No imps are involved, so it can't be *absolute* chaos. It's merely 'utter' chaos.

I swoop in via the patio door to find my parents flipping out. Dad's having a—mostly—controlled conversation with Dalton, demanding he find Sam, while Mom is running around in circles generally losing her mind. The girls are sitting together halfway up the stairs to the second floor. Sierra looks furious, but isn't doing or saying anything. Rather, she's got both arms around Sophia, who's bawling.

As soon as I walk in, everything pauses.

"Sarah!" shouts Mom. "Have you seen your brother?"

"Sam didn't come home from his friend's house." Dad hurries over to me. "Jordan's parents have called asking if we've seen him. Daryl's parents didn't and aren't answering their phone."

My phone pings with an incoming text, but I ignore it and give Dalton the eye. "We have a problem."

"Bollocks," whispers Dalton.

Mom pins me with a stare. "You know something."

I glance at the girls on the steps, but only hesitate for a moment. Heck with it. We're all in this supernatural crap together. "Sam's been abducted by a group of vampires from Los Angeles. One of them paid me a visit on my way out of school tonight to inform me of this and imply they'd hurt him if Dalton didn't show up within twenty-four hours."

Sophia's crying stops in an instant. Apparently, learning Sam got taken by vampires and not some random creep has changed her despair into anger. It's kinda weird seeing *her* angry. She usually doesn't 'do angry.'

Dalton bows his head. "Right. Nothing for it then but to go there. This shouldn't have blown back to affect all of you. It's my mess and I'll suss it out."

"*Now* can I take sword lessons?" asks Sierra. "No vampire's gonna kidnap me and keep all his fingers."

Mom bites her knuckle. Dad purses his lips in thought.

"I'd advise against that. At least until you're taller." Dalton glances at her. "Even as an adult, you'd be at a distinct disadvantage in strength and speed. A sharp enough sword might bring the odds closer to even, but…"

"Don't care." Sierra shakes her head. "If a vampire's coming after me to hurt Sarah, I'm *already* gonna be in deep sh—crap. Being in slightly deeper poop isn't gonna matter."

I can't help but share some guilt. New vampires aren't supposed to cling to their mortal life. This is why.

Dalton either reads the mood in my head or on my face. Rather than head out the door, he steps closer and puts a hand on my shoulder. "Buck up, lass. This isn't your fault. There's no need to regret your choices. Going after my progeny is a bit of an abnormal situation. This lot has some unusual means of expressing their dissatisfaction."

"Dissatisfaction?" I raise an eyebrow. "You firebombed them."

He chuckles. "Aye. And they deserved it. What I mean is, extending the aggression up or down a vampire's Transference line is generally not done without them being directly involved. Since you didn't help me torch the place, it's unorthodox for you to be threatened."

"Yeah, but it happened." I fold my arms.

"I'm merely saying it's not going to be that way every time someone gets cheesed off at me. Though, I shan't imagine I'll be doing much of anything shortly. Fifteen or so on one never ends well for the one."

A storm of emotions rages through me. Dalton's going to go surrender himself to save Sam. I'm angry with him for putting my brother in danger, for exposing my family to something like this. But, I'm also angry at them for attacking the guy who gave me the Transference. Part of me wants to fly down there with him and help fight… even though I suspect it would only result in both of us being torn to shreds. Still, just sitting here saying or doing nothing while he leaves to his death doesn't feel right either.

"I'm going with you."

"Don't, luv. Out of sight, out of mind. They'll kill you to hurt me, then finish me off. But if you stay here where they're not thinking about you, should be nothing to worry about."

"Nothing? I'm worried about Sam. Worried about you," I shout. "What if you go there and get ripped apart? How does Sam get home? And they have no reason to simply let him go."

"Hi," whispers Sophia.

I look over at Coralie descending the stairs. Sophia scooches over to one side, squishing Sierra against the banister, making room for the woman to walk past them down the steps. Sierra evidently doesn't see her as she shoves at Sophia for squeezing against her. Mom and Dad don't react to her either; neither does Dalton. Upon reaching the bottom, she shimmers, an aura of faint light surrounding her form. The 'rents jump back startled and gawk at her. Sierra gets this 'oh, that's what happened' expression and stops giving her sister grief.

"You should not do this." Coralie walks straight up to Dalton. "Sarah's fears are the most likely outcome. They intend to kill the boys once they no longer require them."

Mom looks around for something to punch.

Dad puts an arm around her, staring at the three of us—me, Dalton, and Coralie. "We have the advantage of daylight. What if Allison and I went there during the day when they're stuck asleep?"

"Went where exactly?" asks Mom.

"Umm." Dad glowers at no one in particular. "Wherever they are."

"I do not see your going there ending in any way but tragedy." Coralie offers a sad stare. "They have mortal servants."

"There's no way I'm just going to sit here and wait," yells Dad.

"Dad... Dad..." I put myself between him and Coralie. "Don't yell at her. She's only trying to help."

My father gets a look on his face indicative of imminent disaster. Last time he made that face, he nearly flooded the house. Mom ended up calling a plumber to fix the sink *and* the damage he caused. "I can at least help. Couple crossbows with stakes should do the trick, right?"

I push him back toward Mom. "No, Dad. Stakes don't really work. Trust me."

"So what the hell are we supposed to do here then?" asks Dad. "Dalton goes there, they kill Sam. He doesn't go, they kill Sam. We go there, they kill us... *and* Sam."

"Do you think Aurélie would leave Seattle?" asks Dalton. "The woman could walk into the place and gobsmack every last one of them."

"And possibly risk major problems with the LA elders?" I ask. "I'm sure she'd do it for Sam... but last resort."

Mom and Dad start arguing with Dalton about the situation. Mom's getting all lawyery about it, basically telling him this is all his fault without sounding like she's directly blaming him for being a reckless idiot. Dad's frazzled out of worry for Sam and keeps bringing up new and bigger ways he could possibly fight vampires. Since I shot down his idea for stake-throwing crossbows, he's all about flamethrowers now. Like mounting two of them to his new car. No idea where the heck he expects to get those things in twenty-four hours. Besides, I think they're illegal in California.

The girls whisper conspiratorially with each other about using magic, then run upstairs. My parents and Dalton are too loud for me to make out much of what the girls said, but I don't bother going after them. Any help at this point would be good, even if I don't really expect Sophia to be able to do much.

I check my phone to see who the text came from in case it might've been Sam or one of those vampires using his phone to make a threat. Turns out, it's from Hunter asking me if I've seen Ronan. Oh, dammit. No! How am I supposed to tell him his little brother's life is in danger because of me? No way is that message going by text or even phone call. Gotta do it in person.

"Where the hell are they?" asks Dad. "You seemed to know."

"I imagine they'd want me to go to the place where I left the bomb. However, it's unlikely they are still living there. The place had some remodeling done. It's quite airy and open now." He flashes a whimsical smile. "If a bit blackened."

"They are not," says Coralie in a calm, ethereal voice. "All I see of the ruins are agony and sunlight."

Dalton squirms. "Aye. That wouldn't have been pleasant. But if they're not going to release Sam, what the bloody hell am I supposed to do?"

I grab two fistfuls of my hair, but manage not to scream in utter frustration. It's sorely tempting to call Aurélie and ask her to swoop in on LA and 'layeth the smacketh down' as they say. But, to be honest with myself, it's doubtful she would. Maybe I'm overestimating the political delicacy of the situation. The impression she'd given me months ago when describing things is that different regions of the world fall under the political control of various vampire elders. Control in the sense of vampire kind, I mean. They don't bother with mortals. Usually anyway. Apparently, the Cuban Missile Crisis would have ended in a nuclear strike if not for some strategic mind control.

But… Sam. Yeah, I gotta ask at least.

"I'm gonna call Aurélie. Maybe she can help."

Dalton makes a weird face, glancing up at the top of the stairs.

I've barely got the phone halfway out of my pocket, but I twist around to look—expecting some manner of Sophia weirdness—but it's Blix. The imp stares at me and makes a 'come here' gesture with one finger.

Coralie nods.

Okay, maybe I *don't* need to bother Aurélie.

"Umm, guys. Give me a sec…" I head for the stairs.

Blix darts out of sight.

"What are you doing?" calls Dad.

I pause on the second step and glance back at him. "Getting Sam and his friends back… I hope."

19

THE GRAND LIFE

Blix is waiting for me in Sam's room, staring intently at my brother's tablet.

I guess it's technically his room, too.

When I walk in, he holds the screen up at me, open to the note app. Writing in a scrawl like from a kindergartener spells out: 'will take you to Sam. Go now. Go fast.'

"Blimey," whispers Dalton, behind me.

"Gah!" I jump and whirl, clutching my chest. "You scared the crap out of me."

"Sorry, luv. Habit."

"I didn't even hear you coming."

He examines his fingernails. "I am somewhat practiced at being quiet, though I hadn't been trying to startle you."

"Forget it." I point at the imp. "You don't think they have Sam and the boys at the place you blew up."

"Highly doubtful. It's a ruin now. No real cover."

I scoop Blix up and 'show' him to Dalton. (The imp appears not to mind.) "He says he can find Sam. So, I'm gonna go get my brother and his friends back. Then we can worry about what to do with those vampires."

"Right. Let's go." He nods.

"You're coming?" I blink at him.

"Wait, you're not going to try and talk me out of it? You're supposed to say 'no that's too dangerous for you to go there. It's what they want.'" He puts on a fake look of worry, but I can tell from our thought link he's teasing. Dalton's furious they involved Sam. "Right. Let's go. There isn't much time left. Oh, wait."

"Wait? One second you say we don't have much time, the next, you say wait?"

Dalton extends his fangs and draws blood from his thumb, creating a small puddle in his left hand. "Here, luv. This will help."

"What are you loaning me? Stealth?"

"No. Flight."

"I can already fly."

"Yes, but you're not as fast as me." He winks.

Whatever. I don't have time to argue and there's no deception here, so I grab his hand and slurp up the maybe teaspoon's worth of blood. An electric tingle crackles over my teeth before running down inside me to my stomach, then spreads over the rest of my body.

"Right. Let's go."

Blix flails and babbles. Yeah, yeah. I know. We're going.

"What are you doing?" asks Sierra, from the doorway.

I run over and grab her hand. "Go tell Mom and Dad we have a way to find Sam, maybe skip entirely around those other vampires. Dalton and I are going to LA right now to get him back. And no, you're not coming with us."

She grumbles. "I know. Too little, no real skills. Too dangerous. I wanna go, but I'm not stupid. Okay. Be careful!" Sierra hugs me, then runs down the hall to the stairs.

Blix keeps flailing and babbling.

Sophia's standing in the doorway of her bedroom, face still wet from crying but she has a confident, determined set to her eyes. As we leave Sam's room and go left down the hall to the stairs, she and the imp exchange looks. He gives her a thumbs-up, to which she nods. No time to grill her about it, so I run down to the space by the front door and put on my sneakers before dashing outside and leaping into the air without too much care if anyone happens to be watching. It's late and dark, anyway. Dalton scoops his expensive shoes up and puts them on while flying.

Blix emits a frustrated sigh, then wriggles out of my grip to climb around onto my back. There, he digs his little claws into my shoulders and flattens himself against me. Even without Dalton's loan to boost my flight speed, outrunning imps didn't tax me much. We are going *way* faster than Blix can fly on his own. However, the speed doesn't appear to bother him. Then again, he's not wearing any clothes to be ripped off by wind. My sweatshirt and jeans are handling it well at least.

I figure it's pretty pointless to ask Blix for directions right away. We've got a long ass flight ahead of us, pretty much the entire West Coast. Dalton takes my left hand and tows me into the air. I pour on as much speed as my body will give, and it *does* feel as though the wind is hitting my face much harder than normal. No idea how fast we're exactly going, but it's not stressing me out to keep up with Dalton. While we can't talk at this speed due to wind, telepathy works.

We'll likely be arriving down there with very little time to spare before sunrise, says Dalton into my head.

Yeah. Figured. That we're going to make it there at all without having to stop somewhere to rest is kind of impressive. How fast are we flying?

A titch over 220 miles an hour. I'd strongly advise against sudden encounters with solid objects at this speed.

My mental laugh is loud enough to make him flinch. Yeah, not a problem I'll have often. Is your gift going to last the whole way down there?

Aye, should. 'Tis why I'm holding your hand. Close contact extends it.

Oh. I thought he was trying to comfort me.

That too, luv. None of this should ever have happened. Made a slight miscalculation and the incendiary device didn't ash them all. Still, never imagined they would've gone after you when they couldn't find me.

If they had your blood to use in order to find me, why didn't they use it to find you?

He smiles over at me, lips fluttering. If not for my worry about Sam, the sight of his face would've made me burst out laughing. *I'm sneaky. Not quite to the point of Shadows, though. Those blokes elevate not being seen to a way of life.*

Dalton's trying to be whimsical, but his statement strikes me as sad. They really do need to stay out of sight to protect their existence. I suppose there might be a few places in the country where they could walk around in the open and people would assume them to be a body-modification freak, but if people see them, they'd usually erupt in panic.

We go up high enough to use the coastline for navigation purposes. For most of the flight, the directions are fairly simple: straight. I don't remember where Los Angeles is exactly in California, but Dalton fills me in with a mental image of a map. It's close to the southern border of the state near the coast. So, yeah. Long flight. My class got out at nine, figure the time spent feeding and dealing with that LA thug, then at home… we probably leapt into the air somewhere between ten-thirty and eleven.

If we're doing over 200 miles an hour, the trip's going to take like five hours. I *think* we'll make it to LA before sunrise, but it's going to be dangerously close. The idea I'm flying to my death purely from the sun catching me off guard gnaws at me on the most primal level, but it's irrelevant to protecting my little brother. Considering the outcome for failure and not trying is the same—Sam dies—it's not even a choice. As soon as Blix offered a glimpse of hope, the only thought on my mind was getting there as fast as possible.

Hopefully, Dalton put a little more thought into the timing of our arrival than I did.

The ground races by below, details of the terrain unhidden by darkness my eyes ignore. We're too high up to see much without zooming in, but I don't bother. My attention remains locked on the horizon straight ahead where the black night sky touches the scrolling landscape of mostly grey, dotted here and there with splashes of glowing lights. Urgency to find Sam as fast as possible makes the trip feel ten times longer. Eventually, the seemingly endless spread of green gives way to mountainous spots with a long strip of brown on the left. The sky to my left—the east—is starting to look frighteningly blue in the distance.

We're passing over Mendocino now. Almost to LA. Okay, not almost. Still a long way off, but we're at least in California.

I bite my lip, worrying more about Sam than catching fire.

Dalton squeezes my hand, trying to be reassuring.

Almost an hour—or so I guess—later, he enters a gradual dive, towing me along. It's impossible for me to tell from the air what's where. There's a ton of urbanization on the ground, all of it painfully radiant to my sensitive eyes.

We stop descending at maybe the height of a twenty-story building, flying level for another few minutes before Dalton slows to a stop so we're hanging in midair above what I assume is the San Francisco downtown.

"Umm, you stopped?" I ask.

"Aye. The only advantage we have right now is I'm sure they won't be expecting us to arrive tonight." Dalton gestures at Blix. "If he's got some way to locate Sam, let's do this quick."

Blix gives us both a weird stare that seems like he's annoyed and calling us stupid.

"What?" I ask.

He babbles gesturing wildly at the ground while babbling more.

"Sorry. I can't understand you."

The imp slaps himself on the forehead, emits a sigh, then waves for us to follow while zooming off ahead and a little to the left. Over the next few minutes, he leads us to an industrial district where he comes in for a landing on a three-story factory/warehouse type building, perched atop a half-height wall bordering the entire roof. Dalton and I land behind him.

Blix emits a rapid, whispery babble while pointing at another warehouse across a deserted four-lane street from the one we're on. The other building's windows have all been covered in black spray paint or plywood sheets and the parking area is overrun with weeds growing from cracks in the paving. Despite the overall look of disuse, a handful of newish cars sit parked near the wall. They all look souped-up and foreign. A group of twenty or so people hang out by the cars, only four of them women. At this distance, I can't read if they're vampires, humans, or thralls with any of my supernatural senses. However, at least a dozen are wearing similar clothes and tattoos as the vampires who harassed me in Seattle. Some could still be mortal thralls. The four women don't look like gang members, so they're likely snacks or girlfriends to the mortal thugs. Street racing cars and a big-ass pack of vampires.

Great. It's the Fanged and the Furious.

"In there?" asks Dalton.

Blix nods.

"Oi. Hitting the front door is going to be messy."

"Yeah." I fold my arms. "But if that's what it takes to get Sam and his friends out of there…"

Dalton puts a hand on my shoulder. "I know you're talking entirely out of bravado there, luv. You full well know rushing in is only going to get yourself killed. And Sam needs you not to die."

"I know our odds aren't terribly good."

He chuckles.

I glance at him. "What about that is funny?"

"Maybe you've inherited more from me than we thought. Brits are masters of understatement. 'Not terribly good' odds?"

"I'm pissed."

"Aye. Me too. I think our best chance to get them out without a scratch is for you to take advantage of your unique relationship with the day. Go in there tomorrow while they're stuck sleeping."

My head's shaking no before I even consciously think to do it. "I can't leave the boys in there all night. There's no way I'm going to leave them in there even a minute longer."

"Sarah." Dalton puts an arm around my shoulders and points the other one at the east. "We've got maybe fifteen minutes left before the sun gives us a smoking hot makeover. It would take us longer than that to fight our way through the crowd by the door, assuming we'd win the fight."

Blix squeaks.

"Yes." Dalton nods at him. "I am aware that's a slightly audacious assumption."

"Can you turn us invisible?"

Dalton sighs. "No. My abilities tend to make people look the other way or simply not notice me if I've got stuff to hide around. Won't help much in an open parking lot."

I gesture at Blix. "Was talking to him."

The imp shakes his head.

"He could make a distraction. Maybe down the road? Blow up some transformers?" I point.

Blix gives a thumbs up, but makes a 'waving off' gesture. I take it to mean he *could* blow up transformers but doesn't think it's a good idea.

"Possible, but we don't have the time to take advantage of that." Dalton takes my hand again. "I'm afraid Sam and his friends are unavoidably stuck where they are at least until you are able to get there in the daytime tomorrow. Provided, of course, the sun isn't too strong for you."

I hang my head, sighing. "Yeah. This *is* California after all."

Dalton jumps into the air again, pulling me after him. He doesn't seem to be *too* confused about where to go, though I do get the sense he's checking options more than heading for a particular specific location. Two minutes after leaving the warehouse district, he swoops in for a landing next to a large one-story building entirely painted black. A purple woman silhouette over the doors has cat ears and the words 'Night Kittenz' on it.

"You're not taking me to a vampire kink parlor are you?"

Dalton laughs. "No, it's just a night club. As far as I know, it's run by mortals. However, it's got underground rooms."

My skin crawls at the thought of what must go on in places like this. But… we're at roughly T-minus eight minutes until *foom.*

Dalton pulls out a set of lock picks to attack the front door, but Blix makes a flicking gesture, which opens the lock in an instant.

"Oi. Handy little blighter, aren't ya?"

Blix grins.

We step inside and re-lock the doors. The place has a wall-to-wall cat motif with almost an Egyptian cat-goddess thing going for it. Though, rather than desert browns and gold, it's mostly shades of purple and black trimmed in silver. Dalton jogs across the giant room to a curtained door, zips past it, and leads me down a dark grey corridor to a stairwell flooded with the odor of sweat, foot, and fruitiness. I can't tell if it's spilled drink or stripper perfume.

The hairs on the backs of my arms stand on end as memories of my last attempt to sneak into a night club replay in my head. If I wind up in a dungeon cell again, someone's losing body parts. We go around a switchback in the stairs and through a steel door with a push-bar. A basement corridor of black cinderblocks stretches out for a good distance, with openings on either side roughly the same size as doorways. None is an actual doorway, just openings in the cinder blocks with shower curtains on rods. Sure enough, the smell of sex hangs in the air, but it's not strong enough to suggest people are here right now. There's also an unfamiliar chemical tinge on every breath. I'll assume it's some kind of drug residue, but I've never—knowingly—been around that stuff, so have no idea what the heck it is.

"Heroin," mutters Dalton. "And a bit of meth."

"You take me to the nicest places," I mutter.

We run to the first corner, hang a right, and go down the hall enough to reach the first room with an actual door. Inside, a plain square room holds a plush sofa and a queen-sized mattress on the floor. Two of the corners have leather wingback chairs on either side of a wooden table marked with condensation rings from glasses. In here, the aroma of stale beer overpowers the drugs.

"This'll do in a pinch." Dalton flips the deadbolt on the door, then flops onto the mattress.

In that strange way of knowing vampires have, the foreboding feeling the sun is less than two minutes from rising comes over me. No real time to protest or complain, so mattress it is. I lay beside him kinda like a daughter/sister forced to share a bed. One could say there is zero sexual tension between us, but it wouldn't be entirely accurate.

Is it possible for sexual tension to be so far removed the number is less than zero?

"Ouch," says Dalton, again reacting to my thoughts.

I sigh.

"Teasing. You don't need to explain your feelings. I can feel them."

"That's only a little creepy." I stare up at the plain black ceiling, acutely aware I'm over a thousand miles from home and we've broken into a place I'd never have set foot inside of in a million years otherwise. I also have no damn idea what's going to happen tomorrow. "Is this where I would've wound up if I'd 'died' and not gone back to my family? Running off with you? Sleeping in a different creepy place every night?"

"Aye." He laces his fingers behind his head. "A grand life that would've been. Enjoying the city, moving around whenever we cared to. Going all over the country wherever whim took us. Seeing the sights, the finer things."

"Truly," I sigh more than say.

"You really do prefer the humdrum of home?" He whistles. "Most girls your age can't stand being stuck under their parents' roof, having to follow rules, and they're not even immortals."

I shrug. "Guess I'm a wimp."

"Naw, luv. I think it's sweet." He raises an arm and makes a sweeping gesture in the air. "The grand life is all a matter of perspective."

"Perspective..."

He lets his arm flop at his side. "Aye. In a way, I envy how you can be so happy with such... simplicity."

"Have you even tried the simple life?"

Dalton chuckles like I'd suggested he light himself on fire.

My parents are probably worried sick. They *might* still be awake even. I pull out my phone and send the parents a text: ‹Arrive ok. No time to do anything. Zzz.› Then I send Hunter a text to let him know I think we've found Ronan.

"Blix," I whisper. "Go watch over Sam and his friends, okay? Do whatever you have to in order to keep them safe."

The imp starts gesturing and babbling, attempting to explain something relatively complicated... but I pass out under the irresistible weight of sunrise.

20

IT'S ONLY GRAND THEFT AUTO

The benefits of being a vampire are numerous.

One such benefit is the ability to go straight to sleep when the sun says so regardless of how incredibly worried I am about my little brother. It seems as though one second, Blix is babbling at me and the next, he's gone and some dude is hovering over me with his hand on my neck.

When my eyes snap open, the late-thirties guy—a cop—jumps back emitting a startled yelp. Another cop stands closer to the door, flashlight pointed at me. She's about the same age as the guy, and also looks beyond freaked out. Another woman, older but not elderly, hovers in the doorway holding keys. Long, pewter-grey hair half covers her face.

I sit up and telepathically stab the male cop in the brain, putting him on derp mode. The older woman starts to scream but faints. Miss Cop starts to pull her gun, but I'm in her face before the weapon's halfway out of the holster, holding her arm down while staring into her eyes.

Wow. Okay. This is a little more severe than getting pulled over for driving too fast. We legit broke into some place. But, we're not here to steal, only avoid a fiery death. Also, I'm not above exploiting free take-out. After mentally placing both women on hold, I feed from the male cop. No, his blood doesn't taste like donuts. More like a turkey club sandwich. Probably the last thing the guy ate; the scent of it is all over him.

While I'm clamped onto him doing the lamprey act, I grab his dangling arm and check his wristwatch. It's 2:11 p.m. They woke me a little early, but I'll deal. There's all sorts of ways I could get a pair of cops out of my hair, but I opt for the 'nicest' one. His memory of walking in here to see a pair of dead 'overdosed druggies' lying on the mattress goes into the trash can. Apparently, he'd been trying to check me for a pulse when I awoke. Watching me go from corpse-grey with sunken cheeks to normal and alive looking in a second freaked him out. Go figure.

Yeah, he doesn't need to remember that. There's going to be a report somewhere the older woman called the police about us, so I can't make them forget entirely about being here. I need to give them a dead end. Hmm. Idea. The number of people I don't care for firmly embedded in my mind enough to create believable memories of is a short list. And by 'short list,' I mean one. Scott.

I dredge up a mental image of the asshat and leave the cops thinking they found my dead ex-boyfriend crashing here. When they disturbed him, he pushed the male cop on his ass and ran off. Once I finish the mental implants, I carry the cops one room over—making them think they'd been there all along—and leave the guy on the floor like he'd been knocked down by a fleeing suspect. The woman cop, I drape on the room's sofa, giving her a memory 'Scott' shoved her, too.

The older woman is evidently the owner of this place. She'd found us while doing a quick check of the rooms upon arriving here to start her work day. I also give her a memory implant of seeing Scott's less-evil twin in the other room, and reinforce their thinking the room Dalton and I are hiding in is empty. Also, she will spend the next twenty-four hours believing there's a nasty ghost in the basement and not wanting to be down here.

I head back to our room, ease the door shut, and wait.

Roughly three minutes later, both cops scream 'whoa' like they're in the middle of falling over... and run down the hall shouting 'Stop, police!' Not sure how long they'll spend chasing a literal ghost, but it should keep them away from us. As soon as I can't hear them anymore, I poke my nose out into the hall. Looks like the owner ran upstairs, too. Good.

Well, not really. She won't find us, but the leaden feeling in my bones tells me the world outside is nuclear. A quick trip down the hall to the stairs confirms it. Pretty sure I'd literally burst into flames even staying inside the building on the upstairs level. Grr.

So damn frustrating.

I jog back to our room and shut the door, locking it to keep surprise visitors from coming in. No idea what sort of hours night clubs keep, but it's doubtful they're going to let people in the door this early in the afternoon. I step over Dalton and take a seat on the couch. He's pretty much a dried-out corpse in terms of appearance. Wonder how much of his appearance in sleep is due to age vs. bloodline? When I'm over a hundred, will I look the same way? The cop still had a little hesitation as to whether or not I'd died, hence checking for a pulse. That tells me my appearance isn't as ghastly as Dalton's while sleeping.

The thought should make me feel better, but it doesn't. I'm too worried about Sam.

I check my phone. Sure enough, there's about a thousand text messages from the parents and the beginnings of a novel from Hunter. He stopped by the house soon after Dalton and I left, and the parents filled him in on what happened. Every other message from him starts with 'I know you're asleep and can't reply, but...'

To save time and window-hopping, I create a group chat for both parents and Hunter, to which I send: ‹Just woke up. Am safe. Located boys via paranormal means. Didn't have time to do anything last night except find shelter. Too hot out there to do anything yet.›

Mom sends me an explosion of emojis, several OMGs and ‹why r u waiting?›

Dad sends ‹Will explain 2 Mom about too hot. Keep us posted. Btw— wear a headband.›

I chuckle despite wanting to scream out of worry.

Hunter asks ‹How is Ro?›

‹Not sure yet. Haven't seen them. Going ASAP.›

We trade texts for a while. Both girls stayed home from school today 'sick' with worry. Obviously, Mom called out from work, too. Dad would've been home anyway, but he's not developing program code, too focused on my missing brother. While understandable, asking constant questions about Sam and the other boys is sending their extreme nervousness over the internet and into me. Texting them is making me freak out more and more.

Argh! It's like I'm stuck in a jail cell while my little brother is being gradually tortured to death. I think I understand why some cats claw the crap out of things when they're stressed. The sofa is looking mighty scratchable.

Mom sends: ‹Sophia wants me to tell you Coralie says you can relax. Is that good news? What does she mean? Why would you relax while Sam's in danger?›

Normally, telling someone as upset as I feel to just 'relax' always backfires. However, when the suggestion to chill out comes from a precognitive oracle ghost, it does help a little. I send back a few texts explaining if she's telling me to calm down then Sam's okay for now.

Boy, do I regret the 'for now' part.

My phone's going to melt.

Whistling out in the hall puts me on edge. Minutes later, a short Hispanic woman who obviously has keys barges in on us, pushing a cart of cleaning supplies. She stops short at the sight of corpse-Dalton on the mattress. Before she can scream, I clear my throat. The woman makes eye contact with me—and I promptly make her forget seeing us.

Oh, I also give her a compulsion to let me borrow her iPhone charger and believe this room is already done. She backs out into the hall like a zombie and stands there for the minute or three it takes the mental fog to wear off. Whistling resumes, and she goes into the room across the hall from ours.

I plug my phone in using the borrowed—hot pink—charging cable. Truly, my immortal powers are tools of darkness.

Hours of super frustrating boredom go by. I'd text Blix if I could, asking him for information, but… he doesn't have a cell phone or a pocket to keep one in. According to the internet, twilight's going to start at approximately 5:54 p.m., with actual sunset at 6:23 p.m. Not a whole lot of time to work. I didn't bring a hoodie, but that only means dealing with pain from sunlight. As soon as it's possible for me to tolerate going outside, it's time to start.

The weather app says clear and sunny. There's a shocker for California. At one point in my life, Cali sounded amazing. As scary as the idea of moving down here for school had been, part of me *did* actually look forward to it for being so different. But, yeah, Michelle's probably right. It's quite likely homesickness would've kicked my ass. While I don't see myself bailing out and quitting school after two months like she suggested, I probably would have transferred closer to home after the first year.

For a while, my brain wanders around the idea of if I would've missed the littles. Before my death, we'd had a reasonably normal family dynamic. Older sister thinks her younger siblings are kinda annoying but begrudgingly spends time with them as needed. Sierra liked me more than she let on but kept her distance. Sophia made no secret of adoring me, and cried every time I brushed her off. I used to think it came from manipulation, but now I know it had been genuine hurt. Death really kicked me square in the feels, but would simple college have done the same thing? And yeah, I know it's pointless to ponder, but not thinking about anything is going to leave me constantly worrying about Sam and going more and more stir crazy for being trapped in here.

At 4:45, I decide to test my luck. Dalton's still stone cold, so I leave him be and head out of the room. The daylight coming down the stairs no longer glows like the heart of a nuclear power station, but it's far from pleasant. It does not, however, set off my instinctual sense of panic—which I imagine is quite a bit weaker than other types of vampires. If *any* sunlight meant rapid death for me, it would be a whole lot scarier.

I'd compare going upstairs to jumping into a deep fryer, but never having jumped into a deep fryer, it would be a guess. It's not bright enough that I start smoking at least. Sounds of activity come from doors leading to a staff-only back area, though it doesn't appear anyone is out in the 'public' part of the club yet.

Okay. Here goes nothing.

Clenching my jaw to stop from screaming in pain at the burning all over me, I stiff-leg it across the room to the front door and into a patch of daylight. A little smoke wisps up from my hand, but I'm already in so much pain it doesn't feel worse. Involuntary tears slip out of my eyes, but I force myself to keep going outside.

The only chance I have of getting my brother back alive is to deal with this mess in the daylight.

Blurry shapes bump me from everywhere. It takes me a few seconds to realize they're pedestrians. None of them seem to care I'm stumbling around like a drunk who's also high. More to the point, I basically am a blind person staggering around on fire. Even the waning daylight of a near-cloudless sky is agony to my eyes. The world's washed out to a painfully bright white glare in all directions... like I'd gone to a nude beach in Ireland.

A little hand grabs mine.

Great. Some kid thinks I need help.

Blix babbles and pulls at my arm. Okay, he has *got* to be invisible to humans or there'd be mass chaos going on right now. At least one thing is working in our favor. I let him pull me along since I have no better ideas at the moment.

"You know I'm grounded at the moment, right?" I whisper.

Hopefully, anyone hearing me thinks I'm on a cell phone call to a friend talking about being punished by my parents and not literally grounded due to sunlight.

"*Eebu nomlen bwoo.*"

"Good point."

"*Drr'gu,*" says Blix, unimpressed.

He tugs at my hand, so I walk after him for a little while until he rests my hand on the door handle of a white SUV. The vehicle emits a chirp like the car alarm disarmed itself. A click comes from the lock.

"Seriously?" I whisper.

"*Ooba.*"

Whatever. If I'm going to break the law, why not go big? Stealing a new-looking giant SUV seems like the perfect target for my first moment of deliberate criminal activity. It's actually kind of amazing how little resistance I have to the idea after spending so many years afraid to break even little rules. I mean, really. It's not like I'm defying curfew or jaywalking… merely starting off with a little bit of light grand theft auto. Nothing serious. Sam needs me and I won't allow the police to arrest me. At least, I'll make them let me go once it's dark. I climb in, slam the door, and stare at the dashboard.

"Okay, now wh—"

The engine starts.

"Damn, Blix. That's cool."

"*Norba Neem.*" He grins.

"How is it Sam can understand you?"

Blix pats himself on the chest, then makes an injecting motion to his head.

"You gave him knowledge?"

The imp nods rapidly, his ears thwapping with a leathery flutter.

"And you haven't done it to me because…?"

He holds his fingers to his mouth like fangs.

"Can't do it to vampires. Right."

Thumbs-up. "*Zodu Norba.*"

"Does that mean follow me?"

Blix nods, looks at me surprised, then jumps out the driver's side window.

Wonder how many credits I'd get for learning demonic as a language elective?

I pull out into traffic as soon as it's possible to do so... and drive. It finally occurs to me why Blix picked this particular vehicle after a few minutes when I realize my eyes are only stinging—not boiling. Whoever owns this truck loaded up the windows with tint. Also, it's got plenty of room for Sam and his buds.

And ugh. Crap! I didn't even think about that. *Driving* back to Cottage Lake, Washington is going to take like twenty hours. Screw it. I'll take the boys to the airport and mind-zap us onto a plane. Yeah, I can fly, but not at 600 miles an hour and not carrying four tween boys.

Blix flies a few feet ahead of me, giving me reasonably ample warning before I need to turn.

Unfortunately, being a demon—or daemon—from a parallel world, he's not exactly aware of traffic laws... or the meaning of one-way signs. I nearly have a head-to-head collision with a little old man driving a Prius. The Escalade I've stolen would've run that thing over like a speed bump. Fortunately, we both stop. And, perhaps his heart did as well.

Damn. I'm *really* sorry, but my brother's in deep shit.

I leave the guy grasping his chest, back out of my aborted turn, and keep going straight. Blix guides me left at the next possible opportunity onto another one-way, but it's going in the direction we need.

At 5:07 p.m., I pull over beside the warehouse we landed on last night, cover my hands with my sweatshirt sleeves, and hit the button to turn the engine off. That done, I wipe down the shifter knob and the steering wheel for fingerprints, then hop out.

A tall chain-link fence surrounds the abandoned warehouse the vampires I have a particular problem with at the moment are using for a home. Flying over isn't possible due to the damn sun. Blix rakes a single claw down the fence, tearing open a slice I can squeeze through. Wow, imps can be damn handy when they're not using their abilities for chaos.

Once past the fence, I sneak around the outside of the parking lot. Two of the street-racer type cars are missing, but six remain. Those likely belong to the gang. However, there's no one outside right now, so I hurry over to the front doors.

Blix babbles and waves at me to follow him, shaking his head rapidly as if to say *bad idea.*

Sure, whatever. I'm as weak and vulnerable as a normal mortal right now. If something happens to me, Sam's going to die. Gotta trust the imp. He heads into a narrow gap between the building and a solid fence at the back of the property full of chest-high grass, weeds, and a scattering of trash. Ugh. Looking at it makes me feel fleas and bugs crawling all over me, but I only hesitate for an instant.

Some sixty meters later, we emerge in another parking lot along the rear of the building where a huge concrete truck dock covers most of the wall. Decaying black cushions droop from the edges of twenty individual garage doors, all covered in graffiti and rust. Blix flies up to a normal 'person door' all the way at the right end, closest to the corner where I'm at. A faint *click* comes from the knob, after which, the imp grins.

I grab the chest-high concrete and pull myself up, hurrying around several empty boxes and a pallet jack. The door opens without making too much noise. I'm all too eager to get out of the sun, so I barge right in and pull the door shut behind me. The instant the door closes, my skin ceases burning. Cool air surrounds me along with my abilities coming online. Such a sudden change from inferno to pleasant cool costs me a few seconds involuntarily standing there in relieved paralysis.

Blix rasping snaps me out of it.

Of course the vampires who live here have blacked out all the windows or any other potential sources of light pollution. Though, simply being out of the daylight doesn't let them wake up like I can. Yay for being special, right?

Sigh.

Blix zooms down a corridor and into a massive room full of machines bigger than some people's houses. Voices and video game sound effects echo in the vast chamber. It's a bit confusing to locate the sources based on the reverb, but I'm inclined to think three guys and a woman are somewhere to my right and a distance ahead.

Since I'm online, I float off my feet and glide for maximum quiet. Even sneakers make *some* noise on sand-strewn concrete. At the end of the first giant machine, I peek around the corner. Light comes from a hallway off to the right. Most likely, the mortal thralls are hanging out in a former employee lounge they've no doubt updated with a big TV and a PlayStation or something.

"Go check on the brats," says a guy.

"Hell no," mutters another man. "Not doing that again."

"The bleeding stopped, didn't it?" asks the girl. "Besides, they didn't get far."

I narrow my eyes and give Blix a 'what happened' glare.

The thralls continue discussing whose job it is to obtain food and bring the boys something to have for dinner.

He pantomimes opening a door, running, then dives like a football player making a tackle.

"You tried to help them escape, but they got caught?"

Blix nods and points at the hallway where the sounds are coming from.

"Those people caught them."

Thumbs-up.

"Thralls?"

He jabs his thumb higher.

Damn. So much for using mind control on them. They're already under some other vampire's command. However, being thralls, they're still mortals. So I shouldn't have too much trouble fighting or killing them. At least not literal trouble. Mental/emotional trouble... that's a different story. If need be to protect Sam and the boys, sure I would totally kill someone. For pure spite or to make it easier to sneak past them, I can't do it.

Blix flies over to the corridor and sits on a nearby water cooler, waving at me to follow him. Oh, crap. He's kidding. I have to go past the room full of thralls? Dammit. At least I'm floating silently. I glide across the large manufacturing room, going over conveyor belts and around columns, taking as straight a line as possible.

When I reach the corridor, Blix leaps onto my shoulder like an oversized parrot and points. I keep going. The light and video game sounds come from a break room on the right side, about halfway between the factory floor and an L-bend to the left.

I pause by it and peek in.

The relatively large—probably former conference room—now holds a beat up plaid sofa, giant flat-screen TV, and five cot beds. Three guys and a woman occupy the couch, all focused on the video game. Perfect.

None of them react to me zooming past the door and around the L bend in the corridor. Blix leaps off my shoulder and flies ahead, heading straight for the double doors at the far end a good ways down, past numerous other side rooms. While no sound comes from any of the closed doors, they give off a tangible sense of presence that tells me I'm amid a nest of vampires. They're all still trapped asleep by daylight, but one wrong move on my part might cause a cascade awakening in frenzied panic. Bad idea. As dumb as jumping head first into a wood chipper.

Jaw clenched, I keep floating to the end of the corridor.

Both doors open on their own when the imp gets near them, revealing another manufacturing area. This one's much smaller with tiny machines —only the size of cars—set up in neat rows interlinked by conveyor belts. Signs on the walls indicate clean suits are required here. Many try to be cute or humorous, portraying 'dust' as a growling monster that needs to be contained.

Within seconds of entering the room, I catch a whiff of sweaty socks, fart, and chocolate. Yep. Boys. The weaker scents of Sam, Ronan, Daryl, and Jordan lurk beneath the less pleasant aromas. Small whispering voices plot another escape attempt. Hearing them lights a fire at my butt. I fly over the machinery toward the voices, not caring if my brother's friends see me breaking the law—of gravity. I've already stolen a truck tonight.

A wall of steel gridding blocks off the rear left corner of the manufacturing floor, some kind of security cage. Judging by the empty shelves inside, probably where the factory kept expensive parts for whatever they made. The boys are sitting on the floor in the middle of the locked area, arranged in a circle like they'd gone camping.

Sam, as ever, has a blasé look to him, as if this whole experience is no big deal. Ronan's eyes are huge and he's trembling. Daryl's throwing off anger more than anything, and nursing a new fat lip. Grr. Jordan has his head in both hands, elbows on his knees, and his back to me.

I land before anyone sees me flying and rush up to the door.

"Sare!" whisper-shouts Sam, his expression brightening. "See, you guys? I told you she'd find us."

21

EARLY RISERS

The other three boys all jump to their feet.

"What's she gonna do?" whispers Daryl, gesturing at me. "She's just your big sister. We've been kidnapped by vampires."

"Uhh, guys… there's something you should know about Sarah," says Sam.

"She likes girls?" asks Jordan.

"No, dork. She's not gay." Sam sighs. "You remember last June when people thought she died for a couple days?"

"Yeah," mutters Daryl and Jordan at the same time.

Ronan stares at me with this 'please don't let us die' expression.

I stare at my brother.

"What?" asks Sam, looking at me. "They've seen these vampires. And you're just gonna make them forget it all anyway."

"Wait, hang on there just a sec." Daryl raises his hand, giving me side eye. "Your sister ain't no damn vampire. Or she'd be dead to the world. Sun ain't down yet."

"Sam…" I rear back to stomp-kick the security cage door, but Blix gets in the way.

The imp points at his ears, then at the door out. Grr. Good point. If I bash that door open, the thralls will hear.

"Well, open it then," I whisper.

Blix makes a finger gun and 'shoots' the cage door. The lock emits a *clank*.

"Ooh! It opened again." Jordan points at the door.

Ronan moves up beside him. I swear those two boys could be brothers —or at least members of a tween band. Both are scrawny and blonde, except Jordan's hair is short and he's got blue eyes to Ronan's green. Did I mention Sophia thinks Ronan's cute? Yeah. There's a reason I didn't. I really don't want to think about that.

"Come on. We gotta get out of here." I pull the steel mesh door open, but it emits an ear-destroying squeak.

Blix face-palms.

The boys rush out. Eff it. I start running for the door, weaving among the conveyors and work stations... but the instant I hear multiple sets of footsteps in the hallway coming toward us, I'm airborne. Need to keep any violence as far away from the boys as I can.

Daryl and Jordan both gasp in awe.

"Holy crap! Your sister *is*... something," blurts Daryl.

I land at the double-doorway out of the room right as they burst open. One of the mortal thralls stops short, gawking at me... clearly not expecting to see someone who isn't a tween boy. He's holding a crowbar like a sword, but doesn't make a move to swing it at me. The other three aren't too far behind him, running down the hall. As expected, his brain is hidden behind a wall of interference from the vampiric blood giving him power.

Time seems to slow to a near halt as my body kicks into fight mode.

I don't want to straight up kill these people. For all I know, they've been enthralled against their will. But they look like gang members. They also locked my brother and his friends in a big cage. Second but—we need to get out of here *now*.

Sorry, bud.

Before he can recover from the shock of seeing me, I sprout claws and fangs, growling while trying to make my eyes glow red.

The two guys farther down the hall nearly fall over each other trying to stop and go back the other way, screaming 'oh shit!' repeatedly. Unfortunately, the woman merely slows to a walk and gives me a look like she found a lump of dog poo she's responsible for cleaning up. The big dude in the doorway raises the crowbar and lunges forward, hacking down at me. He's not too much faster than a human, which makes it easy to dodge aside. I take the merciful approach and merely punch him in the head rather than claw his throat out.

The crowbar clatters to the floor in front of me as the guy sails off his feet. He flies a good distance before landing on his chest, out cold. Might've cracked his skull a wee bit. But, hopefully, he'll recover from that better than multiple gaping wounds. The woman pulls a gun.

Oh, hell no. I dive flat to the floor, grab the crowbar, and roll into a throw, aiming for the gun.

Unfortunately, the amount of practice I've had at crowbar throwing is pretty limited.

Like, this is the first time I've ever attempted to throw a crowbar at someone to disarm them.

I miss the gun by a few inches—up and to the right.

The crowbar spears into the woman's gut, stopping when the hooked claw end makes contact with her hip. Oops. She staggers backward. I rush in and grab the crowbar in one hand, gun in the other, yanking the bar out of her while squeezing the wrist until she drops the weapon. Stupid bitch *still* takes a swing at me. I mostly get out of the way, but her knuckles graze my temple.

For no particular reason, a fluorescent light fixture falls off the ceiling and beans the woman across the head. It doesn't knock her out completely, but it staggers her enough the fight leaves her eyes. She backpedals, clutching the hole in her gut where the crowbar had been.

The boys collect behind me.

"Gross," whispers Jordan.

"Wow." Ronan stares at me. "This is getting dangerous, isn't it?"

"A little," I mutter. "C'mon."

I only make it one step past the doorway before another man comes zooming around the corner up ahead and runs at me. He's got the same face/neck tats as the idiots who came after me in Seattle. The instant our stares meet, I know he's a vampire, not a thrall. Crap to the power of ten. Either these guys set their alarm clocks early or I didn't have enough damn time before sunset.

Crowbar isn't going to help me much here. I chuck it over my shoulder and pop claws, hoping none of these guys have them and might hesitate because of how much they hurt. Sure, it's unlikely odds, but my chances of bluffing my way out of here are probably better than fighting all of these guys at once. "Back off. I'm taking my brother and his friends home... or I'm taking as many of you with me as I can."

The vampire shakes his head. "Just had to get involved, didn't you?"

"I *wasn't* involved until you jackasses made me. This was between you guys and Dalton, but now, you've attacked my family."

"So?" The guy raises an eyebrow. "Am I supposed to be scared of you?"

"Under normal circumstances, probably not. But I'm past caring what happens to me. You wanna take on a vampire willing to do as much damage as possible before they die? Bring it. Sure, I might lose. But, ask yourself... are these four boys worth spending the next six months in agony?"

Unfortunately, the vampire decides to bring it.

He hurls himself into a charge, pulling a knife off his belt on the way. I manage to evade his first stabbing attack, but he came in with a lot more speed than the thralls. This guy's a little faster than me but not by a whole lot.

The boys scramble behind the nearest conveyor for cover... except for Sam. He runs out to grab the crowbar I dropped.

Growling, the vampire lunges again in a series of slashing and stabbing attacks. His greater speed forces me to give ground while dodging, backing up a step or two each time I duck. There's no opportunity for getting in an attack. Oh screw it. It's just a knife.

I abruptly reverse, rushing him when he goes to slash me again. My metaphorical balls cost me a gash on the left arm but I land eight claws on his chest and shred downward, reducing his shirt—and most of the skin under it—to a ruin of tattered bloody ribbons. He howls, gasping at the pain he obviously hadn't expected. I take advantage of the opening in his defense to jam my hand into his gut and randomly grab. Hey it worked for Aurélie, right?

He throws his head back and screams in anguish, then clocks me across the face with his knife hand. I fly sideways into a dried-out water cooler near the doorway, crushing it. The empty plastic bottle bounces off into the room, emitting a hollow drum-like rattle.

The vampire storms after me, but wipes out hard, eating floor. He went down so fast it looked like another vampire swept his legs out from under him. That has Blix written all over it. The fall gives me a chance to get back on my feet before the guy's on top of me. We spring up at the same time.

"Such a bitch," he growls.

"I warned you. No one fucks with my family."

Sam gasps.

Yeah, yeah. I know. Mom's gonna be mad at me for cursing.

El Douchey comes after me again with the knife. I try to twist under it, but he's still a bit too fast and manages to stab me in the shoulder. Hurts, but not as much as claws—or a shot to the heart. Snarling, I grab his right bicep in both hands and rip my claws down the arm to the wrist, digging them in with all the strength I can give myself. A few of my nails scrape bone.

The dude shrieks like the blonde bimbo from a horror movie and staggers back, gawking at his twitching, useless right arm. Okay, that is seriously, seriously gross. It looks like one of those 1960s bead curtains made out of meat strips. However, instead of freaking out and leaving, he goes into this insane rage and flies at me, grabbing a fistful of my sweatshirt, pushing me back into the wall.

His useless arm dangling, he pins me in place with one hand and extends his fangs. Of course, being close to an angry vampire with claws is the last place he should be. I grab for his face, slicing my three-inch nails into his cheeks and throat.

Sam runs out from hiding and charges up behind the guy, walloping him in the back of the knee with the crowbar. "Get off my sister, creep!"

Hot blood rolls over my fingers, gushing out of the ruin of this dude's throat. He's *still* too strong for me to throw off, so I keep on ripping.

Another guy with face tats stumble-runs in, a bit of grogginess to him from a sudden wake-up. This guy's carrying a katana. He spots me shredding Moron One and hurries over to chop my arms off, but doesn't get far before his foot flies out from under him and he fumbles the sword. The katana hits the concrete floor with a loud metal *clank*, and somehow —in absolute defiance of physics—*bounces* away from him multiple times like a rubber ball.

The man holding me roars when Sam whacks him in the other knee. He lets go of my shirt and spins on my brother, hiss-growling past his fangs.

Sam holds his ground defiantly, not even the slightest look of fear in his eyes—and tries to nail the guy in the balls with an upswing. The vampire catches the crowbar, stopping it cold. Blix dashes over to the katana, swoops down to grab it, then flies toward me. Growling, the sword's former owner floats back to his feet, but stops short staring in confusion at the sword apparently moving on its own. Or maybe he can see Blix and has no damn idea what he's looking at.

The vamp I've mostly shredded grabs Sam by the throat with his one usable arm. My brother starts pulling a Gordon Freeman on him, swinging the crowbar so damn fast it's a blur. Alas, a ten-year-old doesn't quite have the arm strength to crack a vampire's skull with a crowbar, especially when taking such rapid, unfocused swings.

I leap at him, nabbing the katana from Blix on the way and swinging at the guy holding Sam. My attack slices into his leg, stopping against his right femur with a dull *crack*. He emits a growl of pain and sinks down on one knee, groaning, still holding Sam by the neck. The other boys pop up over the conveyor belt and start throwing smallish metal objects at the vampire while shouting at him to let go.

The gang thug who lost the katana rushes at me. One of the metal rods the boys threw abruptly swivels around all by itself and gets under the guy's foot, tripping him again. Thank you Blix. Sam continues bashing the guy holding him over the head.

"You little shit," snarls the guy.

Sensing he's about to snap my brother's neck, I let out a war cry and hack at the arm. The other vampire launches himself at me like an undead meat torpedo, flying into me from the side at the same instant my blade slices his buddy's arm clean off at the elbow (more or less). Sam scrambles back, the severed limb hanging from his throat like a macabre necktie.

Sam peers down at it. "That's rather disturbing."

Vampire Two fly-carries me most of the way across the room. We crash against the wall—the bastard using me as a cushion—hard enough to crack cinder blocks and break a few of my ribs. Fortunately, I only pretend to breathe, so I don't have the wind knocked out of me. The hit causes him to bounce away, though he lands on his feet and grabs my hand.

"*¡Consigue tu propia espada, puta!*"

"What?" I grunt. "I took French in high school."

The guy pauses to give me a stare of 'really?' before tugging at my hands, trying to get his sword back. Mostly, he drags me around by it.

"Oh, you want this?" I abruptly let go of the blade.

His own strength flings him over backward the instant I'm no longer resisting, his arms and the blade up in the air leaving his chest undefended. I fly-leap after him, shredding my claws down his front and landing seated on top of him, straddling his hips. *This* I have training for. Grandma Sheridan had a cat that used to destroy her cushioned furniture.

The guy howls as I rake and shred at him, digging into his guts like a dog trying to bury a treat. The katana is too long for him to get the blade around on me in a proper swing, so he tries bonking me on the head with the handle, but it doesn't bother me. Blood and fragments of flesh go everywhere from my cat-on-sofa technique. A sharp pain jolts down into my left side. I ignore it, thrusting my hand up under his ribs until I grab hold of his pulsating heart—and crush it between my fingers. As soon as my claws reduce the hot lump of muscle to bacon strips, he goes limp and flops flat on his back.

It's at that moment, kneeling here with my right arm up to the elbow in vampire, I finally notice he'd plunged the katana straight down into my left shoulder. I got lucky, it only pierced my lung—missed my heart, but I think the tip went in so far it scraped my hip bone.

Ouch.

I extract my arm from him with a gooey slurp, grasp the katana, and draw it up out of my body. Surprisingly, it doesn't hurt much at all coming out. There are probably a handful of jobs I could theoretically handle in my current state of existence as a vampire. 'Katana scabbard' is not one of them.

The remaining thug, his one arm shredded to tatters, his other half missing, lays motionless on his front, perhaps having succumbed to blood loss. Sam makes a face like he stepped in dog poo, grasps the forearm dangling from his neck, and tugs it off.

"You okay?" I ask.

Sam waves the severed arm at me, then chucks it aside. "Make me forget this happening. I don't want to remember some dude's cut-off arm touching me."

Ronan, Jordan, and Daryl all stare at me, their mouths open.

I stand and limp over to the 'disarmed' vampire. Just to be sure he won't cause more problems, I lop his head off with the katana. Don't want him springing awake starved of blood and savaging the boys.

"What the heck is going on?" blurts Daryl.

"Nothing you're going to remember." I stare into Sam's eyes and remove the severed arm from his memory.

Dalton zooms in the double doors, skids to a stop nearby, and stares at me incredulously.

I blink at him. "What are you doing here?"

"I could ask you the same thing. You didn't wait for me to get up?" He sets his hands on his hips and exhales. The guy has the look of someone whose alarm clock failed, woke up way late, and went from dead asleep to being at work in about fifteen minutes.

"No. Wasn't the plan for me to get in and out of here before they woke up?" I rub my shoulder. "Ow. That's gonna be sore for a bit."

He eyes the katana, then plucks a large knife off the belt of the vampire with half an arm left. "You know what you're doing with that thing?"

I shrug. "Nope. Course, I don't really know what I'm doing with claws either."

"We can work on swordplay sometime, assuming of course we make it out of here." He waves us toward the double doors. "We need to—"

Rapid footsteps, the clicking of guns readying, and a whole lot of cursing echo in the hallway outside.

Dalton slams the double doors and braces himself against them. "So much for that idea."

A sneaker squeaks behind me.

I glance over at Sam holding the crowbar, the other boys all having armed themselves with pipes or metal rods.

Wham!

A heavy impact bounces the doors inward, but Dalton holds his ground.

"No way!" I point at the boys. "You four stay back."

Another slam nearly throws Dalton to the floor.

"Crikey, they're a touch cheesed off." He widens his stance. "Best attack is to stab them in the brain. That'll knock them—" He lurches forward when the vampires outside hit the door again. "Unconscious. Heart's not too bad, but it's only a momentary stun."

I already know cutting the head off doesn't cause unconsciousness, or even paralyze the body. Yeah, the total stuff of nightmares. Gotta damage the brain to knock a vampire out.

"What are we gonna do?" asks Ronan.

"Find a window?" asks Daryl.

Sam shakes his head. "There aren't any or we would've made it out last time. We had to go down the hall but got caught."

Blix babbles.

"He wants us to go to the bathroom," says Sam.

"He's gonna need to hold it," I mutter.

Blix face-palms.

"Any ideas?" I ask, staring at Dalton.

"Only one, and it's not very good. Gonna need to fight." He grunts, pressing himself against the doors, holding back the constant hammering.

Someone fires a bullet through the door, missing his ear by an inch.

"You ready?" asks Dalton.

"Boys! Get down," I shout.

The kids scramble around behind the conveyor.

I grab the katana in a two-handed grip. "Yeah. I'm lying, but yeah."

"Move to the side. Don't stand right in the way or you'll get shot."

"Okay." I hurry to the right, near the wall in an ambushing position.

"Oi. 'Ere goes."

Dalton mouths three... two... one...

22

A SHORTCUT'S A SHORTCUT

Dalton times it so he moves an instant before the mass of vampires outside rams the door again.

Without his resistance, the crowd of Scions slams the doors open hard enough to bend the hinges. The first three spill forward, landing on their chests, other vampires behind them stumbling as well. Dalton pounces on the one nearest him, stabbing his knife into the man's ear. I hack the katana into the head of a thirtyish woman wearing punk clothes, nearly cutting her head in half. She twitches, fangs out, and goes still.

Vampire unconsciousness looks fatal, but she'll get back up in a few hours.

The dude in the middle does a push-up so hard it flings him to his feet. He evades Dalton's knife and rolls away from me when I slice at him. Another guy jumps on me from the right, knocking me flat and riding me like a toboggan for several feet across the bare concrete floor. As soon as we stop moving, he puts a gun to the side of my head, but I elbow his arm aside an instant before he fires. The bullet bounces off the floor—and I'm pretty sure my eardrum exploded.

A faint high-pitched war cry accompanies Sam charging in and Conan the Barbarian swinging his crowbar over his head like a two-handed sword. He lands the curved part right on the vampire's wrist, shattering it and making him drop the handgun. Somewhere to my left, grunts and growls come from Dalton taking on a group all by himself.

The dude on top of me glares at Sam, but the distraction lets me throw him aside. I levitate to my feet, flying after him—and thrust the sword up his nose as he crashes to the floor. A quick twist elicits a *crunch* and a spurt of blood from his mouth.

"Make me forget seeing that, too," says Sam. "After."

"Look out!" shout Daryl, Ronan, and Jordan at the same time.

I instinctively jump in front of Sam and raise the sword to defend myself—but they were talking to Dalton. Fortunately, the guy who got the drop on him from behind with a shotgun experiences a misfire.

The weapon only *clicks.*

Oh, Blix... I could kiss you.

I charge at the guy, but another vampire comes at me from the left swinging a machete. Parrying with a sword is so far out of my skill set I don't even try, relying instead on dodging. This guy doesn't feel faster than me, which could mean he's relatively new. However, he's had a lot more practice fighting with a blade, so I end up giving ground, moving away from Dalton and the other six or so vampires going after him.

Sam runs up behind him and nails the guy in the shin with the crowbar. The strike is trivial, but it hurts enough to make the guy shriek and stumble—which gives me an opening. I fake an overhead swing to lure his defense up, then pull the blade back and thrust it into the underside of his chin. A few inches of katana pokes out the top of his skull. His eyes cross. Blood runs down the blade and foams from his lips. Growling, I push forward, slicing the blade a few inches deeper into his head before tearing the sword out and letting him collapse flat on the floor. Wow, this thing is sharp.

"Sarah! Right!" yells Sam.

A blur comes at me. I dive backward away from it, going horizontal in midair as another machete passes over me. The vampire swinging it stumbles forward, unprepared for his strike to hit nothing but air. Rather than chase me, he rushes straight for Sam.

My idiot brother raises the crowbar to defend himself—but a steel conveyor belt roller comes skidding across the floor and slides perfectly under the guy's foot. He wipes out and lands on his back. I pounce, spearing the katana into his eye hard enough to chip the concrete floor under his skull.

Dalton jumps on a guy with a one-armed hug, looking like a pair of drunk friends—only he stabs the guy in the chest, then up under the chin before throwing him into the path of two more vampires rushing at him together. The body takes the one on the left down, but the other gets past him.

Bang.

Another gunshot comes from my right—and the hot stab of pain in my chest is a pretty clear indication of who they fired at. I hurl myself to the left, trying to avoid a short, wide-necked Hispanic dude in the doorway firing twice more at me; the first bullet hits me above the right boob, the second misses.

Boom.

Most of the skin on the face of the vampire who shot me disintegrates in a bloody splat. Naked red skull stares at me—well as much as someone with no eyeballs left can stare. He howls, mostly in anger, and grabs at his face.

Thump.

I glance left. Sam's flat on his back holding the shotgun that failed to head-explode Dalton. His facial expression looks like a chemist who got an unexpected (explosive) result in the lab. I'm sure his shoulder is in pain, but he looks more bewildered at his failure to anticipate the strength of the recoil.

At least the dude who shot me had a smallish gun. The two holes it put in me burn a bit but don't slow me down. Rusty rapiers stuck into me hurt more. Dalton's bleeding from several slashes, stabs, and gunshot wounds. Four of the vampires around him are limp on the floor, but the remaining two are pushing him back.

The one Sam de-faced with the shotgun starts shooting randomly. Several of his bullets hit his buddies, as well as Dalton. Most clank off the various conveyors and machinery in here. Screams of panic come from Sam's three friends. My brother rolls over onto his front and crawls under the conveyor, abandoning the shotgun. Guess it hurt too much for him to dare try firing it again.

I dash over to the shotgun, landing in a skid on my knees, and drop the sword nearby. Nothing happens when I pull the trigger at the guy still unloading his 9mm all over the place.

"Pump it!" yells Sam.

What? Oh. Duh. Umm. I try to do that 'pumping' thing they always have characters in video games and movies do. Really, this ought to be easy. I've played enough *Call of Duty*. Apparently, the games are not a perfectly accurate recreation of reality. Who'd have thought video games aren't the same as actual combat training? Grr. Finally, I apply the right amount of force to the right thing and the handgrip slides back, ejecting a smoking plastic shell and chambering a new one.

Aha!

No-face dude is out of ammo and flailing at the air. So, I pivot to the left and fire low at the two thugs corralling Dalton. The guy on the left steps on something that makes him fall right as I pull the trigger. My shotgun erupts with the same loud *boom* as before but doesn't kick anywhere near as bad as I expected. Half the guy's head liquefies into a reddish splortch. If he hadn't fallen over backward, I would've hit him in the ass.

"Thanks, Blix!"

He babbles something in a happy tone.

The other vampire stabs Dalton in the gut, but apparently, fell for a trap. The men hit each other at the same time, only my sire rammed his knife into the other guy's ear. Puree brain is instant lights out for a vampire—or anyone else, really. We just get back up after a few hours.

Dalton throws the guy off to the side and looks around while I pump the shotgun again and put another blast into No-Face's head. The second hit goops the interior of the skull, knocking him out. I pump it again before swapping it to one hand and grabbing the katana in my left.

"This is a damn mess. Is that all of them?" I ask.

"I don't think so, but it's still not quite completely dark. We need to get out of here right now." Dalton waves for the boys to follow and rushes out into the hall.

It's nothing short of a miracle the boys don't hesitate to run past the mangled, bleeding bodies we left littered around. Oh, it's such a good thing I can play with memories. Might even let Dalton deal with this since he's had a lot more practice at it. Don't want anything resurfacing in the kids' heads for a nightmare. It's weird to say, but the sword felt more useful than a gun. Well, maybe not the shotgun, but handguns? Sierra might have something with wanting to learn how to actually use a blade after all.

One of the gang vampires springs up unexpectedly as I run past him toward the hall. He jumps on my back, sinking his fangs into my shoulder. Holy shit that burns like a son of a bitch. I'm screaming before consciously realizing I'm screaming. Dalton skids to a stop and starts running back toward us.

All four boys attack the guy with their crowbar and pipes. The combined assault is apparently painful enough he lets go of me to deal with them, shoving me forward before whirling on the boys. He grabs Ronan and Sam by their shirts and pulls them up off their feet.

I spin, put the shotgun against the back of his head, and fire.

The blast of liquefied vampire head showers Daryl and Jordan with gore. An eyeball bounces off Jordan's forehead. Sam and Ronan sink back to their feet as the strength leaves the vampire's arms.

Oh yeah. There is going to be *much* rewriting of memory later.

Daryl throws up. Apparently, the poor kid's mouth had been open.

"He's not dead," I say. "Just... *very* unconscious."

Dalton grasps me from behind. "That's bloody disgusting."

"We're deleting everything from their memory."

"Aye. Absolutely. C'mon." He tugs at my arm.

The two gore-drenched boys are too shell-shocked to do anything more than stand there gawking, so I hit them with a mental compulsion to follow me. Sam and Ronan sprint after me down the hall while the other two kinda zombie-walk.

We race past multiple doors on both sides. Blix screams from behind. He's gesturing with all four limbs and his tail at a door with a standard men's bathroom icon on it.

"Not now," I yell. "We gotta get out of here."

Blix scream-babbles.

"Sare!" shouts Sam. "He says we're gonna die if we don't go in there."

"Crap. Okay. Dalton!" I do a one-eighty and run back to the two stunned boys, dragging them faster than they're able to walk into the mens'. Since my hands are full, I punt the door open and go inside.

Four stalls stand on the left, two of the doors missing. A pair of urinals hang from the wall straight ahead, and there's a counter on the right with three sinks and three rectangular mirrors. Fortunately, it doesn't stink too badly in here, though there is a lingering air of urine, likely soaked into the floor from before the place was abandoned.

Sam and Ronan zoom inside, hurrying over to me.

"Sarah?" calls a distant echoing voice that sounds an awful lot like Sophia.

"What the hell are *you* doing here?" I shout.

Dalton barrels in the door, slams it, and leans against it. "Oh, this feels familiar, doesn't it?"

I exhale hard. "Just a bit. Am I hearing things or did my kid sister just call for me?"

Blix nods and points at the mirrors.

"Oh, crap... seriously?"

The imp flails and chitters at me.

"Umm, Sare?" asks Sam. "He says he was trying to tell you he could've brought you and Dalton down here inside the mirrors in like a half hour so you didn't have to fly all night."

"Ugh. My fault. I was in a hurry." I grab Daryl's head and stare into his eyes. "Dalton, will you fix Jordan?"

"Bit busy with the door here, luv," whispers Dalton, a hint of manic high-pitch to his voice.

Sure enough, the banging has already started. At least he's got a better position there with one foot braced on the sink counter and only a single door to hold shut.

I hurriedly wipe Daryl's memory of everything that happened from the time they walked out of the security cage to right now. Can't do much about the blood all over them... but I can always fix it later—if we make it out of here.

Dalton holds the door while I go from boy to boy, deleting all the vampire stuff. I leave them remembering a gang from Los Angeles who a friend of mine pissed off abducted them in a bid to get me to turn against him. Except for Sam, they don't remember anything about vampires. In my brother's case, he only loses witnessing gore, basically turning it into a PG action movie. He still shot the one guy, but the vampire flew over backward so fast he didn't see the wound, just a bloodless video game bad guy going down.

There.

The boys will remain sane and not need—much—therapy.

"Sarah!" shouts Sophia.

I jump and spin.

My kid sister's blonde, angelic face peers at me from the center mirror above the sinks, kinda like one of those magical paintings in *Harry Potter* that move. The mirror isn't very large. I'm not the biggest person in the world and I don't think it's going to be possible for me to fit. In fact, asking Daryl to squeeze through it might be pushing things.

Literally.

I'm going to have to push him.

"Soph? What the heck? That's so damn dangerous. Why are you in the mirrorverse alone!"

"I'm not alone." She leans to the side, revealing Sierra—who's wearing a red headband. "And Coralie is here, too. She's helping us stay safe... and find you. Come on!"

The glass in front of her shimmers, for an instant appearing like thin plastic film before disappearing entirely. Sophia reaches an arm out into the bathroom.

"Uhh, Soph, there's no way Dalton or I can fit into that little rectangle." I glance at Sam. "But the boys should make it."

Banging at the door pauses. A gunshot goes off in the hall outside, leaving a slight bulge in the door behind Dalton's head. Multiple *pings* echo and someone yells in pain. Heh. Maybe that'll convince them not to try shooting anymore.

"Uhh, are you serious?" Jordan stares. "What the heck is that?"

"No way." Daryl shakes his head hard enough to make his somewhat chubby cheeks wobble. "That's seriously messed up."

Ronan jumps up on the sink without hesitation and climbs into the mirror. "Come on, guys. I do this all the time. It's fine. There's cool stuff in here."

Another pound at the door leaves a bigger dent, and nearly breaks the hinges.

"Ooh, he's a strong one," mutters Dalton.

"C'mon. Go." I point. "Hurry. It's a safe way out. Blix, go with them to make sure they stay safe."

Blix salutes me and zips across into the mirrorverse.

Coralie appears in the room beside me. "Safe is debatable, but it is likely less dangerous than your current situation."

Sam jumps up on the counter and dives into the mirror without hesitating. I grab Jordan and chuck him through the opening before facing Daryl. He starts backing up. Ugh. No way is he going into the mirror struggling, so I hit him with the same mental stun I use before feeding, then heft his semiconscious body up like a log and stuff him in. As expected, he gets stuck at the gut. Trying not to hurt him, I shove as gently as possible while increasing force. The kids pull his arms.

The door flies open, throwing Dalton forward onto the sink counter.

A small group of vampires force their way in right as Daryl's legs slip into the mirror. This sight, as one might expect, stuns them into staring. Okay, maybe I'd been wrong. *I* could probably fit into the mirror, but I don't want to leave Dalton alone.

He jumps off the counter, grabs me, and starts trying to shove me into the center mirror. "Go!"

"And leave you alo—?"

One of the gang vampires shoots at the portal mirror, but the bullet goes in rather than smashing the glass. Sophia screams in startlement. Two other vampires rush at me and Dalton while the other guy keeps shooting at the mirrors. Glinting shards of glass rain down over the sinks from the other two.

My first instinct is shotgun, but I forgot to pump it after the guy in the hallway. With little time to think, there's no choice but to drop it and rely on the sword. Dalton gets into a close-range knife fight with the other one while I wave the katana around like I've got a bee in my pants, trying to keep the guy back.

A lucky shot at the portal mirror cracks the metal frame, causing a minor explosion of paranormal energy. The blast wave is powerful enough to knock us all to the floor and bend the stalls.

"Dammit! That was our shortcut... guess we're in for some bad luck now," I mutter.

"Technically," says Dalton from the floor, "the bloke who smashed the mirror's in for the bad luck." He casually inserts his knife into the ear of the vampire on top of him, twists it, and yanks it out. "Quite rude if you ask me."

The one on top of me grabs my wrist, pinning the katana to the floor. He thinks he's got me, but... surprise bitch! Claws. I slash my left hand at his face and neck. The guy leaps back, shrieking in pain. Dalton tosses the 'unconscious' one off him, then absorbs three bullets to the chest from the guy in the doorway who broke the mirror.

"Must you?" asks Dalton with a sigh. "This shirt was expensive."

The guy glances down at his gun as if it malfunctioned.

I spring upright, moving to attack the guy I clawed, but he punts me in the chest, launching me backward. My ass lands in a wall urinal and I crack my head against the top part. Grr. Disgusting. At least it's been dry for a long time. Dalton throws his knife, burying it in the forehead of the guy with the gun. Screaming mostly out of anger, I let off a war cry and rush at the other one, sword high. He catches my forearms, stalling the blade a few inches away from the top of his head.

This one's noticeably stronger than me. Trying to overpower him and slice into his head is about as productive as attempting to push over a skyscraper with my bare hands. We sway about, almost nose to nose, the guy trying to throw me off my feet again, but I manage to keep myself relatively in place with flying.

The *ka-chook* sound of a shotgun echoes in the bathroom.

His eyes go wide. "Oh shi—"

Boom.

And… I'm wearing his head. His brains are in my hair. I wipe the gook out of my eyes and peer over the smoking neck stump at Dalton's cocky grin. Speaking of cock, he attempts to pump the shotgun again, but makes a sour face at it and drops it.

"Broke?"

"Out of ammo." He grabs his knife back from the one guy and takes a second one off the belt of the shotgun decapitation victim.

"Can I ask a stupid question?"

"No question is stupid but the one you don't ask," says Dalton in a posh accent.

"Thank you, motivational poster guy." I shake my head. "Is it normal for a head to entirely explode when hit with buckshot?"

"Hmm. No. Definitely kind of unusual. Must've had some special ammunition."

"Right." I look at the smashed mirrors. "Damn. So much for that. And you wouldn't have fit anyway. Not leaving you alone in here."

Dalton tries to close the door, but it's a little bent and won't fit the doorjamb properly.

"What do we do now?"

He glances back at me. "Well, we either try to stay in this room until sunrise in hopes you'll wake up before them and drag me out of here… or we fight our way out now."

"Fight?" I gawk at him. "Wait, you mean there's more of them?"

"By my count, yes. But it's quiet. Maybe they've decided to be smart and not all sleep at the same place." He examines his fingernails. "Nothing quite like a large incendiary device to make vampires reevaluate their procedures. Let's get out of here."

I nod.

We haul ass out of the bathroom, run down the hall around the L bend… and skid to a stop in the huge outer room full of massive machines. A line of vampire gang members stands in our way, like fifteen or twenty of them. Giant machines hem us in on both sides, and there's enough superstructure overhead to make flying fast difficult. They'd surely catch up to us before we made it to the door.

"Umm… I think we're fighting now," I whisper.

Dalton tosses and catches his knife. "Aye, looks that way."

OF COURSE

He glances at me. *Sarah, make a hole and get the heck out of here. This isn't your problem. I don't want you to get hurt over this.*

I think about the katana stabbed into my shoulder so deep it scratched my pelvic cradle. "Too late."

The gang vampire in the middle of the line steps toward us, glaring at Dalton. He's the only one of the men to have long hair. Though the guy doesn't look any taller than the others, and he's not overly muscular, he gives off an air of power the rest of them lack. Fortunately, it's nowhere near as strong as Aurélie's. I saw her get really pissed once at a social event, and she leveled the entire room with a wave of mental radiance. No one dared to even speak.

"The *pendejo* is ours now, Armand," says one of the three women among them, flashing an irritating smile at us.

"Wait." I point at their apparent leader. "Your name is Armand? Like seriously?"

Armand peels his melting scowl away from Dalton and turns it on me. "You have a problem with my name?"

His thick Spanish accent is almost enough to make me laugh despite the really crappy situation. "Not a problem really, but come on, man. Every vampire movie ever made names the dark, broody guy 'Armand.' Couldn't you come up with something more original, or were you trying to be campy on purpose?"

Armand snarls.

"That was perhaps not the best thing to say," adds Dalton, whispering behind his hand at me.

"Not trying to do anything there. I'm serious. Armand? Really?"

He roars and lunges at me.

This guy... yeah, he's way faster than me. Before I know it, there's a hand around my neck and I'm against the wall, dangling off my feet. Must've slammed me pretty hard since the katana went flying out of my grip and my back hurts. He's holding me up by one arm, not all too impressive for a vampire. We're strong as heck and I don't weigh a lot. He's probably about to say something condescending—but he's evidently not prepared for me raking at his forearm. His fingers snap open in response to the pain of my claws tearing into his skin. Wow, I guess it's true. Claws might be rare or absent entirely for Scions. They have no idea how much these little bitches hurt. I drop back to my feet and fly straight up to avoid being grabbed trying to go around him.

Gotta give the guy credit... he didn't scream in pain or even grimace much.

Dalton's a two-knife whirlwind, eyeball deep in angry vampires. For a second or two, I stare in total awe like I'm on the movie set of *Pirates of the Caribbean*. Blades of all sizes, including one legit cutlass, flash in a continuous ballet of bloodletting. Only the red spurts hanging in the air or a few scraps of severed cloth seemingly floating give away we're all sped up. Some of the vampires appear to be moving in mild fast-forward to me, though Dalton is faster than them—mostly. Armand *feels* stronger.

Fortunately, he can't fly, or doesn't bother. I'm not sure if the gang has lost interest in 'the kid' or they simply don't notice me hanging out up in the rafters, but the whole crowd converges on Dalton. Armand can't get to him due to the sheer number of other vampires surrounding him. Even without a mind link to my sire, I know he's worried—he's not making any wiseass comments each time he stabs someone. Really, he's actually kinda good at that. The knife in his left hand, he almost exclusively uses for defense except for a few surprises when he spins around like a bullfighter to avoid someone. Already, five gang vampires are out cold, bleeding from head wounds.

I can't believe no one's shot him yet. Either this group didn't bring guns or they're trying to keep it quiet enough to avoid police showing up, merely for the inconvenience of having to send them away or kill them.

Also, I can't sit up here and watch them overwhelm him.

Okay, time to help. I target one of the vamps on the opposite side of the crowd from Armand. Hey, I'm not a chicken, but there's also no reason to be stupid about this. Five-month-old vampires don't pick fights with centenarians. Like something out of one of Sierra's video games, I jump off the steel rafter and dive-bomb him, the katana held over my head in both hands.

The combined force of my drop plus as hard a downstroke as my arms are capable of splits the guy in half from the top of his head to the middle of his gut. No one's as shocked to see this as I am. Well, maybe the guy I hit is, but he's not going to be seeing much of anything for a few days. Fortunately, the melee is so chaotic only two vampires notice me nearly cutting their pal in half—and they both come after me.

I try the parrying thing since the chick's got a knife in her hand, which is a lot shorter than my blade. She yanks her hand back fast enough to evade the katana, and stabs at me before I can recover my swing. My attempt to dodge turns it into a slash raking over my chest and right thigh.

Merely a shallow cut, only about an inch deep. Ouch.

The guy stabs me in the left kidney, pulls his blade out, and tries to get me in the head. Good thing for me my legs give out from pain. His blade goes over my head. I fall in a spinning motion and rake the katana around in a slash, taking his right leg off an inch below the knee.

Howling, he falls over backward, calling me all sorts of unpleasant things.

"Not bad for a baby," mutters the woman right before kicking me in the face.

Oh, that's a broken jaw.

I go from sprawled on the floor in front of the guy to like twenty feet away, crumpled up against one of those giant machines in an instant. Pretty sure I slid across the floor, but I don't remember it. The blood smear I left behind is fairly compelling evidence. Dazed, I push myself up, but the bitch comes out of nowhere, grabs two fistfuls of my hair, and proceeds to pound my skull over and over into the metal machinery behind me.

After the seventh time my nose bounces off the metal, I get my hands up to brace against the greasy steel. She keeps pushing, but we're either an even match in strength or I'm starting to panic. Another vampire walks up behind us with a metal baseball bat balanced over his shoulder like a cocky major leaguer who thinks he's going to hit a home run.

Grunting, I push with both arms and a foot at the machine, but the bitch holds me down while the guy wallops me in the left thigh, breaking the bone. That hurt so much I barely even feel anything more than an endorphin high.

There may have been a few more hits from the bat, but they don't register in my memory.

Next thing I know, someone's dragging me across the floor over to where Dalton lays semi-conscious. He looks like he got run over by a city bus, two taxis, and a high school marching band. I'm probably in similar shape, though the pain is coming from so many places at once I can't tell what hurts more.

The vampire bitch tosses me to the ground next to Dalton.

Armand strolls up to stand near our heads, arms folded, an arrogant sneer on his face. He observes us for a moment, savoring his victory. I really want to taunt him about being such a total badass for needing twenty-on-two to win, but my jaw hasn't knit yet.

This isn't good.

Oh, aye, says Dalton in my head. *Appreciate you trying at least. Important thing is the boys are okay.*

Yeah. My heart sinks at the thought of my family losing me again, that grief I tried to spare them from by going home. Better me than Sam. I glance at Dalton's bloody face and think, 'Hey, you're not bad at the fighting thing.'

He chuckles, spraying goopy blood from his lips.

Armand squats, grabs a fistful of Dalton's shirt, and pulls his limp body up so they're face to face. Our mind link tells me he's overacting being injured to the point of paralysis, but we're surrounded by at least twelve—and both pretty battered. Even if he catches Armand off guard, it's probably not going to matter. Then again, if we're dead anyway, no reason not to try.

"Ahh, the fancy rat," says Armand. "Thought you could make short work of us. I despise mercenaries. There's no creature as low as a man who'd sell his allegiance. You fight for nothing but greed."

"Nope," I rasp. "There's lower."

Armand whacks me across the face with the back of his left hand. "Quiet."

I snarl and start pushing myself up, but two vampires grab my hair and shoulders, pinning me to the floor. "What's low is a coward who abducts children as bait. Dalton came here to—"

He slaps me again, setting off an explosion of pain in my face and a gusher of blood from my nostrils. Yeah, that's a broken nose. Oh, I really don't like this guy. In fact, if by some miracle this isn't my last night alive, it's tempting to ask that Petra bitch to make him one of her 'art projects.' Alas, she doesn't torment vampires, only mortals.

But it's a good example of how much I hate this guy right now, wanting him to be on the receiving end of her.

"Hit her again, your hand's going up your arse," rasps Dalton.

Armand laughs. "You, my friend, are going to have a date with the sun… but only your legs. Tomorrow will be arm day. Then the rest. And, that cute little one you brought along as an apology gift will be a nice—"

A curtain of darkness races from right to left behind Armand. His neck bursts into a geyser of blood as his head falls forward, tumbling, long black hair trailing after. The wraith-like apparition swerves back and flies at me. Both vampires holding my arms release their grip and dive to the floor screaming.

Glim appears out of the blackness, standing behind a third gang vampire. As smoothly as the soldier he used to be, he grabs the guy, one hand muffling his mouth while he rips the man's throat out with the other.

"Cor blimey!" blurts Dalton. He shoves himself up, overpowering the two vamps holding him and swiping the cutlass from Armand's belt before the body finishes collapsing over forward.

The woman who'd beat the crap out of me grabbed the katana—nice of her to keep it close, right? I jump on her while she's prone on the floor trying to avoid the big scary shadow monster illusion. Claws are sharp and mega-painful, but metal blades are still better for piercing bone. Still, while sitting on her back, I grab her head in both hands and mash her face into the floor repeatedly, gouging at her head with my claws. Payback's a bitch, right? As soon as she stops moving, I extricate my fingers from the holes they made in her skull, grab *my* katana, and leap upright.

Well, mostly upright. My left femur is still not quite back to full strength. Okay, so I'm levitating in a generally standing position until I can put weight on that leg.

Bat-man decides he wants to finish what he started and comes after me. I swing the katana like I'm trying to chop his aluminum bat in half. The tactic works, deflecting his attack. He tries again and again, our weapons clashing in a series of loud sparking *clanks*. Alas, I have a normal katana, not some overblown Hollywood super weapon. It doesn't cut the baseball bat in half. While we keep trading swings, various curses and groans come from everywhere. Dalton and Glim fighting are a disorienting blur since my attention is entirely focused on this guy with the bat.

A few pained screams make me smile, since they didn't come from either of my friends.

The guy swings for my head; this time when I block, my blade scrapes down the bat and shears most of his fingers off. Bats don't have hand guards. He shrieks as the metal club goes flying, falling silent as soon as I stab him in the face, a good nine inches of katana sticking out the back of his head.

Before I can pull it out of him, a shrieking female vampire with gang tats jumps at me from behind and left, raking her claws down my back as I fail to twist away in time. Imagine getting sliced by red hot razor blades covered in petulant wasps. Yeah. This hurts so much I invent new curse words to yell while staggering forward and tossing the unconscious vamp off my sword. The bitch rakes at my stomach when I spin to face her, but I'm angry enough not to care. Taking the hit gives me the perfect opening to cut her head in half with a diagonal downward swing. The one eye she has left blinks at me before she collapses.

My everything hurts. Claw marks on my back and stomach burn like the wounds had salted alcohol in them. Only concentrating on using flight to keep myself upright prevents me from landing in a heap, and even doing that is starting to feel exhausting.

Glim disappears in puffs of illusory black smoke only to reappear behind or near other vampires and give them a nice up-close look at his massive claws. Dalton, now in possession of a proper sword rather than a knife, disarms and head-stabs six vampires one after the next. He's still using a knife in his left hand as a defense tool, and it's mesmerizing to watch him so effortlessly deal with these idiots. The remaining four are so freaked out by Glim 'teleporting' around they run off in a panic.

"Sarah?" Dalton, cutlass held high, turns in place, surveying the area for any more threats. Seeing none, he lowers the weapon and looks at me. "I'd ask if you're okay, but that's a stupid question."

I glance down at myself. My clothes are a bloody, shredded ruin. There's not much left of my top except for a scrap of fabric draped over my shoulder and the former collar. No idea where my bra went. Claw bitch ripped my jeans so bad they've fallen around my knees, but hey at least my panties survived, even if they are completely blood-drenched.

Dalton's outfit didn't fare much better. Wow. He's wearing tan silk boxers covered in small blue teacups.

"My apologies for taking so long to get here." Glim retracts his astoundingly long claws back to their usual merely epic length and walks over to us. "Information traverses the shadow realm much more slowly from this far away."

I raise my arms to hug him, but stop. No, it's not being topless. Strangely, it doesn't bother me as much as it should. After everything that's happened since my Transference, standing here boobs-out barely registers as awkward. I'd even hug him like that. But no, it's more than my wardrobe malfunction. I'm a bloody mess. Touching him would cover him in gore, plus sting like hell. "No problem at all. Late help is still awesome. Don't think we were going to make it this time otherwise."

He pats me on the cheek. "I hate seeing you like this."

"Thanks. Yeah, I hate seeing me like this, too. Not your fault I got my ass kicked. Still kinda new at this."

Dalton shows little reaction to my exposed chest. He spent eighty some years among the unseemly characters of London's night life. He's seen so many prostitutes traipsing about topless in lounges or brothels that the sight of boobs has become boring to him. Also, he still thinks of me as too young.

"Okay, now what?" I ask, finally lowering myself to sit. "How long is it going to take my leg to knit?"

Dalton's presence in my mind tingles, probably examining my injury somehow. "An hour or so. Maybe two."

"Great."

Sigh. I get into a claw fight and end up basically limping away naked. Of course. Every damn time.

THE MOON POND MOTEL

Dalton grasps my left arm and helps me up.

"What?" I glance at him. "We're not waiting an hour?"

"No. I've got another idea of a place we can go to clean up. This lot will wake eventually. Though… hang on, luv."

Dalton, wearing the shredded remains of a tweed blazer and shiny silk boxers, drags Armand's head and body across the room to the door. Guess someone's going to have a date with the sun after all.

Glim stands near me, arms folded, watching the inert vampires.

"So glad you found us," I say, still resisting the urge to smear blood all over him with a hug. "So it took a couple hours for you to feel this happening from Seattle?"

He flashes a jagged smile. "Not exactly. The farther off it is, the longer it takes to propagate across the shadow. It's not a linear thing. News from a hundred miles might take a few hours. Two hundred miles, a day or so."

"Uhh…" I stare up at him. "We're over a thousand miles away. You wouldn't have heard anything from the whispers."

"I didn't. At least nothing beyond Dalton's original involvement with these vampires. Your father found me on the roof and asked me to help."

"Wait. What?" I gawk. "Dad? He found you? On your roof? How the heck did he even know where to go?"

Glim chuckles. "I knew he was looking for me, so I allowed him to find me. He drove without knowing exactly where he was going, but found me nonetheless."

"Nice. You're more of a friend than anyone deserves."

"Don't belittle yourself, Sarah." He crouches to examine my wounds. "You should recover without any scarring. Though, you will need a good deal of blood, and soon."

"Yeah. Pretty sure I'd feel damn hungry right now if I wasn't in so much pain." My attempt to laugh stops short at a feeling like a hundred needles in my stomach. "Ow. Guess I should feel lucky only a few of these guys had claws."

Glim looks around at the carnage. "Yes. Scions are the least likely to have some of the Old World abilities. Their bloodline relies more on modern technology, sort of an evolutionary abandonment of vestigial traits. Why use claws when swords and guns are much more effective? Why fly when cars exist? Less developed night vision because of electricity. And so on, so forth."

"Right... Is that also why they're stronger and faster than me?"

"Somewhat. Though you are still quite young."

"Don't remind me." I chuckle. "Ow. Hey, can you take us back home the easy way?"

He mulls for a moment, then cringes. "The length of the trip might have unintended consequences on one who is not a Shadow."

"Ugh. Really? Like what?"

"I am perhaps being overly protective of you." He pats me on the head as if to make fun of his treating me like a kid. "Our energies are about as opposite as possible."

"Right. Life and death." I frown. "But I don't care about that."

"It would pain me to see you start to inherit some of my curse. Too much time spent in the realm of shadow could affect your appearance."

I lean against his leg, trying not to get too much blood on him. My numerous wounds from metal blades have already closed and stopped bleeding, but the claw marks continue seeping. "I don't think you're cursed."

"That is kind of you to say. Kinder of you to sincerely believe, but it does not escape me how most regard our appearance."

"Yeah, well, they're buttheads," I mutter.

Glim chuckles.

"We can fly home tomorrow," says Dalton while walking back over to us.

The sight of him wearing boxer briefs, dress socks, expensive shoes, and little else while carrying a sword sets me off laughing.

"Aye, amusing. We're both in our knickers, luv."

"It's the sword, the accent, and the blood all over. You look like you walked right out of a Guy Ritchie movie."

He examines himself for a moment, shrugs, then points the cutlass at the guy who had the bat. "We should relocate ourselves before Frankie two-thumbs wakes up."

"Eww." I grimace at the guy's mangled hands, every finger except his thumbs cut off close to the knuckle. "Weird to think they're all going to grow back."

"Aye. T'will. Even the lass you gave a melonectomy to." Dalton wanders over to the half-decapitated woman, grabs the upper third of her head and sets it back on top of the rest of her. "There."

He really does have a soft spot for women, even if that bitch tried to kill us. Putting the pieces back together will probably let her wake up in mere hours instead of weeks to regenerate the missing portion of her head. So weird. He planted a giant firebomb which nearly killed her weeks ago, yet now he's helping her.

"They won't be a problem without Armand"—Dalton chuckles—"that was brilliant by the way."

"What?" I ask.

"Teasing him about his name. Rather annoyed him."

I float up to stand on my intact leg. The break is itching like a bastard, which means the bone is starting to knit, but I'm still not going to put weight on it yet. "Well, it is such a stereotypical name for a 'head vampire,' isn't it?"

"Precisely why it annoyed him so much. How many 'Armands' do you think grow up in South Central LA?"

"Not many."

Dalton grins. "That's why it ticked him off so much. Bloke probably saw a movie, thought it sounded all sorts of scary and impressive... and you made a mockery of it."

"We still got our asses handed to us." I limp over to him.

"T'was a bit of a rough punch-up, but those blokes got their arses handed to them." Dalton points the cutlass at the inert vampires. "We're still standing."

"On one leg, but okay. I'll take it."

"C'mon, luv." Dalton takes my hand, then faces Glim. "I am in your debt, again, good sir."

Glim's yellow glowing eyes sparkle. "Among our kind, a favor owed is the most valuable commodity."

"Are you seriously suggesting we go outside like this?" I ask.

"Briefly," says Dalton.

"Bad." I sigh at his boxers. "Must we?"

"I've got some replacement clothing stashed at a motel nearby."

"What about them?" I point at the vampires on the floor. "Bloody beats nothing."

"Bloody clothes will still attract the wrong kind of attention. And we'll be stuck having to dispose of them. Someone finds a wad of bloody kit somewhere, they're going to call the cops."

"Kit?" I ask.

"Clothes." He guides me to the door.

Glim follows. "No one will see either of you."

"Thanks." I smile at him.

The three of us head outside and take flight. Dalton leads us most of the way across the swath of glaringly bright city to the northern end. We come down in sight of mountains, near a decent-sized lake kinda shaped a bit too square to be natural. Probably a human-made reservoir.

Glim accompanies us all the way to an old motel that doesn't look like it's had a paying guest since the late 1970s. An old-school sign stands atop a metal pole at the outer corner of the lot. Hollow metal letters filled with smashed neon tubes read, 'Moon Pond Motel.' The large L-shaped building, half the rooms missing their doors, wraps around a modest parking lot. I think there's a bullet hole or six in the sign as well. Dalton heads toward a room on the left side, about midway down the longer wing. While Glim and I wait by the door, he pops up to the roof for a moment, returning with a key he'd evidently stashed up there.

The key still works, and we step into a reasonably-intact room for an abandoned motel. It doesn't even stink *too* bad. No power, but we don't need lights.

"Glim?" I ask. "Can you please go check on my brother and the other boys? I'm not completely confident in my ability to alter memories. Maybe make sure my attempt to get rid of all the gore and weirdness they saw sticks?"

"Of course. Will you two be okay?" Glim looks around at the room.

Dalton opens a drawer on the bureau and holds up a garbage bag. "Yep. Clothes are still here. Armand will be up in smoke, and the others likely won't have the stones to do anything without him. Plus, we're at the ass end of San Fernando now. Even if they try looking for us, we'll be gone before they find us." He drops the bag into the drawer. "Shower first."

"What about that Academic using blood magic?" I ask.

"Armand."

I gawk. "*He* was an Academic?"

"They're not all 'nerdy wizards in robes' you know." Dalton gestures at the bathroom. "Ladies first."

Glim bows at us and disappears in a whorl of black smoke.

"Thanks." I hurry into the bathroom, close the door, and shed the torn remains of my clothes. Of everything I had on, only my socks and sneakers escaped intact. Top is straight up *gone* as is the bra. My panties, though not physically damaged, have soaked up so much blood they look like I used them to clean the floor at a shotgun murder scene.

Eager to rinse the blood off my body, I hop in the tub and turn the water on—wow it works—and stand there in the spray. The initial shock of ice cold water fades to neutral temperature once my body adjusts to the freezing chill. Yay for one of the paradoxes of being an Innocent. I feel cold initially, but if it persists—as with a morgue cooler—it shifts to feel like room temperature. Any vampire could rock a bikini in Antarctica and not mind. I'd feel cold for a minute or two first. On second thought, it might actually be *too* cold. Anywhere a body could legit freeze solid is probably not a good idea for even a vampire. But who knows? We're magic... so maybe we won't freeze.

Claw wounds hurt when they happen, and they burn pretty much continuously until they heal. Having shower jets pummeling at the gaping slits all over my back and stomach is a new level of ouch I hadn't been prepared for. Fortunately, the cuts are mostly shallow and only damaged the underlying muscle in a few spots.

They're going to hurt for days, but at least none of the damage is anywhere not normally covered by clothes. The 'rents are going to notice I'm in pain, but at least they won't *see* it. After rinsing off as much as possible without soap, I cut the water and step out of the tub to discover the room has no towels.

This shouldn't surprise me as the place is abandoned. But it's still annoying. Grr. I squeegee my hair with my hands over the sink, happy to see the runoff is blood-free. In a total 'oh hell with it' moment, I grab my bloody rags, clean socks, and sneakers, then walk into the outer room wearing only a crisscross of claw wounds and water... and nearly scream at the sight of five black gang members in the room.

None of them react to me at all, continuing to stare into space.

Dalton's clamped onto one of the men, feeding. He shifts his gaze to me. *Three for you. Two are mine.*

I don't even have time to be mortified before the idea of feeding drags some primordial monster out of the deepest recesses of my brain. Like Lilith herself, I pounce on the nearest guy in flagrant disregard of being stark naked, and feed. Hot blood surges into my mouth as soon as my fangs pierce him, tasting like awesome. The true extent of how hungry I'd become after such a royal beating robs the blood of any real flavor. Fire scorches the lines of my claw wounds, making me squeeze the poor guy, snarling out my nose as I desperately pull the blood out of him as fast as possible.

I don't even realize I'm literally *sucking* at his neck until a mental poke from Dalton snaps me out of the feeding frenzy before I've consumed a fatal amount. Usually, the arterial spurting is enough and I don't need to treat the person like a giant Capri Sun pouch.

"Oh, shit..." I seal the bite wound and step back from him, shivering. "Wow..."

"Aye. Little hungry. 'Tis why I brought three for ya. I had a nosh outside already before I found this lot."

The second man I bite is far more normal in terms of feeding experience. In the absence of manic hunger, his blood tastes like a cheeseburger. After taking a safe amount from him, I move on to the third man who—bizarrely—tastes like the chicken and pasta casserole thing Mom makes.

Once finished feeding to the point of feeling slightly overfull, I stand there awkwardly dripping, not entirely sure how it's possible for me to tolerate standing around like a wood nymph in front of a room full of strange men. Maybe it's because the claw wounds hurt so damned much I'd rather be naked than let cloth touch them.

Or perhaps I've simply stopped caring. Nah. Can't be. I'm not centuries old yet. *That* level of blasé to nudity takes a while... or drugs. Or growing up somewhere like the Amazon rain forest.

"All set then?" Dalton smiles.

"Yeah. Thanks for the Five Guys."

He tilts his head. "Pardon?"

"It's a burger chain. Never mind."

"Oh." He taps his fingers to his forehead in an 'I should've caught that' sort of gesture, then programs the men to wander off somewhere and forget ever seeing him or being here.

After, he heads into the bathroom for a shower. I sit on the end of the bed, not entirely wanting to touch it, and air dry. With a recent blood meal in me, the claw wounds finally start closing. It hurts almost as much as suffering them in the first place, but I manage not to scream—though I do come close to crushing my knees from gripping them so hard. About twenty minutes later, open wounds have become red lines. They're still way tender, but at least the air blowing over my skin doesn't feel like a storm of razor blades.

Eventually, Dalton emerges from the bathroom. Our mind link tells me he's uncomfortable being naked together with me, so I don't look at him. Unlike me, he has no problem putting clothes on while still soaked from the shower. Plastic trash bag rustling comes from my left and behind. A wad of fabric hits me in the arm and flops to the bed.

I'm dry enough... mostly. So I pick up the bundle. It's a *Starsky & Hutch* T-shirt and a pair of khaki cargo shorts. Wow. Sensing Dalton has already gotten dressed, I peer back at him. He's wearing a *Transformers* T-shirt with Optimus Prime on it and an equally awful pair of shorts.

Predictably, the shorts he gave me are his size. They're going to fall off me unless I hold them up, but it beats nothing. I pull them on, add the shirt, and stand, feeling like the world's biggest dork—from 1981.

"Wow."

He raises an eyebrow. "Rockin' threads, what?"

"Hah. Seriously. We look like the nerds in my dad's movies."

He holds up a finger. "It's camouflage."

"What?" I blink. "Camouflage against what, style?"

"No one looking for me would dream I'd wear something so ghastly."

I smirk. "Where did you get this stuff, Goodwill?"

"No. It came off the store shelf new... a few years ago. Been stashed here a while."

"Oh, just a bit." I brush at the shirt which smells like wood drawer and plastic bag. Weird to think I'm the first person probably to wear these clothes. Also, amazing they haven't dry rotted. Then again, 1980 wasn't *that* long ago.

"So, now what?" I head over to the front window and claw snip some of the curtain cord to make an improvised belt. These shorts are so dweeby they've got belt loops. "You know, I think it would be *less* embarrassing to just go home naked than let anyone who knows me see this outfit."

Dalton laughs. "That, my dear, is exactly why they are camouflage."

"Yeah, maybe if we went to a con or something. No… wait. We'd still stand out there." I point at the window. "We have a slight problem. This room isn't light sealed, and it's facing east. Great choice by the way."

"Couldn't be helped. It's the most structurally intact room and still has running water." He hurries to the door and sets the deadbolt. "The bathroom is sealed off though. We'll sleep in there."

"Ugh. My back hurts already from hearing you say that."

Dalton starts to explain how it won't matter to us, but I raise a hand.

"Yeah. I know. Still hurts to think about."

Dressed like the two least popular kids in school from thirty years ago, we hang out in a motel room for a couple hours, waiting for sunrise. It's too late to call home, so I send basic 'we're okay' texts to the 'rents and Hunter. After, we sit on the bare mattress talking mostly about how Dalton's so good with a sword and knives. While explaining the sort of 'rogue's life' he had as a mortal and for many years after becoming a vampire, he decides to give me some pointers on how to use a cutlass.

"Katana's an entirely different style. Haven't a bloody clue about it." He picks up the blade and looks at it. "No idea where those wankers got this, but it's probably a real one."

"As opposed to what? Plastic?" I laugh. "Of course it's a real sword."

"No, I mean a cheap 440 stainless knock-off. This is an actual Japanese katana. Probably quite old. One of those cheap ones wouldn't have sliced clear through a man's leg like that." He pauses. "Well, perhaps with a vampire's strength behind it, but still."

"Okay neat. So I've got a legit sword."

"Probably worth a few thousand bucks, though you should keep it."

"Wow. Okay."

When the sun starts getting close to rising, we retreat to the bathroom, keeping the swords close at hand. For added protection against any light leaking in under the door, we end up in the bathtub together. Dalton, ever the gentleman, goes in first. I climb in on top of him and try to get as comfortable as possible… which isn't very comfortable at all.

Physical comfort doesn't matter much since once the sun comes up, we're out.

INNOCENT BYSTANDER

I open my eyes to a featureless wall of grey metal a few inches in front of my face.

And my clothes are gone. Although, nudity is probably a style upgrade over what I had. Still. Ugh. Someone found us and I'm in a morgue cooler… again. I check my arm and sure enough, there's a plastic bracelet. Oh, seriously!? They put me down as Jane Doe with an age of fifteen. Sigh. My life is teenager hell, constantly being thought of as a kid younger than I am. Grr. Might as well get this over with.

I brace my hands against the wall behind my head, rear my legs back as much as I can move in the tight space, and mule-kick the door. Escaping is much easier than the first time, mostly because knowing I'm a vampire lets me skip all the confusion, and I'm not freaking out at being trapped in a small space with no clothes.

The cooler door flies open with an echoing *bang*. I shove the sliding tray out and hop down to stand on a frigid tile floor in a relatively bland 'medical type' room. The whole wall behind me is covered in square cooler doors. Not much stands out as unusual except for a trail of small bloody barefoot prints leading from the counter on the left out the room's only door. They're not *too* little. Smaller than my feet, definitely not Dalton's. Clearly not from an adult either.

Uh oh.

This doesn't feel like a normal morgue. Did the Persons In Black grab me? Or maybe thralls working for another group of vampires? I creep along the trail of footprints, careful not to step on them since they appear wet. The plastic swinging door opens at my touch without a sound, revealing an immaculate hospital-white corridor marked with more red footprints.

I pad out, bizarrely at ease with not having anything on. Soon after leaving the cooler room, soft suckling noises draw my attention to a left offshoot from the corridor not far ahead of me. The footprints lead around that corner. Pretty sure a freaky sight is waiting for me, but I keep going anyway.

Hesitant, I stop at the corner to gather my nerve, then step around.

Two tween girls, one blonde and one with light brown hair, kneel on either side of a big guy in medical scrubs who appears dead, his vacant stare upturned at the ceiling. The blonde girl's in an overly elaborate doll dress while the other kid's wearing a T-shirt, jeans, and sneakers. The barefoot prints lead right to the life-sized doll, but her gown is so voluminous it covers her feet.

"Crap," I whisper.

Both girls detach from the man's neck and look at me.

My little sisters grin, blood dripping off their fangs.

Sierra points at a catatonic guy slumped against the wall to the left. "We saved you one."

"I'm dreaming."

"Yep!" chirps Sophia.

My eyes snap open again—for real this time. I'm still on top of Dalton in the bathtub. He makes for a really bad mattress. Even more so when he's all grey and corpselike. Sunlight leaks in under the door, but it's not too bad to me. Kinda feels like a space heater running a few feet away. Even the glare reflecting off the old linoleum floor would probably cause Dalton's skin to smoke. Despite my curiosity, I don't test the theory. He probably appreciates that.

I get up out of the tub and sit on the toilet with the seat fully closed, turning it into an uncomfortable chair. My claw wounds still sting, but the pain has lessened enough it doesn't occupy ninety percent of my brain. According to my iPhone, it's 2:58 p.m. Considering the beating I took, waking up this early is pretty surprising. Gotta be nerves. Weather app says it's deadly outside, but at least the predicted sunset time for Los Angeles is around five, so I don't have *too* long to sit here.

With nothing else to do but suffer a couple crappy hours of boredom trapped inside a tiny motel bathroom, I check texts. The 'rents replied. Sam (and his friends) are back home, safe. Dad comments that he's happy I played mind games with them. Guess it means he figured out they don't remember certain details no kids their age should witness. Kinda obvious given the bloody mess on Daryl and Jordan's clothes.

It hits me the boys knew they'd been abducted by vampires. Guess the gang hadn't made any effort to conceal themselves. While it *could* imply they planned to erase memories, more likely, it had been their intention to kill the boys all along as Coralie said. Whatever guilt I had at slicing them up dies fast. In fact, if I could tolerate going outside right now, more of them would get sun baths.

Hopefully, Armand woke up for a few seconds as the daylight burned him off the face of the Earth... like a laser removing a wart from someone's ass.

My fingernails click on the screen as I send a text to the group chat with Hunter and my parents. ‹I'm okay. Will be going home as soon as we can catch a flight. Kinda stuck at the moment due to a little light problem.›

‹Understood,› replies Dad.

Mom sends, ‹What happened? I'm worried.›

‹Too much to type. Will explain in person. Hope the boys are okay.›

My parents and Hunter send multiple rapid texts confirming the kids got back okay, having emerged from the mirror in Sophia's bedroom. Glim showed himself to Dad again, and according to him, 'checked my homework.' I take that to mean memory tweaking. Jordan borrowed some of Sam's clothes so he didn't go home a bloody mess. Alas, Daryl couldn't fit into my brother's stuff, so he ended up stuck hanging out in one of Dad's T-shirts while Mom ran his clothes through the laundry. Glim made sure the boys didn't remember being covered in gore.

The motel room's outer door opens with a loud *thud,* probably from being kicked.

Crap.

I toss my phone back onto the remains of my jeans and grab the katana. If someone opens the bathroom door, I'm probably going to catch fire. Best thing for me to do is back all the way up against the wall behind the toilet, the farthest possible place from any light coming in.

Multiple people enter the outside room, all talking in Spanish. I don't understand most of what they're saying though *la droga* and *mucho dinero* are pretty obvious. Great. I'm stuck in a bathroom while a drug deal goes down on the other side of a flimsy wall. Okay, nothing to panic about. Just need to stay quiet. This is merely an abandoned motel. Not like we broke into their house or anything.

Spanish discussion mutates into Spanish arguing over the next fifteen minutes. Guys start shouting at each other and pounding on furniture. Not sure if understanding them would be scarier or calming. I can't overhear anything that would get me in trouble for knowing, but it also means I can't tell what's going on. Fortunately, it doesn't really sound like they're going to get violent, more like guys having an argument over which sports team is better—wait, sports arguments sometimes get violent, especially when beer is involved. Granted, I doubt they're actually quibbling over football. More likely, the particulars of the deal.

Pre-vampire me would've been terrified being this close to legit drug dealers. Whether or not the stereotypes of what men like this would do to a young woman are true, I'm a wimpy little suburban kid not prepared to be around this level of criminal activity. Or *was*. They're still mortals. However, if sunlight really hits me, I'm going to be in deep crap. Even the little bit coming in under the door is almost robbing me of my powers. As in, if I walk three steps closer, I'm back to mortal strength and a too-real vulnerability to permanent death.

All I have to do is stay quiet until they leave. Drug deals don't take too long, right? They'll be gone soon. About ten minutes after I have that tragically incorrect thought, someone approaches the bathroom.

Dammit!

As soon as the door opens, I'm nerfed. If the dude sees me holding a sword, I'm probably going to get shot in the face. I stash the katana against the wall to my right, hidden behind the toilet. Still in easy reach if needed, but not waving around in plain sight.

The door opens in a blinding flash of heat, but it's not as painful as expected. I don't smolder, though the bathtub begins filling with meat-scented smoke. A Hispanic guy in his early twenties stops short on his way to the toilet, one hand on his zipper, staring at me.

Against absolutely everything about my nature, I put on a harmless, sexy face and whisper, "Hi there. Why don't you close the door and we can have a little fun?" I lick my lips, suggesting a particular activity. Come on, pal. Close the door and get close enough for me to make you forget seeing me.

He stares at me for a few seconds, then rushes over to grab my arm before dragging me out into the main room. Six other guys stand around the exposed mattress, which contains several bags of what I assume to be narcotics of some kind. Hmm. Guess the 1980s printed T-shirt and shorts don't exactly work for alluring. Or it's that 'looking too young' thing getting in the way again. Grr. Okay, think, Sarah. Time to put my childish face to good use. Maybe they'll feel sorry for me.

The guy holding my forearm rambles in Spanish at the others, gesturing at me and the bathroom. In the brunt of late-afternoon sun partially muted by motel curtains, my odds of doing anything except trying to play harmless are nil. So, I stand there trying to look scared and nonthreatening while lightly tugging at his grip, more out of protest than sincerely attempting to get away from him.

A scrawny guy with something attempting to be a goatee dangling from his chin walks over and puts an enormous silver-plated handgun to the side of my head. "The hell you doin' here, *chica?*"

"Umm..." I grind my toes into the rug like a kid. "Just hitchhiking up the coast. Found this place and decided to crash here for a while. Didn't know it was your room. I'm sorry. I don't know any Spanish, so I have no idea what you guys said before."

"Yo, you crashed here?" asks the guy with the gun to my head.

"Yeah."

He raises an eyebrow, glancing to his left. "In the freakin' bathroom?"

I manage an awkward smile and shrug. "I've got a funny thing about windows. Can't sleep in a room with any."

"Yo, that's messed up," says the guy holding me.

"Yeah, it kinda is. So, umm... I really don't care what you guys are doing here. I'm only trying to get home, okay? I didn't see anything."

The dude with the gun looks me up and down, his lip twitching like he really wants to laugh at my ridiculous outfit but is trying to stay 'hard.' After a moment, he pulls the gun away and lowers it. "Fine. Get outta here, kid."

"Umm. Thanks, but I really can't go outside yet. I've got a nasty allergy to sunlight."

"Heh." The guy holding my arm lets go and mock-punches my shoulder. "Like a vampire?"

Holy crap that hurt. His knuckles hit me right where the katana went in yesterday. Guess it's not fully healed yet. I bite back the involuntary pain tears and force a smile. "Yeah, heh. My friends call me that all the time. Umm, seriously though. If you guys don't mind, can I just hide out in the bathroom? Really don't want any trouble and I'll be leaving California tonight. No problems."

"You're one weird kid," says the guy with the gun.

"Yeah. Guess I kinda am."

One of the other guys sniffs the air and mutters something about 'carne asada' while patting his stomach. Ugh. He smells Dalton roasting.

"Aww shit." Arm-grab guy brushes a hand at my face, moving my hair. "Dude. She's turnin' red. Girl ain't lyin' about that sun thing."

The front door flies open, revealing the silhouette of a man holding a briefcase surrounded by nuclear sunlight. "Yo, yo, yo!"

Next thing I know, I'm standing atop the bed amid a cloud of smoke, snarling, my claws out. Blood spatter decorates the walls in wide, sweeping trails. The front door is closed again, two bloody hand smears leading down to the corpse of a tall black guy in a tank top and jeans. The guy who dragged me out of the bathroom cowers under the little table by the front window, staring up at me. Gun dude who was going to let me go, fainted right where he'd been standing. The other four gang members are ripped up and either unconscious or dead. I'm—once again—covered in blood, only it's not mine this time.

Arm-grab guy babbles in rapid Spanish, probably praying.

Fleeting memories come back to me, mere still-image snapshots while I raged out of control, lost to a panic-frenzy of exposure to deadly levels of sunlight. Despite the three or four dead guys around me, my thoughts go back to when Mom barged into my room and made me hiss from sunlight. Had she been in arms' reach at the time, I might've lost control and hurt her. Okay, relax. I'm not a threat to my family. Dad tinted the basement windows. It's not possible for anyone to send me off on an out of control freak-out while I'm in my bedroom.

At least one person is dead by my hand, maybe five.

"Dammit."

I jump down off the bed and approach arm-grab guy, the only one in here other than me who's still conscious. He whimpers, mumbling something about la Diabla.

"Relax. I'm not going to hurt you." I lean down and grasp his arm, coaxing him out from under the table. "Just don't open the outer door, okay? Bright sun gives me panic attacks."

The guy looks around at the carnage. "Y-you call this a panic attack? What the hell are you?"

I usher him to the bathroom. "Maybe not the standard definition, but yeah, I panicked."

As soon as we're in the bathroom, I shut the door and push him back against the innermost wall. The entire area behind the shower curtain is full of smoke from a smoldering Dalton. As soon as I'm online, I dive into the gang dude's mind.

And wow. The instant the sunlight hit me, my skin turned grey, my eyes lit up red, and I flew around growling in a deep, demonic tone like an angry mountain lion. That poor black dude walking in died first since he had the misfortune of being between me and the door. Arm-grab guy didn't see much else before he screamed and dove for cover other than their contact from the supplier collapsing dead against the door and sliding to the ground. He heard me lashing out at his buddies but didn't look.

It's easy enough to erase a recent memory, even one so emotionally scarring. Of course, I have to put something in my place to make it permanent. Leaving a hole in time with zero memory can lead to his brain unlocking what I made him forget months or years down the road. It's tempting to make him think the dead guy in the doorway came in shooting, but I don't want to start a gang war. For another thing, he died to claw wounds not bullets.

So I do the most ridiculous thing I can think of: this guy remembers a small group of ninjas attacking them with steel claw gloves.

Once I'm certain the implant stuck, I compel him to collect all the drugs and crap on the bed and go home. It takes him a few minutes to snap out of the fog and mechanically follow my compulsion. As soon as he leaves carrying the narcotics, I head out and drag the dude with the gun into the bathroom. It's a lot of work considering my strength is merely normal and I'm not a big girl. Eventually, we're in the bathroom with the door closed and he's all mine to do with as I wish.

And no, I don't have anything fun in mind. Merely erasing memories.

He might be a drug dealing gang thug, but he was going to let me go and didn't try to grope me or anything. I'm glad he survived. As far as his memories go, he never saw me at all and remembers ninjas coming out of nowhere to attack everyone in the middle of their deal. Then, I send him home.

After he leaves, I check the remaining gang members. One of the four is dead, having bled out from a lucky (or unlucky as the case may be) claw slash to the side of his neck deep enough to rip open the carotid artery. The others all appear to have fainted from pure terror.

It's butt-busting work, but I drag each survivor to the bathroom to escape the sun and fiddle with their memories. Roughly an hour and a half later, everyone left inside this motel room is dead. One unlucky tall-as-heck Jamaican dude, one Hispanic gang member, and two vampires. I re-secure the deadbolt on the outer door and run to the bathroom, pulling the shower curtain aside to reveal a standing column of dark grey smoke. Coughing, I wave my hands to disperse the cloud a bit, then lift Dalton's stiff-as-an-Egyptian-mummy body out of the tub and lean him against the wall in the corner. That done, I strip and hop in the shower. Twice, my socks have escaped bloody ruin. This time because I'd left them in the bathroom. I might be dead, but sleeping with shoes on is still kinda weird.

My second shower is *far* more pleasant since I'm no longer covered in trenches of torn skin for the water to needle at. Once I'm blood-free, I hop out of the tub and proceed to wash the short and shirts in the sink. Kinda sad the first time anyone wore these clothes they end up doused in gore. Even if they're hideous, they don't deserve to be ruined. There's only so much water can do, but it does lessen the bloodiness from *'Texas Chainsaw Massacre'* to 'highly unfortunate accident with ketchup.'

Again, I sit on the closed toilet while the dreadfully dorky T-shirt and shorts hang over the shower rod to dry. At least iPhone games keep me from completely losing my mind at the boredom. None of my wildest nightmares ever included spending a whole afternoon naked in a strange motel bathroom playing phone games with a dead body leaning on the wall nearby.

At 4:59 p.m., Dalton rapidly regains color and slumps into a heap.

He winces from the hard landing on his butt, glancing at me with one eye open. "You're naked. Did something happen I don't remember and would woefully regret?"

"Nope." I smile, my attention still focused on the phone game.

He exhales in relief. "Ahh, brilliant. Why am I on the floor?"

"Because you're not stiff as a plank anymore."

"That doesn't explain why I'm out here and not in the tub."

"Needed to shower. Figured you'd prefer to remain dry. Besides, standing on top of you while showering would've felt all kinds of wrong."

"Ahh. Yes. I suppose it explains why you're starkers. Why did you have to shower?"

"Clothes got bloody. Had to wash them too."

He stands and plucks the *Starsky & Hutch* T-shirt off the shower curtain bar. "This is washed?"

"Fine. Rinsed. There's no detergent here."

"Ahh. Right. It's merely damp now." He tosses it to me. "Dare I ask what happened that you got bloody again?"

While putting the shirt and shorts back on, I explain the drug deal interrupted by ninjas. Dalton laughs himself to tears since he can also see the ridiculous mental image of ninjas I implanted in the gang members' heads. Okay, so I had *Mortal Kombat* on the brain. Still snickering, he uses his shirt to wipe around the bathroom, eliminating possible fingerprints. I put my socks and sneakers on. With any luck, I'll be able to avoid another dousing of blood.

He whistles at the sight of the room. "You did a right proper Jackson Pollack on the walls and ceiling."

"The muse was impossible to resist." I fold my arms. "Woke up this afternoon and just thought the place needed some color."

Dalton shakes his head. "This motel is off the list of safe spots."

"I think you need to reevaluate what 'safe' means. A bunch of guys randomly showed up to work a drug deal. And how many 'safe crash spots' do you have?"

"Oh, a handful." He winks. "C'mon. Let's get out of here."

When we leap into the air, Dalton heads south. I'm about to question his direction sense but he explains via mental link he intends to secure us some less suspicious clothing, then slip onto a commercial flight. Cruising at almost 600 miles an hour is a whole lot faster than we can fly. We could've taken a ride on a plane to get down to LA, but I guess neither one of us had functioning brains due to emotion that night. Anyway, flying commercial is more comfortable. However, we'd stand out too much in this dork couture, especially with bloodstains on me.

We head to a Macy's.

"Stay close to me," mutters Dalton.

"Okay."

Cameras don't pick me up. If you stay near enough, they'll not see you either.

Oh, cool. Must be one of those neato things Lost Ones can do that I can't, right?

He smiles.

I hover beside him like 'Overly Clingy Girlfriend' while we grab reasonable replacement clothes and head for the changing room. It's not even awkward at this point to get dressed in the same stall with him. We're both focused on task and eager to get the heck out of California as fast as possible. Dalton snaps all the anti-theft stuff off the garments, leaves them on the bench, and we walk out as though we'd come in wearing those outfits. We're not carrying bags and we left the swords outside on the roof before going in. No one gives us a second glance on the way out.

We collect the blades and fly toward LAX.

You'd think it would be an issue to walk into an airport carrying swords, but Dalton tells me to hold it close to my body and stay with him. We breeze past the ticket counter and go around the security checkpoint like cops. No one seems to notice this or care. Upon locating the next flight leaving for SEA-TAC, we lurk around the boarding gate for a while and simply walk on with the rest of the passengers, using a bit of mental influence to keep the flight crew from noticing we don't have boarding passes.

A minor snafu develops with someone whose seat we took, but Dalton smooth-talks it over by saying we had standby tickets, so we move to an unoccupied seat a few rows closer to the tail. Wow. I'd say this is the first time in my life being on an airplane, but I technically died five months ago.

It's strange to be flying without the wind in my hair, but hey, the airplane's offering a huge variety of in-flight meals.

KINDA ROUGH

Vampire flying from SEA-TAC airport to Cottage Lake is much nicer than our initial trip down to LA. The airline saved us three hours. Dalton and I land on the deck behind my house a little after eight at night. My intro calculus class has already started—and I never had a chance to do that metric crapton of homework for it. Honestly, my desire to rush to school is pretty minimal after everything. I need to see my family.

Ugh. I missed classes on Thursday, too. Going to school really gets in the way of being dragged into vampire warfare.

"Well then." Dalton faces me. "With Armand"—he makes air quotes at the name—"destroyed, that lot shouldn't be much to worry about. I think I'm going to remain in the area for a while, but no need for me to impose on you for sleeping space."

"Cool. Glad you'll be around."

He scratches an eyebrow. "Ehh, sorry about the whole Sam thing."

Grr. I lean toward him. "What do you mean 'the whole Sam thing?' They almost killed my little brother."

"Sorry." He stares at the deck.

"No… that it happened isn't your fault. It's their fault. I'm just freaking out over it. I'm not upset with you. Well, maybe a little for brushing my little brother's kidnapping off as a 'thing.' Really, I'm not mad at you for this."

"That's good to hear." He gives me this playful but apologetic look. "Brits are prone to understatement. Can't help it. Not trying to downplay what happened."

I huff. "Yeah, I know. Again, just frazzled. Thanks for helping get him back."

"There's absolutely no way I could have done anything else." He gazes off into the sky. "I know what you're thinking, but that was a different me and a different time."

"Yeah. It's still kinda weird seeing you fight."

"How do you mean?"

"Oh, I dunno. The sight of you actually *good* at something is kind of a new experience."

Dalton sticks his tongue out at me.

I chuckle.

"There's a mild difference between ineptitude and being unlucky. The streets were kinda rough where I grew up. Worse even with the crowd I wound up with. Had to learn the knife early or you'd end up with one stuck in a sensitive spot." He looks me up and down. "For a newbie, you didn't handle that katana too badly. 'Course, you've got a bit of my blood in ya. Hmm. C'mere a tick."

I step closer, one eyebrow raised. "Wwwwhy?"

Dalton rests his hands on my shoulders and stares deep into my eyes. Images flicker like a slideshow in my mind that starts off like a gritty, depressing version of *Oliver Twist* with knives and tween boys stabbing each other as well as grown men, moves on to the dingy slums of Whitechapel in the late 1800s, and jumps through scenes from both World Wars. Everything is from Dalton's point of view when he'd been in the middle of a knife or sword fight. My muscles twitch as if my body's trying to participate as well, but none of the images last long enough for me to react.

The bizarre experience leaves me a bit dazed and contemplating foot position and balance. I need to grab him to keep from falling over sideways from dizziness.

"Whoa," I whisper. "What happened?"

"Sires can pass certain bits of knowledge to their progeny. I've tried to give you as much of what I know about fighting with a blade as I can. You'll not attain mastery overnight, but you should retain some of what I just tossed into your bean. Once the bewilderment fades, you'll at least know the pointy end goes toward the bad guy."

"My head is spinning too much to think about it."

"Aye. Normal. Tomorrow or the next day, you'll realize you don't feel like such a newbie with a sword in your hand. Least I can do for the trouble I caused."

I rub my forehead. "Feels so weird."

"Well, you should go inside and let your parents stop worrying."

"You're not going to come inside to see Sam at least?"

Dalton fidgets. "Well, I suppose I could. Don't want to impose."

"My parents aren't going to bite your head off for this. They know it's not your fault." I pull him toward the patio door. "And you do know you can stop by to visit when you don't have a vampire gang wanting your head on a post, right?"

"Aye." He chuckles as we go inside. "Will keep that in mind, luv."

PERMISSION TO LIE

My parents leap off the sofa and run over as soon as we walk into the living room.

Mom and Dad collide, hugging me at the same time. Dalton stands a safe distance back while they go through various stages of freaking out before returning to controlled calm. Naturally, they want to know everything that happened, so I start explaining.

While I'm in the midst of telling the 'rents about the drug dealers, Sophia, barefoot in a normal white-and-pink dress as opposed to the gothic vampire princess doll gown I keep dreaming her in, pads down the stairs and walks up to me. "The boys are waiting for you upstairs."

"What?" I ask.

"Except for Sam." She smiles.

"What? Why?"

Sophia tilts her head. "To make them forget what happened. Coralie showed me how to put people in a mental fog."

I blink. "You know how to magic people into a state of derp-a-tonia? Oh, that couldn't possibly backfire. Nope. Not at all."

She giggles.

"Glim already fixed their memory," says Dad. "Are the boys *still* upstairs?"

"Well, that explains why Daryl's mother keeps calling." Mom rubs the bridge of her nose. "Didn't we send them home last night?"

"Yeah, but they came back over." Sophia bites her lip, looking unsure of herself. "Coralie showed me how to open the mirrors whenever I want. It's a lot faster to go places. She also helped me navigate. It's really tricky to figure out what places match the real world, but she kept us from getting lost. It only took us like an hour to walk to LA."

"Wow, incredible." I whistle.

"Not really," says Sophia, looking down. "We almost died like six times. It's only a little safer than taking an Uber with a stranger driving."

I gawk. "I don't think you'd come close to death six times in an Uber."

"Possibly in New York City," mutters Dad. "Or Jersey."

"The fire spiders even made Sierra scream." She cringes.

"You're not to go into hazardous alternate mirror dimensions alone, young lady," says Mom. "Not until you're at least eighteen."

"Sorry, Mom. It was an emergency! And, I wasn't alone." Sophia shivers. "I'll never go in there alone. It's too scary. *Fuzzydoom* is in there. You don't have to worry. I'm too much of a chicken."

Dammit. If I didn't grab Blix and run outside, we could've been there, done, and back in one day. The little bugger probably would've taken us right to the mirror in that bathroom. No wonder he was flailing when I carried him outside. He'd been trying to tell me to go to a mirror. Of course, had we done that and managed to slip in and out clean, Armand— ugh—would still be after us. At least my clumsy solution solved the problem permanently, even if I did get super lucky. It's possible the story the parents got contained some embellishments, so it didn't sound like we almost died.

"So the boys are all here?" I ask.

Sophia nods, then takes my hand and pulls me upstairs to Sam's bedroom.

Mom and Dad make hesitant noises rather than actual words. Dalton floats up and over the sofa back and settles in to relax.

Once we're upstairs, I whisper, "Glim already erased their memories."

"Sorry. They came over today to hang out and I didn't know they already forgot." She fidgets. "Oops."

We enter Sam's bedroom. He and Blix are sitting on the rug absorbed in the PlayStation. Ronan, Daryl, and Jordan sit nearby, all three of them gazing into space.

"Sare," says Sam, not taking his eyes off the screen. "Soph broke my friends."

"They're not broken." Sophia shakes her head. "Just like on pause. I didn't know they already forgot stuff."

Mom and Dad walk in.

Blix emits a faint *eep* and zooms under the bed to hide.

"Are they okay?" Mom waves her hand in front of Daryl's face. He doesn't react.

"Sarah," says Dad. "You might need to make the boys' parents forget they went missing for a night."

"Jonathan." Mom shakes her head. "They missed school. There's a record of that absence. Their parents already know the boys were abducted by someone looking to hurt Sarah."

"Exactly my point." Dad folds his arms. "The police are going to be by eventually to interview us about why someone would want to abduct them over something connected to our daughter. They're going to want details we can't give them without sounding insane or compromising Sarah's secrecy."

"Okay, fine." I hold my hands up in surrender. "I will rewrite parents. What story are we going with?"

"We got lost in the woods?" asks Sam.

"Nah. Can't overuse the woods excuse." Dad rubs his chin.

A grin spreads over my face. "I could blame ninjas again."

"Pirates are cooler," says Sam.

"Ninjas?" Dad glances at me. "Hold on, are you holding a katana?"

"Yes."

"*Why* are you holding a katana?"

I shrug. "Because I haven't put it down yet."

He groans. "Sarah…"

"One of the vampires tried to take my head off with it. I objected. Mine now."

"Fair enough." He reaches for it. "Can I see?"

I let him take it.

He pulls it a few inches out of the scabbard and whistles. "Wow, is this authentic?"

"Yeah… how'd you know?"

"The wavy pattern of lighter metal along the cutting edge. That, and it's got a much more gradual taper. This thing's worth a fortune. Don't lose it." He snaps it back in the scabbard and hands it to me.

Mom waves to get everyone's attention. "Hello? We're still trying to figure out how to rewrite people's memories here. Can you just make the whole thing go away?"

I rub my chin. "That would involve tracking down and visiting every teacher or school staff person who knows they missed school. Impractical. Easiest to make them all think they had like a twenty-four-hour bug or something and spent the day home sick."

Mom nods. "I can't believe I'm condoning lying like this, but yes. That's ideal. Nothing for the police to care about."

Wow. The world really is broken. My parents are not only giving me permission to lie, they're telling me to.

THE VELOCITY OF KITTENS IN SPACE-TIME

I dive into the brains of the three catatonic boys, replacing the entire abduction event with a relatively boring memory of being stuck home feeling sick with a mild cold-like disease. No need to make it overly miserable. Again, I let Sam keep the truth without gore.

Mom walks back in with a small, grey kitten sitting in her hand. "Sophia. What is this?"

"Umm. That's Klepto. She's mine."

"Mew," says Klepto.

"When did I say you could have a pet?" asks Mom in a stern tone.

Panicked, Sophia whines, "But Mom! Sam has a demon! You can let me have a cat."

"What!?" shrieks Mom.

"Eep. Oops." Sophia shrinks in on herself. "I mean frogs."

"No way, young lady. Back up. What did you mean about demons?"

Sophia faces me. "Sarah! Help!"

"Blix isn't a demon. He's a daemon," says Sam. "And he's not a pet. He's a friend."

"What the heck is a Blix!" shouts Mom.

"Mew," says Klepto, licking her paw.

The imp pokes his head out from under the bed and flashes a toothy smile at the 'rents. His droopy ears *do* kind of make him look cute in a gargoyle sort of way.

Dad edges back toward the door. "Don't make any sudden moves. I'll be right back with the weed eater."

"No, he's cool." Sam waves Blix over to sit beside him. "Don't hurt him. Please?"

Mom blows up yelling at Sophia for sneaking a cat into the house without asking permission and Sam for keeping an imp. Sierra screams that if Sophia and Sam can have pets, it's not fair she can't get a dog. Sam—not screaming—grumbles at Sophia for telling the 'rents about Blix.

Dad holds his hands up like a traffic cop saying, "Guys! Guys! Guys!" but no one gets quieter or stops arguing. Sierra moves on to screaming about stupid frogs in the stupid bathtub and how much cuter dogs are than frogs. Sophia merely stands there crying and begging to keep the kitten while Mom yells at her.

Finally, the guilt and noise build up too much for her and Sophia lets out this glass-shattering high-pitched shrieking scream. An eruption of brilliant white-purple light blobs sprays out of her and hangs in midair like a hologram of a radial tie-dye shirt centered on her. By the time her lungs run out of air and she opens her eyes again, the room has gone quiet. Everyone except for me, Blix, and Klepto appear to be frozen in time.

"Whoa... what the heck?" I gaze around at the odd glowing blobs everywhere.

"Mew?" Klepto licks her paw.

"Wow," whispers Sophia. "It worked."

"What did you do?"

Sophia runs to me and grabs my hand. "*Please* make Mom okay with me keeping Klepto!"

"You know I won't use my abilities on you guys. This includes the parents. *Especially* the parents."

"But you're an immortal." She bites her lip. "Just this once. Please?" She sniffles. "I can't lose Klepto! I love her!"

The tiny kitten purrs and weaves around Sophia's ankles, rubbing.

"I might be an immortal, but I'm still their daughter. Having the ability to make people do what I want them to do doesn't change that as long as I'm still under their roof, I need to follow their rules."

"Aww." She looks down. "Please?"

"Wait... why did you name the kitten Klepto?"

"Because she steals stuff. All the things that keep going missing in the house? I found out it was her. She's stashed them all under my bed where she nests."

I exhale in relief. At least one thing going wrong here had an innocent explanation. "Okay. No problem. Look, you're going to have to talk it out with her, but I'll help."

"Okay," says Sophia to the floor.

"Oh, one more thing." I poke a finger into her forehead. "You shouldn't disrupt the space-time continuum over a kitten. That's probably going to end up pissing something off."

She almost smiles. "I didn't. I interrupted it to stop a huge argument. I hate it when we fight. We used to argue all the time before Scott stabbed you. We're not supposed to yell at each other. I hate it. Families shouldn't scream at each other." Sophia starts crying.

I hug her until she calms down a minute or two later. "It's okay. Just... undo whatever this is before one of those big powerful guardians of the time flow or whatever come knocking."

"Okay."

"Did you freeze the entire universe or just this room?"

"Umm. Just this room probably. I don't have *that* much power." She closes her eyes in concentration. The past few minutes rewind rapidly right before my eyes, slowing as Mom walks backward out of the room with her empty hand positioned as if holding Klepto.

The kitten, sensing obligation, teleports from the floor by Sophia's feet to Mom's hand.

Oh, crap. She's *rewinding* time. "Umm. One more thing. Don't say anything about Blix being here, okay? He's friendly, Mom and Dad do *not* trust imps, and Sam would be heartbroken if he had to go away."

Sophia, concentrating too much to speak, nods once.

As soon as Mom's out in the hall, the weird lights disappear.

Time resumes.

Mom walks in with the kitten in her hand. "Sophia. What is this?"

"Umm, you know how I'm getting magic training?" asks Sophia in a timid voice. "That's Klepto. She's part of my magic training. I'm still not sure if she's a real cat since I kinda made her out of powdered mushrooms."

Mom's facial expression would be perfect if a random stranger walked up and slapped her across the face with a slab of raw salmon then ran off skipping and singing to himself while farting rainbows.

"Mew," says Klepto.

Dad glances sideways at a lingering fragment of pink-purple light. It fizzles away almost as soon as he looks directly at it.

"So this isn't a kitten despite looking and acting like a kitten?" asks Mom.

Sophia grinds her toes into the rug, trying to look adorable. "I'm still trying to figure that out. Most people who can do magic have special pets. She's important. I promise I'll keep her out of your way."

Klepto disappears from Mom's hand, reappearing on her shoulder, then rubs her head against Mom's cheek. "Mew."

"That cat just teleported," says Dad.

"Only two feet. Not very impressive as teleportation goes," says Sam.

I bury my face in one hand. Stay calm. Don't get upset. Don't freak out. This is what I wanted. Staying home. My family might be growing weirder by the month, but they're awesome. And holy crap! My kid sister just rewound effing time.

Wow... I really feel sorry for her future boyfriend. He is never going to win any arguments.

PLAYING CATCH-UP

Monday evening after my English lit class is over, I head across the building and downstairs to Professor Heath's office. Calculus problems are *still* dancing around in my head from the night before when I marathonned that massive amount of homework. He doesn't have class on Mondays, but he's available to talk to students. The guy literally lives on campus since he's another vampire.

Problem there is I can't simply make him believe I didn't miss his class last Thursday.

Of course, the upside is I can explain the actual truth.

I knock on the doorjamb.

"Enter," says Professor Heath in an overacted grand tone.

When I poke my head in, he waves me closer. I step in, shut the door behind me, and flop in the chair near the desk. "So, about last Thursday."

He leans back, rubbing his chin. "I assume you weren't sick."

"No. A gang of anarchist vampires from Los Angeles kidnapped my little brother." I explain what happened, though leave out the magic and mirror stuff, crossing my fingers he won't ask about it. "So, I was hoping you'd be okay with excusing the absence and giving me whatever catch-up work I need."

"That's not a problem." He smiles in a grandfatherly way. "Making accommodations for students with unique needs is nothing new. Your needs are merely a little *more* unique than most. But I understand."

"Whew."

"How did you fare with your instructors for the Friday classes you missed?"

I fidget, a little uneasy admitting to another teacher I mind-controlled his peers. Then again, he's a vampire so he'll understand. I hope. Can he report me to the administration for that? Is mental domination of a professor against the student code? "Umm. Already spoke to Professor Garcia and Dr. Mercer. They gave me the make-up assignments and think I had a family emergency."

"Technically, you *did* have a family emergency." Professor Heath smiles.

"Yeah, well… they believe my father put himself in the emergency room over a mishap with a power tool."

He laughs. "I take it that's not beyond the realm of possibility?"

"Mom doesn't let him play with anything too dangerous." I grin.

"Anyway…" He shakes his finger at me. "Naughty. You shouldn't mind control your professors. We wouldn't, err, want to threaten the sanctity of higher education or anything." His serious expression lasts for a few seconds before he starts laughing.

Relieved, I crack up, too. "Ugh… I hate vampire politics."

"So do I. Why do you think I'm here?" He winks and leans back again in his chair. "Someday, you'll come to realize there are two types of vampires. The type who adore the politicking, and the ones who spend the rest of their immortality wishing they'd remained mortal." He ponders for a moment, then smiles. "I suppose there's also a third kind. People like you and I who don't mind what we are so much and keep mostly to ourselves."

"Yeah. What about the Lost Ones? They keep to themselves, right?"

He chuckles. "Oh, they still have politics. Merely their own set of rules. They call themselves free spirits and anarchists, but they're not. They only object to the Old Guard's idea of how to run a vampire society."

"I think Dalton's pretty independent."

"Sure, not everyone within a given group is a perfect example of that group. After all, some college students are capable of independent thought."

I laugh.

"Speaking of immortality, how are you holding up?"

"Fine." I draw in a big, useless breath, and grin. "Better than fine, actually. Maybe even happy. Can't say I'd have made the choice to become a vampire if I had been given the option in the absence of being murdered, but turns out, this is pretty damn cool."

"That's good to hear. You know I'm available if you ever need an ear to listen or want advice." He glances at his wristwatch. "At least I will be here for another decade or so before migrating to a new school."

Thoughts roll around in my head for a moment before aligning to one concrete truth: I am genuinely happy despite everything that's going on. "Cool. I'll keep it in mind. Really, I'm pretty content, even with the bumpy parts. Though…"

He raises an eyebrow. "Hmm?"

I smile. "Things are surely getting strange lately."

Professor Heath laughs. "Indeed. Most people in the world live on the very outer surface of existence. They have a limited view of reality and are satisfied to cling to their version of reality, disregarding everything in conflict with it."

"Are you talking about politics or religion?" I ask.

He chuckles. "Oh, no. We'd be here for years. I'm referring to the reality that you're coming to know. Vampires, caves that lead to other dimensions, *trolls* even. Our reality is but one of an uncountable number of possible realities. And even within the boundaries of our dimension, there are vast amounts of truths that few among the living are capable of accepting."

"Next you're going to tell me faeries are real."

He wags his eyebrows.

"Seriously?" I stare. "Ugh. Please don't let Sophia find out."

"What about unicorns?"

Professor Heath whistles innocently. "Depending on where you look, perhaps."

"Dragons?"

He nods once. "But they're no longer in this physical reality. You'd have to go through a doorway to find one."

"Wow… What about a second season of *Firefly?*"

He raises his hands. "Hey, now. Don't get crazy. The universe does have limitations."

I sigh. "Darn. Oh well. I should get going, got some stuff to do."

"School work?"

"That, too… but I need to hunt down some parents and change their perception of reality."

"All right. Don't do anything a twenty-year-old version of me wouldn't do."

I pause halfway to the door and glance back at the Grateful Dead and Led Zeppelin posters on his office wall. "That will require making certain assumptions."

"So does life. Or unlife, as the case may be."

"Heh. True. Good night, professor."

He waves.

I head out down the hall toward the stairs. Yeah, my life has truly taken a turn for the weird. But, honestly, except for dialing down the danger to my family, I really wouldn't change anything about it.

Sunlight is totally overrated.

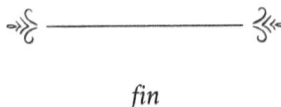

fin

ACKNOWLEDGMENTS

Thank you for reading the seventh book in the *Vampire Innocent* series. Sarah's story will continue soon.

Additional thanks to Lee Sheridan for editing and Alexandria Thompson for the cover and interior artwork.

ABOUT THE AUTHOR

Originally from South Amboy NJ, Matthew has been creating science fiction and fantasy worlds for most of his reasoning life. Since 1996, he has developed the "Divergent Fates" world, in which *Division Zero, Virtual Immortality, The Awakened Series, The Harmony Paradox, and the Daughter of Mars series* take place. Along with being an editor at Curiosity Quills press, he has worked in IT and technical support.

Matthew is an avid gamer, a recovered WoW addict, Gamemaster for two custom RPG systems, and a fan of anime, British humour, and intellectual science fiction that questions the nature of reality, life, and what happens after it.

He is also fond of cats.

Visit me online at:

- Facebook: https://www.facebook.com/MatthewSCoxAuthor
- Amazon: https://www.amazon.com/author/mscox
- Pinterest: https://www.pinterest.com/matthewcox10420/
- Goodreads: https://www.goodreads.com/author/show/ 7712730.Matthew_S_Cox

Email: mcox2112@gmail.com

OTHER BOOKS BY MATTHEW S. COX

Divergent Fates Universe Novels

Division Zero series

- Division Zero
- Lex De Mortuis
- Thrall
- Guardian
- Harbinger
- The Shadow Fixer
- Neuroshock

The Awakened series

- Prophet of the Badlands
- Archon's Queen
- Grey Ronin
- Daughter of Ash
- Zero Rogue
- Angel Descended

Daughter of Mars series

- The Hand of Raziel
- Araphel
- Ghost Black

Virtual Immortality series

- Virtual Immortality
- The Harmony Paradox

Prophet of the Badlands Series

- Prophet's Journey

- Prophet's Mercy

Divergent Fates Anthology

(Fiction Novels - Adult)

The Roadhouse Chronicles Series

- One More Run
- The Redeemed
- Dead Man's Number

Faded Skies series

- Heir Ascendant
- Ascendant Unrest
- Ascendant Revolution

Temporal Armistice Series

- Nascent Shadow
- The Shadow Collector
- The Gate to Oblivion
- The Queen of Discord
- The Burning Alchemist

Vampire Innocent series

- A Nighttime of Forever
- A Beginner's Guide to Fangs
- The Artist of Ruin
- The Last Family Road Trip
- The Phantom Oracle
- How Not to Summon Demons
- Ordinary Problems of a College Vampire
- A Vampire's Guide to Surviving Holidays
- An Introduction to Paranormal Diplomacy
- A Vampire's Guide to Adulting

- How to Stop a Vampire War in Six Easy Steps
- Ancient Vampire Death Cults and Other Annoyances
- Hunting Vampires for Fun and Profit
- A String of Seriously Unlucky Events
- The Summer of Completely Usual Strangeness
- Demonic Crisis Management for the Modern Vampire

Standalones

- Wayfarer: AV494
- Axillon99
- Chiaroscuro: The Mouse and the Candle
- The Spirits of Six Minstrel Run
- Sophie's Light
- The Far Side of Promise anthology
- Operation: Chimera (with Tony Healey)
- The Dysfunctional Conspiracy (with Christopher Veltmann)
- Of Myth and Shadow
- The Girl Who Found the Sun

Winter Solstice series (with J.R. Rain)

- Convergence
- Containment
- Catalyst
- Catacombs

Alexis Silver series (with J.R. Rain)

- Silver Light
- Deep Silver
- Silver Quarrel
- Silver Crucible
- Silver Heart

Samantha Moon Origins series (with J.R. Rain)

- New Moon Rising
- Moon Mourning

- Haunted Moon

- Moon Master
- Dead Moon
- Lost Moon
- Vampire Destiny
- Infinite Moon
- Vampire Empress
- Moon Elder
- Wicked Moon
- Moon Blade

- The Devil's Eye
- The Drifting Gloom
- Dark Mercy
- Primal Wrath

- Blood Moon

- Broken Ice
- Broken Wing

- The Elementalist
- The Black Rose
- The Wakefield Curse

- The Witch and the Hangman

Zeb Clemens series (with J.R. Rain)

- The Beast of Devil's Creek
- Wanted: Undead or Alive

Young Adult Novels

The Eldritch Heart Series

- The Eldritch Heart
- The Cursed Crown
- The Sapphire Soul

Evergreen Series

- Evergreen
- The World That Remains
- The Lucky Ones
- Nuclear Summer
- The Nuclear Frontier
- The World We Make
- The Threat Unseen

Progenitor Series

- Out of Sight
- Out of Mind

Diary of a Teenage Fey
(Short story series)

- Elder Horror
- The Hag of Barrow Falls
- Babysitter's Nightmare
- Lharakki
- Bauble for a Soul
- Simulacrum

- Amorphous
- Manticore

Middle Grade Novels